PLAGUED LANDS

PLAGUED LANDS

NIKKI BROOKE

CROW
KNIGHT

Published by Crow Knight Film and Publishing Realm
Melbourne, Australia

First Edition

A catalogue record for this book is available from the National Library of Australia

ISBN for paperback: 978-1-7635881-0-3
ISBN for ebook: 978-1-7635881-1-0

Cover design by The Book Designers

For those who believed a lie, only to awaken to the truth, stronger and more powerful than before.

One

WE'RE ALREADY DRESSED IN our hazsuits because, although the bus is protected, we're forbidden to leave the decontamination center without them on.

My rubber gloves squeak against the hazsuit while I try to massage my sore arms. I wince at the sound. The worst part is the headpiece; while I'm sitting, the suit bunches up so the visor digs into my chin. If the hazsuit fit better, it wouldn't bunch up—but we can't afford custom-made suits.

My muscles still ache from yesterday's work. For two days straight, we've been washing the glass bubble that surrounds the Sparkle Sector. I've been assigned the worst job: cleaning the underside of the bubble. The only way to get the job done is to squeeze in uncomfortably where the sphere curves into the ground. And I still have three more days of it.

I groan. *El mejor trabajo.*

Everyone else on the bus looks just as tired. Old Henry sits across the aisle, his eyes closed as he leans his head against the back of the chair. As usual, he's stealing a few minutes of sleep while the bus travels around the city.

Behind him sits Liam with his new girlfriend—what's her name? Kelly, Kaylie, Kerry? Something like that. She's a new window grunt, quietly whining to Liam about her sore muscles. I wish I could tell her the pain goes away with time. At least she's lucky she only works half the week—my brother and I don't have that luxury.

Most people have their eyes closed, like Old Henry, preserving their energy for the day ahead.

I try to relax, so I look outside the aseptic bus, but it's hard to see anything through the dusty bus windows. I can just make out the decrepit remains of the Old City. The desert has eaten up most of the buildings over the years since the city was abandoned. What's left sticks haphazardly out of the wasteland, looking sad and neglected.

The other side of the bus boasts a view of the glass bubbles surrounding our city, Neustin. The bubbles are aflame as they reflect the rising sun, sparkling in brilliant oranges and reds. They wouldn't sparkle so brightly if we didn't work so hard to clean them. Even through the window grime, I have to squint against the brightness.

I close my eyes. It's nothing I haven't seen before, anyway.

The peace doesn't last long. Something knocks me in the gut, jolting my eyes open.

"Would you quit moving about?" I cry.

I massage where my little brother, Sebastian, elbowed me. He isn't helping matters. He's jittery and bouncing in his seat; and every time he moves, he bumps another of my tender muscles.

"I can't get comfortable, Martina," Sebastian groans.

"That's because you keep moving," I say through gritted teeth. *"¡Quédate quieto!"*

He grumbles under his breath, continuing to squirm. My frown darkens. I watch him fiddling, his face screwed up in discomfort. I want to stay angry, but I can't. It's not his fault. He's only eight years old. He shouldn't have to do this kind of manual labor. Nobody should. He's probably just as sore as me. Or worse.

Poor kid. I collect him into my arms, impeded slightly by the bulky hazsuit. His helmeted head rests against my chest and I grit my teeth as he squirms a little more, but eventually, he relaxes.

They always get us young ones to clean under the bubbles. We're the only ones small enough to reach the glass where it curves toward the ground. The gap is so narrow, the only way to clean it is by lying on our backs. We reach over our heads to wash and squeegee the cursed windows, scrubbing them until our arms ache—until they're so clean we can see up the skirts of the rich snobs inside.

I'll be too big to do this within the year. At least, I hope so. I never thought I'd still be doing this at sixteen, but I'm short for my age. I want to move up in the world and advance to cleaning the top of the bubbles. Still strenuous work, but not nearly as exhausting. No more lying on my back, holding my sore arms above me for hours on end; at the top, I'll rappel down the bubbles to clean them.

I hope I get the promotion soon.

Poor Sebastian has years ahead of him. Years of crawling into those small gaps and having nothing but shaking, aching arms by the end of it. The best he can hope for is an early growth spurt. I pray he'll be so lucky. Papá had been tall. Maybe he'll take after him. I nag him to eat his protein bars, repeating Papá's slogan: "It'll make you big and strong." I don't refrain from repeating it whenever I can.

Lulled by the motion of the bus, I start to drift off. Images flicker before me, my mind too foggy to focus on any of them—Mamá's warm, smiling face; the broken remains of the abandoned city; a heaping plate of Papá's *sancocho*; the rich snobs of the Sparkle Sector, with their perfect, smug faces, who never spare me a glance while I clean the windows that protect them.

Suddenly, Sebastian jumps forward with a gasp.

My eyes fly open.

Sebastian is staring intently out of the window. His helmet blocks his face, so I can't see what direction his eyes are pointing. I look out the window, searching frantically to find what made him start. I stiffen.

¿Qué?

A man walking alone.

A man. Alone. *Outside.*

This can't be real.

His black boots disturb the desert floor, kicking up dirt around his legs. His *unprotected* legs. No hazsuit. He's wearing only a pair of jeans and a t-shirt.

This can't be right.

I adjust my visor to get a better view. The bus is moving away from him fast, but I catch another glance. No mask, no helmet, no suit. His face is fully exposed. The wind tousles his long, dark hair.

The bus turns, obscuring the man from view.

Sebastian twists around in his seat. His eyes are round, a mirror of my own. "How?"

I look around the bus. No one is paying us any attention; Old Henry is still asleep, Liam and his girlfriend—Karrie, Kylie?—are still talking quietly with their heads together. Everyone else is either asleep or falling asleep. No one is staring in a panic out the window, looking for the man in the desert.

A few minutes later, we pull up outside the Sparkle Sector, at the section assigned to clean. The bus stirs. Eyes open, arms stretch, and slowly, the workers make their way off the bus.

Old Henry continues to snore quietly.

I shake his shoulder and his eyes flicker open.

"We're here," I say with a smile.

The fog of sleep dissipates from his eyes. He returns my grin, even though he doesn't have much to smile about. Just another long day of washing windows. He may not have to climb under the bubble like me, but it's still hard work.

As I go to leave, I feel a tug on my hazsuit. I turn to find Sebastian, his eyes still giant orbs. "Martina?"

I shake my head. "I don't know."

We get off the bus and I try to act normal. No one will believe we saw a man in the desert unprotected. And even if they did, we don't need them to impose additional disease screening on us. Not when the man came nowhere near us.

Usually I start the day by going to the rear of the bus to collect a bucket of water. My body moves mechanically, following the same old routine. But my eyes betray me, scanning the distant ruins of the Old City. What if the man comes over here? He could spread a disease.

I pull Sebastian close. "Work beside me today, okay?"

He nods, but his eyes are also on the ruins.

"Good health, Marty," Liam says, filling his own bucket of water next to me. He smiles as I cringe. I hate it when he calls me that—and he knows it. Whenever I hear the nickname, I feel like the weak child I was when we first met. "Coming to the park tonight?"

"I'll be there."

He chuckles. "No shaking, okay?"

"I said I'll be there." I'm not afraid to fight him; he doesn't realize how much I've been practicing without his help.

Liam holds his fist out to Sebastian, who eagerly bumps it with his own.

"You too, little man," Liam says. "I'll teach you a few moves as well."

It'll be good for Sebastian to learn more self-defense. *He might need it*, I think with the mystery man is still fresh in my mind.

Old Henry hobbles toward the water tank. He's not as strong as he used to be, and his back is bent even before he's collected any water.

"I've got this," I say, grabbing his water bucket and hauling it over to his section.

"*Gracias*," he says with a thick Neustin accent. Since he found out that Sebastian and I are from Colombia, he always tries to speak to us in Spanish. It's a sweet gesture that never fails to make me smile.

I collect another couple of buckets for Sebastian and me, then we head toward our section. Side-by-side, we crawl under the glass bubble, disturbing a handful of black beetles that scuttle away.

Sebastian doesn't complain. He never does once we get started. He gets straight to work, lathering the glass overhead with soapy water.

As we work, clearing away the recent buildup of dust and dirt, the inside of the Sparkle Sector comes into view. Through the glass, a stone's throw away, some kids are playing. Wealthy kids, of course. Everyone in the Sparkle Sector is wealthy. Only a bit of glass separates us, but that simple fact makes them seem worlds away. They're busy running around and playing games, or have their eyes glued to their personal comms units, probably taking school lessons. They're the lucky ones who can afford an education. They've never had to work an hour of their lives, let alone a ten-hour shift, like Sebastian.

They're oblivious to the world Sebastian lives in. The world *we* live in. They don't even see him through the windows, scrubbing away at the glass, cleaning every spot until it shines. All I want is for Sebastian to have a life like theirs. To play games, to go to school. No kid should have to work as hard as he does. No kid should have to work to live.

If they don't notice us cleaning beneath them, then I doubt they'd have noticed the mystery man, either. But what if someone has? What will happen to him? Will the guards go looking for him? Will they put him in quarantine or just leave him to wither and die in the desert, exposed to all manner of viruses and diseases? I've never heard of someone like him, someone surviving outside without a hazsuit. There's no saying what the authorities will do if they find out.

The outer doors of the decontamination center clank shut behind us.

The bus sits in the middle of a chamber with thick steel walls, each embedded with large fans. Before we're allowed to leave the bus, the air in the chamber is sucked out and replaced with clean, filtered air. The process takes about five minutes and, of course, Sebastian is restless. At least this time he has good reason. We're both eager to get off this bus and finally talk about what we saw, but we've still got several procedures to go through before that's possible.

A beep sounds, meaning the chamber is now full of clean air and we're safe from any airborne diseases.

The interior doors of the chamber open and the bus drives into the terminal. It parks next to a row of other buses that have either just arrived from other bubble cities or are preparing to depart.

Three short beeps sound, signaling the bus is unlocked.

I drag myself off the bus as quickly as I can, only slightly slower than Sebastian. We race through the unlocked pedestrian exit to the next stage of sanitization.

Individual decon stations line the far wall. People move in and out of the stations as they prepare to enter and exit the center. Red and green lights over the doors indicate which are in use.

We find two available next to each other, enter our PINs, and wait for them to be approved. The PINs send a message to storage to deliver our civilian clothes once we're purified. They're also a security measure. Without a PIN, no one can enter Neustin. I never really considered the need for security before. It's always been just a part of the daily routine. Now, though? A horrifying thought enters my mind: what if it's security against people outside? What if the man tried to infiltrate the bubble? He would infect us all.

I strip off my suit and throw it into the decontaminator machine to wash and dry it.

A shiver runs down my spine, but it's not from my lack of clothes. With each step of the cleansing process, I'm even more confused about how the man is still alive. We go through so many precautions to keep us healthy, to keep anything outside from coming in. It's unthinkable someone could be outside, walking around without hindrance.

While my suit is sprayed with antiseptic and other chemicals, I use the shower to scrub away any possible germs that could have penetrated the suit. The hot water spurts from several ports in the ceiling and walls of the chamber, stinging as it hits my bare flesh. I itch all over from the antibacterial soap. But itchy skin is better than dying from disease or spreading contagions throughout the community.

How has that guy survived without all of this?

Some workers use a soothing sterilized moisturizer to reduce the itchiness, but Sebastian and I can't afford it. All our money goes toward food and medications to keep us healthy. To keep us safe from infection. We already forego a meal sometimes to pay for the meds.

Once I'm red, raw, and itching from the shower, I walk through the chamber to the scanner. A laser runs over my naked body, searching for any remaining germs. I wish I could cover my breasts, but the machine will beep embarrassingly if I do, and I won't be allowed to exit. My skin crawls. Anyone could be watching the scan.

I breathe a sigh of relief when the scanners don't detect any anomalies—but why should they? Of course I'm healthy. The man didn't come anywhere near me.

A short beep sounds and I move to the next chamber, where I can finally dress again, this time in comfortable civilian clothes. I hurriedly put on my ratty old jeans and a t-shirt, which are all sterilized, of course, but a far cry from respectable.

When I'm dressed, I find my hazsuit ready and waiting for collection. With a push of a button, I send it off to storage until it's needed again tomorrow morning.

"Ready?" Sebastian is at my elbow, hopping from foot to foot. Under his cloth mask—his favorite one with a robot jaw printed on it—his cheeks are pink from scrubbing them. His black hair is still damp, flopping over his eyes. He flicks it off his face, but it flops straight back over his eyes.

I nod. I'm just as ready to get out of here as he is. I shoulder my backpack and put on my own face mask—plain red—and hurry Sebastian out of the decontamination center.

We're wordless as we march through The Nix. Unlike the Sparkle Sector, The Nix is a patchwork of rundown sheds, even near the edge of the bubble, the most sought after area. The residents have tried to animate their homes with cheerful colors; one has blue walls and red shutters, another has orange plant boxes that border a yellow apartment, while its neighbor favors pink and green. They remind me of the neighborhood in Colombia where I grew up, which was as bright as a rainbow and covered in beautiful art.

The evening sun makes the colors even more vibrant. Although they're in disrepair, the houses are pretty, all the same. But I don't have time to appreciate how pretty it looks. I jog across the concrete streets with Sebastian in tow, weaving in and out of crowds, taking shortcuts down narrow alleys, not stopping until we reach the edge of the bubble.

Sebastian reaches the window before me. He splays his fingers against the glass and squashes his face against it.

"Do you see anything?" I don't wait for an answer. Instead, I mimic him, bringing my eyes as close to the glass as I can.

The glare from the sun is so great I can't see anything through the glass. Not to mention it's filthy. Our bubble doesn't get cleaned regularly like the bubble surrounding the Sparkle Sector. No one in The Nix has money to spare for window washing. Layer upon layer of dirt and dust veils the glass, making it nearly impossible to see through.

I find a section that isn't as dirty. Even so, all I see is the vague outline of the sunken buildings in the distance.

I push away from the window with a huff.

"Did you see anything?" Sebastian asks.

I frown at my brother. Is that hope in his voice? What is he hopeful for? The man is going to be dead by morning. Nobody can survive outside that long without dying from disease. There is no hope for him.

I shake my head and squeeze Sebastian's shoulder. He slumps forward, resting his body against mine.

I tuck him under my arm. "Let's go get our meds, *hermanito*."

Two

THE LINE IS LONG when we arrive at the med-bay. Our detour to the bubble window cost us precious time. Now we'll have to wait over an hour to get our evening meds.

I spot Liam and his girlfriend—Klarice?—near the front. Where we should be. Sebastian and I usually race out of the decontamination center to beat the rush.

We reluctantly join the back of the queue.

It doesn't take long for my body to scream in protest. My limbs are so heavy they're dragging me into the ground. Our tiny pod might not be the biggest or most comfortable home in the world, but now it seems an unattainable heaven. I can't wait to flop down onto the bed. Even if I do have to share it with Sebastian.

Sebastian—restless as ever—hops from one foot to the other.

"Would you stop it?" I mutter under my breath, sparing an apologetic glance at the woman behind me. She doesn't seem to notice. Well, I don't care if he's not disturbing anyone else; he's annoying the hell out of me.

"I'm bored, Martina."

"What do you want me to do about it? We've still got ages to wait."

"Humph!" He leans into my body and gives me the most maddening hug ever.

I wriggle out of his grip. "If we don't get our meds, we might catch a disease or a virus." A bit more gently, I add, "You don't want to get sick, do you?"

He shakes his head.

"Well, how about you go wait over there?" I point to a spot outside of a shop selling face masks, home crafts, and a variety of junk. "Come back when I'm near the front of the line. You know they won't distribute your meds to me, so you'll need to be here."

"Okay." He starts to edge away.

"And here." I hold out my comms unit. "Play some games. But keep an eye out for me, okay?"

His eyes light up. He doesn't get to play games very often. We only have the one unit between us and the datanet is expensive. I can't afford to buy him an education. Not even self-paced courses or access to historical data. There's so much we don't know about the world simply because we don't have the money.

Sebastian takes my comms unit and squats by the shop front. Within seconds, he's absorbed in his game.

I wish it could always be like this for him. Just a normal kid playing games, not one that must work to put food on the table. When we first arrived in Texas, I wouldn't allow Sebastian to take on work. But the money I made was barely enough to cover the cost of our meds. So we tried to save money where we could. We stopped using the datanet. Then we started skipping meals. Sebastian became skinny. Even after I gave him most of the food from my own plate. Soon all his childish puppy fat had wasted away and his ribs stuck out unnaturally. We needed to buy more food.

He started working with me as a runner, carrying buckets of water and sponges from the bus to the workers cleaning the bubble windows. He learned quickly, and a year ago he joined me washing under the bubbles. It's still hard to see his little body pushed to its limit, to see him dragging his body along at the end of each grueling day.

Still, at least now I don't have to worry about leaving him alone. The Nix isn't safe. Especially for a child. He could be snatched and sold, and there's no telling what they'd do to him. I see the bruised kids on the streets, hiding their heads when anyone comes near, darting into dark crevices seeking safety.

My stomach lurches at the thought of his broken body.

A cough sounds, making me jump. The woman behind me is pointing at the line, which has moved forward considerably. I hurry to close the gap.

I look at where Sebastian sat down. He's not there. I scan the area, looking for the familiar robot jaw mask. There's red, blue and rainbow masks. Masks that look like birds and butterflies, others that look like superheroes. But not a robot one. I can't see Sebastian. Perhaps he's with someone we know? I look up and down the queue, but there's no one I recognize. Liam's long gone and so is Old Henry.

My heart beats faster. There's too many people around, sitting on steps and at tables, lounging in cafes and bars, milling around the pop-up craft market, watching a street performer play drums on an old bucket. He could be anywhere, lost in the crowd.

Maybe I should leave the line to look for him. But I hesitate—there's only a handful of people ahead of me. If he's not with me when I reach the counter, they won't dispense his drugs to me. We'll have to rejoin the back of the queue, and it's almost as long as it was when we first joined it. On top of that, if he doesn't take his meds, he'll be at risk of catching something and getting sick.

I take a deep breath, trying to calm down. Sebastian isn't a silly young kid anymore. He's smart enough not to talk to strangers. If he was nabbed, surely I would have heard him scream? But the crowd is full of noises, so I can't be sure.

Only one person stands in front of me.

"Sebastian!" I call.

I look at the man in front of me, willing him to stay at the counter a little longer. But he moves to leave, holding his sachet of pills. He flings back his head, swallowing the pills with a mouthful of water, and walks away from the counter.

The pharmacist behind the counter nods her head at me. I drag my feet toward her, ignoring her impatient stare.

"Scan your thumb," the pharmacist barks.

"Can I collect my brother's medications too?" I ask.

The pharmacist doesn't hear me; she's busy doing something inside her booth. After a moment, she looks back at my thumb reading. Realizing that I haven't put my thumb on the scanner yet, she repeats, "Scan your thumb."

"I need to collect my brother's meds, too."

She scowls. "You know the rules. I am only authorized to distribute medication to individuals who have scanned their thumb."

"He was right here," I plead. "He's only eight. He just got bored in the long line and left. Can't you distribute his meds to me just this once? Please?"

"No," she says flatly.

"Oh, come on! I'm his sister! I'm basically his mom. Surely you're allowed to give them to me?"

The woman is expressionless behind her mask.

I bang my fist on the counter. "I've waited in this line for over an hour! He's a kid. You can't expect a kid to wait that long. Of course he's run off."

The woman looks over my shoulder at the line behind me. "Miss, there are other people waiting. Scan your thumb or leave."

I am tempted to tell her I'm not leaving until she gives me the meds, but there's a guard standing a few yards away. One word from the pharmacist and I'll be forcibly removed. Resigned, I scan my thumb. I might as well get mine while I'm here.

The pharmacist presses a button, then a sachet of pills slides across the counter with a vial of water. I snatch them up. I'm about to swallow them when something touches my elbow.

"Sebastian! Where have you been?" I don't wait for his response. I grab his thumb and place it on the scanner. The pharmacist taps her nails on the counter, frowning at both of us. Another sachet is distributed.

"That will be twenty-four credits," the pharmacist says.

"Twenty-four?" I shake my head. "It was only twenty credits yesterday."

"Yes," she responds like she's talking to a child younger than Sebastian, "but today there is an extra pill, and you have to pay for that."

I notice the additional blue pill in each sachet. "What's it for?"

"Protection against the new Azutine virus. There is an outbreak in the Linto quarter. It's mandatory."

This damned virus is going to cost us four more credits every day. How will we afford that? The pharmacist doesn't care; she waves her hand impatiently over the ID pad until I enter my PIN and pay. I have no choice. I need to keep Sebastian safe, and that costs money. We'll just have to ration our food.

Sebastian and I lower our masks, swallow the bitter pills, and then leave the counter. The pharmacist turns her attention to the next person before we're even out of the way. There's not a moment to spare for the two of us or our problems.

I take a moment to digest the pills—and the additional costs—before rounding on Sebastian.

"Where were you?" I snatch the comms unit from him.

"I … I …" Sebastian's eyes are wide with alarm. "I went back to the window. I wanted to see the man again."

I sigh. His words are like a bucket of water thrown over my fire. I understand his curiosity. I want to know more about the man, too.

"Did you see him?" I ask, unable to hide my interest.

He shakes his head. "Do you think we'll ever see him again?"

"I don't think so, *hermanito*. He's probably very sick already."

Sebastian's head falls and he shuffles his feet.

"He's probably *loco*." As soon as it leaves my lips, I realize it's no comfort at all to think of the man as crazy. I pull Sebastian into an embrace and kiss the top of his head.

"*Vamos!*" I say, changing the subject. "Liam is waiting for us in the park."

"Do we have to?" Sebastian moans.

"I thought you wanted to go?"

He shrugs. "I did. But I'm tired now."

"Well, I'm not going to give Liam the satisfaction of thinking I shaked out." I ruffle his hair. I don't tell Sebastian the other reason I want to go. After that scare, he could do with some more fighting practice.

His shoulders slump.

"We won't stay long, and then we'll get some dinner." I wrap my arm around his shoulder. "And find out what's with those latest blue pills."

"They were gross." Sebastian sticks out his tongue and bares his teeth. I laugh at his deranged expression and then snap his mask back up over his mouth.

There's already a pair fighting when we arrive at the park. If you can call it a park. It's really just a concrete courtyard with a handful of trees. Not like the lush gardens some of the other quarters have.

Liam turns from the small crowd and greets us, bumping each of our fists. "Hey little man, hey Marty."

I roll my eyes.

"You're late," Liam says. "I thought you'd shaked."

I chuckle. "And miss the chance to beat your skinny butt?"

I recognize a few other people in the crowd, and they come over to bump fists or knock elbows with me and Sebastian. We don't kiss people on the cheek in greeting like we did in Colombia. People fear it will spread germs.

"We're next," Liam shouts above the crowd when one fighter taps out. The crowd feels alive, mumbling in anticipation. They part to let us through to the center.

Liam and I lather our arms with sanitizer gel. It doesn't matter that we recently went through the decontamination center—it's standard procedure before the hand-to-hand fights.

I turn to face Liam, and the crowd closes in around us.

When I first started fighting Liam, I was weak and hopeless. I lost every time. But now our fights are the kind to draw in a crowd; it's never certain which of us will win. Liam has taught me well.

I keep light on my toes, leaning forward, like I would if I was dancing salsa. My muscles are taut and ready. Despite what Liam might think, I'm not scared. My heart beats steadily in my chest.

Liam lunges. He often attacks first, he's so impatient. But I don't mind—I win more frequently this way.

I block his blow and he grabs my wrist with his other hand—exactly like I anticipated. I twist and duck before flipping him over my back the moment he's caught off guard. Within seconds of the fight starting, he's on the ground with me on top of him.

His eyes crinkle in a smile above his mask.

I shake my head, feigning disappointment in him.

We stand and prepare to fight again. The best of three rounds wins.

The second round goes for longer—long enough for me to work up a sweat. For a while, I have the upper hand. But then the mystery man pops into my head and I lose concentration. Liam clocks me in the gut with his elbow. I know he can hit harder, but it still smarts.

Before long, Liam has me in a headlock that I can't get out of. I tap out.

So it's even; we've both won a round. I narrow my eyes and take my stance. I push the mystery man out of my thoughts. If I'm going to win this round, I need to concentrate.

Even though I know the odds are against me if I move first, I do it anyway. I lunge at his torso, trying to knock him backward. But I'm only five foot four. I'm not big or heavy enough for that to work. It's a stupid move.

Or, at least, that's what Liam thinks.

He goes to push me down, but I've ducked lower than he expected. I spin my leg around, trying to knock his from under him. But he anticipates my move and jumps over my leg.

I'm off balance, so it's easy for Liam to tackle me to the ground. I flail and buck, but he has me pinned down. I can't move. With a frustrated cry, I tap out.

"Nice move," he laughs, climbing off me.

I scowl. He holds out his hand to help me up, but I slap it away. How could I make such a stupid move? I should know better.

I stand up and am met with an influx of pain. It could be from the day's work or the fight, but I'm determined to ignore it.

Some of the crowd cheer as we walk away, relinquishing the park to the other fighters.

We lather ourselves with sanitizer gel again, as we do at the end of every fight. When Liam's done, he turns to Sebastian. "How about you, little man? Ready to learn some of those moves I taught your big sister?"

Liam goes through some defensive moves with Sebastian. Despite not wanting to come, Sebastian enjoys himself. He always does.

I watch on grimly. If anything ever happens to Sebastian—I suppress the images of the street kids, with their sunken eyes—then these moves will be useful. He's learned a lot since we started taking lessons from Liam. But he's still so little.

Before long, my stomach is growling and I don't think my legs will hold me up much longer.

Sebastian and I head across the square to the diner. It's packed, as usual. We find a table, and this time Sebastian stays where I leave him, eager for me to return with food. When I place the tray in front of him, his face falls. Even though it's the cheapest place to eat in The Nix, there isn't much on the menu I can afford. Especially with this new pill to pay for. The best I can get is a bowl of stew—more water than food—with chewy meat and wilted vegetables, as well as two dinner rolls. But Sebastian doesn't complain. He offers me a spoon before he scoops a small piece of meat into his mouth.

"We can pretend this is Papá's *sancocho*," I suggest.

Sebastian doesn't say anything, just keeps chewing.

"Do you remember Papá's cooking?" I ask.

He shrugs. My heart caves in a little. He's too ashamed to say it, but I can tell his memories of our parents are fading.

I swallow some stew, then make a face at him. "Well, this isn't quite as nice."

He grins and makes a face back.

Three

A PLEASANT CHIME, *DAH duh dum*, signals the evening's health announcements. We continue to eat as Dr. Lederman, the health minister and CEO of PMC Life Tech, materializes on every screen around the diner, including our comms unit. He wears a black shirt that's too tight on him with a shiny blue tie tucked into it. Yesterday it was a candy red tie. Why he bothers wearing such brightly colored ties is beyond me. It's not going to make his announcements any more cheerful. Maybe it's part of his mission to appear young. But no amount of trendy clothes can help him with that.

"We've had three confirmed deaths from the Azutine virus today," Dr. Lederman says, delving straight into the happy news.

People at a nearby table gasp, their hands flying to cover their already masked mouths. I barely stir; the deaths don't come as a shock. Azutine is a new virus and has killed no one before today, but I knew someone would die within the week. Someone always does soon after a novel virus is detected.

I watch Dr. Lederman's artificially inflated lips as he continues, "The Azutine virus poses an inherent risk to our community." It's hard to tell if this news affects him at all. His voice is neutral and his face carries no emotion. I doubt it could express emotion even if he wanted to, with the amount of anti-wrinkle and filler he's injected into his forehead, cheeks, lips and who knows where else. I don't know why he bothers—it doesn't work. He still looks like an old man. A creepy old man, with features that barely look human anymore.

The diner is quiet. Even the waitstaff pause; everyone is watching the headline news.

"We are still tracing the origins of the disease, and one hundred citizens are under strict quarantine. We have asked the residents in the Linto quarter to adhere to standard lockdown procedures and maintain an 8 p.m. curfew. Of course, the Linto quarter will be off limits to all other quarters until further notice. Your cooperation helps keep each and every one of us safe."

I feel bad for the Linto quarter. The Nix quarter has been in lockdown before and it is tough. They enforce restrictions on everything, from the number of people allowed in the diner at one time, to how often and how long you can leave your home each day. They only allowed us out of our pod for two hours per day. And our pod is only made for a single person. It's too small to stand up in and only wide enough for a single bed. Stuck in such closed quarters, Sebastian and I were going crazy by the end of the week.

To make matters worse, we earned no money that week in lockdown, which meant we had no food. Any money we'd saved up was spent on medication. We lived on pills and water for the week. The scent of food wafting from the diner's kitchen reminds me of how empty my stomach had felt. How much I had longed for food.

Remembering that week almost makes me feel better about spending money on the additional blue pill, but then I look at Sebastian, who's already licking clean his bowl, and my stomach rumbles.

"... attacks the liver as well as other organs, poisoning the blood." Dr. Lederman is still talking about the horrific new virus. "The blue pills," he flicks his tie, and it's now obvious that his tie is the same color as the electric blue pills, "act as a blood stabilizer, a little like iodine in water; it stops the spread of poison in the bloodstream, preventing the virus from taking hold."

His pouting lips manage to smile, which is supposed to be reassuring. It misses the mark. "We've included the blue pills in your evening medication sachets at the small price of only 2 credits per pill, because your health is priceless!"

I snort. It seems to me our health is worth 2 credits, at least.

Nobody else in the diner looks like they can afford the pills either; their clothes are well-worn, like mine, and there's a hungry, hollow look in too many cheeks. Some men nearby frown, shaking their heads and exchanging worried glances. One of the waitresses, Rosa, is muttering to herself, unaware that she's talking out loud. I catch her eye and give her a smile, which she weakly returns.

Some diners, though, seem to accept the news. A couple a few tables down are nodding their heads, clearly in agreement with Dr. Lederman.

I look at Sebastian, who seems to be the only person in the diner oblivious to the news, still licking his bowl as if more stew will miraculously appear.

"Don't shake on those pills," Dr. Lederman says. "They could save your life."

I roll my eyes. You can't *shake* on medication, only people. His pursuit of youth is so ridiculous.

The minister turns to an update on other viruses in circulation. He talks about the usual stuff—the current rate of infection, active cases, treatments, and the state of quarantine. The diners lose their attention, returning to their food, and I only half listen myself. We hear these reports daily, and while I want to stay up to date with the news, right now I'd rather be tucking myself and Sebastian into bed.

"*Hola*, Martina." My eyes snap open; I didn't realize they had started to droop. I look up to see Rosa collecting our empty bowls. Her eyes smile above her mask.

"Good health to you both," she says.

"Good health, Tía," Sebastian and I say in unison. She's not our auntie, but it's polite to call her Tía.

"That Azutine virus sounds pretty horrific, doesn't it?"

"Don't they all?"

Rosa looks over her shoulder, watching as her boss ducks into the kitchen. When he disappears, she pulls out two dinner rolls from her apron and holds them to me. "Here. Shh."

Sebastian looks at them hungrily. I try not to do the same. I should be too proud to take them. I wish we didn't need her charity. But I'm too hungry to object.

"Thank you," I murmur, hiding the rolls in my backpack. Determined to change the subject, I ask, "How's your husband?"

"Oh, *está bien.*" She brushes her bangs out of her eyes. "His hands are almost healed, so he'll be back at work soon."

Rosa's husband usually works in the diner too, but a week ago a vat of boiling oil burst onto his hands.

"They could fix his burns that quickly?"

"The doctors are *maravillosos.*" Rosa's eyes take on a dreamy look.

"Please tell him good health from us."

Rosa smiles and hurries away with our dirty bowls and silverware.

The minister has finally finished his miserable evening announcement. He signs off with his usual salutation, "May we all stay healthy and safe." His warped, bloated face fades from all the screens.

Sebastian's head droops toward the table.

"*Vamos*, let's go," I say.

Outside the diner, I pass him one of the dinner rolls. His face lights up as he takes it, but his eyes still squint with sleepiness.

As expected, as soon as Sebastian crawled into our pod, he fell asleep, and is now sprawled out across the bed, leaving only a small corner of it for me. I've been twisting my body around him for hours, but I can't get comfortable. I just can't stop thinking about the man in the desert.

The image of his rotting body plagues my mind. Because he surely died out there. Maybe that's what some people do—they go outside to die.

I turn over, only to find Sebastian's foot in my face. Grumbling, I push his foot away, but end up with an elbow poking my side instead. I wish I could afford a place with room for two beds. Or *at least* a bigger bed. But that won't happen anytime soon. Not now we have to squeeze in the cost of those stupid little blue pills. If only they promoted me to abseil cleaning; it pays much better. I'm sick of waiting. I've done the training; it's just a matter of waiting for a position to open up.

Sebastian's chest rises and falls. At least sleep comes easy for him, despite sharing a bed with me. I wish he could get an education, or at least more access to the datanet so he could learn *something*. He could get a manager's position someday and do more than just grunt work. The managers at the decontamination centers are well respected and earn decent amounts. Sebastian could have a good life if he got a job like that. He could even move to the Bama quarter, with its beautiful gardens. I've seen him looking at the gardens through the windows as we wash them, a wishful look on his face. They're not as nice as the gardens in the Sparkle Sector, but he could have a peaceful life there. A life that doesn't involve cleaning windows.

He squirms, a frown forming between his brows, but he doesn't wake up.

An alternative to that pleasant life invades my mind. A life where he slogs, day in and day out, cleaning windows. Breaking his back. Eventually breaking his soul. Struggling to get by. A dead-end life with no future. I know that's my future. It's all I have to look forward to. Even if I get a promotion, I'll still be stuck cleaning windows for the rest of my life. Unless I wander off into the desert alone and die from disease. Just like that man.

I try to relax into my pillow, but the thoughts don't stop.

He must have had a death wish. That's the only explanation. There can't be any other reason to be outside the bubbles without a hazsuit. But he had looked so casual, like he didn't have a care in the world, strolling along as if he was in one of the Bama quarter gardens, completely safe. Maybe that's what it looks like when you've got nothing left to care about.

If Sebastian hadn't seen him too, I would believe I'd imagined it. I've never heard of anyone going outside without protection. Voluntarily, that is.

A shiver runs up my spine. My parents certainly didn't end up outside by choice. I see flashes of the Colombian bubble as it crumbled; the last glimpses I had of my parents, with their terrified, stricken expressions.

I shake the images out of my head.

But I can't get rid of the image of the solitary man quite as easily.

My eyes fly open. Sleep isn't eluding me; it is completely and utterly avoiding me. The more I try to sleep, the more awake I feel. Even with my exhausted body, my mind just won't turn off.

I throw off my bed covers. Sebastian doesn't flinch as I climb over him to the pod door. I pull on some shoes and put on my mask before I leave; it's illegal not to wear one in The Nix quarter. Sebastian won't miss me if I go for a short walk, but I still quietly close the pod door as I exit.

Our pod is part of a group of twenty pods built above a curry restaurant. Even though the restaurant is closed, the sweet spices still permeate the air as soon as I'm outside. I ignore my rumbling tummy and climb down the access ladder, past the lower pods and the shop front.

This area of town is never completely quiet at night. Neon signs flicker, inviting people to unsavory activities, and claiming complete health for all clientele. A few food vendors are still open, peddling tacos, samosas, pizza, and kebabs—satisfying the hungry late-night patrons willing to pay the premium prices. Cries and shrieks pierce the air as someone trips over their high heels or a beer bottle slips from drunken fingers and smashes to the ground.

It's not the safest spot for a relaxing walk, so I hurry out of the area. Before long, I reach quieter streets. I wander aimlessly from street to street. The neon signs give way to quaint window shutters, houses lined with flowerpots, and doors that are tall enough to allow visitors to enter without stooping, unlike my pod. The night reduces the colors of the houses to shades of gray. Occasionally, a street lamp lights up a home in vivid color, but it washes back to gray at the edge of the light.

There's no one around. No drunken giggles. Just the soft hum of air being pumped into the bubble's atmosphere, keeping the air clean and the temperature an even 72 degrees.

In the tranquil setting, my mind finally feels like it's unwinding.

I turn a corner and behold the deep black of the bubble's window. It stretches high over my head. I catch my breath. My mind wasn't winding down after all but deceiving me into returning to the edge of the bubble.

The blackness beyond is intimidating. I approach slowly.

As I come closer to the glass, all I can see is my own distorted reflection and the glimmer of street lamps. I stare at myself for a moment. My mask hides most of my face, but my eyes are large and wide awake. My curly hair is a mess after tossing and turning in bed.

I squint, trying to look through my reflection to outside, but it's all a blur.

I edge closer. The light from inside the bubble, although dim, creates a glare on the glass, making it impossible to see any details in the darkness. I edge even closer until my face is a fraction of an inch away from the glass. I cup my hands around my eyes, trying to block out all the light and glare.

Night stretches out beyond. I cannot see the desert or the Old City. It's just blackness out there. I don't know what I expected. Lights? Movement? A man staring back at me?

I shudder.

It dawns on me that if there *is* anyone outside, they'll see me clearly, even if I can't see them. Even in the soft glow of the street lamps, I'll stand out like a beacon against the shadows of night.

I take several quick steps backward.

I realize I'm in even more light where I'm standing, so I back up further until I reach the line of houses.

Pausing for a moment, I stare out at the emptiness through the windows. Maybe it's not so empty after all. I can't shake the feeling that someone *is* watching me.

Something catches my eye. Movement. A shadow darker than the night.

I go cold despite the perfectly controlled temperature. My heart knocks at my ribcage.

Get a grip!

I search the dark for another movement, a shadow, a light—anything. But it's fruitless. There's nothing. I walk backward from the window, surprised to find my legs wobbling, until I'm hidden by the shadows of the houses. Then I glance back over my shoulder several times as I hurry away.

The streets have lost their tranquility. The shadows could hide all manner of horrors, and I actually look forward to the neon lights of my neighborhood. At least it's deep within the bubble.

I don't dawdle on my way home.

Four

I LAY ON MY back with a squeegee and a sponge, reaching above my head to clean the underside of the bubble. Soapy water drips down, smudging the visor of my hazsuit. I'm wedged in pretty good to make sure I get every inch; I'll get in trouble if it's not cleaned properly.

I keep having to go back over sections I've already done because of spots I've missed. It's unlike me; I'm usually efficient. But my concentration keeps wandering. Every second, I'm tempted to lower my arms and drift off to sleep.

It's frustrating. Last night I couldn't sleep, no matter what I did. Now that I want to be awake, I can barely keep my eyes open.

I wish Sebastian were here. His talking and whining would help keep me awake. The one time I need him and he's stationed somewhere else. Typical.

I'm not worried about him, he knows what he's doing, and I trust the other window grunts to get on with their jobs and leave him alone.

My right eye twitches. I want to scratch it, but it's impossible in the hazsuit. To annoy me even more, a swarm of miniature flies keep buzzing near my face, landing on my visor and blurring my vision.

Suddenly, the light above gets blocked. Some girl inside the Sparkle Sector has come right up to the window, gazing at something off in the distance.

I try to keep working, but it's hard to see what I'm doing with the light blocked. Doesn't this idiot realize I'm trying to work here? All she needs to do is look down through the window and she'll see me. She could stand anywhere else by the window, but of course, she chooses right above me. Some people are just born stupid.

The light pirate is a dark-skinned girl wearing high heels and an expensive looking pink dress; if she takes one step closer, I'll be able to see up it. I hope she doesn't. I don't feel like looking at her stupid lacy underpants.

With a huff, I wipe away the drops of water from my visor with the sleeve of my hazsuit and return to work. At my movement, she looks down, right at me. Our eyes lock.

Her pouted lips form an "oh" of surprise and she jumps backward.

My cheeks burn. I don't want her to think I was spying on her. Or looking up her dress. I was here first; she encroached on me!

I try to avoid her eyes, but it's impossible to look away. She isn't wearing a face mask—no one does in the Sparkle Sector—so I can see she's incredibly pretty. She might be a little older than me, maybe seventeen or eighteen. Her black hair is elaborately braided across the top of her head and around her crown, with a silver chain woven through it.

I frown at her. She just stares back at me with her mouth still agape, like the stupid pet goldfish I had in Colombia. She might be everything I wish I was—tall, slender, gorgeous, rich—but at least my brain is still bigger than hers.

I reach the squeegee over my head and pull it down the length of the window and then repeat the action, all the while keeping my eyes on her. She continues to stare. Is her life so boring and empty, with all her money and fancy clothes, that it's entertaining to watch me wash windows?

She looks over her shoulder. She hurriedly speaks to someone behind her, though I can't hear anything through the glass. Then she looks at me again. She cocks her head, a slight crease forming on her brow.

Usually, I'm ignored by people inside. It's like I don't exist to them. Why is this girl still staring at me?

After a moment, she takes a deep breath and sashays away, out of view.

I suddenly feel uncomfortable in my suit. My sweaty skin sticks to the fabric. I tap the regulation unit on the arm of my suit. The temperature is an even 72 degrees Fahrenheit, as usual. So why do I feel so hot?

I tug the material off from my skin, hoping it will help the air circulation inside my suit. It doesn't.

I return to work, feeling even more frustrated than before.

"Martina?" Sebastian calls.

It's been an hour since I saw the gawking girl. I'm tired, hot, and hungry, although it's not time for our lunch break.

"What do you want, Sebastian?" I don't bother hiding the impatience in my tone.

"There's a man out here."

"*¿Un hombre?*" Is it the same one from yesterday?

Both Sebastian and I had searched through the bus windows this morning when we left The Nix, traveling around the bubble city, past the Bama quarter, to the Sparkle Sector. But we saw nothing strange.

Dropping my squeegee and sponge, I shuffle out as quickly as I can. I jump to my feet when I'm clear of the bubble and scan the horizon. There's no one there. I'm about to complain about this to Sebastian when I notice a man standing behind him. He's in a hazsuit, and the truth dawns. Sebastian wasn't talking about the mystery man. He meant this man. He's from the bubble washing company; their logo is printed on his hazsuit. He must be a manager. Only managers have company hazsuits.

"Martina Monsalve?" the man asks.

"Yes, sir." I nod. "Good health to you."

"Good health." He nods back. "Congratulations, we're promoting you to abseil duty."

The man turns and walks away, leaving me gaping. When he sees I'm not following, he tilts his head in invitation to join him.

"With the lockdown of the Linto quarter," he says, "we're short of qualified abseilers. We should have got you up there this morning. Now we're behind schedule, so we need you up on the bubble ASAP. We'll get you outfitted at the decontamination center. You'll need a harness and utility belt with bungee straps. Understood?"

I nod. He seems to appreciate my efficient response.

"Good." He reaches a sterile truck, gesturing for me to get in the passenger seat. I follow him in a daze. I'm being promoted. Unbelievable. Is this the chance I've been waiting for?

As I reach for the door, I hesitate, remembering Sebastian trailing behind us. I spin around. Sebastian is waving his hands, shooing me into the truck with a massive grin on his face.

"I'll see you later!" I return his grin and swing into the truck.

My hands are shaking. Although I've scaled the domes before during training, it feels different this time. This time I'm being paid for it. Almost double what I was paid before. It's not fear that has me vibrating, but exhilaration. I'll finally be able to afford a decent meal for Sebastian. I don't have to worry about the cost of the extra blue pills. We'll have enough.

It won't be enough for Sebastian to quit washing the bubbles, but he'll be able to take weekends off. He'll have some time to be a child, some time for learning. He'll have a chance to become something other than a window grunt, something more than me.

I climb up a miniature access ladder on the side of the Sparkle Sector's bubble. My safety cable is attached to the pole that runs alongside, protecting me from death if I slip. It's slow progress. I have to stop for each breaker to transfer my carabiner onto the next rung, which is often. But at least I'm safe.

When I reach the top, I'm out of breath. I take a moment to slow my heart rate. The plaque at the top tells me I'm standing on the Bush quarter bubble, but I know it as the Sparkle Sector.

Somewhere far below, Sebastian is washing the underside. Within are the wealthy citizens of Neustin. They're living their comfortable lives, in velvet lounges under jeweled chandeliers, eating fresh meat and sipping on cocktails. Not that I can see all that from here, the internal towers and luscious plants block the view of the street.

I see the tops of all four bubbles that make up Neustin, as well as the corridors that connect them. But it's not them that interest me. From up here, I have a clear view of the Old City. The ruined buildings, half-sunk in the desert, with sands rolling over them like bed covers bunched under a chin. An occasional building stands taller than the others, bearing its scars of abandonment. The sun is high, so the forsaken buildings cast almost no shadows.

A bird flies overhead, soaring over the ruins, then dives into them to catch its prey; probably a desert mouse.

I search for other signs of life. Through gaping doorways and empty windows, over hills, and in the groove that might have once been a riverbed but has long since dried up. I never realized how large this city used to be. It stretches out for miles. So many people must have lived there—much more than the population of Neustin. But it's empty now. There's no people, no movement, nothing; not even the whisper of a wind. Even the bird has disappeared.

I can't waste any more time staring out at nothing. I get back to work. The last thing I want is to be accused of shaking off on my first day. I strap in my ropes and gear on the anchors, just like I was taught, and I turn my back on the Old City. I plant my feet and lower myself, pulling back on the rope as I step down the glass to the windows assigned to clean. Other workers dot the bubble doing the same. I select a self-soaping sponge from the gear that hangs at my waist and start washing.

I spend the afternoon rappelling down, stopping at each square of curved window to wash it before moving onto the next. Then I climb the bubble again and clean the next row of windows.

I have never felt more alive, more free. The world seems so much bigger from up here. It's the opposite of being squished into the wedged spaces under the bubble. Out here, there is so much space.

By the time I reach the bottom for the second time, the sun is lowering, but I start the climb back up the bubble all the same. I get paid per window, so I don't want to waste any time.

"Monsalve!" The washing manager calls up to me from the ground. "We're done for the day. Get down here!"

I pause from my climb and look down at him, considering whether to tell him I want to keep working. Will that show diligence or disobedience? I'm not sure, but I'm eager to start my third abseil. But as I look down, I realize how dark it's gotten. The shadows stretch far into the Old City, which is now veiled in gray.

Except for a spot of brightness.

A light; the glowing, flickering light of a flame. Someone has started a fire in the Old City. It's a long way from the bubble, so I can't see it clearly. There must be someone there, tending it, but I can't see them. It's just a spot of orange glowing amongst the ruins.

"Monsalve!"

I look down at my manager. His arms are folded as he impatiently waits for me. After one last glance at the fire, I figure I won't find any answers from staring at it. So I secure my gear and do two long and quick bunny hops to the ground.

"You did well today, kid," the manager says gruffly. "But don't overdo it. I'll get canned if you're out too late."

"Yes, sir." I don't admit the reason I hesitated; I'd seen signs of life where no one should be able to survive.

Five

Last night, I was able to provide a decent meal for Sebastian and myself. Rosa got a shock when we ordered our feast. We indulged in crisp vegetables, steak and even had ice-cream for dessert. Neither of us has had ice-cream since we left Colombia, though I doubt Sebastian even remembers that.

We gorged ourselves and then rolled into bed to sleep. Sebastian's smile stretched from ear to ear the entire time. I haven't seen him smile like that in a long time. We can't afford to eat like that every night, but it was worth a little splurge to see that smile light up Sebastian's face.

I didn't mention to Sebastian the fire I saw in the Old City. I don't want to get his hopes up, as it couldn't be the mystery man. He'd be so sick by now—or dead. But it can't be anyone else, either. Surely there's no other person in this world so stupid as to leave the safety of the bubbles? It makes no sense. It mustn't have been a fire after all, just some light reflected off scrap metal. It's all absolutely normal. Nothing to concern myself over.

I considered going to the edge of the bubble again last night, in search of a fire, but I was lulled into sleep by the fullness of my belly before I could really think it over. It's a wonder what a good meal can do for a decent night's sleep.

Now I'm back on top of the bubble, abseiling down it with my squeegee hanging from a cord at my waist. My body aches differently than usual. It isn't used to this kind of work. But it's better than being squeezed under the bubble with my arms over my head. I know my body will get used to this ache in time. Even if it doesn't, the extra money is worth the pain.

After the fourth climb up the bubble, my calves burn and my glutes are tight. All the weight of the gear presses down on my waist, making it harder with each climb. But when I abseil down again, my focus is all on the job at hand. Scrubbing the windows and wiping them clean.

I am still near the top of the bubble when I hear someone shouting.

There are no other abseilers nearby. I look down to the ground and see the washing manager waving and shouting up at me. He's too far away to hear what he's saying. Surely he can't possibly be telling me to finish again? There's at least three hours of good light left. Is he trying to stop me from earning more? Maybe I'm going too fast and he doesn't want to pay me that much.

Regardless of what he wants, I can go as fast as I want. I turn back to the windows and continue washing. He can't trick me out of my money.

He shouts again, but I keep working. He's barely audible at this distance, so it's easy to ignore him and continue cleaning. I finish the third window and lower myself to the next.

I'm scrubbing at a big glob of bird poo baked onto the glass when I realize it's more than just the manager shouting now. Multiple voices join the racket. I glance down. The manager is standing with two other abseilers, all of them waving up at me. They look like flowers blowing in the wind, waving their arms like that in their white hazsuits. The dust of the desert swirls up and around their feet, blowing across their bodies and then hiding them from my view.

It's windier than usual.

I return to scrubbing the bird poo. I've worked through worse.

The spot is almost clean when a big gust of wind hits me, pushing me off the glass. It spins me around and flings my back-side hard against the bubble.

For a moment, I can't breathe. All air has been expelled from my body.

My heart is beating fast and hard when the pressure in my chest finally eases and I gulp in air greedily.

I'm facing out toward the Old City, but I can barely see it. Clouds of dirt and sand swirl through the air, obstructing my view. I look down at the other abseilers. They're barely visible through the dusty wind. They've given up on me and are racing for the truck.

I need to get off this bubble now!

I try to turn around to face the bubble again, but I'm hindered by all my gear. I'm like a beetle floundering on its back. I try to untangle myself, but the wind pins me to the glass.

A gust blows me diagonally across the glass, but I don't fall because my rope is hooked in place, clipped behind my hip.

My breath sounds ragged, echoing inside my suit. Even though the suit is tightly regulated, filtering the air outside so I always have ample oxygen, I can't get it into my lungs fast enough. My heart thumps against my chest, trying to escape the confines of my ribs. For a moment, I can't move. I just stare out at the horror forming before me.

Dark clouds roll over the sky, obstructing the sunlight, turning the world gray. The clouds swiftly dissipate and reform; like cream stirred through coffee. A flash of lightning shines white before being drowned by the clouds. Dirt and sand rise from the land. The sand hisses as it collides with my hazsuit.

I firmly plant my gloved hand on the glass behind me. The rubber sticks to it and I'm able to stop from gliding across the glass again. Hooking my leg up, I use both my foot and my right hand to push hard and flick back around to face the glass. The wind tries to whip me back, but I flatten against the bubble, eliminating the chance for it to get under me.

The problem is, to abseil down I need to unclip my rope and lean away from the glass. The rope will feed through the descender, allowing me to lower to the ground. But if I do that, I risk creating a sail for the wind with my body and it could blow me straight out into the open air.

I could die out here.

What will happen to Sebastian without me?

I hope he's back inside the decontamination center by now. It would've been easy to collect him from under the bubble and drive the team back to the center. If I hadn't been so stubborn and stopped working when the manager called, then I'd be there with him now.

Pressing my fingers onto the glass, I prepare myself to lean back and unclip my rope. I do it one handed, my other hand still pressed to the glass, and without leaning out far at all. I try to feed the rope through to lower myself, but the rope keeps catching because of the angle I'm at. It's designed that way to stop anyone falling straight to the ground if they let go of the rope or if their clip fails. I need to lean away from the glass.

My hazsuit flutters violently in the wind, despite the thick material. I look over my shoulder, but dirt and debris batters my visor, blinding me. I brush it away with my sleeve, but more takes its place.

Something larger is suddenly there, rushing at me fast. I duck but it still clips my shoulder, jarring me so I let go of the rope. I fall a foot, but the rope catches again, slamming me against the glass. Neither the glass nor my hazsuit break; they're too sturdy.

The storm is getting worse.

I can't see a way out of this mess. I pull my knees up to my chest and angle myself away from the glass as much as I dare. The rope feeds through. I breathe a sigh of relief and start crawling backward down the wall. It's slow and hard work. I can't see the ground; my vision obstructed by the waste coiling around me. It's impossible to tell how much further there is to go. All I can do is keep moving, descending gradually, inch by inch.

My hands ache from gripping the rope so tightly, and my shoulder throbs where it was hit. I hope my suit isn't ripped. Even if I survive the storm, I might not survive the diseases. I push down these thoughts; I can worry about that later. Right now, I need to focus on surviving. I grit my teeth and continue down the bubble.

I don't see it coming this time. Something large barrels into me at such speed I don't have a chance to react. I'm flung away from the glass. For a second, my rope goes taut.

Then it snaps.

This is it. I'm going to die.

Sebastian.

Did he survive the storm? What will he do without me?

I hit the ground.

I lay, stunned, staring as the dirt and sand swirls above me. I'm alive. I must have been much closer to the ground than I realized.

Rolling onto my side, I stand up. My body is whole, intact; I'm not torn limb from limb.

Wind and dirt pummel my back as I start walking. I need to get back to the decontamination center.

Something catches my eye. A movement that doesn't look like debris.

I can barely see, but it looks like a person. Another window washer? Maybe it's the mystery man. Whoever it is, they're running the wrong way and they'll get hurt out here.

I take off after them.

"Hey!" I yell, though it's useless yelling with the storm raging. "Hey! This way!"

They're a blur, a shadow in the storm. I can't tell if they're wearing a hazsuit. It's dark and there's so much dirt in the air.

The shadow disappears into the Old City. What are they thinking? Maybe they think it's safer in there, but it's not. Any one of those old buildings could come crashing down in this storm.

I hesitate. Should I leave them and go back? Sebastian is waiting for me.

I look up at one of structures. It's partially shrouded by the flying sands and dirt, but its shadow still looms over me. I look back over my shoulder. The bubble city is only a blur beyond the storm.

The person is probably huddled somewhere just inside these ruins, waiting out the storm, not knowing the danger these old buildings pose. Sebastian is inside, safe. I can warn this person. Help them. Sebastian will have to wait a little longer.

I run into the Old City.

Dirt whips up the time-worn streets, and it's even darker among the crumbling buildings. I've never been in the Old City before, so I slow to a jog to navigate my way. Debris litters the streets. There are piles of bricks, steel beams, and little hills of sand. The storm continues to whip sand into the air and I'm grateful for my hazsuit's protection.

I squint through a darkened doorway; the frame is broken, and the door hangs off its hinges. Inside, the building is as much of a mess as the streets; the upper floors have caved in, some walls have toppled over, and it's all covered in a thick layer of dirt.

I can't see anyone inside. Have they kept running? I continue searching.

There! A moving shadow in the distance. They're running so fast, I'm forced to sprint after them. I follow them down streets and around corners, sidestepping and leaping over hurdles of wreckage.

"Come back!" I scream, though my voice is lost in the uproar of the storm. "You're not safe in here!"

Something flies past my head. I duck.

I'm going to get killed out here.

My foot catches on something, sending me sprawling to the ground. Through the darkness, I can just make out what I tripped on; an old sign with large, faded letters spelling 'STUBB.' I don't know what it means, and any other letters have long broken off.

I look up. The figure has disappeared. I want to follow, to stop them from going deeper into the dangerous ruins, but I don't know where to go. There's no telling which way they've run.

There's nothing I can do to help if I can't find them, so I pick myself up and turn around.

My blood goes cold.

Where am I?

I take a few tentative steps, but I can't even tell if I'm going back to the bubbles or further into the Old City. The city bears down on me, the ruins high and looming. It could be day or night, with the raging storm obscuring the sunlight. I have to admit it—I'm lost.

I take off running again. I have no clue where I'm going, but I can't stand still, waiting for the storm to pass. All I can do is keep moving. Maybe I'll find my way out.

It comes without warning—the sound muffled by the rumble of the storm. At the last moment, I see it; bricks falling around me. I dive out of the way as a building crumbles.

Something hits me in the head and everything goes black.

Six

"Is she alive?"

Light shines through the gaps in the dirt that rests on my visor.

"I can't tell," says a different voice, older sounding. "She must be hurt, at least."

There are hands on my body, touching me, feeling up and down my limbs.

I cough. "Get your hands off me."

The hands disappear instantly.

"Well, she's alive," the second voice declares.

I move my head and the dirt slides off my visor. I'm greeted by an influx of sunlight. I squint. The glare causes a sharp pain in my eyes right to the back of my skull. My head throbs as I look around.

The sun has just started to rise. I'm lying in a patch of sunlight between the shadows of broken buildings, pressed up against a brick wall. I'm surrounded by dirt and sand and large pieces of wreckage where the building fell. The bubble city is nowhere in sight, blocked from view by the ruined buildings.

Two figures stand nearby. Their shadows stretch out like long-limbed aliens. They watch me warily, bodies tense, like they're ready to flee. Neither wears a hazsuit.

I lift myself onto my elbows and instantly regret it. My head swims. I rest it back against the wall and breathe through the sensation. I wish I could rub my temples, but my helmet is in the way.

"Are you okay?" the figure closest to me asks. It's the owner of the second voice.

He's my age, around sixteen or seventeen. His dark hair hangs to his waist, ruffling slightly in the breeze.

My eyes widen. He's the mystery man.

Not a man after all, just a teenager. His thick eyebrows are creased. It's hard to tell if he's concerned for me or distrustful. Instead of a hazsuit, he wears blue trousers and a yellowing cotton shirt. The top buttons are undone, revealing a firm chest.

I look away, trying not to blush. He's practically naked without a hazsuit.

The other kid is just that—a kid. He's older than Sebastian, probably thirteen or fourteen. He looks like he's related to the older boy; both have the same dark hair, brown skin, and high cheekbones. But instead of a scowl, this kid is grinning from ear to ear like a fool.

I frown at them. "I don't know," I finally answer, almost choking on my words because my throat is so dry. It's a fair question—*am* I okay? I really need to figure it out. I start by wiggling my toes and fingers and graduate to testing my legs and arms. Every muscle throbs dully, but as far as I can tell, nothing is broken.

I make myself sit up the whole way. The effort makes the world spin.

My next problem is to figure out if I am infected. Unbroken bones are well and good, but it's all for naught if I'm about to die from disease.

The two boys watch me as I read the stats on the arm of my suit, checking for punctures and functionality.

Ruptures: nil

Air filtration: functional

Water supply: 61.4%
Sustenance supply: 37.6%

I shake my head, dumbfounded. I was sure I was going to die in the storm, but I've come out relatively unscathed. Something must have been on my side. With no ruptures in my suit, it appears I won't die from disease, either. I can get back home. Back to Sebastian. I let that sink in.

"Where am I? Where's the city? Where's Sebastian?"

"I don't know who Sebastian is, but you're about a mile from Neustin," the older boy says and points in the direction which I suppose Neustin is.

I take a deep breath. Sebastian would have spent the night alone, not knowing if I'm alive or dead. I hope he had the sense to get his meds. Hopefully he made it to the diner. He would have had a few credits left over for food, but maybe Rosa would have taken pity on him, sitting there hungry without me, and snuck him some dinner rolls. At least the rent on our pod is paid for the month, so he won't be kicked out just yet. I'll be back before that happens.

Every cell of my body rebels when I move it. But I manage to stand up, though I'm forced to hold the wall for balance.

The younger boy steps away from me while the older one takes a step closer. He reaches out as if to help me, but then seems to think better of it, though he doesn't move away again. His arms are hovering near me, as if he's waiting for me to topple over. And with the weight of my suit and harness, I might.

"What are you doing out here without hazsuits?!" I blurt out. I would love to take my hazsuit off and move freely without its bulky weight. But I'd be exposing myself to all the potential pathogens in the air. The thought is enough to send shivers up and down my spine.

The older boy straightens, frowning, while the younger one grins even wider. I can't decide which one of them I like less.

"We're not slaves to the pharmacists," the older boy says.

I gape. "What is that supposed to mean?"

"We don't live in the bubble cities, and we certainly don't wear those stupid suits." He looks me up and down, an eyebrow raised as he appraises me. I feel so clumsy and clunky under his gaze.

"Don't be ridiculous," I say. "How can you survive? You'd be dead." I hesitate. "Well, you will be soon, anyway."

"I'm alive, aren't I?" He presents himself as evidence, his arms sweeping wide.

I glance again at his strong, exposed chest. And look quickly away. "For now. Where are your suits? Did they get damaged in the storm, so you took them off?" As I talk, I realize how wrong I am. I saw him two days ago in the desert, just as unprotected as he is now. But there's no way he's been out here all this time without a hazsuit.

The older boy shakes his head. "I told you. We don't wear those stupid suits."

I huff, pushing away from the wall, away from him. But as I put pressure on my left foot, I yelp. A sharp pain runs up from my ankle. I stumble, but before I fall flat on my face, the older boy grabs my shoulders, steadying me.

"I'm fine, I'm fine." I brush him off now that I've regained my balance. He stays nearby, ready to catch me. I frown at the ground.

"You've hurt your ankle," he says in a sour tone, "maybe sprained it."

"It'll be fine in a minute," I lie. Tentatively, I step down again. I can't put any weight on it without the pain shooting up my leg. I breathe through the pain and try again, but the result is the same.

The two boys mumble something to each other, but I don't catch what they say. They're probably laughing at me.

"What?" I ask.

The older boy turns back to me. "He was just wondering where you expect to get to on that leg?"

"I'm going home," I say. "Where else would I be going?" I shake my head. These kids are seriously dumb. There is nothing around here for miles other than the city. I'll die of thirst or disease if I stay out here any longer.

"I don't think you're going to get far on that ankle."

"I'll manage. I have no choice." Although I try to hop, the pain becomes too much after moving only a few feet away from the wall. I take a breath. I'm aware of the boys watching me, but I try to ignore them. Trying again, I take an awkward mix between a hop and a limp. I only make it a few yards before I'm huffing and sweating. The effort has taken minutes. Just to go a few yards.

"You're not going to get there without help," the older boy says.

"And the way is blocked," the younger one pipes in, still grinning.

I take another step, ignoring them, ignoring the riot of pain. I stop, letting the pain return to a harsh throb. They're right. I won't make it back alone. If the way is blocked, that means I'll have to climb over rubble, dangerous even if I wasn't injured.

I bite my lip. Despite not wanting to ask for help, Sebastian needs me at home. I'll die out here if I don't get back soon.

I look at the older boy. "Will you please help me get back home?" I probably could have sounded sweeter. But at least I said "please."

"I want to, but I can't."

"What?" I gape at him again.

"I'm sorry." He shrugs his shoulders again. I can see this is a habit of his. "We can't put ourselves in that kind of danger."

"What are you talking about?" I say, my voice rising. "What danger?" I don't care that I'm angry. Even if I do need their help, these boys are proving to be a waste of space.

"We have no suits, right?" he says slowly, as if I'm a child.
"No. So?"

"So," he takes an exasperated breath, "if they see us, the pharmacists will claim we're infected and kill us." He raises his eyebrows, waiting for me to agree with him.

"What a load of bull," I say. "That's the stupidest thing I've ever heard. They will *help* you, not kill you. But you'll die if you stay out here, so you have to come with me, anyway."

"Oh, man." He runs a hand through his long hair. "You're so brainwashed, bubble girl."

We stand a couple of yards apart, staring daggers at each other. I can't believe what I'm hearing. It doesn't make any sense, and my confusion only makes me grumpier.

After a moment, the young boy mumbles something to the older one. I hear the word "die" and "help" but don't make out the rest. My stupid helmet is muffling his words. The older boy shakes his head, but after a little more mumbling to his companion, he turns back to me.

"We'll help you," he says. He glances back at the younger boy, who nods his head in encouragement. "Yeah, we'll help you. But!" He points his finger at me. "We'll do it on our terms."

"What do you mean by that?"

"We'll help you get back there, but not straight away. We'll need to go at night. Until then, you can come with us."

I don't understand. The way back will be even harder to navigate in darkness. But I don't have a lot of choice. I need his help. I nod my agreement.

"Okay." He takes a breath, as if he needs the extra air to muster the strength to help me. I understand the feeling. It's taking all of my strength to let him help.

He comes to my left side, puts his arm around my waist, and loops my arm over his shoulder. It's clunky with my suit on, but I can still appreciate the width and power of his shoulders. I lean into him and do a practice limp forward. He takes the bulk of my weight and I only feel a dull pain. This will work.

I realize I don't know where he's taking me. If we're not leaving until nightfall, I don't understand why we can't stay where we are. But I feel like I've tested his patience enough, so I say nothing. I just limp along by his side.

The young boy grins even wider as he skips ahead of us.

I'm sweating despite my air-conditioned suit. The shadows have gotten shorter. We walk among the veins of the Old City's buildings, ducking under steel beams, climbing over small mounds of dirt, all with the help of the older boy. The landscape has changed little; we could be in the same place as earlier. We're still within the Old City's ruins, the broken buildings surrounding us all looking the same, covered in dirt and sand.

Neither of them has said a word to me since we started walking. Occasionally they mumble something to each other, but I might as well be a sack of potatoes.

My body is sorer than it's ever been, worse than any day working on the windows. It's battered and bruised and limping along takes more effort than I imagined, even with the older boy's help. I press my lips together and push on.

But after a few steps, my good leg buckles. I tumble down as if the potatoes have come loose from the sack. The older boy tries to catch me, but I slip from his fingers and hit the ground with a whomp.

"Are you okay?" His eyes are wide with concern as he reaches for me.

I slap his hand away. "No thanks to you."

He squats down in front of me. "I'm really sorry." His genuine concern looks stupid on his face. "I should have realized this would be hard for you."

"It's not hard," I say.

"Oh, of course it's not." The corner of his mouth twitches. "I mean, with your ankle, and the storm—"

My glare cuts him off.

"Anyway," he says after a moment. "Will needs a rest."

"I do not!" The younger boy says. For once, he's not smiling.

The older boy makes a shushing sound, and the younger one's grin returns. The younger one, Will, joins us in the dirt. He pulls out a canteen and takes a few big swigs before holding it out to me. "Water?"

I frown. "Uh, no." Doesn't he realize I can't drink anything outside of the suit? I'm completely sealed up. But he continues to hold it out to me. "I can't with the suit on," I explain.

Will shrugs and takes another sip. They *must* be related. The shrugging thing is probably a family trait.

"Do you wear that thing all the time?" Will suddenly asks.

"Of course not," I say. "I take it off once I'm in the decontamination center."

"But aren't you thirsty? Don't you want some water?" He holds out the canteen again. He inclines his head, the same way Sebastian does. I feel a sharp pang somewhere in my gut.

"Thank you." I try to inflect a bit more kindness in my tone. "I can't. I don't want to be exposed like you."

Will's eyes open wide.

"I'm sure you'll be okay," I say hurriedly, "but I think it's best to be cautious."

Will nods along with me but I'm not sure he understands.

"Here." I hold out my arm so he can see the controls. I click a button and a straw extends inside my helmet to my mouth. I close my mouth around it and take a sip. "This is how I drink water while I'm in the suit."

Will eyes my suit with a mixture of awe and distress. Maybe these boys really didn't go out in hazsuits. I brush the thought aside. No one could survive out here for long.

"Wow," Will says. "How do you eat?" He moves closer to see the controls better and I show him the different functions. How a soup-like nutritious meal can also be fed through the straw, which is what I usually have for lunch; how I can regulate the temperature with a click of a button; how I can regularly check the suit is intact so there's no chance of contagion.

The older boy doesn't say anything, he only watches us. I think he is just as interested as Will, but doesn't want to show it. Still, his eyes follow my fingers as they tap at the controls.

After drinking the water and soup, I feel a lot stronger. "We can keep going. That is, if you wouldn't mind helping me up?"

The older boy stands up and gently lifts me to my feet, hooking his arm around me again and providing support.

"It's not too much further," he says.

"Where are we going?"

"You wouldn't believe me if I told you."

He was right on both counts. Ten minutes later, I barely believe my own eyes.

There are people. Lots of people. Moving in and out and between several tents nestled on the edge of the Old City ruins. None of them are wearing hazsuits. Some stand at the outskirts of the camp, holding guns, watching as we approach. Many are dressed similarly to Will and the older boy; jeans or sturdy trousers, with light long-sleeved shirts rolled to the elbow and big hardy boots. There's a mix of men and women, old and young, some light, some dark. It's as varied a mix of people you'd find in The Nix. But it's clear these people have not come from the bubble city.

The tents blend into the landscape, ranging from browns to reds to beiges. Clothes hang on lines between the tents, and bags of their belongings sit by the entranceways. A handful of beaten-up vehicles—far from sanitary or airtight—sit at the edge of the camp.

Will's smile has grown even bigger, which doesn't seem possible. It almost splits his face as he glances between me and the camp. His chest is puffed up with pride. But he doesn't have a hint of arrogance. Not like the older boy, whose expression clearly says, "I told you so." My own expression transforms from wide-eyed to a scowl, when I notice his smugness.

But then I see *them*. I inhale sharply.

Animals. There are tall four-legged animals tied up at the side of the camp, grazing on dry grass. I have never seen anything like them. Even though they are stationary, I see their power; the muscles in their legs are formidable.

"What are they?" my voice comes out as a whisper.

"They're horses," says the older boy, frowning as if I'm stupid.

The horses tear grass from a stack, their lips flapping around their strong teeth as they chew. I'd heard of horses. I'd even seen pictures of them on the datanet when we had more access in Colombia. But I thought they were extinct. These are much more marvelous than any picture I had ever seen.

"Nathan!"

A woman strolls toward us. As she comes closer, I see her hair is long and dark like the two boys, though hers is streaked with white. She doesn't have their height though; even the younger boy is taller than her, and she must be at least fifty. Though it's hard to tell. The woman's eyes are crinkled, making her look stern and friendly at the same time.

"Nathan, who is this person? Why have you brought them here?" She addresses the older boy, who has lost all signs of haughtiness. He still has his arm around my waist, helping me stand.

"She's been injured by the storm, Mother Jessica," the older boy—Nathan—says. "She can't walk without help."

"That doesn't explain why she's here." The woman walks right up to me, peering through my visor, inspecting my face.

"She's the one that chased me in the storm. She was trying to help me." So it *was* him in the storm. "And she would have died if we left her. It upset Will."

"And you too, I suppose?" She presses her lips together, nodding at Nathan. "Well then, we'd better get her a seat."

Nathan continues to help me hobble along, leading me into the camp. I attract the curious eyes of the people. Some openly stare, stopping in the middle of their chores.

I stare back. They're a melting pot of people. Many dress like Nathan, in trousers and loose shirts, but one woman wears a dress that flows around her ankles, like her blond hair floats around her shoulders. An older man wears a large hat that shades his eyes and his bushy beard. I've never seen someone with such long facial hair; it's more common for men to be clean shaven in the cities because it's more comfortable under their masks. Others are dressed in shorts; their legs bare to the elements. I blink at them.

Nathan eventually stops outside a tent and helps me sit down on a stool. Once I'm settled, he sits in the dirt a few feet away. Will plonks down next to him. The woman continues to stand, hovering close to me.

"What's your name, child?" she says, looking down at me.

"I'm not a child!"

The woman presses her lips again, though it's hard to tell if from amusement or contempt.

"My name is Martina Monsalve," I say with formality. "And yours is?"

"They call me Mother Jessica. You can call me Mother, if you prefer." Even though her voice is stern, it feels strangely welcoming.

I bow my head. "Good health to you, Mother."

She tuts in response. I ignore Nathan and Will's guffaws.

"Now it seems you've hurt your leg?" Mother doesn't wait for me to answer. She kneels in front of me, taking my booted foot in her hands. She feels along my leg, up and down the muscles, squeezing in places, causing me to grimace, but I avoid flinching and I don't pull away.

"You're a tough one, aren't you?" Mother says.

I don't know how to answer, so I don't say anything.

"It's a shame we can't take your suit off," Mother continues. "I think we could get you fixed up pretty quick if we did."

"I can't!"

"No, of course not." Mother stands, bringing a hand to her chin. "It only feels like a mild sprain; nothing serious. Best for you to rest and keep it elevated for now. It's going to be a bit sore for a while."

I take a gulp of air and nod. How will this impact my trip back to the bubble? If only I could walk back without help.

Will jogs off, disappearing between the tents, but is back almost instantly carrying another stool. He places it in front of me and then tenderly lifts my leg onto it. I smile in thanks.

"Now you just rest, drink some water, and we'll figure out what to do with you." Mother leaves before I can explain that the boys have agreed to return me to the bubble after nightfall.

Seven

Will and Nathan sit nearby while we wait for Mother's return. Will draws in the dirt with a stick and Nathan pulls out a switchblade and a piece of wood. He whittles away at it, further perfecting the shape that appears to be a horse.

The community continues with what they were doing before I arrived; clearing away the mess and debris that must have blown in with the storm; repairing and re-erecting tents and structures.

Not everyone's working. A group of five or six kids poke their heads out from behind tents, giggle, and then disappear again. Another child runs from behind one tent to another in a poor attempt to hide from my sight, all the while gaining a better view of me. I laugh as two kids crash into each other, too busy staring at me to notice where they're running. They pick themselves up and dust off the dirt, before one of them gives the other a small shove and they both run off to hide again.

Then something black and furry rounds the nearest tent, running straight at me. It runs on four legs but is much shorter than the horses and it doesn't stop when it reaches me. I close my eyes and brace for impact. It jolts against my suit and I open my eyes. The thing is bouncing on its hind legs, its toothy mouth and long tongue aiming for my face. It licks my visor and I almost fall off the stool.

"Argh, help!" I shout.

Will is laughing as he pulls the animal away by a collar adorning its neck. "Roscoe, stop! Sit." The animal obeys and sits on its hind legs, peering up at Will with a look that could only be called a smile.

"It's a dog," Nathan informs me. His tone isn't as superior as it was earlier. Instead, he seems more curious than anything. He watches me carefully as I rearrange myself on the stool again with my leg up. "Have you ever seen one?"

I shake my head. I've heard of dogs, but just like horses, they're like mythical creatures. There isn't the capacity for animals in the bubbles. The closest thing to an animal is the protein farms, where animal muscles are grown in incubation chambers. But they certainly aren't what you would call *alive*.

The dog is panting, its tongue lolling from its mouth. When Will sits down again, the dog lowers himself, resting his head on Will's lap. He scratches the dog behind its ears.

"What does it do?" I ask.

"Roscoe?" Nathan smiles. "Not much at all. Pretty much what he's doing now, the silly mutt."

"What's the point in keeping him then?"

Nathan frowns. "He's a pet."

I frown back, but say nothing.

"Haven't you ever loved something just for the sake of it?" he says.

Of course, I love Sebastian. And I loved my parents. For some reason, I'm not sure this is what he's talking about, so I stay silent.

Will throws a stick and Roscoe runs after it, skidding clumsily in the dirt and snatching the stick from the ground. He trots back with the stick in his mouth, dropping it in front of Will, who throws it again. Roscoe looks so proud of himself each time he brings the stick back. How he gets so much enjoyment out of running and fetching, I can't figure out; it seems so pointless. But

I find myself laughing at his goofy antics. Will and Nathan laugh along as well. Eventually the dog flops down again, exhausted, but panting happily.

"Do you want to see around the camp?" Nathan looks at me strangely. It's like he is trying to figure me out. But what's to figure out? He's the strange one, not me.

"I'd like to," I admit, "but how can I? My ankle is too sore."

"We can put her in the wheelbarrow." Will's voice is high with excitement. I don't know what a wheelbarrow is, but I soon find out. Will disappears for a moment then returns pushing a wheeled contraption in front of him.

"I'll help you in." Nathan's voice is quiet, and his cheeks a little pink. He leans down and picks me up, cradling me in his arms for a moment before laying me in the dipped tray of the wheelbarrow. I busy myself with getting more comfortable in the contraption and making sure my foot is still elevated. Better that than focusing on Nathan's easy strength.

Nathan hands me a cushion from inside the tent to slide under my calves so they can rest comfortably on the edge of the wheelbarrow. Once I am secure, Nathan takes the handles and pushes the wheelbarrow—and me—forward. Will walks beside us, and even a few of the other kids follow behind.

We weave between the tents, Nathan ducking under clotheslines, and skirting around stools and workbenches.

I stare wide-eyed at it all.

It is beyond my wildest dreams. I never would have thought it possible for people to live out in the wilderness. But here they are. A huge community of people *and* animals. Not one of them look sick. In fact, they look healthier than anyone in the bubble cities. Their skin glows; their bodies muscular and fit.

They look at me with as much curiosity as I look at them.

"Why are they staring at me?" I ask.

"It's not often they see people in these weird suits." Nathan flicks the shoulder of my hazsuit. "We stay clear of the bubble cities. We might see them from afar, but we don't go close enough to see the people inside, or their bizarre clothes."

"This is normal!" I protest.

"Not to us, it isn't."

"Well, we only wear these outside. Inside, we're dressed just like you." Some of us, anyway. I think about the girl in the fancy pink dress; anyone from the Sparkle Sector would stick out like a sore thumb in this camp, not to mention The Nix.

"I find that hard to believe," Nathan says.

I try to turn around to look at Nathan, but the movement disrupts the balance of the wheelbarrow. Feeling it tilt, I flick back around to face forward again, gripping the sides of the tray.

"Steady." Nathan chuckles as he rights the wheelbarrow.

He has a pleasant laugh—deep and throaty. I prefer it to his usual haughty frown.

"I saw someone near Neustin," I say, after a while.

"Really?"

"Yeah, it was you. A couple of days ago. At dawn."

"Oh ... I didn't think anyone saw me. It was very early." Nathan is quiet for a moment, then says, "It's not safe for us to go near the cities. If we're spotted, the guards might come after us. It could put us all in danger."

He sounds hesitant. I wish I could see his face, but I don't risk turning around again. Will keeps quiet too.

"Then why would you go near the city?"

"I ... I shouldn't have."

We reach the edge of the camp and I see the horses up ahead. I forget our conversation in the excitement of seeing them again.

"Can we ..." I point at the horses. It feels weird saying, "Can we see the horses?" Even with them standing in front of me, it still doesn't seem real that they exist. I may as well be asking to see a unicorn.

Nathan steers the wheelbarrow toward the horses. They're bigger than I first thought, and I start to regret asking to see them. What if they try to eat me? Or—my stomach lurches—what if they jump on me like the dog did?

But they do neither. One of them completely ignores us. Another looks up briefly and then continues to chew its grass, like we're not here. The third looks at me inquisitively. I flinch away when it lowers its head near to me.

Nathan chuckles again. "It's okay. She's just saying hello." He rubs the nose of the giant beast. The horse lets him, slowly blinking her eyes, as if she enjoys it.

"You can do it too," Will says, reaching for my hand.

I shake my head.

"She won't hurt you," says Nathan, still patting the horse's nose. Will approaches her and rubs along her neck.

I really want to touch her too, but I keep my arms close to my chest. Her fur looks shiny and velvety; a beautiful rich brown. Her eyes are enormous; they seem to see everything around her, like they hold some kind of wisdom beyond my understanding.

"Okay," I say. I reach toward the horse's neck; it seems safer than her nose. Slowly, I edge closer until my fingers brush lightly against her fur. My gloved fingers can't quite feel the softness of the fine hair, but I marvel at the sight of my own fingers making the short strands move on her neck. I lean forward, careful not to disrupt the wheelbarrow, and place my whole hand against the horse. I feel the powerful muscle beneath my fingers; the slight curve of the muscular tissue as I run my hand down the length of her neck.

A breathy laugh escapes my lips. I'm *actually* touching a horse. A horse!

Nathan's hand has moved up the horse's nose and is rubbing her forehead now. I move to touch its nose in his place. As I reach up, the horse does a quick snort and shakes her mane. I pull my hand back quickly.

Nathan and Will laugh, and after the moment of shock passes, I laugh too.

"That's incredible," I breathe. I'm too nervous to try again, but I'm satisfied. I touched a horse—*¡Es increíble!*

Nathan maneuvers the wheelbarrow under the cover of a tarp hung near the horses and leans against a rusty truck. He crosses his arms casually over his chest, assessing me.

"You look impressed?" he asks, and the smug look is back.

"I am." I'm not ashamed to admit it. I'm still marveling at the horses, watching them rip at the bundles of grass, their teeth circling as they chew. Their lips flap as their heads lower for another bite. "I didn't think they existed anymore. How did you find them?"

"My family has kept horses for hundreds of years," Nathan says. "For as far back as you can imagine. Way before the global pandemic." He gestures to Will, who has found Roscoe and is playing with him again. "Will and I are descendants of a Native American tribe called the Zuni. The Zuni had a reservation where they grew crops and kept animals like horses and cattle.

"Of course, the tribe almost died out during the Yeran pandemic. But a few survived who continued to tend animals. When they joined up with other people who survived, the Terrene Folk, they brought the animals with them."

"So, you've always lived here?" I say. "Like this?"

"No, not here," he laughs. "This is just the roaming community. There's a lot more of the Terrene Folk back in New Mexico."

"*More* people?" My jaw drops.

"Lots more," he says, the smile still playing on his lips. "But to answer your other question, yes, we've always lived like this. Some people here, and in New Mexico, found the Terrene Folk over the years and joined us. And some have been in the community for generations.

"We're all family now. We all look out for each other. All of us contribute, share food and goods. We work to make sure that everyone has what they need."

I am still processing the fact that people can live outside of the bubbles. To find out there is a large community of people outside too, living lives that seem to be better than Sebastian's and mine—it's inconceivable.

I can't deny that the life they live is appealing. Horses, dogs, freedom, the open plains—I wish I had all this. What a life it would be for Sebastian. Playing with other kids, playing with a dog like Will does. Being part of a community, like we had in Colombia. People around to care for him, not just me. It's a future I had never dreamed of before because I never thought it was possible.

My head feels heavy; my mind clouded with questions.

"How?" The word falls from my lips.

"That's a long story." Nathan pushes himself away from the truck and returns behind the wheelbarrow. "Let's go see some more."

He leads me through the camp again, though this time in a different direction. It's just us; Will and the other kids must have tired of us. We pass people working in all different capacities, from cleaning clothes to cooking food, repairing vehicles, and making things out of wood. They all look up from what they're doing as we pass. Some are curious, but I get the distinct feeling that a lot of them don't want me here. I squirm under their gaze and shrink further into the helmet of my hazsuit so it's harder to make eye contact.

It's a relief when we reach the edge of the camp and are no longer under their scrutiny.

I look out away from the camp. I've never seen this view before; the Old City ruins have always blocked it. And it's beautiful.

The desert stretches out as far as I can see. A wide-open expanse of nothing. Just the earth and the blue sky. A bird of prey circles in the distance. It sees something, dives, and disappears from view. Other than that lone speck, nothing else moves.

"It's so peaceful," I whisper. It seems wrong to talk any louder and disturb the tranquility.

"That's why I love it." Nathan's voice is quiet too.

I shift in the wheelbarrow, trying to get into a more comfortable position to enjoy this moment. But my back has started to ache, and despite the cushion under my leg, the tray still digs into me.

"Do you want to get out for a bit?" Nathan asks.

I nod in response.

He comes close, leaning down to collect me. He's touched me often today, but something has changed since we first met. Maybe because he doesn't seem as haughty anymore, or at least, it doesn't bother me as much. I don't want to bite his head off every time he shrugs or frowns. What is wrong with me? This annoying arrogant boy is now taking pity on me by showing me around his camp and I start ... what? Swooning?

I catch his eye and look away quickly, trying to shove the silly thoughts away.

I slide my arm around his shoulder without looking at him again, holding tight as he easily lifts me out of the wheelbarrow and sets me on the ground.

"Why does your community travel?" I ask. "If you don't like the bubble cities, why do you go near them?"

"There's a few reasons." Nathan pauses. "The main reason is to scavenge from the old cities. That's what our nomadic community does. We travel to different places and find things we can use back on our reservation. You'd be surprised at some of the things we find in old cities and ruins."

"Like what?"

"Lots of things. Electronics, useful materials, books."

"Books?"

"Yeah, you do know what a book is right?" He raises an eyebrow at me.

"Yes ... in Colombia we could access them through the datanet. But I can't afford them now."

He shakes his head. "We find physical books, printed books, not digital ones. There are a lot of boring ones, but some are very interesting." He's no longer measuring his words. He speaks with excitement. "The most valuable thing we look for is fuel. That helps us run our vehicles and other things back on the reservation."

"Fuel? Why would that be in the old cities?"

"Well, sometimes we find old cars and trucks, but the best is when we find old airports. They're like goldmines. I read about airports in the books, actually. Did you know that before the Yeran pandemic you could fly in machines through the sky? They were called airplanes. And they used fuel to fly."

I look at him sideways, wondering if he's teasing me.

"It's true! I've seen them at the airports where we find the fuel. They don't look like birds or anything, just huge metal machines with wings."

I can't help but imagine birds with metal wings anyway.

"And there was all this other technology before the Yeran plague too. Self-driving cars, robots, people even went into space!"

"In the airplanes?"

"No, in different machines called rockets." He excitedly animates his story with his hands.

I shake my head, struggling to imagine it all.

"Where is it all now?"

He shrugs. "Most of it is just wasting away in these old cities. Supposedly, a lot of knowledge was lost when so many people died. And the people remaining were only interested in health sciences." He breaks into a sneer. "So the focus was on building those bubble cities and the technology needed to run them."

"At least there were pharmacists," I say, "and medical people left. Without them, we wouldn't have been safe from other plagues."

Nathan glances at me out of the corner of his eye. He opens his mouth to say something, closes it again, and then asks, "Don't you think it's weird that the only technology advancements have been in the medical sector?"

I frown. "But that's what's most important."

"I agree it's important, but you miss out on so much living in that bubble. You miss out on this." He waves to the sky above him. "The bubbles cities were built, the decontamination centers, the vaccines, the medicines, all to help you live right? But are you really *living*?"

We both fall silent.

If what Nathan says is true, we lost a lot more than people's lives with the Yeran pandemic. *If* it's true—and that's a big 'if.' Our society *is* advanced. We have comms units, body scanners, the datanet, not to mention we're safe from diseases with all our meds and the amazing glass bubbles to shield us. How could our ancestors have had more? I can't imagine such a world. But why would Nathan lie? If he's right, it was all lost. Just because of some microorganisms.

My fingers trail through the dirt, leaving grooves behind. My hazsuit remains clean, as if the dirt never touched it. That's what it's designed to do, to stay clean. What would happen if I took it off? I could touch the horse with my bare hands, really feel its fur. I could feel the wind in my hair, the same way it blows Nathan's hair away from his neck. I could let the dirt get under my nails, the same way it stains Nathan's fingers.

The uncleanliness doesn't seem to bother him at all. It's not just the grubby hands. He's not worried about catching diseases. He doesn't wear a hazsuit or a face mask. He doesn't keep his distance from other people. It gives him an air of carelessness, but also freedom.

"Why aren't you sick?" I blurt out.

"You can't believe everything they tell you, bubble girl."

"What does that mean?"

"Just that you're fed a load of lies." Nathan leans back on his hands in the superior manner he has a habit of. "Well, surely you've figured this out by now?"

I don't respond; I don't understand what he's talking about. But I don't want to give him any more fuel to work with and look more foolish.

My silence is answer enough, though. He explains, "PMC makes money out of people being sick. The more people that are sick, the more products they can sell. They make up these lies so people will keep spending money on their products. The diseases aren't real; it's just the way they can keep control." He talks as if it's all common knowledge. As if it's not an awful thing he's accusing the pharmacists of.

"No," I say, my mouth agape. "That is the most farfetched thing I've ever heard."

Nathan shakes his head. "Then how do you explain that I'm not dead right now? I'm not wearing one of those suits and I'm outside. Why haven't I succumbed to one of the horrible diseases they tell you is *so* deadly?" His eyes are wide and mocking.

"I don't know." I hesitate. "Maybe you have some kind of immunity or something."

"To *all* diseases?" His eyebrows almost reach his hairline. He thinks I'm just a silly girl. And maybe I am. I can't explain how he is alive, or how any of his community is surviving outside of the bubbles.

"But I know people who have died from being exposed," I say, "and even now one quarter is in lockdown because of an outbreak. How do you explain that?"

He shrugs. It's his turn not to know the answers. "Maybe the pharmacists are killing them."

I snicker. "You're really suggesting that the doctors and pharmacists sworn to protect us, that heal us with medicines every day, are also responsible for killing people?"

"Yep!" He almost sounds cheerful.

I shake my head. There's obviously no convincing him, so I say no more on the subject. Nathan says nothing either. He must think I'm so naïve. But I can't deny, his story makes me feel uneasy.

I glance at him, trying to read his thoughts, but his eyes catch mine and we both look away quickly.

I keep looking at his face from the corner of my eye. It's hard to do it surreptitiously through the visor, so I pretend I'm taking in the view around us. It's strange to be able to look at a stranger's face in full, especially so close. In The Nix quarter we all wear masks, so I usually only see people's eyes. Despite their steely expression, his eyes are surprisingly beautiful. They're dark, flecked with gold and red, framed by long eyelashes.

Sometimes I get the chance to spy on people in the Bush quarter that don't wear masks, but that is usually from a distance, or distorted by the curved glass of the bubble. The only faces I get a good look at are other windows grunts that wear hazsuits like me. And even then, their faces are obstructed by the helmets and visors.

It's only Sebastian's face that I get to see without something in the way. His big eyes; his dark hair that flops over his forehead; his round face, still so childlike, even with a strong chin forming as he grows up. I'm already missing him; it's hard to believe it's only been a day.

Sebastian would love to pet the horse or play with the dog. I wish I could bring him here. Even if we were allowed, we wouldn't have the time. I'll have to work extra hard to make back the wages I've lost yesterday and today.

"You seem to have a nice life here," I break the silence, and my grim thoughts.

"It can be tough sometimes, but it's pretty great." He grins. "You really liked the horses, huh?"

"Yeah," I exhale, "they're spectacular. Magical."

"Maybe you can ride one."

"What?" I exclaim. "You ride those things? That can't be safe."

Nathan chuckles. "Of course we ride them. But you're right, it's not always safe. You need to be respectful of them, treat them right, and if you do, they'll show you respect in return."

I like his laugh. It waters down his arrogance, and he actually seems likeable.

His mouth moves like he's about to say something, but then he closes it tight. He looks away, scratching his head. He murmurs, "Why don't you stay here ... with us?"

My eyes go wide.

"I mean, you'd have to help around here," he says, still not looking at me, "and learn how to survive in the wild. But I think you could do it."

I don't respond.

He quickly fills the silence. "I'm sure Mother Jessica will say yes, and she'll convince the other adults to let you stay, too. You could get rid of that silly suit." He grins.

I frown. If I lose the suit, I could die.

It is a tempting thought. Living free under the skies. No longer wearing hazsuits and face masks. No more itchy antibacterial soaps and humiliating decontamination center scans. A chance for Sebastian to run and play.

"I can't." I look away. I inspect the creases in my gloves. Tiny cracks in the outside material are like veins through the white, not deep enough to affect the integrity of the suit, but just enough to show it's not brand new. They would be invisible if it weren't for my sudden scrutiny.

"Why not?" Nathan says.

I continue looking at my gloves. It's not just to distract myself from the fantasy. I don't want Nathan to know how much I would like to take him up on his offer.

"You can't still think that you'll die if you take the suit off?" Nathan presses.

I click my tongue, looking up at him. "There's a chance of that. But it's not the main reason."

"Then what?"

I sigh. "It's my little brother. Sebastian. He's still in Neustin. Or at least, I hope he is." I pause, waiting for some flippant remark from Nathan. For once, his tongue is tied. "I'm hoping he got back inside the city before the storm hit. He's only eight. I'm all he has in the world."

His eyes soften. It's not a look I've seen on him before. He swallows before saying, "Where are your parents? Why don't they look after him?"

"They died." I stare into his eyes so he understands the importance of what I am saying. "They died from diseases when they were exposed outside."

His face goes through a mixture of emotions; pity, horror, confusion, and ultimately, disbelief. His eyebrows contract and he shakes his head.

My anger hits me like a punch in the face. "You think I'm lying? You think I'm a liar? Just get me back home and you'll never have to see me again!" *And I'll never have to see you again!* What kind of person doesn't believe someone when they confess their parents are dead? He seriously thinks I would lie about my parents dying?

I avoid looking at him as I struggle to my feet. His hands are on my waist, trying to help me stand, but I push them off, the force of which makes me stumble. But I manage to stay upright and hobble to the wheelbarrow where I ungracefully climb in, careful not to put pressure on my tender ankle.

Quietly, Nathan says, "I'll take you back to the camp so you can rest."

We travel the distance in silence, entering the camp again. Sooner or later I'm going to have to break the silence. But I'm embarrassed. Not because I care about our conversation, but because I have to do my business.

I finally talk myself into it. "Do you have a bathroom or something?"

"I'm sorry?" I'm not sure if he didn't hear me because I spoke quietly or if he doesn't understand.

"A toilet?" I repeat a little louder, but still hushed so only he can hear.

"You can go to the toilet in that thing?" he says loudly. I look around to see if anyone else heard. People *are* glancing at us.

I feel my cheeks burn. "The suit discards it," I say through gritted teeth.

"Come on, I'll show you to the latrine."

When we arrive at the secluded spot, he helps me out of the wheelbarrow and I totter to a makeshift shed. He waits outside while I wish a disease had breached my hazsuit and was eating my flesh from the inside out. It would be preferable to leaving the shed and having to look at Nathan's smug face again.

But he doesn't look at me when I exit, which makes it worse. Now I feel like there really is a reason for me to be embarrassed. I shake my head. I shouldn't be embarrassed about going to the toilet. If it bothers him, then that's his problem.

He doesn't speak again until we get back to the tent and then he only says, "You can lie down inside. You must be tired." Then he helps me out of the wheelbarrow again before rolling it away, leaving me alone to watch the camp go about their duties.

Eight

From inside the tent, I watch the campers. I have my foot propped up on a cushion, keeping it elevated in the hope that I'll be able to walk on it tonight.

I feel useless watching other people work while I lounge around. I'm not used to having so much time to do nothing, and I quickly get bored. As the day wears on, I get increasingly anxious about getting home to Sebastian. I count the minutes, waiting for the sun to set. When the skies finally begin to darken, I keep an eye out for Nathan or Will, but I don't see them.

Night arrives, and still no one comes. Have they forgotten they'd promised to help me get home? Instead, someone has started a fire in the pit between the tents and people gather around it.

Over the fire, a man has strung some kind of meat that is roasting as he rotates it. I can't smell the food, but my mouth waters anyway. The nutritious soup in my suit, while *nutritious,* is hardly the tastiest meal. While the meat cooks, more of the community joins around the fire, sitting on stools or on the ground. There must be thirty or more adults plus a handful of kids. I see Nathan, Will, and Mother Jessica arrive and take a seat. I catch Nathan's eyes, his expression unreadable. He quickly glances away and doesn't look up again.

Once the meat is cooked, it's distributed to everyone around the fire. Potatoes are dug up from under the ashes, put there before the fire was started. The people also crunch on a green vegetable, but I can't tell what it is from this distance.

My mind plays tricks on me, making me believe I can taste the juicy meat. My stomach feels hollow. I take a sip of my nutritious soup held within my hazsuit, but it does nothing to satiate me. It only makes my hunger worse.

Beyond the fire, the horses stand silently, their coats glowing from the fire. I prop myself onto my elbows to see them better, longing to touch them again.

A shadow blocks my view. I look up to see Mother Jessica standing outside the tent. She steps inside, hiding Nathan and the others sitting around the fire. Will is with her, peeking out from behind. He's not smiling for a change.

"How are you feeling, Martina?" Although she asks it kindly, there's a sternness to her demeanor that confuses me.

"A lot better, I think," I say. My body is stiff and bruised and worse than ever, my ankle is aching, and my shoulder is tender where I was hit by flying shrapnel. But I can't admit any of this to Mother. Despite how I feel, I want to get back home as soon as I can.

"Really?" Mother raises her eyebrows.

"Well, I'm still a little sore, but I can make it back to the city. I know I can."

"I'm sure you're determined enough to try, but ..." Mother pauses.

My head swims with what she's about to say. There should be no "buts"—I am going back to the city. There's no "buts" about it.

Mother's expression is grim. "... but I can't let you."

"You can't *let* me?" I feel the heat of rage building inside me. I suspected something was wrong, but I didn't want to believe it. *Couldn't* believe it. I have to get home.

"I'm sorry, Martina," she says, but she doesn't sound very sorry; she sounds like a teacher simply stating the facts. "But we can't trust you. If the city authorities find out we're here, they'll send the military. They'll try to eradicate us, Martina. Do you understand? They won't stop until they've killed us all. We can't risk it."

"Don't be ridiculous," I say slowly, shaking my head as if I can shake Mother's words away. She truly intends to stop me from returning home. I refuse to believe it. But she genuinely seems to believe the authorities will demand their deaths. For no reason! Now I understand where Nathan gets his outrageous ideas from—Mother has been brainwashing him. I don't know what motive she has for spinning this garbage. She's crazy. They all are. And I'm stuck here with them.

"You're keeping me prisoner," I spit.

Mother shrugs—it's definitely a family trait, along with the madness. "Not exactly. But you must stay with us a while longer. If you still want to return to your bubble city in a couple of days when we've packed up camp and are ready to leave, then we'll help you return." She smiles kindly, as if she's bestowing a generous gift. "I know you tried to help Nathan in the storm—this is all we can offer in return."

"If? If?" My voice is a screech, but the only response I get from Mother is her backing away from me and outside of the tent. "My brother needs me. Why would I *ever* want to stay here?"

I watch Mother leave. I target all my pent up energy at Will, who stands by the tent flap, looking pitiful, fiddling his hands and avoiding my stare.

"You're shaking out on me?" I shout at him. "You said you would help!"

"Shaking?" He frowns at the word, but before I can explain, he continues, "I'm sorry, Martina. I will help you." He glances at me before looking back down at his hands. "But I can't just yet. I can't disobey Mother. And ... and I can't put the camp at risk."

"Just leave me alone." I plonk back on the pillow.

Will looks at me one more time—he really looks different without a smile—and leaves.

I lay there for a while, dreaming of sneaking away and returning to the bubble city without their help. I know I can't walk the entire way, but maybe I can steal one of their horses. Nathan said you can ride them. But he also said that you need to show them respect, and maybe stealing one wasn't what he meant by that. And truth be told, they scare me too much to ride one.

Maybe I can steal one of their vehicles. But if the way is blocked, a vehicle won't be any help. I spend a bit of time testing out my ankle without standing up, but it is definitely too tender to walk on it very far alone.

I give up on my fantasies of escaping and stare out at the dying fire outside my tent. Most of the community has dispersed, but a few remain chatting quietly with the light flickering across their faces.

I notice an elbow of someone sitting just outside my tent. I swivel around to get a better look and can just make out his face in the dark. It's Nathan. He must be keeping guard and making sure I don't flee. As if I could. It infuriates me even more to know that he's the one that's been assigned to guard me. He must think it's hilarious that silly little me can't go anywhere.

Instead of sleeping, I imagine all sorts of diseases he could catch that would make the last few days of his life a living hell. Oaten would give him painful pustules all over his body. Supposedly, REKS feels like your gut is on fire.

When I do eventually sleep, it's restless. It's uncomfortable in my suit, and my body aches constantly, especially my ankle, but it's my mind going round and round that's the bigger problem. I constantly worry about Sebastian alone in the city, and I can't quiet the questions I have about the Terrene Folk. How have I never heard of them before? We've always been taught no one can survive outside, everyone knows that. Maybe no one in the bubble cities know about them. But Mother mentioned the authorities. She said if they found out about the camp, the authorities would send the military to kill them. Does that mean the authorities know about the Terrene Folk? Why have they never told the rest of us?

Nathan said there's more of them, these nomad people. It's hard to imagine what their reservation is like. Is it just a bigger version of this camp? Maybe they have houses like we have in the city. Do they have more animals? They have horses and dogs here. What other extinct or mythical animals exist on their reservation?

By the next morning, I haven't worked out any of the answers to my questions, and I lay in the tent for hours, the questions continuing to plague me. If only I had something to distract myself, but they've left me alone in the tent.

My fingers play with the threads of the blanket, waiting, until I'm so fed up, I slap the blanket away from me. I cross my arms as I stare out of the tent, my brow furrowed.

A man with red hair meets my stare. Instead of being warded away, like I hoped, he detours from his path and comes toward me. He's dragging some cloth behind him. I sit up quickly and shrink further back into the tent. These people are keeping me hostage; I don't know what they're capable of.

He looks to be in his fifties, but his skin is more weathered than I'm used to, so it's hard to tell. He's covered in freckles, so many it makes his skin look darker than it is. His red hair has a lot of gray running through, which still surprises me to see. So many people in this camp have whites and grays in their hair. But back home, few people keep their natural hair color. Especially at his age—the moment a white hair appears, they reach for the hair dye.

"Hi Martina," he says with a broad smile. "I'm George."

I feel like telling him to go to hell.

He ducks his head and comes into the tent. Inside, he's too tall to stand up straight, so he keeps his head bowed. He looks a little comical with his head tilted like that.

"I bet you like keeping busy, don't you?" he says, with an infuriatingly warm grin.

I don't smile back. I want to hate him. I try to summon a deeper frown, but the best I can do is purse my lips. Watching this grown man bowing so comically and smiling so warmly is melting my iciness. I bite back the nasty words I want to say about the Terrene keeping me captive.

"Anyway," he says, "I thought you're probably bored? I can see you are." He winks at me. "So I brought you something to do."

He drags in a large piece of beige material. It's coarse and matches the fabric my tent is made from. He dumps it across my legs, then hands me a small box. I take it gingerly, confused as to what he's asking me to do.

"It's not particularly fun, but it is helpful," he explains. "There's a rip in this tent. It happened during the storm. And you look like you're clever enough to fix it. There are needles in the box, and all you need to do is stitch the length of the tear back together. You do know how to sew?"

I nod. I've had to sew plenty of Sebastian's clothes back together over the years to avoid buying new ones.

"Great! I knew I could count on you. Thanks!" He ducks back out of the tent before I have a chance to refuse his request. Why would I want to help him when his people have refused to help me? I push the fabric away and cross my arms, resolved not to help them.

My resolve doesn't last long; boredom takes care of that. I gather the thick material back up and find the tear. Selecting one of the large needles, I set to work mending the tent.

I work for a few hours, but all too quickly I'm finished. I get restless again as the rest of the day slowly progresses.

"Hi!" Will tentatively steps inside the tent. I cross my arms in response and give him a look that would frighten any self-respecting child, but Will doesn't budge. Instead, he sits down next to me.

"I thought you might like some company," he smiles.

I huff in response.

"Okay, well maybe you just want some entertainment then." His smile widens. He sticks two fingers between his lips and lets out an ear shattering whistle. I jump with a curse. I don't know what he's playing at, but it's not my idea of entertainment.

There is a scuffling noise outside. Seconds later, Roscoe, the dog, races into the tent and jumps on top of me.

"Umph." I let out a grunt when he lands on my stomach. He licks at my visor as if it's the tastiest treat on earth. Will, laughing heartily, eventually saves me, pulling Roscoe away. Roscoe doesn't seem very perturbed; he sits on his hind legs, looking back and forth at me and Will, his tongue drooping out from his toothy grin.

Despite myself, I let out a small giggle.

"I knew he'd make you smile," Will says without any of the arrogance of his big brother. His goofy smile mimics the dog so much that I can't help but laugh again.

"I'll show you some tricks he can do." Will goes onto his knees. He gets Roscoe's full attention and puts on a performance for me. Will says "down" and the dog drops onto his belly. Will says "roll-over" and Roscoe rolls onto his back. I'm amazed to see the dog obey. Will goes through several more commands, like shake, speak, jump, and every time Roscoe performs in kind.

"I didn't know dogs understood English," I say.

Will chuckles. "I've never heard it put like that before. But I guess they do. At least a few words, anyway. But they are very limited. Like Roscoe doesn't understand what I'm saying now. You can train them to react to select words."

"That's amazing."

"You can try if you'd like."

"Can I? What do I do?" Roscoe sits patiently, watching Will and waiting for his next command.

"Try getting him to shake hands. Just hold out your hand and say shake." Will demonstrates, and Roscoe puts his paw in the palm of Will's hand.

I sit up further and face Roscoe. He looks at me expectantly.

"Shake," I say as I hold out my hand, palm up. Roscoe looks at me for a second—his ears twitch and his head tilts to the side—and after a moment's thought, he places his paw into my waiting hand.

I squeal with pleasure. "Oh my god." Hearing my excitement, Roscoe jumps up and licks my face again—or tries to, smearing saliva all over my visor—all the while wagging his tail.

Suddenly Roscoe stops, looks out the tent, and before I know what's going on, he's disappeared. I look out to see where he's run off to, but instead I lock eyes with Nathan. He'd been watching the whole exchange. Smiling. But it quickly fades.

I expect him to walk away and continue to ignore me like he has all day, but he walks into the tent. His demeanor isn't as sickening as it had been; he actually looks sheepish with his eyes lowered, watching his fingers twist and entwine around each other.

"I hope you're feeling better?" Nathan says, shooting a quick glance at me.

"Yes," I say, and it's the truth this time.

"That's good." He swallows. "We'll be having dinner soon. Um, I know you can't eat it, but you're welcome to join us around the fire."

I'm tempted to give him a biting remark and declare I'd rather be alone, but I'm too bored. The thought of spending several more hours on my own in this lonely tent will send me mad.

Before I respond, he says, "Mother Jessica is going to tell the origin stories. I'm sure you'll enjoy it."

I accept with a curt nod.

Nathan deposits me onto a log near the fire and sits next to me. Will plonks down nearby. Most of the community has joined us, but they keep their distance from me. George winks from the other side of the fire. Mother Jessica is the last to join, and she sits on a stool in the middle of the gathering.

"Thank you all for joining me," Mother says. "Tonight it is timely to remember the past."

She doesn't look at me when she says it, but we all know that this is for my benefit. "It's always worthwhile remembering where we came from, how the world came to be the way it is, and teach our children the history of the world."

As she speaks, food and drink are handed around. I am a little distracted by it. My tongue involuntarily glides along my own lips as I watch Nathan eat some juicy looking meat.

"... and the people were greedy, selfish; all they cared about was making money and the growth of the economy," Mother Jessica is saying when I pay attention again. "They didn't care about the people dying around them. They abused the environment;

countless animal species were killed off, made extinct; and people continued to get sicker and sicker.

"The people didn't change their habits. They continued their lives as normal; wastefully and greedily." Mother Jessica's voice is grave. She stares into the fire as she speaks. "At first, they could contain the viruses that spread the world; SARS, Swine flu, Ebola, and COVID-19. Then came CRS-T8, which swept the world and wasn't contained. Millions of people died and millions more were infected. The spread was hard to detect because people were contagious before any symptoms showed. But people refused to wear masks, wash their hands regularly, or keep distant from each other, which caused the disease to spread more and more."

This was no different from the history I knew. And it's why we are now so careful in the bubble cities, being meticulously clean and wearing masks in the largely populated sectors.

"Eventually, a vaccine for CRS-T8 was created and distributed to the billions of people around the world. It saved many of them. PMC Life Tech made billions of credits from the creation and sale of the vaccine, and made even more money from preventative medicines in the following years. These drugs were supposed to protect the population from future diseases, and they did for a time.

"But once the initial fear of CRS-T8 was over and the people felt safe again, they stopped taking the medicines and vaccines, and PMC's profits dropped. The greedy corporates and executives didn't like that. They liked their private jets, fancy clothing, and big houses."

I remember being taught that people stopped taking the preventative medicines; it had been drilled into me from an early age as a lesson to always take my medications. But I'd never considered how it would affect profits. I want to reject Mother's words, but they make some sense. The people of that era were greedy. We had all been taught that was the downfall of man. So why would that exclude the PMC executives?

I shake the thought away. Of course, the pharmacists weren't the same. Their choice of profession was evidence they wanted to help people. They were different.

"It wasn't long before another virus, a deadlier virus, was detected. The Yeran virus was highly infectious. People started dropping like flies. Everyone was scared. They started buying medications and vaccines again in bulk. Profits soared for PMC Life Tech once again."

Mother takes a breath. "We can't be certain where the virus came from, but it's suspected it was created by a secret division of PMC and it got out of hand."

I gasp. But I'm the only one who's surprised. People are nodding their heads; they've heard all this before. How can they believe Mother? Anger at their stupidity heats my blood, and I'm not sure how much more of this I can listen to.

"People spoke out about PMC. Even other pharmaceutical companies denounced them. But PMC had too much power by then and those people were silenced. Plus, the world was in chaos with the Yeran virus running rampant. It wiped out the human population, leaving only a small percentage of survivors. And, the PMC executives rich.

"We lost so much during this time; people, animals, cities, technologies. The plague devastated the world."

Mother glances at me. "PMC were the ones who built the bubble cities under the guise of keeping humans safe from disease."

This is true, too. I remember my history lessons back in Colombia. I was taught that PMC injected funds into the construction of the bubble cities. But it was told to me as if they were heroes, not the villains.

"And what they didn't tell the population was the Yeran virus had died out. They didn't give people a choice of where or how to live. They used fear to convince the people that the bubble cities were their only option. But it wasn't. Small pockets of people escaped their grasp when they herded the rest into the bubble cities. The Terrene Folk remained free.

"Over the decades, the people in the bubble cities have been exposed to a variety of deadly diseases and viruses. There's been thousands of deaths. But the Terrene have remained healthy. The people in the bubble cities spend billions of credits every year on preventative medications. The Terrene Folk do not, and yet we remain healthy."

Mother nods her head as if someone has asked her a question, or maybe she sees my confused expression. "Yes, sickness still exists, but it's treatable and doesn't wipe out large numbers at once. The Terrene Folk use our own remedies to prevent colds and flus and heal the body. We use medicines when necessary, not every day. We don't need to live in a bubble city to survive."

Her face turns to stone. "PMC Life Tech lies to their citizens. To keep their secrets and remain in power, they cannot allow their citizens to know that the outside world is survivable. They cannot allow communities like ours to exist. PMC have hunted the Terrene Folk. They have killed our kindred. They have started a war against us. But we won't lie down and die!"

I jump as her last sentence is repeated around the fire. "We won't lie down and die." A few fists are pumped into the air.

I frown. How can they believe this? Somehow, I'm not as angry as I was when Mother first started talking. No, the anger has been overtaken by confusion and maybe a little fear. Fear for them or for myself, I'm not certain.

It seems Mother Jessica's story is finished and the people around the fire applaud her before dispersing, their meals finished.

I remain where I am, thinking about what I've heard. It's incredulous; it goes against everything I've ever been taught. How can they explain my parents, who died when they were exposed to the outside world?

But I have to admit, there's one problem with what I've been taught; I have always been told *no one* can survive outside. But here is a community of people doing just that. And if they are to be believed, there are even more of them out there, surviving. And not just that, *living!* Why hasn't PMC Life Tech or the health minister ever mentioned this? Why isn't anyone doing something to allow the entire population to live like this?

I'm still chewing on this thought when Nathan kneels in front of me.

"Hi Martina," he says shyly, his voice almost a whisper. "I have some great news for you." He swallows before continuing. "The road has been cleared and the camp will depart at first light. So we can help you get home tomorrow." He smiles.

Despite myself, I smile back. He's quite cute when he's chagrined. Although I'm still upset they've kept me from Sebastian for so long, I'm grateful that I'll be going home tomorrow. The thought that I might not get home had been plaguing my mind for too long.

"I was thinking," Nathan says, then falters. He glances around, looking everywhere but at me. "Since it's your last night with us, would you, maybe, like to go for a ride with me? On a horse?"

My eyebrows hit my hairline.

"It's safe, I swear," he says quickly. "It's just that, I know you haven't ever done it and I think you'd like it."

"Are you sure it's safe? My ankle is bad enough; I don't need any more injuries."

"I swear I'll keep you in one piece." And he smiles, knowing I'm going to accept.

Nine

"This is Jerry." Nathan introduces me to a white horse. I marvel at its glossy coat, which seems so soft, all I want is to reach out and touch it. Not for the first time, I curse my hazsuit.

Nathan tells me the best way to mount the creature. I'm awkward, especially since I can't put a lot of pressure on my left foot. My hands rest on Jerry's back and I do a little hop, but as I try to mount, Jerry's head swivels to look back at me. I flinch away, hopping backward with a small shriek.

Nathan chuckles. "It's okay, Martina. Jerry won't hurt you; I promise. Do you want to try again?"

I nod silently, taking a deep breath and steeling myself. I approach Jerry once again. This time, he ignores me when I use his back as leverage to launch myself. But I don't get enough height to throw my leg over like Nathan instructed, and I slide back to the ground.

"Nice try," Nathan says. But I know he's just being kind. I must look ludicrous to him. "Let me help you." He comes forward, interlacing his fingers and lowering them to my shin level, making a step for me. "Put your right foot into my hands, and I'll propel you upward. Then you just need to swing your left leg over."

Even with his help, it's difficult. I put my right foot into his hands and he lifts me up. I almost fall backward, but steady myself against Jerry's body, then swing my leg around.

It's completely ungraceful, but all Nathan says is, "Good."

Then in one fluid movement, Nathan leaps from the ground and settles behind me on the horse. My cheeks flare at the ease in which he does it compared to my labored effort. He encircles his arms around my body and takes hold of the reins; it's almost like he's hugging me. My cheeks get even hotter. He clucks his tongue, and the horse begins to walk.

I grip the saddle and focus on slowing my rapid heartbeat. I'm glad he can't see my burning cheeks through my hazsuit.

As the horse walks, my weight shifts slightly from side to side, but it's easy to stay seated, especially with Nathan's arms securely around me. Through the fabric of the hazsuit, I feel that he's totally relaxed, which is the complete opposite to me. My body is on edge, stiff as the metal beams that hold up the glass bubbles. The ground looks a long way down. I experience a feeling of vertigo, which surprises me. I never felt this when I was at the top of the bubble. Maybe it's because I don't have my abseiling gear with me, fixing me in place. I'm totally reliant on Nathan to keep me safe.

Night has fully arrived, and the tops of the tents are only illuminated by the moon, though Nathan navigates the horse around the camp with ease. He doesn't stop when we reach the edge of the camp, but continues into the desert.

"Hold on," he whispers.

I clench the saddle tighter just in time. The horse takes off at a faster pace. I bump along, disorientated, unable to make out anything because of the movement and darkness. Hopefully, Nathan and Jerry know what they're doing. I grit my teeth.

After a short trot, Nathan slows the horse again.

"Are you okay?" he asks, a hint of humor in his voice.

I chuckle. It's a nervous laugh, or maybe slightly hysterical—my emotions are all over the place. "I think so." I marvel at the fact I'm riding a horse. It was only yesterday I found out they existed, so this is beyond my wildest dreams.

But as much as I want to enjoy this moment, I can't stop thinking about home. I miss Sebastian. And I miss when everything made sense. What if everything I've been taught is a lie?

My mouth has gone dry.

I fear I'm missing a chance to live free like Nathan. I must go back to the bubble city—I will never leave Sebastian alone—but I can't deny a part of me wishes I didn't have to. To live freely among the Terrene Folk. Truly live. But if I stay out here, I might die from disease.

"Look up." Nathan's voice is husky in my ear. He pulls on the reins and brings the horse to a stop.

I take a sharp breath of filtered air. The galaxy is spread across the sky, looking like milk stirred through dark oil. There is an impossible number of stars that I've never seen before. From inside the bubble, only a handful of stars are bright enough to see through the glass.

"Come on." Nathan dismounts before helping me down. Then he lowers himself all the way to the ground, lying flat on his back. He shrugs. "It's a nice way to watch the skies."

Awkwardly, I do the same, lying down next to him. He's right; I can see the stars without craning my neck. There's a moment of silence as we both take in the incredible sight.

"I owe you an apology," Nathan says softly.

"Okay," I whisper back. Although no one is around, it seems proper to speak quietly out here, to be gentle with the silence.

"When you said your parents died from going outside, I didn't believe you. I'm sorry."

"And you believe me now?"

"Yes." He pauses. "I spoke to Mother, and she explained that many people who live in the bubbles don't survive outside them. She mentioned something about antibodies. What she means is that me and the rest of the Terrene Folk have built up immunities from being exposed to minor diseases over time, like colds and flus, but because the people from the bubble cities haven't been exposed, they're more susceptible to sickness. They could die, just from a simple cold. Have you ever had a cold?"

"No. I've never been sick. Well, not like that, anyway. I've had a headache before. And some vaccines make you feel really crappy for a while, and they have medicine to help that so it's not so bad. But I don't think that's what you mean." I take a shaky breath—the thought of getting sick, being in quarantine, dying—the only thing worse is imagining Sebastian sick.

"No, it's not," he says. "But it's incredible."

"What do you mean?"

"It's incredible that you've never been *really* sick. You've never had a cold. A real cold."

"Why did Mother tell me that story tonight? If what you say is true about antibodies, my people will die if we're exposed outside. We can never be like you."

"She told it so you'll know the truth! They're still lying to you. Don't you want to know the truth?"

"Maybe." I'm not sure if ignorance really is bliss. Not now that I've seen what it can be like outside of the bubbles. Free and under the stars.

"And anyway, some people *do* survive. Some people who have joined the Terrene once lived in the bubbles. And they're okay now. They didn't die. They just need a bit of time to adjust to life outside."

"Really?" I didn't mean to inject so much hope into my tone.

"Really! George is one of them. And people should know that. Plus, we're sick of being hunted. We just want to live in peace. I wish we could ... I mean ... never mind."

"What?"

"I don't know. I guess I wish they would just leave us alone." He seems like he's holding something back, or there's something more he'd like to say, but I don't push him. I'm too concerned with my own thoughts. It really is possible to live outside. George is proof someone from the bubble cities can survive. But how can I know if I'd be one of the people who dies or one that survives? And what about Sebastian? Even if I can get him out of the bubble city, would he survive? I must be crazy to even consider it. There's too much risk. I don't even know if I can trust these people.

After a while, Nathan breaks the silence. "Tell me about your parents."

I take a moment to think how to respond. "Papá was funny and Mamá was serious." It doesn't feel like enough. They were so much more than this. But I wasn't ready for the question. How do I explain to Nathan the beautiful, incredible people that were my parents?

"How did they end up outside?"

"We lived in Cali in Colombia. A few years ago, the bubble collapsed. The city didn't have individual sectors like Neustin, so once the bubble was compromised, the entire city was infected."

"How did you survive?"

What is this? An interrogation? But I answer him anyway. "Mamá was an anchorwoman for the Colombian news. She found out before most people that there had been some kind of explosion and the bubble was in jeopardy. It might have already been breached. Before she announced it on air, she rang Papá to warn him and told him to get us kids out of the city. She had connections to get us through the decontamination center and onto a bus."

Nathan was silent, but now he had opened the floodgates I couldn't stop. "I remember being in the kitchen with Papá and Sebastian. I was doing my homework at the table and Sebastian was bothering me, the little *pendejo*. He kept asking what I was doing. It was a math assignment, so of course he didn't understand it. He was only five. I kept telling him he wouldn't get it, but he kept asking anyway. Papá was making arepas, and we had the TV tuned onto Mamá's channel, waiting for her to come on and read the news. We would watch her every night." I smile at the memory, but tears well in my eyes.

"Instead, the comms unit rang, and she was on there, yelling at Papá to get us out of the city. She didn't say goodbye to us. She must have known she was a goner already, but she was more concerned with our survival. She yelled at Papá to get us onto a bus leaving the decontamination center." I cringe, remembering her voice screaming through the comms unit.

"Papá raced us across the city, but the decontamination center was already quarantined. Because the city of Cali is just one big bubble, the decontamination center is the only area they can isolate from the rest. But Mamá had already organized help. She knew a center manager who sneaked us through a repairs access shaft. It was supposed to be locked down too, but the manager overrode it and we got through just in time. Papá was too big to get through the shaft. It wasn't made for people, only machines. Luckily, Sebastian and I were small enough.

"I remember Papá's sobs. How they echoed down the shaft as he called his goodbyes." My voice is tight; it's hard to speak. "He kept urging us to keep going. I didn't want to leave Papá behind." I sniff. "But he convinced me it was best for Sebastian.

"Inside the decontamination center, people were boarding their buses, ready to depart." Tears well in my eyes, but my voice has taken on a neutral tone, like it's someone else talking now. "It was chaos. Every bus was preparing to leave. There were so many people running around, trying to get on buses, trying to find their loved ones. I guess not everyone made it to the center in time, because there were some spare hazsuits. Sebastian and I were lucky. We put them on and got on the next bus leaving town. We didn't know where it was going. There were loads of buses. All going to different cities. The bus took us here, to Texas.

"We had nothing with us other than our stolen suits," I finish.

Nathan is silent for a moment, his dark brows creased. "Then how do you know for sure your parents died? Maybe they could still be alive?" Nathan sits up to look at me. He seems excited that he might be right. But he's not.

A tear spills over, sliding down the side of my face to land in my hair. I look away from Nathan. "No," I say. "I know they died. Mamá was a news anchor, remember? Well, when Sebastian and I got into Texas, we went in search of information. We didn't have to look hard. It was on every screen throughout the city. It's big news when the total population of a bubble city is exposed."

I try to steady my voice. "And Mamá was still reporting it. People from other cities, safe in hazsuits, filmed it all. She obviously wasn't wearing a hazsuit. Or even a mask. She had already been exposed, so there was no point. And it was a great story, wasn't it?" I can't hide the bitterness from my voice. "Watching the famous anchorwoman waste away. Watching her describe the deaths of every person from the Cali bubble. Even her husband's death. We lost our whole *familia. Nuestros tíos y tías,* and *mi abuela.* Eventually the news station ran a memories reel of Mamá's most popular news moments as a way to say goodbye." I sniff, shaking my head. "I guess I should be grateful that I'm alive."

"Sor ... I'm sorry," Nathan says, stumbling over his words. "I can't believe I ever doubted you. I'm ... I'm so sorry you had to experience that."

My tears burn hot trails down my cheeks, pooling in my hair. My breath is shaky. I take a few deep breaths to help steady myself. This is something I have never shared with anyone before. I rarely get close enough to people. Even Sebastian and I avoid talking about it. I don't know why I revealed it to Nathan.

Nathan stays silent but reaches out his hand to take my gloved one. My heart thumps with delight, despite its pain.

We don't say much more while we gaze at the stars, but eventually Nathan suggests we should go.

When we get back to the camp, Nathan slides off the horse. I miss the feeling of him behind me, but then he holds out his arms to help me down. I savor the moment when his strong hands touch my waist, steadying me. They let go too soon. But he doesn't move away.

His black eyes bore into mine, as if my visor doesn't stand between us.

"I wish ... I wish you weren't going tomorrow. I know you have to go, but ... well, it would be nice to get to know you better."

He turns and walks Jerry away.

"It would be nice to get to know you too, Nathan," I say to his back, surprising myself.

He glances back at me with a small smile and keeps walking.

Ten

"Martina? Martina, wake up!"

I open my eyes and find Will pulling on my uninjured foot to wake me.

"Is the camp ready to go?" I ask sleepily, but quickly waking up.

"Almost. We just need to pack the tents. Everything else is ready. But that's not what I was going to say. Come see this."

He helps me out of the tent where Mother Jessica is waiting, holding a comms unit.

"Where did you get that?" I ask.

"That's not important," Mother says. "You need to see this."

She holds it up so I can see the screen. It's showing the local news reel for the city. Dr. Lederman, the health minister, is talking to the camera, and in a square projected beside him is a picture of my face. It flicks between one with my red mask on, and one without.

"What?" I ask.

Nathan joins us and looks over my shoulder at the comms unit. "What's going on?"

I turn up the volume. "... missing since the storm hit," Dr. Lederman is saying, "she is assumed to be infected and must be quarantined if found. Repeating. Martina Monsalve went missing outside the bubble during the storm. If spotted, do not approach her. She could be highly contagious and must be quarantined.”

“But I’m not sick,” I say.

“I’m sorry, Martina,” Mother Jessica says, “but I think your life is in danger.”

I exchange confused glances with Nathan and Will.

“I believe PMC have become aware of the presence of the Terrene Folk,” Mother says, “and they suspect you’ve found out about us. It explains why they won’t wait to see if your suit has been breached; they will put you straight in quarantine. We’ve seen this happen before.” Mother paces. “They put people in quarantine who they want to dispose of. It’s easy for them to claim death by disease. In fact, the people they do this to do actually die from disease. However, it’s a disease they have administered to ensure the person dies.”

“But why?” I say quietly.

“So you can’t tell the world about us. So they can keep their power and their lies and their secrets.” Mother’s eyes burn into mine. “Believe me, Martina, you won’t survive the week.”

I back away from her, shaking my head. “I have to go back! I have to get back to Sebastian.”

“You could stay with us,” Nathan says.

“No!” My voices rises. “I can’t, Nathan. I ... I need ... Sebastian needs me. I can’t leave him alone. Anyway, I could die if I stay.”

“But you’ll definitely die if you go back.” His face is creased; his brows lowered with worry, but eyes flashing with anger.

“You don’t know that!”

“There’s a good chance you will,” Mother says calmly.

“I need to take the chance. For Sebastian. I have to try.”

Mother considers me for a moment, then nods.

Nathan shakes his head. “Martina, I know you want to help your brother, but it will be at the cost of your life.” He spreads his hands in a gesture of pleading. "You can't really be considering this."

"I'm not." My voice is hard. "I've already decided. I'm going back. I'll find a way to help Sebastian. I have to."

Nathan starts to protest again, but Mother lays a hand on his shoulder, stopping him short.

I sigh in relief. At least I have Mother's acceptance, and she's not going to hold me here against my will.

"There may be another way," she says. "You can enter the city using an alias."

"You mean a different name?" I ask. "But I need to enter a PIN to get through security."

"We have one you can use," Mother nods, as if the plan is all coming together in her head. "You'll need to enter via the Bush quarter. The PIN we have won't work in any other sector. If you keep your head down, you can go through to the other quarters from there and reach your brother."

"The Sparkle Sector? But I don't have the clothes for that. They'll spot me a mile away."

"The PIN you'll enter will allow you to take the owner's clothes, dress as her, and use her name. She'll be out of town, so won't be needing them."

"Who is she?"

"Dr. Katherine Marshall."

"A pharmacist?"

"Yes."

"You can't be serious!" But she is serious. I can see it on her face. She really expects me to go into the Sparkle Sector posing as an elite pharmacist. I guess if I get through the decontamination center no one will even know I used her PIN. I could just be another rich member of their society. It all rides on me getting through the decontamination center. And if Dr. Marshall is renowned, no one will be checking her comings and goings. The elite get a level of privacy the rest of us don't have. I doubt they ever have cameras on her when they scan her for contagions, like I'm almost certain they do in The Nix's decontamination center.

Even though it turns my legs to jelly, I agree to her plan. I must be crazy.

I bounce in the seat of an old pickup truck as it weaves its way through the Old City. There's enough space between collapsed buildings and rubble for the vehicle to weave around unhindered. It must have been a road at one point. Now it's littered with the bones of the Old City and blanketed with sand.

Nathan is driving. He drives quickly; it would be dangerous for him to go any slower. Mother wants the community out of the area in case PMC attacks. Nathan needs to drop me off near the Sparkle Sector and then get back to the Terrene Folk as soon as possible.

Before I left the camp, Mother gave me the PIN I'll need to get through the decontamination center. I'd love to use their comms unit to call Sebastian, but it's pointless. Sebastian doesn't have a comms unit and mine is stored in a locker at the decontamination center with the rest of my stuff.

As Nathan waited for me in the truck, Mother held me in an unexpected embrace. Her voice was weighed with importance as she said, "Remember what you've learned here. Witness the truth."

Will grinned as he said goodbye, although it wasn't as wide as it has been. "I hope we'll see each other again one day," he said, hugging me tight.

Nathan hasn't said a word during the drive. He's probably still fuming that I'm going through with this plan and haven't agreed to stay. I keep silent, too.

We're close to the edge of the Old City when Nathan pulls up behind a brick wall. "This is as close as I can get you," he says, finally breaking the silence.

I stare out the window at the crumbling city. It's strange that I used to find it so mysterious; now it just looks like a bunch of old, crumbling buildings and piles of sand. There's nothing special about it.

"Thanks," I eventually say when it's clear Nathan has nothing more to add. "I'll just go then."

"Martina, wait. Please don't be like that."

"Like what?" I snap and immediately regret it.

"I'm sorry. I'm just worried about you." He reaches out for my hand and I let him take it. "I understand you have to do this, I just … I wish you didn't have to. But I *do* understand. It is important you know that. I would do the same for Will."

I squeeze his hand. "Thank you. That means a lot."

"We're still a little way from the bubble. The buses pass through that route." He points to an opening between the abandoned buildings, much larger than the route we've taken, where the rubble appears to be cleared away. "They slow down considerably through this section, so you'll have time to make your move." He hesitates. "Are you sure you can do this?"

"Yes," I say. My ankle has improved significantly over the two nights with the Terrene Folk. I still have a limp, but I can put a lot more weight on my left foot now.

We get out of the truck.

"Be careful, bubble girl," Nathan says, his eyes drilling through mine. His thumb rubs along my gloved fingers. It sends a shiver up through my suit. For a second, I think it has malfunctioned, giving me an electric shock.

I try to say goodbye, but my throat closes around the words. Without thinking, I reach up and brush his hair off his face.

My heartbeat races and I look away with cheeks burning. I can't believe I did that. Even with a glove on, I've never touched anyone so intimately before. But still, I wish I could have touched him without my gloves and really know how soft his hair is.

We lock eyes, and I smile when I realize he's blushing too.

I try to memorize his face. I'll probably never see it again. His long hair, his dark brows that are always frowning, and eyes that seem to see through me.

I turn and limp away.

When I reach the bus route, I crouch in the shadows of a building so they won't see me. I glance back to where I left Nathan, but his truck is already gone. Only the dust in the air shows where he'd been. I'm on my own.

I stay crouched for what feels like an age, but it has probably only been twenty minutes or so. We timed my arrival with the bus timetable.

The way has been cleared of rubbish to allow buses to pass easily through the Old City, but the buildings on either side are still a mess of broken walls, fallen signs, and piles of wood and metal. I'm squatting in what might have been the foyer of a building, now only a dark hole.

I hear the crunch of tires on gravel.

I perch on the balls of my feet, ready to pounce.

A dusty white vehicle rounds a corner. I inhale sharply—even though I was expecting the bus, the sight of it still sends my heart into overdrive. If I don't time this right ... the image of my broken body under the wheels of the bus flashes through my mind.

It is coming slowly, just like Nathan said it would. It rolls past my hiding spot, leaving a cloud of dust in its wake.

I sneak up behind it, ducking low and using the dust as cover, so I can't be seen through the back window. I match the pace of the bus and ready myself. Before I can change my mind, I leap, latching onto the back, my fingers gripping the windowsill. I can only pray my fingers aren't noticed by the passengers. I have to hunch uncomfortably, so my helmet doesn't poke up above the window.

My toes rest precariously on the bumper. Any sudden movement and I'll be sent flying off the bus. I don't feel very balanced, and after a few seconds, my fingers ache from the effort of holding on. But I don't let go. I can't let go.

The bus continues its slow drive through the Old City, past buildings with faded signs, a few words still visible—discount, trader, bikes, apple. I don't know what any of it means. It seems weird to have a whole building just for fruit.

The bus suddenly leaves the ruins. Without their shadows, I feel exposed. The sun beats down on me like a spotlight. I cower into the bus further, wishing I could turn invisible. I'm relieved that I haven't been spotted yet; the bus would stop if someone saw me. I pray it stays this way.

I glimpse the ugly gray entrance to the decontamination center, but keep my head low, not daring to peek from my hiding spot. I hear the clunk of metal on metal as the outer door of the decontamination center opens.

I hold my breath.

The sun disappears as the bus slides inside. I look up to see the metal roof of the decontamination center, with its many fans whirring furiously. The outer door closes behind us. I shut my eyes tightly, as if that helps me be more invisible.

The chamber is slowly filtered with fresh air. Every inch of me burns from holding on to the bus. I'm tempted to let go, to discreetly step down from the bumper. Maybe I won't be seen now we're inside. But I can't risk it. Better to wait until the bus has parked and other passengers are around. Then I can hide in the crowd.

My legs shake from the strain. My ankle aches more than it has in the last twenty-four hours.

Finally, the inner doors clunk open, and the bus moves into the parking terminal. It parks next to another white bus, stained orange by the desert.

I wait until I hear the bus door open before I step down.

The passengers disembark and the area is filled with people; men and women turned genderless in their white hazsuits, only a couple children among them. I walk into the crowd as if I'm just another passenger. Some of them mill around, waiting for luggage. Others head straight to the individual decon stations. I follow them, trying to walk as casually as I can.

When I reach an empty station, I enter the PIN with shaking fingers.

78654*1

Nothing happens. The station stays locked. Don't panic. I must have hit a wrong key; my hands are shaking so badly. I memorized the PIN before leaving the camp, but what if I got it wrong? I shake my head. That's not an option. There is nowhere for me to go. I can't just leave the way I entered. The only way is forward.

I steady my hands and enter the PIN again.

78654*1.

I hold my breath.

The door beeps. A clunk indicates the door is unlocked. I open it, releasing my breath once I enter the small chamber beyond.

My knees are weak and fear sits in the pit of my stomach while I go through the usual procedures; stripping off my hazsuit and throwing it into the decontaminator machine for washing and restocking; then scrubbing myself in the shower using the antibacterial soaps. My heart is racing throughout it all, despite the normalcy of it.

For a moment, I take pleasure in the warm water against my skin. After being trapped in my hazsuit for the last few days, the feeling is delightful. But I don't linger. I'm eager to get out of the center quickly.

I pat myself dry and spot the sterilized moisturizer dispenser. I've never used it before. It's always been too expensive to even consider. But this time, Dr. Marshall is paying. I dismiss the idea as overindulgent. Is it really necessary? I've never used the moisturizer before and I've been fine. Itchy, perhaps, but fine.

But Dr. Marshall would use it. And I must do my best to keep up appearances. With a grin, I pump out some of the smooth liquid and lather it over my body. It's instantly soothing, easing the sting of the soaps. I close my eyes and breathe in the sweet smell, like fresh apples. If only I could afford to use this every day.

Once I'm washed, dried, and moisturized, I move into the scanning chamber. I steady my breath. If I'm going to be discovered, it will be here. If anyone is monitoring the scanners, they'll instantly notice I'm not Dr. Marshall. As usual, I'm tempted to cover my breasts, but I know I can't. I try to relax while the laser runs over my naked body.

I'm shivering as I wait for the machine to clear me as uncontaminated. But what if I'm not? Maybe my hazsuit was really damaged in the storm and I *am* infected. My skin tingles as the lasers run over it, despite the fact that I can't feel a thing.

Beep.

I jump, then shake my head. It's only the machine beeping to indicate that I'm free of germs. The next set of doors open, letting me into the dressing area.

Dr. Marshall's clothes have been delivered, and they are beautiful. A silky cream pantsuit that falls delicately over my hips.

The trousers are far too big and long, but I pin them in place with some bobby pins I find in Dr. Marshall's belongings. I tuck a white shirt into the pants and cover the pins at my waist with the matching cream jacket. The outfit is topped off with white high heels.

I eye the heels. I've never worn high heels before and these look like they'll add several inches to my height. They're a tripping hazard. Even if I didn't have an injured ankle.

I rummage around Dr. Marshall's belongings, finding jewelry, a handbag, and, thankfully, another pair of shoes. This pair is flat, made from a material so soft they could be slippers, but the jewels running along the side of them assure me they're not. I slide them on, relieved. I also slip on some of the jewelry, not because of their value, but to complete the disguise. And then I pin my curly hair back with some more bobby pins and a jeweled clip.

I look at myself in the mirror. I have no idea what Dr. Marshall looks like, but I doubt it's anything like the hollow-cheeked, sunken-eyed girl staring back at me. The lack of food must be affecting me more than I realized. I glance at Dr. Marshall's makeup, wondering if I can make myself look less corpse-like. But I have barely any experience wearing makeup—I could end up making it worse.

I search her belongings for a face mask before I remember they don't wear face masks in the Sparkle Sector. Why would they when it's the cleanest quarter with the smallest population in Neustin? I feel exposed, not just because I'm not used to walking around without a mask, but because I could use the extra bit of disguise.

She doesn't have a backpack, so I assume she leaves the additional things, like her extra pair of shoes, here in the center. I pack up her stuff and reenter her PIN so that they go back into storage, along with my ancient hazsuit. Then I rush out of the decontamination center as quickly as I can without drawing unwanted attention.

The Sparkle Sector is beautiful. Little streams, dotted with goldfish, run along the side of the white marble paths, the clear water bubbling pleasantly, creating a musical backdrop to my walk. Green fronds and colorful flowers hang overhead, not too bushy that they block out the light, but creating a sense that I'm outside in nature.

I breathe in deeply. The streets are perfumed with the flowers and greenery. There's no sickly sweet scent of too many people, nor the pungent smell of disinfectant. And there's certainly not the smell of booze and spices that surrounds my pod in The Nix. The Sparkle Sector smells clean and fresh, the air easy to consume, without any of the overpowering scents of cleaning products.

Clean white walls peek out from behind the ferns and every so often there's an ornate wooden door, the entranceway to private residences. Sometimes a small bronze plaque states the name of the family's residence; Peterson, Sanchez, Smith, Jeyarajah.

I marvel at the extravagance of it as I walk along, looking for the corridor that connects it to the other quarters. I know I can't get to The Nix directly from here, and the Linto quarter is most likely still in lockdown, but I should be able to go through to the Bama quarter that then connects to The Nix.

The streets are almost empty; there's nowhere near the amount of Sparkle citizens as other quarters. There are two people walking leisurely ahead of me, both immaculately dressed, strolling past some large green leaves. I want to hide my face and drop my head, but I can't. People from the Sparkle Sector don't walk like that. Instead, I try to mimic the struts of the people in front. They walk slowly, almost lazily, with their heads high. They walk as if they own the world.

When I walk by, they cast a glance in my direction. Even slowed down, it seems I'm walking too fast. I smile at them, but they don't return it.

I spot some cameras hidden in the decorative foliage. My heart beats harder. Anyone could be watching me. Did they spot my faux pas? I slow down even more, trying to look as if I've got nowhere to be but here.

My ankle aches from trying to walk normally. I feel my limp becoming more pronounced with each minute. My palms sweat and I feel a tingling on the back of my neck, like someone's eyes are on me. It's an effort to avoid looking over my shoulder. It will only draw more attention.

But the sensation doesn't go away. I risk a brief glance behind, hoping it looks casual.

Two guards look straight at me. They're following behind at a distance. Neither react when I look back at them. I want to bolt, but I restrain myself. Maybe they're not really looking at me. Maybe they are simply doing their normal rounds of the quarter and are not interested in me at all.

It's all I can do not to quicken my pace.

I keep walking, searching for any signs of the corridor that connects to the Bama quarter, but I can't see any street signs. No indications at all of where to go.

There's a path to my left. I look back at the guards as I turn onto it in the most nonchalant way. They haven't gained on me at all, but my eyes lock with one of them. My heart skips a beat. I break eye contact as I disappear down the path.

It's narrow enough that the fronds almost create an archway overhead, touching in the center and blocking out some of the light. The stream has disappeared, but the white walls of the private residences still run along behind the greenery on both sides of the path.

A footstep echoes on the marble. The guards must have followed me down the path. Frantically, I look for a place to go, to either hide or run. If I try to run on my injured ankle, the guards will quickly catch up. But I'm small. If I can find somewhere they can't squeeze through, I might have a chance.

But there's nothing that will do the job. Only white walls. Not even the ferns are dense enough to hide me.

My eyes flick left and right, up and down, looking for a solution.

Then I spot it. Marshall.

The name is printed on a bronze plaque attached to stately double doors. I stroll toward them purposely, as though the home was always my destination. On the security pad next to the doors, I enter the numbers 78654*1 and pray to God the doors open. My prayers are answered with a soft click, and the doors swing wide.

Once inside, I press a large black button on the wall that closes and locks the automatic doors. As they swing shut again, I see the two guards stroll past. They don't even glance in my direction, and in a moment, they're gone, obscured by the closed doors.

I let out a sigh and lean my head against the door, allowing my heart rate to slow.

"Mom?"

My heart stops.

Eleven

"You're a little short to be my mother," the voice says.

I turn around slowly.

I'm standing in the entranceway of a grand home. The entranceway itself is the size of the diner back in The Nix. A bejeweled chandelier hangs from the ceiling, casting slivers of rainbow light across the marble floor. An ornately carved table stands across from me, boasting a bouquet of white flowers, and two archways lead into other rooms on either side of the entrance. There's a grand staircase, trimmed with stained wood and gold. And coming down the staircase is a beautiful young lady.

I instantly recognize her; she's the stupid girl that stared at me through the window when I was washing the underside of the bubble.

"Well, hello again," the girl says.

I'm frozen like a cockroach when it's caught crawling under a rock. She continues down the stairs.

She wears impossibly high heels, but she walks effortlessly. A pale blue dress offsets her dark skin, and is strategic in length to reveal enough of her long legs without it being too short. Her hair is elaborately braided around her head again, with sparkling jewels woven in. More jewels are on her arms and fingers, hanging from her ears and around her neck. She drips wealth.

She appraises me at the same time I do her, and I can't help but feel like I come up short. Literally. Even if she wasn't wearing high heels, she would tower over me. I must look ridiculous in the oversized pantsuit, which I realize now must belong to her mother.

She reaches the bottom of the stairs and comes toward me. She stops a few feet away, keeping her distance.

I stand up straight, out of the crouch I didn't realize I was in. But even at my full height, I'm still half a foot shorter than her.

To my surprise, a smile plays at the edge of her lips. "You don't seem sick to me," she says.

"What?"

"Your face is all over the news warning us to keep away from you if we see you." Her voice is clipped, enunciating everything the way posh people do. A little like how my Mamá spoke when she was on air. "They want to quarantine you. But you look perfectly fine to me." Her mouth slides into a wider smile. She cocks her head. "You don't talk much, do you?"

"I..." I clear my throat. "I'm just trying to figure out if you're going to report me."

"Not right now," she says. "Why don't you come away from the door?" She turns her back to me and strolls into the room on her right. I consider bolting. But if she isn't going to turn me in just yet, then maybe I can use her. She might be able to help me reach my brother. So I follow her.

I enter a living room with plush silver carpet and drapes. She perches on the edge of a white armchair and gestures for me to take the chair opposite her. I remain standing near the doorway.

The smile continues to play around her lips as she considers me. "Since you're wearing my mother's clothes and you somehow got into our home, I assume you used her PIN to sneak back into the city?"

I maintain a neutral expression. Better if I don't confirm my guilt.

"And that would mean you got through the decontamination center with no contagions detected." She nods to herself. She clearly doesn't need my confirmation. "So why do they want to put you in quarantine, Martina Monsalve?"

My name coming from her mouth sounds both foreign and musical. I stare at her, unable to formulate a response.

"If I wanted to turn you in, I could have done so already," she continues. "So you might as well talk to me."

It's true; she could have had me arrested already. Someone this rich would have servants in the house. One shout from her would bring people running.

If I'm going to get her help, I'm going to have to tell her something. So I sit down on the seat across from her.

"What's your name?" I say, not sure where to start. "You know mine. It's only fair that I know yours too."

Her lips twitch. "I'm Persephone. Persephone Marshall."

"Dr. Katherine Marshall is your mother?"

She nods.

"I can't tell you how I got her PIN," I say. It's not a complete lie; I don't know how Mother Jessica got a hold of it. "But I needed it. I need to get to my brother. He's in The Nix quarter and if I end up in quarantine, I won't see him again." I pause, wondering if I should say what I'm thinking. For some reason, I do. "And I might wind up dead."

"But you're not sick?"

"No. But I don't think that matters." Maybe it's silly talking about this with someone I don't know, but I feel I have no choice. My hands turn clammy as I keep talking. "I know something that the pharmacists don't want anyone else to know, and they might kill me to stop me from telling anyone."

I've finally come to the realization that Mother Jessica was right. PMC must know about the Terrene Folk. There is no other explanation why they would want to quarantine me without testing me for contagions first. They know, and they want to keep it secret.

"What do you know?" Persephone's smile has gone. She seems to take my words seriously.

"It might put you in danger if I tell you." And I don't know if I can trust you, I want to say.

"So? Why do you care what happens to me? You don't even know me."

"I don't want anyone to be hurt!"

She smiles at my outburst, then nods, as if she's reached some kind of conclusion. "You look like you need some food and water." She stands and disappears into another room. I wonder if she's gone to alert someone, but she returns before I have too long to stress about it. She carries a tray holding a jug of water, two glasses, and a plate of biscuits, and places it on the coffee table between us.

She pours me a glass of water and gestures for me to eat the biscuits. I wonder if they're poisoned, but think better of it. She didn't have time to poison them in the short time she was gone. My stomach does the thinking for me, grabbing a biscuit before I can second guess myself.

I finish them quickly. The biscuits are sweet and buttery, a much better quality than what is available in The Nix, even if we could afford them. The water tastes incredible—I didn't even think water had a taste. But after drinking the stale water from my hazsuit for three days, this water tastes delicious.

Persephone refills my water and waits patiently as I drink my fill.

"Thank you," I mutter, and mean it. After days of eating nothing but old soup, I truly am grateful for the food.

"My pleasure." Persephone beams. "What are you going to do once you find your brother?"

"Um, I don't know yet," I say.

"Won't you be putting him in danger if you see him?"

"I guess so. He's probably as much at risk if I do nothing. He's got no food or money to buy food. The rent will run out on our pod in a few weeks and then he'll be out on the street. Maybe I can get him …" I stop myself before I say "outside." I'm not sure if I want to answer the questions that would raise. I'm also not sure I want to take Sebastian outside, not with the health risks. But if he stays here, he might starve to death, become homeless, or get kidnapped. Maybe it's better for us to take a chance outside. And the reward if we survive is so much greater.

"Anyway." I shake my head. "I need to check he's okay."

"I might be able to help with that," Persephone says with a twinkle in her eye. "We can call him on my comms unit."

My face falls. "We only have one comms unit between us, and it's in my locker in The Nix decontamination center."

"Then we'll look for him on the security feeds," she says, as if it's not a problem at all. She sees my look of surprise and giggles. The sound is like chimes tinkling. "My mother has access, and *you* happen to know her PIN, so it shouldn't be a problem. We'll find him."

She stands and leaves the room and I limp behind. She goes back out to the foyer to an access pad on the wall below the stairs. The door is so subtle, I hadn't noticed it before.

Persephone nods at me and I enter her mother's PIN. The door swings open.

The small room is dark, the only light coming from several screens that line the back wall. Images of the different quarters are projected on them. People wearing colorful masks in The Nix; business men and women rushing around the Bama quarter; the vacant streets of the Linto quarter in lockdown, with only the guards patrolling them; the pretty paths of the Sparkle Sector, with its citizens idly strolling in expensive dresses and suits.

My mouth is agape. "Why does your mom have all this? I thought she was a pharmacist?"

"She is," Persephone says. "But she's very senior and that gives her certain privileges. She uses this for infection control. You know—makes sure everyone is staying in quarantine and not spreading any diseases." She grins at me and rolls her eyes. "She'd just love you! Avoiding quarantine, sneaking into the Bush quarter, and busting into her home. She would burst a blood vessel or two."

I turn back to the screens. There are several dedicated to watching The Nix. I search for Sebastian and his familiar robot printed mask.

"There's even more views." Persephone leans over me and I catch her flowery scent. "Just press this button to flick between the views."

When she steps back, her scent lingers; rose, jasmine, and a hint of something else. I'm preoccupied by it for a moment, but I blink my mind back into focus, and continue searching the screens for Sebastian.

It's Sunday, which means he won't be working, but he might be inside the pod where there are no video cameras.

"Ah ha," I mutter when I find the view of our street. I see the curry restaurant and can just make out the row of pods above it. All the doors to the pods are closed, so it doesn't give me much information. I continue to flick through the views, while leaving that screen focused on my home street.

I flick through Nixo Square, the med-bay, and the diner, but don't see Sebastian in any of those locations.

While I continue to search, Persephone sits quietly beside me. I'm aware of her eyes on me, not the screen, but I refuse to let it bother me. My gaze flicks across the many screens, over and over. Where is he? I rack my brain to think of his usual spots.

I jolt. I catch a glimpse of a red shirt, like one Sebastian owns. But before I can confirm it's him, he disappears from view.

"Did you find him?" Persephone says.

"Maybe," I say, my eyes glued to the screen. "I saw a kid in a red shirt that might be him."

Persephone leans forward to look, too.

I flick through different views of the same area for several minutes. Neither of us talk until Persephone says, "There?" She points to a kid in a red shirt near the windows of the bubble. I can't quite tell if it's him.

"You can zoom in," she says, doing it for me by leaning across and pressing a different button.

"Oh!" My hand flies to my heart when I see the robot printed mask. "It's him!"

He strolls slowly along the edge of the bubble, constantly looking outside. Maybe searching for me. My eyes well up. He's okay.

"Thank you, Persephone," I whisper, tearing my eyes away from the screen for a second so I can look at her. She's smiling broadly; I return the smile, before my attention goes back to Sebastian.

"What's that he has in his hand?" Persephone says. "I think he's holding a comms unit."

She's right. Somehow, he's gotten hold of a comms unit. I start, realizing it means I can call him. Persephone is already holding out her comms unit. I take it from her with a look of gratitude.

I dial my own number, assuming that he somehow retrieved my comms unit from the decontamination center. Before pressing the last number, I pause. What if my phone is being monitored? Am I putting us both in danger right now?

I press the last number anyway. It's worth the risk.

There is no sound coming from the video security feed, but I see Sebastian's reaction when it rings. He jumps and almost loses his grasp on the unit before answering.

"*¿Aló?*" He holds the unit in front of him and his masked face fills the screen of Persephone's unit.

"Sebastian!" I cry. I turn my back on Persephone to create a small amount of privacy.

"Martina? You're alive?"

"Yes, I'm alive. Oh my god, are you alright?"

"I'm fine, but I miss you, Martina." His eyes fill with tears. "I've been looking for you outside. Where are you?"

"I'm in the Sparkle Sector."

Sebastian's eyes widen.

"I had to sneak in here because they want to quarantine me," I explain. "But I'm not sick." I pause. "Sebastian, I think they want to hurt me."

He frowns. "Why?"

"Something happened. Outside." I glance over my shoulder at Persephone and lower my voice. "Do you remember that man?"

Sebastian visibly swallows as he nods.

"Well, PMC don't want anyone to know about him," I say, trying not to reveal too much in front of Persephone. "I'm scared I might be in danger. But I need to see you and make sure you're safe. I'll be there soon, *hermanito.*"

"No, you can't!" Sebastian shouts into the unit, then more quietly, he says, "Guards are following me, Martina. They'll find you. So ... don't come here."

"But ... I have to. You need to eat! And your meds." I hesitate. If the Terrene Folk are right, then Sebastian probably doesn't need all his daily medications. But if he doesn't take them, he'll get in trouble with the authorities, and they'll accuse him of being sick. For now, it's better that he keeps up the pretense while I figure out what to do.

"Martina," he draws out the last syllable of my name in a way that says he thinks I'm ridiculous, "I'm not stupid. I've been using your PIN. How do you think I got your comms unit?"

I chuckle. "So you've been spending all my money, have you?"

"I promise I've been careful," he says seriously.

"I know, *hermanito*. It's okay. I'm glad you did. You need to eat!"

"So don't come back here, okay?" he says, sounding just like me when I'm bossing him around. "I'll be fine."

"Let me work out a plan. And I'll call you back soon. In the meantime, please stay safe. Don't do anything silly."

"Aww, Martina!" He sing-songs.

We say our goodbyes and end the call. Sebastian has grown up a lot since I saw him days ago. He's taking care of himself, showing initiative I didn't think he had. He's grown up more than I realized.

I turn to Persephone—she wasn't even pretending not to listen—and hand her back her comms unit.

"So ... who is this *man*?" Persephone raises her eyebrows.

I purse my lips.

"You might as well tell me," Persephone says. "You're going to need help, and I'm the only chance you've got. Don't you see that even if you get back to your brother, you're still going to have some major issues? It seems like there's a bigger issue to be solved here."

She's right. My biggest problem isn't how to get back to Sebastian anymore, but what to do afterward. How can I keep both of us safe? PMC will not stop looking for me unless they think I'm dead. Maybe I can fake my death. But it probably won't help me. I need to earn a living to feed both of us. Somehow, I have to convince PMC that I know nothing, so I can go back to my old life. But if they catch me, I'll be dead before I get the chance to convince them of anything.

Sebastian and I could leave the bubble city. Join the Terrene Folk. We might survive, but we might die as well. Can I take that risk?

I shake my head. No. I'll never risk Sebastian's life. I only have one real option. I have to expose the truth. I need to inform citizens that PMC Life Tech have been lying to them. If everyone knows that a community of people are surviving outside the bubble cities, then PMC will have no reason to kill me; their secret will already be exposed. Then the people can choose what life they want to live, inside or outside. No longer will they have to blindly follow the life handed to them by PMC.

I'll need help to expose them. I need proof to convince the people. But who can help me?

I look at Persephone. How can I trust her? She doesn't even know me. But she's already helping me and has offered to keep helping me. And she's right—I do need the help.

"That man ..." I hesitate. "He was outside the bubble."

For the next hour, I tell Persephone all about the Terrene Folk; how I found them after I was lost in the storm; how they're a large community traveling past our city, but have an even larger community on a reservation somewhere unknown to PMC Life Tech.

I feel uneasy telling her the truth. I am breaking the trust of the Terrene Folk. But by helping myself, I might help them too.

I explain how they've been persecuted by PMC, hunted, and killed. And I tell her of their beliefs about PMC; the control they wield through fear of diseases and the lies they've told. How they milk money out of people to stay rich, while people in The Nix wither and die from starvation.

I avoid telling her about Nathan. I don't know why, but I blush as I skim over his contributions to my story.

She listens to it all intently, occasionally asking questions. Although she wears no mask, her face is unreadable. It doesn't tell me if she believes me or thinks I'm *loca*.

But the more I speak, the more I start to relax.

When I've finished, Persephone is quiet for a moment. Finally, she says, "You really *do* need my help." She stands and starts pacing. "Honestly, no one is going to believe you if you just tell them that story. And PMC could say that mental illness is a side effect of a new disease. They could easily cover this up."

"So, you don't believe me?" I can't hide the disappointment from my voice. Of course she doesn't believe me. I was crazy to tell her everything. To think she might help me.

"I didn't say that," she says calmly. "But we need proof that it's true."

We. I feel a spark of hope. If she helps me, I might just have a chance of surviving this.

"We need to investigate," Persephone continues. "The chemistry labs might have information that can help, and we can get around using Mom's PIN. They're used to seeing me there anyway, so we might not even need to use Mom's PIN. I could ask around or—"

"Why are they used to seeing you there?" I interrupt.

She stops pacing and looks at me. "I'm a student pharmacist."

I recoil. She's the enemy. Her and her pharmacist friends are killing people. And I've just told her everything I know about them.

She holds her hands out in a placating manner. "It's okay," she says. "I'm not yet one of them."

"Yet?" I hiss.

"I guess they haven't let me in on their secrets yet. I'm not exactly a favorite with Dr. Lederman. The only reason I have my internship is because Mom has sway."

My body is tense. I feel myself readying to run. "Why doesn't Dr. Lederman like you?"

"He hasn't liked some of my suggestions to reduce the costs of medications. I think they should be more affordable for the people in The Nix quarter."

"Why do you care?"

"I guess I'm like you, I don't want anyone to be hurt. It seems to me that the prices are hurting people. People like you and your brother, not having enough money to eat."

I settle in my chair again. Maybe she's not too bad if Dr. Lederman doesn't like her.

"I'll go to the lab and see what I can find out," Persephone says. "You can wait here."

"I'm not waiting here alone," I say. I can't imagine anything worse than waiting here wondering if she has alerted the guards. "Where are the chemistry labs? I'll go myself."

She frowns. "They're at the PMC headquarters, but I don't think it's a good idea for you to go alone." She paces again. "If you go out looking like that, then you're bound to be recognized. That suit is way too big for you, which *will* attract attention, and then you'll be recognized as the wanted girl on all the newscasts. But we can work around that." A small smile appears on her lips.

I swallow. What have I gotten myself into?

Twelve

"THIS IS YOUR *BEDROOM*?" I exclaim.

Persephone has taken me to the top level of her mansion and into the biggest bedroom I've ever seen. Her bed is three times the size of my entire pod. But the room still has plenty of space to spare, even with the dresser and chaise lounge.

Persephone merely shrugs at my outburst.

It's the opposite of my dreary pod. It's not just the size and furniture. Everything is sparkling white, so bright it almost hurts my eyes. But there are dashes of color to break through the whiteness; hints of pink in the stitching and lining of the furniture; subtle threads of gold in the pillows and curtains.

She opens a wardrobe that could house a large family. The wardrobe is filled with expensive clothes, shoes, jewelry, coats, shawls, hats and other regalia. It's more clothes than one person can wear in a year.

I can't help but wonder what she'd think of my pod. It's not even big enough to fit all her shoes.

Persephone rifles through her clothes, while I try not to gawk at her bedroom. She eventually comes out holding two dresses, one in white and the other in sunshine yellow. She holds them up against me. After a brief appraisal, she nods and pushes the white one into my hands.

"Try this on," she commands.

I wait for her to close the wardrobe doors, leaving me inside with some privacy. Once the doors close, my body slumps, glad for a small reprieve. I didn't realize how tightly coiled I was. I close my eyes for a second, trying to wash away the fear and embarrassment. What am I even afraid of? This dress or Persephone? I try to tell myself it's Persephone. I still don't know if I can trust her. But I want to.

I eye the dress and my muscles tighten. The dress is like the one Persephone is wearing; a tight bodice with a skirt that flares out in an A shape. With a grimace, I put it on.

The straps are wide enough that they just cover my shoulders, but none of my arms. And the neckline is low enough to show a hint of bust. The edge of the skirt is lined in lace and falls lower on my short legs than her long ones, grazing my knees. I must look like a child playing dress-ups.

The material is soft; softer than I could imagine any material could be. My fingers press into it, making small dents in the fabric until I pull my fingers away, and the fabric smooths out once again. The dress whispers a sigh as I move, and it shifts across my body like a gentle caress. It probably costs more than a year of wages, and Persephone is willingly lending it to a fugitive deadbeat.

I take a moment to calm my nerves again before exiting the wardrobe.

Persephone breaks into a grin. I look away, my cheeks burning. I knew it. I look like a fool.

I turn to go back to the closet, but Persephone pulls my arm, forcing me to stay. She's still grinning at me; this must be her idea of fun.

"Sit," she says, and pushes me onto a stool.

In seconds, she's wielding magic wands. She brushes color onto my face, lines my lips and eyes with pencils, and carefully applies glossy lipstick. There's no mirror around, so I can only imagine what I must look like. A clown, probably. I've never worn so much makeup in my life. It feels wrong on my skin.

She moves onto my hair, pulling my curls into intricate patterns across my head, weaving plaits through and over each other, in a style I imagine is similar to her own. I blink through the tears; she's not gentle as she tugs on my head. I don't know how long I wait—hours, months, probably—but I grow increasingly anxious. This feels like far too much work to do on one human being. Is this a normal amount of time to spend on somebody? Surely she doesn't do this every day to herself?

Persephone finishes my hair by threading in white pearls that match my dress and then clips a complementing pearl bracelet on my wrist. Her fingers brush the inside of my wrist as she pulls away, sending a shiver through my body. I've been so focused on how much of a fool I must look like, I almost forgot how close she is. Now I can't ignore it. Her flowery perfume is all I can breathe. She adjusts the pearls in my hair, sending shivers up and down my body. She touches up my makeup, applying another layer of gloss with her fingertip. My lips turn to fire. I look anywhere but at her, which is hard to do when she's so close.

She moves away a moment and my body thrums. I let out my breath and coax myself to relax. It doesn't work.

She's too close again. And her pink lips hover just above me. What now? How many more layers of makeup and ornaments does she have to add before she's done? I just want her to move away and take her intoxicating floral scent with her.

Persephone leans forward, her hands reaching around me as she clasps a pearl necklace to my neck. Little sparks prickle on the back of my neck at her touch.

She glances down at me as I stare up at her. I've never seen someone as beautiful as her. That's what it is. That's why I'm acting all tetchy and weird. It's because we don't belong in the same room.

I look away.

What am I doing? How stupid of me to think I can look upon a goddess without burning to ashes. I have no business fantasizing about Persephone. She's way out of my league. I'd have better chances surviving outside than being with her. I shake my head, trying to rid these thoughts. I have much more important things to worry about than a girl. Investigating PMC, for one thing.

Persephone steps back, pursing her lips as she eyes me up and down. I look down at the floor, resolved to keep my eyes off her. It's important to keep my wits about me. I need to concentrate on the task at hand; finding evidence against PMC Life Tech. There's nothing more important than keeping Sebastian safe. I can't let a girl invade my brain.

Persephone doesn't make it easy for me. She grabs my hands, sending lightning up my arms, and pulls me to my feet.

"I'm done," she says with a satisfied nod.

She pulls me over to a giant floor-length mirror. I drag my feet. I don't want to see what she's done to me. I'll never be like her. I'm not graceful or beautiful. I don't hold myself with poise. My voice doesn't sound like music. My legs don't reach the sky, mine only reach my hips, which aren't that far from the floor. I'll never look like I belong in her world.

"Do you really think we're going to fool anyone?" I ask. "Dressing me up in these clothes, with this hair? I feel ridiculous."

"You would fool me," Persephone breathes. Her hand on my back pushes me toward the mirror.

A stranger stares back.

The makeup, the dress, my hair; I've been transformed so much I wouldn't even recognize myself if I didn't know this is my own reflection. I look completely different to the wanted girl in the news reels. The girl they're looking for had tired eyes; now they're bright, full of life, and larger somehow. Some trick with makeup? Or do my eyes actually look like that?

The girl in the news reels has a round face, but the one in front of me has prominent cheekbones and a defined jaw. I can't believe I'm the person reflected in the mirror. My curls are gone, replaced by braids. My lips look full and pouty in a red rouge. My body looks womanly, with my waist cinched tightly. This is not Martina Monsalve.

Persephone chuckles quietly. "Told you."

"I ... I ..." My mouth gapes.

She beams and I can't help but smile, too.

"We just need to get you some shoes," she says. She disappears into her wardrobe to collect a pair of strappy, bejeweled shoes.

I balk at the sight of them. "I can't wear them! I'll fall flat on my face."

"Nonsense," she says. "You'll get used to them within a few minutes."

"It's nice that you have such confidence in me. But I couldn't walk in those on a good day, and you obviously haven't noticed that I'm limping with a sprained ankle."

"Oh." Her face falls with the realization. She turns back to her wardrobe without another word.

I appraise myself again in the mirror. Yes, no one will recognize me. Even Sebastian would do a double take. I glance back at Persephone, but she's disappeared deep into her wardrobe. She's so willing to help, but—I look to the door and back—she's a pharmacist. I can't forget that. Even though I want to trust her.

I slip my feet back into her mother's shoes. After seeing Persephone's shoes, they seem almost plain. Luckily, they're only a slightly different color than my white dress. Surely not noticeable enough that people will think much of it.

I tiptoe to the bedroom door and sneak out, glancing back to see if Persephone is following, but she's still inside her wardrobe.

I rush down the grand staircase and out the front door, only slowing down once I'm outside.

I try to walk at a leisurely pace, but my body is tense, wanting to flee. My chest tightens as I walk; I feel bad about leaving. Persephone was helping me. At least, I think she was. But I can't be sure. Not when she's one of them.

She did seem kind. Maybe I should have stayed. However, even if she is trustworthy, I'd only be putting her in danger.

I hold my head higher. I've done the right thing. Continuing down the pristine path, I nod to myself.

The path ends and opens onto a larger one. The larger street is also lined with gardens and streams. Shadows of ferns stretch across the path. I marvel at how serene the place is.

A man and a woman walk toward me, the first people I've seen since leaving the Marshall home. If I was in The Nix, I would have passed several dozen people already. But here, the streets are almost empty. The sight of them makes my heart pound even harder.

Although I've seen how different I look, I can't help peeking at their faces to gauge if they recognize me.

The man is unmasked and clean shaven, his hair slicked back off his face. The woman's hair is in braids, similar to mine, and weighted down by so much gold I hear it tinkle as she passes. They don't even glance in my direction.

I let out a breath. I hope every encounter goes as smoothly.

The street widens and opens onto a public square. Light pours down, unhindered by the greenery growing around the plaza. There are more people here, but it's still quiet compared with The Nix. There aren't long lines at the med-bay, nor at the restaurants that surround the square. People dressed as immaculately as Persephone—as immaculately as myself—mingle leisurely. Everything looks more expensive than anything I could ever afford. Even the air smells different here. Purer, like it's been filtered twice as much as in The Nix.

To my right is a tower of greenery with a stream of water falling from the top, causing a rainbow to pierce the air. The burble of the waterfall is melodic, adding to the serenity of the place.

It's the complete opposite to Colombia, which was bright with colors, people singing, and street dancing. But I must admit, the Sparkle Sector has its charm.

I pause, taking in all the splendor. No one else seems to notice the beauty. I keep walking. How can these people live in a place so beautiful and not stop and appreciate it?

I veer away from the square. I need to find the PMC Life Tech building—it will be in the business part of the quarter—I need to figure out which way that is.

After some time wandering the Sparkle Sector, which more than lives up to its nickname, I finally see something of interest up ahead. The corridor to the Bama quarter. It looms like a dark void, its metal walls a stark contrast to the white walls of the Sparkle Sector.

I take a step toward it.

Sebastian.

Although he said not to go to him, the temptation is strong.

Then I spot the guards. There's several of them on both ends of the corridor, closely watching anyone that approaches. I try to hide in the shadows of some greenery.

I watch as a man travels through the corridor from the Bama quarter. He's not dressed as immaculately as the men in the Sparkle Sector, but he still looks respectable. A guard stops him before he reaches my end of the corridor. After some discussion, the man pulls out his comms unit and shows the guard something on it. The guard looks at it for some time and eventually allows the man entry into the Sparkle Sector.

I turn away. The scrutiny might not be as intense coming from the Sparkle Sector going into the Bama quarter, but I can't risk it. All it takes is one guard to recognize me.

At least I know roughly where I am now. The Bama quarter sits in the west, and I know the business district is to the south of the Sparkle Sector—I've glimpsed it through the windows. So I turn to my left with more purpose than before.

Soon, the streets transition from the winding paths to straight structured roads. Gone is the greenery; here the streets are lined with sharp, square buildings. I've entered the business district of the Sparkle Sector.

The PMC building isn't hard to find; it stands taller than every other building. The letters 'PMC' are emblazoned on the outside, impossible to miss.

I don't allow myself time to second guess my choices and head straight to the entrance. The sliding doors open automatically and I step inside the large foyer.

It's so different from the rest of the Sparkle Sector. The walls are black marble, not white, and it's completely empty. Nothing decorates the space, other than another PMC sign on the back wall, printed in dark red letters. As if the giant letters outside didn't make it clear which building you'd entered.

A short corridor to the left leads to a row of lifts and a directory. Level two: Auditorium; level three: Storage; level four to eight: Hospital and Laboratories, and so on.

To call a lift, I enter Dr. Marshall's PIN and hit the button for level four.

When the lift doors open on level four, I'm stunned from the bright whiteness of it. The whole place is white, not white like the walls of the residential area, those walls had a soft feel about them. These walls, as well as the ceiling and the floor, are a hard white. It hurts to look at it.

Overhead, blue signs state the names of each ward: Cardiology, Maternity, Oncology, Hematology.

I don't discriminate between the wards; I wander through each of them.

I've never been in a hospital before, so I try my best not to stare wide-eyed. The bitter scent of disinfectant and cleaning products burn my nostrils, but they mask other more sinister smells coming from the humans populating the building. The smell of sickness.

It goes against my instincts to stay in a place filled with sick people, but I push back on my impulses and keep walking.

Many of the rooms are lined with beds. Each bed is positioned several yards from the next, and white curtains hang around them, creating little temporary rooms to fabricate privacy for those within. There are some that are closed, but most of the curtains hang open, allowing me to look at the people lying in the beds. Sometimes they have machines and contraptions hooked up to them. I have no idea what these machines do other than beep and whir occasionally.

People are walking around just like me, dressed in normal Sparkle Sector attire, so it makes me feel less conspicuous. But it's not them I'm interested in. It's the doctors, nurses, and pharmacists in their white lab coats.

I watch a doctor speaking to a woman lying in a hospital bed. The doctor is gentle when she leans over the woman, flashing a light into the patient's eyes. When she straightens, I hear her say, "You have nothing to worry about. I've done this procedure once or twice." Then she winks at the woman, who visibly relaxes.

I walk past a pharmacy, similar to the med-bay in The Nix. It's hard to believe my ears—the pharmacist behind the counter sounds genuinely concerned when he says to his patient, "Now, you understand you need to take these meds with food? They'll make you very sick if you don't." I remember the unfeeling pharmacist at The Nix's med-bay, who wouldn't give me Sebastian's meds when he wasn't there. Maybe we got a dud pharmacist. The pharmacist here seems to be more compassionate.

I remember my face plastered on all the news reels and know that not all of them are nice. But these medical professionals truly seem to be helping people. Do they know PMC is lying to the population?

A nurse hurries past when he sees a patient stumbling up ahead. The nurse gently puts his arm around the patient, helping the patient to walk; like how Nathan helped me limp to the Terrene camp. I smile.

As they disappear around a corner, I see a new sign ahead: Microbiology.

I rack my brain. I don't know much, but I know microbiology often deals with bacterial and viral infections. My heartbeat quickens. I might find what I'm looking for in this ward.

I push through the door. It's obvious right away that this ward differs from the rest. There is a large glass chamber ahead, with several people in lab coats working inside. They're bent over stations with microscopes, petri dishes, beakers, and computers. I'm protected from them by the glass wall that separates us.

There are no patients around, so I stand out like a beacon in my civilian clothes. Still, I lean closer to the glass in the hope I can see the information on their computers.

"What are you doing here?" A guard on my side of the glass approaches.

"Oh, I'm sorry." I suppress my Colombian accent and try to adopt the posh accent common in the Sparkle Sector. It's almost cringe-worthy how bad I sound. I smile through it, hoping I look innocent and apologetic. "I must have made a wrong turn."

The guard frowns, her eyelids lowering suspiciously. "Then you best head back from where you came."

I glance at the glass room. If I could just see what they're working on. Although it is anything but inconspicuous, I lean forward; I'm so close to the information I need. I have to stall.

"Isn't it fascinating?" I frantically look for something that could help me. I only have seconds, but I can't make sense of the images or text on any of the computer screens.

"Miss," the guard says. "You have to leave now."

"Oh, just one moment more, please," I say, eyes still glued to the window. "It's so interesting."

"It's for your own good." She takes hold of my elbow and pulls me away from the window. She looks at me properly for the first time, frowning. "Do I know you?"

"I ... I don't think so."

She continues to study my face. Helpless, I stare back.

This is it. I'm busted.

I haven't found what I needed. I'll be sent to quarantine. Sebastian will be lost.

Thirteen

All I can think of is her grip on my elbow. I need to get it together and think of something fast.

"Oh, that's right," I say, trying to sound casual. "I've seen you a few times at that restaurant ... hmm ... you know the one. What is its name?"

She watches me a moment, her head cocked. "Do you mean Wink?"

"Yes, yes, of course. Wink. It's a lovely restaurant, isn't it?"

"Oh, yes." She smiles and lets go of my elbow. "It's a nice one. But you had still best be on your way."

"Of course." I turn away from the glass. The guard isn't going to let me stay, and I don't want to test her patience. I'll have to figure out some other way of getting the evidence I need.

Suddenly, the double doors open. Persephone walks through, her head high as if she owns the place. She glances at me briefly, then says to the guard, "Good health to you, Guard Debbie." She nods at me. "I see you've met my cousin, Arlia."

"Oh, you know this girl, Miss Marshall?"

"Since we were little children." Her charm is completely unflawed by her lie.

"We just discovered how much we both enjoy dining at Wink," I interrupt, before Persephone's lie can undermine my own.

The guard smiles.

"Yes, that is a pleasant restaurant," Persephone says, then turns to me. "Arlia, you took a wrong turn back there. I'll show you the way."

I smile to the guard in goodbye and quickly follow Persephone out of the ward.

Persephone stalks along the hospital corridor, her heels clicking on the hard floors. My shorter legs have to hurry to keep up with her long stride.

"What are you doing?" I demand.

"The same as you, I suspect," Persephone says with a quick glance back at me. She lowers her voice. "Looking for evidence against PMC Life Tech."

Before I can respond, she stops outside a door.

"Lucky I came along when I did," Persephone says. "You might have been busted."

"I had it handled," I say tightly.

She raises one eyebrow, then enters a PIN into the security pad. There is a whoosh of air and mist curls around the edge of the door as it unlocks. Persephone opens it and walks inside. I hesitate before following. With a soft click, the door swings closed behind us. A sucking noise indicates it's sealed and locked.

We've entered the room beyond the glass. The place is square, sporting the same harsh white walls as the rest of the hospital and the disinfectant smell follows us in here. There are several metal workstations and people in matching lab coats working at each of them. Guard Debbie is on the other side of the glass, her back to us.

We walk down the length of the room, passing people measuring liquids in beakers, squeezing chemicals into vials, looking through microscopes, capping and storing test tubes.

"This is where we do tests on different vaccines and medications," Persephone explains. "We have the viruses contained in an isolated room at the back there. They cannot be removed from that room, so we're safe here. These facilities are so good that they have never recorded a contamination breach. This room is sealed too, just in case."

I look to the back of the room where she indicated. There are glass doors with locks and checks before you can go through either way.

"Hi Robert," Persephone says to a man who is switching between squinting into a microscope and writing notes on a screen. He straightens up at the sound of his name and turns the screen off.

"Persephone." He smiles. "Good health to you. What a pleasure to see you today." He seems to melt under her gaze. I don't blame him. "I didn't think you had another session with us until Wednesday?"

"Officially, I don't," Persephone says smoothly. "But my cousin is only here for a short while and I wanted to show her the labs. May I present my cousin, Arlia?"

"Good health to you, Arlia," Robert says. "Where have you come from?"

My heart races. I don't want to say Colombia because it might spark some recognition. My brain scrambles for an answer. "Mexico." I pray he doesn't know the difference between our accents.

He opens his mouth to respond, but Persephone interrupts. "Can you please show us what you're working on?"

"Oh." Robert looks from his work and back to Persephone. I can almost see the clogs working in his brain as he searches for the right words. Finally, he says, "I'm testing a new drug to combat the Azutine virus."

Robert twists his hands in nervousness. I can't decide if this is the way he always acts around Persephone—she can be disarming—or if he's trying to hide something.

"You see," Robert continues, speaking a little quicker, "this new virus is awful. It can kill someone within days. Quite horrible to see it. It attacks the liver and then poisons the blood, turns people's flesh to goo."

I swallow; he doesn't paint a pretty picture.

"You've seen someone die of it then?" Persephone says, sounding only mildly interested.

Robert gulps. "What?"

"You said it's quite horrible to see someone die from it."

"Oh, no, that's just what I've been told. I haven't seen it myself." He turns away from her and starts clearing up his workstation. "I need to take these samples to the freezer." He picks up a rack of test tubes filled with liquids and hurries away.

When he's gone, I murmur, "Did he seem on edge to you?"

Persephone nods and moves to the microscope. "Yes, and I want to know why."

She takes a moment to look through the microscope. When she pulls away, a slight frown creases her brow. She moves to the screen and turns it on. She flicks through images, zooms in and out, and goes back through the history, eyes darting around as she takes in the data.

I hiss when I see Robert returning. Persephone flicks the screen off and steps away from the workstation, moving quickly but still maintaining a casual air. I don't know how she does it. With the same calm poise, she moves to the other side of the room. I follow wearily. She approaches another chemist but says nothing this time. Instead, she stands a short distance behind, looking over their shoulder at the screen.

After a few moments, the chemist looks up. She squeaks. "Oh hello, Persephone."

"Good health to you, Deepa." Persephone gives her a winning smile. "I'm showing my cousin Arlia, around."

I try to express the same charming smile. It has some effect, as Deepa smiles back at me.

"That looks interesting." Persephone nods to the screen. "Is that the Azutine virus?"

"Um ... yes," Deepa says. "But I'm a little too busy to chat today, Persephone. Maybe you can move along now?"

"Of course." Persephone nods and moves toward another workstation. But our way is blocked.

Three men stand before us. They're without lab coats; instead, they wear immaculate dark suits. The closest has paired his with a bright yellow tie and a too-tight shirt.

My eyes rise to his artificially tanned neck, which is wrinkled in a way that his face is not. The skin around his face is pulled taut, an attempt to give him a more youthful appearance that his neck has already debunked. His lips are grossly engorged, swollen, and stretched in a way that looks painful. It takes a moment to realize he's smiling.

Before us stands Dr. Lederman—health minister of the city and senior executive of PMC Life Tech.

He's the one looking for me.

He wants me in quarantine.

And he knows *all* the secrets of the city.

"Good health to you, Miss Marshall," Dr. Lederman inclines his head to Persephone.

"Good health, Dr. Lederman," Persephone croons. "How lovely to see you."

"Working on your day off, are you?" He clips his words with precision.

"Just showing my cousin around." She gives him a closed-mouth smile.

His eyes flick to mine. I don't look away as he holds my gaze. Every cell in my body has twanged to attention, in fight-or-flight mode. I try to relax, but my heart pounds in my chest, making my breath quicken.

I'm too scared to look away. Can he see right through me? Does he know I'm the wanted girl? I pray that my disguise is enough. It's worked so far.

His gaze lowers from my eyes, looking at my lips, and then lower, slowly trailing down the length of my body. My skin crawls. I feel naked; the same feeling as being under the scanners in the decontamination center.

"Your cousin, you say?" Dr. Lederman says. If he could raise his eyebrows, I'm sure they'd be raised right now.

"Let me present, Arlia Alquez," Persephone says. "She's only here for a short while and is interested in my work."

"A pleasure to meet you, Arlia. Good health." Dr. Lederman holds out his hand for me to shake.

I look at it with shock. We don't shake hands in The Nix; the risk of spreading germs is too great. But this is the Sparkle Sector, where everything and everyone are immaculately clean.

I reach out, hoping he didn't notice my hesitation.

I try not to squirm; his hand is cold, his fingers too smooth. I want to let go, but his grip is tight. It's like shaking hands with a scorpion. He could strike at any moment.

"We haven't met before?" He finally releases my hand. "You look familiar."

I tense, then try to smile. "No, sir. I'm sure I would remember that."

He chuckles throatily. "I'm sure you would." No doubt he thinks he's being charming. He turns to Persephone. "I admire the passion you're displaying for your work, Persephone, but you shouldn't enter the laboratories on days you're not scheduled to be here."

He's going to make us leave. I can't allow that; we haven't found the evidence we need. If we get kicked out now, we may never find the proof we need to secure my freedom.

My panic gets the best of me, and I blurt out, "Why? We won't cause any harm."

His eyes flick back to me. He's possibly frowning, but it's hard to tell; his forehead has been stretched smooth. I doubt a single wrinkle could form.

"Of course not," he says, his tone amused, though his eyes are cold and searching. "There are many dangerous viruses being tested and worked on throughout these laboratories. It's a danger to have you both here."

"Even if the viruses are in isolated containment areas?" I instantly regret talking. I need to keep my mouth shut.

"Yes," he says. He turns back to Persephone. "It's time you took your cousin and left. Now."

"Yes, sir." Persephone's face is as expressionless as his is. She turns around and stalks away, tugging on my skirt as she goes. I let her lead me to the door. Once we're outside the room and the security door has closed, I wheel on Persephone.

"They're hiding something in there," I say.

"Yes, they're definitely hiding something." Even though we're alone in her bedroom, Persephone's voice is quiet. "Both Robert and Deepa lied to me. Robert said he was working on a drug, and Deepa said she was looking at the Azutine virus. But both of them were looking at the same thing, and it was a new virus I've never seen before."

"You could tell all that at just a glance?"

"Yes, I've seen the Azutine virus before, and that wasn't it. I'm positive it's something new." She tilts her head. "And Dr. Lederman seems extra suspicious."

"What are we going to do?" I whisper. "We still have nothing that can expose PMC or Lederman."

"We need to go back to PMC." She paces around the room. "We need to get into Dr. Lederman's offices. We'll go tomorrow." She nods decidedly and sits down at her dresser.

She's braver than I thought. I should have given her more credit from the start. My heart feels heavy, weighed with regret. I shouldn't have run away. She's proven I can trust her.

I tug at the silky nightgown Persephone gave me to wear to bed. Like the rest of her clothes, it's softer and finer than anything I have ever owned. It slides through my fingers like the smooth petals of a flower.

"It looks nice on you," Persephone says as she removes her makeup and unbraids her hair.

Blood races to my cheeks. I collect up the loaned dressing gown and wrap it tightly around me.

I sit on the plush chaise lounge. Persephone has prepared it as a bed for me, with pillows and a soft warm blanket.

"Are you sure you won't take the bed?" Persephone asks. "I really don't mind sleeping on the lounge."

"No, *gracias,* I'm fine here," I say, eyeing her massive bed. I would get lost in the monstrosity of it. The chaise lounge is the same size as the bed in my pod, which is more than enough space as I won't be sharing it with Sebastian.

When she has finished taking off her makeup, I glance at her bare face without being too obvious about it. Even without makeup, she is beautiful.

I quickly look away.

She slides into her gigantic bed, I lay down on my pillows, and the lights go out.

I stare at the ceiling. I try closing my eyes. My mind is abuzz with thoughts. I hope Sebastian is okay. Was I recognized at the PMC headquarters? How can I keep Persephone safe?

I squeeze my eyes shut in frustration. As tired as I am, I cannot fall asleep. There is too much going on in my head. I toss and turn.

"Are you awake?" Persephone whispers.

"Yeah," I whisper back.

"I can't sleep."

"*Yo tampoco,*" I grumble and sit up.

Persephone sits up too, turning on a lamp. She runs a hand through her hair and down her face. With her hair unbraided, her curls float around her face, glowing in the lamplight like a halo. She looks ethereal. Like a goddess.

"Since neither of us are sleeping," Persephone says, "why don't you tell me more about yourself?"

"There's not much to tell," I say. "I'm pretty simple."

"Tell me where you're from and how you ended up living in The Nix with your little brother."

With a shrug, I proceed to tell her my story. I tell her about my home back in Colombia in the city of Cali. I tell her how the Cali bubble collapsed and how I escaped with Sebastian. I talk about my job as a window grunt, being promoted to an abseiling washer, and my hopes that it will provide enough money for Sebastian to have a better life.

"Tell me more about your life in Colombia," Persephone interrupts. "Let's get our mind off the crappy stuff for a while. Maybe it will help us sleep."

"What do you want to know?"

"What did you do for fun?"

"Um, I don't know." It seems so long ago. I try not to think of it often; it usually makes me too sad. But something feels different. The way Persephone is looking at me, how excited she is to hear about it all, brings to mind some of the good stuff.

"My Papá was an amazing cook," I say. "¡*Qué rico*! He would make arepas all the time. It's like a bread made from cornmeal. Oh, and don't get me started about his empanadas. They were the best in the city!" I can't stop from smiling thinking about it. I can almost taste his food, smell it, feel the crispy empanadas in my hands.

"Did you cook too?"

"Me? No!" I laugh. "I take after my Mamá in *la cocina*. Cooking is *not* my strength."

"What were you good at?"

A memory pops into my head. I remember trying to practice some salsa moves. I had made Sebastian practice with me. He was probably about four years old and barely came up to my elbow. It was pointless because he couldn't lift his hand up high enough for me to spin underneath it. But he had been such a little gentleman about it and kept trying. Luckily, Papá interrupted us before either of us ended up flat on our backsides. He took me into his arms and spun me around in a way that made me feel graceful. Even when he upped the pace, I kept up, my feet flying to the music. It was such a rush. I grin at the memory.

"I was good at dancing," I say, blushing.

Persephone's eyes light up. "What kind of dancing?"

"Cumbia, Merengue, and of course, Salsa—it's a very popular dance back home."

"I've always wanted to learn salsa! Will you teach me?" She climbs out of bed as she speaks.

"Now?" I blush even deeper.

"Do you have something better to do?" She laughs, then glances at my ankle. "Well, as long as you're feeling up to it."

My ankle is a little tender after all the activity today, but I climb off the chaise lounge anyway. "Okay," I say, laughing.

First, I teach her the basic steps, moving backward and forward on the count. I stand next to her to demonstrate.

"One, two, three ... five, six, seven." I count as I move.

Persephone mirrors me. At first, she keeps stepping on the wrong count, and we laugh every time she does. But with a few more tries, she's got it. She even starts to sway her hips the same way as me.

"Impressive." I nod, watching her hips sway from side to side like she's drawing a figure eight with them. "You've danced before, haven't you?"

"I've had to learn some dances for balls," she admits, "but not salsa. This is fun. This is a partner dance, isn't it? Can you show me what it's like with a partner?"

I suddenly start to sweat.

I swallow. "Sure."

As I stand in front of her, the blood rushes to my fingertips, making them tingle before I've even touched Persephone. Just the anticipation has my body shivering.

"It's quite easy," I say, trying for a nonchalant air to my tone, but I miss the mark—my voice comes out croaked. I try not to cringe.

"Hook the fingers of your right hand into mine." I hold out my hand to her and she slides her fingers into my grasp. The touch sends electricity up my fingers, all through my body. I grit my teeth, forcing the feeling away. "The other hand goes on my shoulder and I put mine around your back." I step closer, placing my hand on the small of her back. I feel hers rest lightly on my shoulder.

My breath is heavy. She's so close. There are only a few inches between us. I don't dare look up into her eyes.

"It's kind of like a waltz hold," Persephone says.

"*Sí*," I croak, my throat tightening.

The scent of her is intoxicating. Jasmine and rose. How can someone smell so nice? I can't concentrate.

I move in the wrong direction, stepping backward, and she moves forward with me.

"Oops, sorry." I giggle. "I forgot I'm dancing the man's part. I need to go the opposite way to you."

She laughs, and it's a little more pitched than normal. Is she nervous too? I scoff inwardly. Of course she's not. Why would she be?

"Okay, I'll count us in and then you step backward like I taught you, and I'll step toward you."

I feel her nod, rather than see it, because I'm still too scared to look up at her.

"Five, six, seven ..." I count us in, and we start to move. "One, two, three ... five, six, seven. Well done!"

Her movements are fluid and perfectly in time. Her hips go round and round. I feel her back twist slightly with each movement. Her fingers sit delicately in mine. I can barely do more than count the steps and even that comes out dry and breathy. My eyes don't waver from her hips until I can't take it any longer.

"Very good, you've got it." I take a step back from her.

"Will you teach me some turns?" she says, her voice husky.

Finally, I look up at her. Her eyes bore into mine, wide and inviting. I blink and nod, unable to talk.

I show her the steps of a basic spin and then take my place as her partner.

"Let's start with the basic step and then do the turn."

Instead of watching her hips this time, I watch her lips. Without making a sound, she mouths the count along with me. *One, two, three ... five, six, seven.* I wonder if she realizes she's doing it.

I'm not paying attention, and when it comes to spinning her, I'm completely uncoordinated. Instead of spinning her outward, my arm gets in the way, causing her to trip. She falls against me and I catch her in my arms.

Her body presses against mine. So close, I feel her heart beating. It's pounding, just like mine.

Her eyes are wide, dark pools of ink. Her lips mere inches from my own. My eyes lower to them, then dart back to her eyes.

"Sorry," I mutter with a sheepish smile. "I'm not used to doing the man's part."

I let her go and take a slow step back. It takes all my willpower to do it. I'm so tempted to stay there, to lean in further, to allow my lips to brush hers. And if I stay a second longer with her body against mine, I'll do it. I'll kiss her. And then she'll hate me. I'll lose my only ally.

"And I must be getting tired because I'm losing concentration." I move toward my makeshift bed.

"Oh, of course." Persephone takes a step back, too. "Yes, it is late."

Her body is out of reach now. My own still burns from her touch, feeling the loss of it.

I force myself to turn away from her and busy myself with rearranging my pillows. By the time I climb onto the lounge and pull the blanket over me, she has retreated to her own bed and is reaching for the light.

"Good night," Persephone murmurs and switches the light off.

Fourteen

BLACK MARBLE RUNS THROUGHOUT the office level of the PMC building. It covers the floors, walls, and ceiling, making the corridors and rooms seem small and confining, but affirming the opulence of the organization. Added to it are gold fixings and decorations, which scream power and money.

Even with Persephone's help to do my makeup and picking a new outfit—the yellow dress this time—I feel completely out of place. No amount of fancy clothes will change that I don't belong here. Persephone, on the other hand, walks as if she owns the place.

We're in the upper levels, where Dr. Lederman has his office, having used her mom's PIN to gain access. We walk down corridors, peeking into offices and rooms, seeking for something, though we're not sure what. We pass offices with large desks, people sitting behind them in their rich suits and dresses, working furiously on computers. My heart beats harder when I see them, but I follow Persephone's lead and act as if I belong, holding my head high and taking care not to fidget.

No one affords us a second glance. We might as well be invisible.

Maybe it's because they're working hard. Maybe it's because strange people come through this building every day. Maybe they feel safe with the restricted access to this level that they assume we're meant to be here. Whatever it is, they don't seem concerned. One person even passes us in the corridor; the only acknowledgement is a slight nod in greeting, and they continue past, unaware that I'm almost having a heart attack.

Persephone's high heels click against the marble, echoing down the corridor. After several minutes of this, I hiss, "This is useless. We're not going to find anything doing this. We need to get onto a computer or something."

She nods and when we reach the next vacant office, we slip inside. I close the door, though I doubt it will do much good—it's glass and people can see right through it.

Persephone sits in the large leather chair behind the desk. She slides a data pad across the desk to me.

"Sit down," she says, indicating the chair opposite her. "It will look like we're having a meeting to any passersby. And you can go through the files on the data pad while I try to access the computer."

I do as she says, although I don't like having my back to the door.

I touch the screen and it lights up with the PMC logo and the words "Pharmaceuticals, Medicine, and Chemistry Life Tech" underneath.

My fingers slide across the screen, searching file names, hoping for anything that might help us, though nothing makes any sense.

Persephone gets out her comms unit and links it to the computer.

"Have you found something?" I ask.

"No, not really." She frowns. "Just some reports showing the profits for the last quarter. It proves nothing but it can't hurt to copy a few things over."

I return to my screen and almost flick right past it. A file named "Azutine virus." I open the file.

The first pages show a graph and some statistics.

Deaths: 4

Cases: 12 Active

Preventative medication sales: 36 million units at a value of 72.1 million credits

Net Profit: 57.7 million credits

"I need the comms unit," I say. Persephone hands it to me and I copy the report onto it. If we can't find anything else, at least the people will know exactly how greedy PMC really is. There is no need for them to charge so much; they could forgo some profit, but because the citizens have no choice than to purchase the drugs, PMC can charge whatever they want. It's not right; they are robbing us blind.

I flick to the next sheet.

And drop the screen on the desk.

"What is it?" Persephone says with a start.

I can't talk. I push the screen around so she can see.

It displays several pictures of a person labeled "Subject 2." The first picture shows a healthy male, probably around 30 years old. Above it states: "Day 1 after administration of the Azutine virus."

The following pictures show his health rapidly declining from day 1 to day 5, in which his flesh is rotting and falling from his face.

I want to look away. I want to delete these images from my mind. But I need this information.

Day 6 shows the man completely wasted away, barely recognizable as human. His muscles, his stomach, even his face, have all sunken in. His skin is a mess of red, purple, and black splotches; some of it has been completely eaten away, showing the yellow pus-lined flesh beneath.

The caption states: "Day 6 after administration of the Azutine virus, the subject succumbed to death."

"Administered?" Persephone breathes.

"PMC gave this man that virus." My mouth twists with distaste. Gingerly, I collect up the screen and copy the file to Persephone's comms unit. It's exactly what we need to prove PMC is lying.

Persephone gasps. She is staring outside the office.

My blood runs cold.

We're busted. We were so close, the proof in our hands. Soon our fate will be the same as Subject 2.

But the door doesn't open, and guards aren't rushing in with guns held high.

Persephone jumps up from her seat. "It's the health minister," she hisses. I glance around just in time to see his disappearing form. I'm out of my seat and to the door in seconds. I crack it open, sticking my head out to see where he's going. The proof we have only condemns PMC, not Dr. Lederman. If we want to prove he knows all about these experiments, like I suspect, we need correspondence from his office. Without that, he'll just claim he knows nothing about the experiments and continue as health minister.

He disappears into an office at the end of the hall.

"I think that's his office," I say to Persephone. "We should try to get in there when he comes out."

"Agreed. Let's get closer."

We leave the relative safety we've found in this office and enter the hall once more. We don't stroll with as much confidence as we did earlier while we edge toward his office, and our eyes stare unwaveringly at his door. Unlike the other glass doors in the corridors, his is completely blacked out. You can't see through the glass to what's within. I hope Dr. Lederman can't see out from the inside, either.

We're only a few yards away from his door. Every nerve in my body is strung tight like the strings of a guitar, ready for me to pluck them into action.

My ears prick with the sound of footsteps.

Footsteps within Lederman's office, coming toward his door.

Persephone and I scramble. We almost collide with each other in our haste to get out of the corridor. We rush to open a nearby door. Luckily, the room is empty. But the door is see-through again, so we hurry to find a place to hide.

We're in a boardroom. In the middle is a large table, fashioned from more black marble. Instead of legs, an enormous block of marble in the center holds it up. We dash behind it, dodging chairs, until it blocks us completely from view of the door. My ears strain to hear the footsteps move past the door.

Instead of footsteps, I hear voices. There are several of them, and they're just outside the door. Suddenly, the door creaks open.

"Bring some refreshments for the meeting." Dr. Lederman's voice rises above the others.

Persephone's eyes are as wide as mine. It's over. We're going to be discovered. As soon as Dr. Lederman and his colleagues enter the boardroom and take a seat at the table, they will see us. And it won't take long for them to realize I'm Martina Monsalve, a wanted woman.

I search for a way out, my eyes darting wildly in every direction. Maybe we can make a run for it. But I stay crouched. They haven't come in yet. They stand at the door with it slightly cracked. I almost wish they would hurry up and enter, just to get it over with. The anticipation is about to make me explode.

My eyes land on two doorknobs carved into what I thought was a marble wall. But looking closely, I realize it's not marble at all, but a set of black cupboards that run the length of the wall behind us. They're not very tall cupboards, but if we kneel inside and hunch over, we both should fit.

I inch toward them. I know I'm visible if the businessmen bother to look in our direction, but I need to take the chance. Opening one cupboard, I risk a glance at the door, but all I see are the backs of heads.

There isn't a lot inside the cupboards, just some cords and a couple of instruction manuals. I push them to the side to make room for me and Persephone. I wave her over.

For the first time, her cool facade has broken, and fear openly ravages her features. To her credit, she doesn't waste a second. She darts to the cupboard and curls up next to me.

Dr. Lederman enters the boardroom just as I close the cupboard door. I hold my breath, praying he didn't see the movement. There's no shout of concern, no rushing of feet to our hiding space, just the constant gabble of the businessmen continuing their casual conversation as they stream into the room.

Slivers of light come through slits in the doors, cutting through the darkness. I put my eyes to a slit, and the boardroom comes into view. I can't see the entire room, but it's enough.

The boardroom is full of men and women, all in business suits, taking places around the table. I hope to hell they can't hear my pounding heart.

Dr. Lederman closes the door behind them and remains standing at the front of the room. He clicks a button and the screen behind him lights up with a presentation. I can't see the screen in full; I can only make out a small corner of a graph. The same graph that was in the report we copied.

"Good health to you all," Dr. Lederman says. "Dr. Marshall will be absent from this meeting. She's still in Norleans handling the mass quarantine there. So we'll continue without her."

I glance at Persephone. Light penetrates the darkness through the slits, creating three lines across her eyes, mouth, and neck.

I can just make out the rest of her face. Although her eyes are illuminated, they reveal nothing.

"These are the results from the first week since the release of the Azutine virus into the community."

A soft rustle alerts me that Persephone is moving. She raises her comms unit up to the slats so she can record Dr. Lederman's presentation. I pray to God nobody heard her move.

"And although these results look quite promising so far," Dr. Lederman says, "there has been unrest in both the Linto and The Nix quarters."

He walks back and forward in front of the screen, his head bobbing in and out of view.

"They doubt the severity of the virus. We've had people refuse to pay for the Azutine drug and forego the entire med pack rather than pay. We've imprisoned those, of course.

"There will be more that haven't gone to the med-bay to collect their drugs. We are tracking down those people now to arrest them. However, the jail is reaching capacity and imprisoning people is not increasing our profits.

"We need to increase fear in the population." He slams his fist into his palm.

"So, more deaths?" a woman asks, as if she's ordering a coffee.

"Yes, and a public scare," Dr. Lederman says emphatically. "Select two or three people from a public place. More people will be worried they have contracted the virus from being in the vicinity, and they'll be rushing to the med-bays as usual."

I gape.

"Is that really necessary?" asks another woman.

No. It can't be necessary. I can't believe what I'm hearing.

"It's in everyone's best interest," Lederman huffs, as if he has explained this before. "If people stop being vigilant with their medications, we'll have another plague on our hands before long."

"Not if we don't infect people," says the same woman.

Lederman wheels on her. "And what about the colds and flus and other unsavory diseases we had before the bubble cities? Do you want them to come back?" He puffs his chest out in indignation. "Thousands of people died. Do you want that to happen again?"

The woman is silent.

"If a few deaths now will prevent thousands of deaths in the future," he snarls, "then I say it's worth it." He shakes his head and turns back to his presentation.

He's delusional. It's clear he believes what he's saying, and he can't understand why the woman doesn't.

"Should the scare happen in Linto or The Nix?" a man asks.

"Better make it The Nix. Linto is already in lockdown, so the impact won't be as big."

The man nods, noting it down in his comms unit. "And the Bama quarter?"

"Leave it for now," Lederman states, brushing it aside like a speck of dirt. "They'll fall in line. It's always an option later on."

They speak as though they're discussing which windows to clean, not which people to kill. At first, I'm shocked. Then disgusted; my stomach rolling in on itself. But as they continue to talk, discussing places and times, I feel my blood boil. They aren't people. They're monsters. And I want them dead. Every. Last. One.

Their deaths won't be pretty. I'll make them suffer the same fate as their victims: the virus that eats you from the inside out. Days of torture as their bodies turn against them and rot away. And they will die alone—no visitors, no goodbyes. Just like the isolation they've forced on others.

I gag on my thoughts.

But even that horrific death isn't enough punishment for Dr. Lederman.

I'm going to bring PMC Life Tech down. Collecting this evidence is no longer about assuring my safety, but the safety of the entire community. For the safety of Sebastian, Persephone, Nathan, Will, Mother Jessica, and sweet Tía Rosa from the diner.

My heart is still beating hard, but now it beats with fury, not fear. All I want to do is burst out of this cupboard and tear their eyes out. But I hold myself back, clenching my fists and gritting my teeth. Beyond that, I remain still.

As a group, they discuss which public place within The Nix will provide the biggest impact. Once they have determined a time and place—Nixo Square, two days from now—to infect someone with the Azutine virus and sentence them to death, they move on to discussing how it will be communicated to the population; what images and language to use to induce the greatest fear.

I start to ache from my cramped position. My injured ankle is twisted to the side and throbbing. It had been feeling a lot better, but this position is making it worse.

Persephone swaps the hand that holds her comms unit, her arm obviously getting tired. But neither of us dare to move more than the slightest amount. Although there is a lot of discussion taking place, there is no telling what slight noise might catch their attention.

"What of the Terrene scum?" Dr. Lederman asks.

I suppress a gasp. I'm surprised they are informed enough to know the name of the community. It makes me more scared for the Terrene Folk. Maybe there is a spy in the tribe.

"What is their status?"

"They've moved on, sir," one of his colleagues says. "They're heading north-east. Do you want the guards to pursue?"

I feel Persephone shift; a slight change in the stifled air around us. But she makes no noise. Then her fingers are brushing against mine. At her touch, a shiver of electricity shoots through me, tingling up my arm, across my collarbone, and straight down to my toes. Then she wraps her fingers completely around mine and holds on tightly. It's a small comfort while we wait for Dr. Lederman to respond.

He thinks for a moment, then says, "No. Let them go."

I release my breath and mouth a prayer of thanks. Persephone doesn't let go of my hand. She gives me a small smile.

"We'll need the guards to quell this unrest and enforce the lockdown. Our priority is controlling this city."

At least they're safe for now.

The pain in my ankle has increased from a throb to a barrage of pain. I assess the way I'm sitting and whether I can move without making a sound. The pressure is getting worse, to the point it's getting hard to concentrate on anything else. Even Persephone's hand in mine has taken a backseat to my discomfort.

"What about this missing girl?"

I forget my ankle and flick back to Lederman.

"Martina Monsalve?" He says my name like he has a foul taste in his mouth.

"We still can't find her," says a man. "We don't believe she is traveling with the Terrene, so there is a risk she'll try to reenter the city. And there has been some activity in her accounts. Someone has her PIN and is using her credits and her comms unit."

I tense.

"Who?" Dr. Lederman asks.

"We believe it's her little brother. A ..." The man checks his notes. "Sebastian Monsalve. He is a junior window washer, living in The Nix quarter. Looks like they were sharing a single pod together before she went missing."

Persephone is squeezing my hand again. I'm not sure if she's still trying to comfort me or stop me from launching an attack right here and now. I grip her hand in return, perhaps too firmly. I don't dare look away from Lederman.

"Does he know where she is?" Lederman asks.

There's a bit of discussion around the table. I have trouble making out what they're saying, but it seems some believe Sebastian knows where I am, but others are saying there is no evidence of that.

"He's a junior washer, right? And how much does a junior window washer make?" Lederman asks, his voice mocking. His colleagues "um" and "ah" around the table, but he doesn't wait for a response. "Freeze her credits. He won't have enough money for food and meds. If she's in touch with him, it'll flush her out. That is, if she cares for him at all." He snickers and a few of his colleagues join in.

My blood boils like molten lava.

One death isn't enough for this monster. I want to kill him over and over again. A million times. I want him to die of every disease there's ever been, and every disease there ever will be.

"Oh, and confiscate his comms unit. It's not registered to him, so he's using it illegally. That will force her out of hiding to talk to him."

Innocent, unsuspecting, Sebastian. Lederman is right. He won't have enough money for food. He might have just enough to buy his meds so he doesn't get locked up in quarantine too, but only if he works longer hours. I can't think of a way to help him, and I imagine his stomach growing inward again, his arms growing thin, his face taut with hunger.

I don't have a lot of time to expose PMC before he starts withering away. I need to get back to him, and I can't do that until I've neutralized the threat. If I poke my nose out an inch, they'll snatch me up and kill me off in quarantine, airing it on news reels to scare the population into buying their medications.

While I simmer in rage and worry, the meeting turns to discussions about the sales of other medications, but they have no more sinister plans. They must have met their quota of evilness for the day.

I've got to get out of this cupboard! Every second that they drone on about sales and scams seems to drag on for an eternity. I've got to call Sebastian and warn him before they take his comms unit away.

Slowly, I become aware of my body aches again. The pain from my ankle has spread to every muscle and bone in my leg. I need to move to ease the pressure. And I'm feeling jittery with impatience. When is this damned meeting going to end?

Finally, *finally*, the executives start packing their comms units into their jacket pockets and shuffling in their chairs, getting ready to leave the room. By now, the pain is too much; I can't wait a second longer. There's more noise now, as they stand and push in their chairs. I take the risk. I twist my foot out slightly, keeping as quiet as possible, trying to get some blood flowing again.

My foot slips on the base of the cupboard, sliding into the back wall with a soft thump.

The man closest to me looks over his shoulder. I feel Persephone stiffen, her hand still in mine. I don't move a muscle. My foot is now at a strange and even more uncomfortable angle; and it takes all my strength not to move it. My muscles twitch.

The man eyes the cupboards. I hold my breath. He's looking right at me. Can he see my eyes staring back at him through the slits? He makes a move toward the cupboards.

This is it. This is the end. I've failed. I'm so sorry, Sebastian. I'm so sorry.

"Gary?" someone calls from the doorway. "Are you coming for beers?"

The man looks at his comrade, and then again at the cup-board. "Yeah, of course," he says, and strolls out of the room.

Fifteen

We remain frozen in our position until everyone has exited. When the door finally slams shut behind them, my body crumbles in on itself as I finally exhale and move my ankle.

Persephone relaxes too, letting go of my hand. But the feel of her fingers in mine lingers.

She slides open the cupboard doors. Fresh air and bright light rushes in, severing any intimacy between us. I climb out of the cupboard, unfurling my legs and limbs. I stretch and blood rushes back to my ankle, bringing welcome relief.

We stay low; the table blocking us from view.

"Let's get out of here," Persephone says.

"There's no time for that," I say. "I need to call Sebastian."

"But they might come back!" Her eyes are wide and mouth agape.

"I've got to take the risk. I need to warn him before they take his comms unit away. And what if we get caught on our way out? I'll never get the chance to warn him then."

Persephone swallows, grimacing. But she nods and hands over her comms unit.

I keep my conversation with Sebastian brief. I fill him in on the headlines of what we've learned. That PMC are killing people to increase their profits. That they're coming for him, to draw me out of hiding so I can't reveal their secrets. He might be young, but he understands everything.

"You need to keep away from any busy public areas, especially Nixo square," I say. "They're going to infect someone in a busy area, so just keep your distance, okay? And Sebastian, they're going to freeze my account. You won't be able to afford food. And you're going to need to work more hours to pay for the meds. I'm sorry. But you can't give up the meds or they'll arrest you or quarantine you as a health risk. Neither are a good option."

"It's okay, Martina," Sebastian says. "Tía Rosa at the diner has been helping me. She can't give me much, but I'll be okay. And Liam will help, too."

My vision blurs. Rosa barely knows us and is probably struggling to feed herself, but she's still willing to help Sebastian. And Liam has already helped us so much, getting us jobs and teaching us to fight when we first arrived in Neustin. It should be me supporting Sebastian. He shouldn't have to rely on strangers. He shouldn't have to starve. He deserves better than this.

"Hopefully it won't be long," I say. "I'm going to come get you as soon as I can."

"What are you going to do?"

I pause. I haven't thought that far ahead. We might have evidence against PMC, but how can we show that to the population? PMC controls the media, so that won't help us. But Sebastian doesn't need to know this. I want him to stay positive, so he doesn't give up. "I'll work it out. You'll see. Everything will be okay soon."

I sign off and stand up to leave, just as the door to the boardroom swings open.

A suited businessman stands frozen, eyes locked with mine.

Persephone, still hidden from view, snatches the comms unit from my hand, and from the corner of my eye, I see her shove it down her bra. Then she slowly stands too.

My body tenses, ready to fight. There's still a chance we can escape.

Still staring, the businessman takes his own comms unit from his pocket. "I need security in Lederman's boardroom," he speaks into it. "Now."

I was so close. I have the evidence I need. I thought I could save Sebastian. I told him I'd figure it out, that everything would be okay. Only seconds ago.

"What are you going to do with us?" Persephone asks. Even now, her voice is composed; it doesn't shake or waver.

"I'll leave that up to Dr. Lederman," the man says.

At the mention of Lederman, the hair on my arms stand on end. He's going to kill me. Will he kill Persephone too?

There's the sound of running feet, and then four guards storm into the room, stun batons held at the ready.

Lederman strolls in behind. He stands tall, looking down his nose at us.

Rage burns through my veins, but it's not enough to over-power my fear.

"Well, well, Miss Marshall. And Miss Alquez, is it?" He smiles—or tries to with his bloated lips. "I suspect that's not your real name?"

He steps closer, stopping only a foot away from me; a lot closer than what is normal in the Sparkle Sector. His head is cocked as he considers me. "Miss Monsalve, I presume?"

I clench my mouth shut. But I don't need to answer him; the way he nods shows he's certain.

"And what are you doing here?"

I say nothing. Persephone doesn't say a word either—she keeps her head held high as she watches Lederman. Only the slight tremble in her hands reveals she's scared.

"How did you get in here?" he presses. "Whose PIN did you use to get back inside the city? We know you haven't used your own. Who have you spoken to?"

I still don't say a word.

"I'm very disappointed in you, Miss Marshall." He turns his lethal gaze on Persephone. "You had promise ... or so your mother says. I'm yet to see it myself. You're more trouble than you're worth, in my opinion. And this is just one more indiscretion against you. Fraternizing with girls that are supposed to be in quarantine." He shakes his head in mock disappointment, though he's wearing his sickening smile, as if he's pleased at capturing her. She really must have annoyed him in the past.

There's a knock at the door and a young man pokes his head inside. If he's surprised to see the two executives, four guards, and two young ladies, his face doesn't show it.

"Dr. Lederman," he says, "you're late for your next appointment."

"Understood," Lederman says without turning around. The young man disappears. "Since neither of you are very chatty, I'll interrogate you later." He turns around and waves his hands at the guards. "Take them to quarantine."

The guards move forward, closing in on us. Lederman doesn't even glance back as he exits, as if he's already lost interest.

The guards take hold of my arms, and they're not polite about it. My instincts kick in and I try to pull away. But one guard switches his stun baton on—the blue electricity buzzing on the end of it—and waves it in front of my face. I settle down.

I glance at Persephone. The guards are bruising her arms with their tight grips. I squeeze my eyes shut. This is all my fault.

As they lead us down the corridor, the black marble feels even more suffocating, bearing down on us and closing in on both sides. Inside the lift is no better. They take us down a few levels.

The doors open onto stark white walls, like the hospital ward. But this isn't the hospital.

In the foyer are two guards in white hazsuits.

"Dr. Lederman wants to interrogate these two," one guard says, pushing us into their gloved hands. "Make sure they're secure until then."

I narrow my eyes at the suited guards, but they ignore me, dragging us to a small room. It's set up for examinations, with a sink and a gurney against the back wall.

We're shoved inside and the door slams shut behind us. Although I clearly hear the locks turn, I try the doorhandle anyway. It doesn't budge.

I spin around, slamming my back against the door. My hands cover my face as I try to calm myself, taking deep breaths.

Persephone giggles.

I lower my hands, peering at Persephone. Her back is pressed against one wall. She keeps giggling as tears run down her cheeks. Her knees give way, and she crumples to the floor.

I rush to her side, but don't know how to help her. I awkwardly flutter around, reaching for her, then pulling my hand back. I stand up and go to her other side. But still, my hand doesn't touch her when it reaches out. I wish I could comfort her somehow, but I'm not good at this.

She continues to giggle. Her legs are splayed out in front and her hands sit in her lap. She looks like a sad doll. Her shoulders bounce as she laughs uncontrollably.

She had been so controlled until now, keeping everything in check, holding her head high when she must be as scared as me.

Still undecided on how to comfort her, I take a leaf out of Will and Nathan's book and plonk onto the floor in front of her, cross-legged. I want to tell her it will be okay, but I can't. I already lied to Sebastian when I said I'd work it out. That's impossible now. We're stuck in quarantine. Everything Mother Jessica said is true. PMC and Dr. Lederman are monsters, and they're going to kill us. They'll keep their secrets and Sebastian will be all alone.

I look at the door; sturdy and impenetrable. We're never getting out of here.

I hang my head in my hands again. It's no use wishing and dreaming, but I do anyway. I wish Sebastian and I were free; outside, roaming the desert, riding horses, running, and dancing. Healthy. I wish I'd never gotten Persephone involved; she doesn't deserve this fate. I wish I'd just gotten down off the bubble when the storm was coming. All of this could have been avoided if I had.

Eventually Persephone's giggles give way to soft sobs. After some time, those also dissolve. Her breathing slows, and the tears dry on her cheeks. She smiles sadly, but it doesn't reach her eyes. "I never knew." Her voice cracks. "I never knew that's what they were doing. What my mom ..." She gasps as it sinks in. Through gritted teeth, she says, "What my *mom* was doing."

"You couldn't have known," I say quietly.

Persephone looks away, picking at a fingernail. Another tear escapes from the corner of her eye. I watch as it trails down her cheek until it drips off her chin onto her lap.

"Oh, I don't know." Persephone brushes the tear away in annoyance. "She's always been a control freak." She takes a few breaths. "She's always away for work. Cleaning up other cities, getting them in order, making sure all the quarantine laws are being followed. She thinks she's saving the world."

"What did you think?"

"I don't know. But no matter what I used to think, I don't *now*."

We fall back into silence. My mind flicks to my own Mamá. I remember her smile, her warm hugs, showering me with kisses.

I break the silence. "So, where is your father?"

"Oh, he's out of the picture. I think he's in California these days." She appears completely uninterested in her father. I don't understand it; I wish I could spend just one more day with my Papá.

"Mom thinks he's a loser. I never hear from him and he left me with her, so ..." She shrugs. "I don't think either of them know me at all. All they're concerned about are my studies and making it big at PMC. They don't know what I want to do with my life."

"What do you want to do?"

She looks at me with those wide eyes again. "I ... I don't want to be just another pharmacist stuck in a lab, or worse, behind a desk, like Mom. I want to be more hands on, like a doctor ... or a cross between a doctor and a pharmacist, if there's such a thing." She laughs nervously. Not the hysterical laugh like before, just a sad chuckle. "I just want to help people." She looks down at her hands, her eyelashes fluttering.

"Why?"

"Why? I don't know." She sniffs. "But I had to go into The Nix quarter once and it was an eye opener." She glances at me, then back down at her hands. "I didn't know people lived like that until a year ago. It was part of my pharmaceuticals course. We had to work in The Nix hospital because there had been an outbreak of ... well, I don't remember which virus it was. We were studying the patients, collecting samples, doing tests.

"Anyway, I had never been to The Nix before. I thought it was like the Bush quarter, or maybe more like the Bama quarter. But it's not. There are so many people. That was my first impression. And then I noticed the houses, all stacked on top of each other, falling apart. I realized then that life in The Nix is very different from the Bush quarter.

"There was this woman. She was watching me and the other student pharmacists as we walked through the quarter. She was holding a young child. Both of them were skinny. Literally just skin and bones. I heard others point her out, saying she must be sick. But she didn't look sick … just hungry.

"So, I went to a nearby pretzel stall and bought a dozen or so. Her face when I gave them to her, well … I've never seen such happiness before." Persephone smiles. "She was so grateful. Just for some bread."

I know how grateful that woman would have been. The same as I would have been if someone gave me a bag of pretzels when Sebastian and I had nothing, and I was forced to watch him waste away.

"I can't feed everybody," Persephone says, "but it made me realize how much I have that others don't. Afterward, I found out that many people starve so they can afford medications, so I've been advocating for a reduction in price, or at least some discounts. I have *not* been successful, and instead I've only gotten Dr. Lederman's disappointment."

Her grin spreads. I grin, too—I'd rather Lederman hate me than like me too.

"I'm not the only one that feels like this," Persephone continues. "There are others in both the Bush and Bama quarters who are lobbying for change."

"Really?" I ask, my eyebrows raised. I'd never heard of anyone questioning PMC before.

"There are, but they are very secretive, very cautious. They believe something will happen to them if they speak out openly. Like PMC would do something to them."

"Maybe they have reason to think that." I gesture around the room we're in.

"Yeah."

Both of us fall silent, consumed by our own thoughts.

Suddenly, Persephone's eyes narrow and she bangs her fist on the floor. "How dare they?" Her voice is thick with tears, but she projects her words with venom. "They can't keep us in here like this, not when we're not sick."

I run my hands through my hair. "They're going to make us sick," I say, my voice quivering. "We've failed ... I've failed."

"No." Persephone shakes her head. "It's not over yet. My mom won't let it happen."

"She's one of them," I say, more angrily than I mean to.

Persephone pauses. "You're right. But I don't believe she'll let me get hurt."

"What about *me*?"

"That is a problem," she whispers. Then she grunts—even that sounds graceful—and wipes the remaining tears from her cheeks. She pulls herself up from the floor. She paces, her brow furrowed. Her eyes light up as she pulls the comms unit out from her bra. "I still have this! If we can find some way to get this out into the public ..."

"How?"

"I might know someone that can help." She keeps pacing. "My mom is a very influential person."

"She's not going to help expose herself."

"I know!" she says impatiently. "Because she is influential," she speaks like a teacher, slow and precise, "she's often doing stuff with the media. She's the woman behind the scenes when Dr. Lederman broadcasts. She knows these media people. She's friends with them. We've even had them over for dinner."

I picture them all sitting around a stately dining table, laughing at the little people believing their lies, not giving a crap about the deaths or misfortunes of others while they gorge on delicious food.

"So?" I shake the image away. "They must be in on it too. Why would they help you?"

"There's this one guy. I'm sure he's not a part of it. I don't know him that well, but we've sort of become friends."

"Who is this guy? Why would he help us?"

"His name is Daniel. He's a nice guy." She shrugs.

"Is he your boyfriend?" The question is out of my mouth before I can catch it. But my ears prick, waiting for an answer.

"He's just an acquaintance." Her lips tilt with a hint of a smile. "But the point is, he knows a bit about that media stuff. And he agrees with me that the meds are too expensive. So he might know how to get this information out on the air. He might just help us."

"Can you send the evidence to his comms unit?"

"No, I don't have his number. We'll need to get it from my mom's office."

They can't be very close if she doesn't have his number.

"Okay," I say, "so we just need to get out of here, find Daniel, and everything will be fixed." I roll my eyes. It's all so impossible. We're locked in quarantine, even *if* Daniel will help us, we still need to get out of this room.

I pay more attention to our surroundings. The room is relatively empty. There's the gurney, a sink, and four white walls. I glance at the sink again. There's a cabinet below it.

I jump to my feet and go to the sink, feeling hope kindle. Opening the cabinet, I find exactly what I expect—cleaning products. A standard disinfectant and two heavy duty cleaners. One with hydrochloric acid.

Bingo.

"I might be able to get us out of here," I breathe.

Persephone's red-rimmed eyes widen. "How?"

"This is a very heavy duty cleaner. It's essential in a place like this. It can be used on ceramics, like the sink. But not metal." I approach the door with the cleaner. "It contains hydrochloric acid. And hydrochloric acid can burn through metals."

I grin and she smiles back tentatively.

I turn to the lock and pour some of the cleaner onto the metal. The chemical isn't concentrated enough to cause the metal to bubble immediately, but after a few seconds I hear the hissing of the chemical reaction.

"Get comfy," I say, turning back to Persephone. "This may take a little while."

"How long?"

I shrug. "Let's just pray it works before Lederman comes to interrogate us."

I sit on the gurney, watching the lock. Persephone joins me, sitting only a foot away.

We're silent for a moment. My fingers twist in the paper sheet spread across the gurney, while she remains completely still. The silence is uncomfortable, and I struggle to think of something to say.

"What I don't understand," I say, eventually, "is when I went into the hospital, the medical staff there seemed to actually care. It didn't matter if they were doctors or pharmacists."

"Many of them *do* care," Persephone says.

"Then why do they let PMC and Lederman get away with this?" I can't understand why anyone can help people with one hand and hurt them with the other. Do they believe the same theory as Lederman, that they're actually *helping* by killing people?

"I don't think they know," Persephone says. "Just like me. I think only the people in the inner circle know the lies. That lab I work in, everyone in there is handpicked by Lederman. The only reason I have my internship there is because Mom and Lederman are friends." She cringes when she says it. "You see, the diseases are real. It's just that they're manufactured and administered by PMC. But the doctors and most pharmacists don't know that. They're really trying to treat them. Most of the pharmacists are good people. They're working to help overcome these diseases and find cures and vaccinations. I thought I was one of them."

Persephone's eyes are downcast, but I still see tears glistening. She continues, "I should have known better. I worked alongside the people that aren't helping and I didn't see it. God, my mom is involved. I don't know how I'm going to look her in the face again." She wipes a tear away, then looks up and into my eyes. "Martina, I just ... I just want you to know that I'm glad I met you. Despite everything that's happened, I'm still glad."

She bows her head but looks back up at me through her eyelashes.

I don't know how to respond, so I just stare at her.

"I'm in this with you, okay?" Persephone says. "No matter what." She rests a hand on my knee. It burns through the fabric of my dress.

"I ... I ..." I flounder. I want to tell her how grateful I am. I want to tell her I couldn't have done this without her. But I'm too distracted by her hand on my knee to put any of those thoughts into words.

I think back to last night. To when Persephone was in my arms. I glance at her lips. She's so close. I breathe in her jasmine scent.

She hasn't moved her hand. She's staring at me.

I lean ever so slightly closer. Her fingers press deeper into my thigh as she shifts closer too.

I'm transfixed. Her gaze pulls me forward. Her lips open slightly as they come toward mine.

My breathing is erratic. Can she hear my heart pounding? Does she think I'm a fool?

I freeze.

I can't do this.

I jump off the gurney.

"Well, let's see if this lock has corroded yet," I say, turning away from her. That was too close—I could lose her. I bend over, focusing all my attention on the lock, ignoring Persephone as she slowly gets down from the gurney and joins me at the door.

Foam has formed all around the metal.

"Has it worked?" Persephone asks, her voice higher than normal.

"Only one way to find out." I reach for the door handle, keeping clear of the foam, I twist the lever downward. It doesn't move, but it doesn't feel as strong as it did before either. I try again with a bit more strength. It gives a little, but not much.

"We're still trapped?" Persephone says.

I shake my head. "Stand back."

I stand on my toes, spin around, and kick—a fighting move Liam taught me. My foot connects with the handle and there's a clunk as the mechanism breaks. The handle sits crooked in the door, bearing the erosion the acid has caused, and when I reach for it, it's easy to turn it the rest of the way.

Persephone and I glance at each other. Then I inch the door open.

Outside is a stark white corridor with four identical doors, and one more at the entrance. Otherwise, the corridor is empty.

I open the door wider, tentatively stepping out. Persephone is close behind. She stuffs her comms unit back into her bra.

Her back is ramrod straight; I can't tell if it's from confidence or fear. Her breathing is shallow as she tiptoes quietly. I skulk along beside her, my eyes swiveling from side to side, looking for a threat. Praying no one comes through one of the doors.

With each step, our shoes clack on the floor, echoing down the long corridor. Click, clack, click, clack. Every step makes me pray to God that we're going to make it.

We reach the entrance and peek through the door. My heart almost leaps out of my chest. But the foyer is empty, and the lifts are only a few yards away.

"What are you doing here?"

I turn around. A man in a hazsuit steps out of a door, inches behind us. Persephone runs. But I'm not quick enough. The man catches the hem of my dress and tugs. My feet falter and I almost fall to the ground.

Persephone slides to a stop just before the lift, frozen as she looks back at me. Her eyes are wide.

"Go!" I growl. She's got the evidence. Maybe she can still get it out there somehow. Maybe she can bring PMC down without me. And maybe she can do it before I'm killed.

She hits the call button for the lift.

The man pulls me toward him, gripping my shoulders to prevent my escape. "You're not going anywhere."

The lift pings as the doors open. Persephone slowly takes a step backward, but she holds the lift doors open.

I try to pull out of the man's grasp. I twist and pull from my shoulders. His gloved fingers dig into the exposed flesh around my collarbone.

Persephone watches me with pleading eyes, still holding the lift doors open.

"Go," I growl again.

She shakes her head. I want to cry with frustration. She's got the evidence. She's our only hope. If she doesn't leave now, if she doesn't get that evidence out of here, then I'm doomed. And Sebastian is doomed.

But Persephone doesn't move.

I grit my teeth. She's left me no choice.

I take a step back, closer to the man. It takes him by surprise and his grip falters; not enough for me to break free, but enough to unnerve him. And he doesn't see what's coming next. He doesn't understand how strong my arms are after years of washing windows and training with Liam. He doesn't know how hard I can hit.

And he doesn't expect it when my arm swings backward and elbows him in the groin.

His grip loosens. He propels me forward as he doubles over in pain. I'm free.

And I run.

Persephone steps into the lift and I barrel in after her, slamming my hand down on the ground floor button.

"Stop!" the man yells, still hunched over, clutching himself.

But it's too late. The lift doors slide shut.

We don't look back when we escape PMC's headquarters. We keep running until we're several streets away. And even then, we don't stop.

Sixteen

We rush through the doors of the Marshall home and into her mother's security room. Persephone quickly searches her mother's computer, and it doesn't take her long to find the number of her media friend, Daniel. And then we're rushing up to her bedroom.

"I want a copy of this before giving it to Daniel," Persephone says, waving her comms unit. She copies the report and the recording of PMC's executive meeting onto her computer.

I tap my foot. It only takes a few seconds, but it seems like forever. I need to get out of here, even though that scares me. The moment I leave this house, anything could happen. I could be spotted; I could be taken back into quarantine. Or worse. But I'm also scared for Sebastian, and that overrides my fear of leaving. The guards are after him. Will they only confiscate my comms unit from him like they'd planned? Or will they do worse now that I've broken out of quarantine?

My stomach lurches. What if they hurt him?

While the files copy, Persephone reaches into a drawer and pulls out a second comms unit.

"Here. Take this." She hands it to me.

I raise my eyebrows in question.

"Just in case we get separated," she explains. "It's a spare."

My fingers brush hers as I take it, sending sparks up my hand. I ignore it, frowning at the comms unit, avoiding her eyes.

"Persephone?" calls a distant voice.

I freeze. The voice is from within the house. It sounds like a woman.

I whip to Persephone. Her eyes are wide with something that could be terror. Or anger. "It's my mom," she hisses.

"Persephone?" the voice calls again. It's getting louder, sounding like she's coming up the stairs.

Persephone pushes me into her walk-in wardrobe and shuts the door quietly. We share panicked glances before she's gone from view.

I hear Persephone climb on her bed, and I pray she's turned off her computer screen. My mind is still playing catch up when I hear the door open.

"Persephone?" her mother says.

I hope her mother has no reason to enter the wardrobe, but I hide myself further behind some hanging clothes anyway.

"You're home early," Persephone says, her voice only slightly muffled by the closet.

"I would have been here earlier, but there was a problem at the decontamination center." Her mother's voice is deep and clipped. It's the kind of voice that's used to giving orders, and having them obeyed.

"What kind of problem?" Persephone's voice is more pitched than normal. I hope her mother doesn't notice.

"It seems that someone has used my PIN to enter the city," her mother says, sounding annoyed. "So I couldn't get in. I've been stuck down there for hours sorting it out."

"That sounds like a real hassle, mom." Persephone sounds bored. I can imagine her examining her nails while she says it.

"The scary part is that it was that infected girl. What's her name—Martina Monsalve."

I jolt.

"What?" Persephone's bored tone is gone. I hope she at least looks composed. "Does that mean a disease is loose in the sector?"

"No, no, that is unlikely."

Of course, it's unlikely. She knows I'm not infected.

"But I was worried about you," her mother continues. "If she had my PIN, she might have come here." She pauses. "She could get inside the house."

"My god!" Persephone sounds suitably disturbed. This girl really is quite the actress.

"You haven't seen anything suspicious?"

"No!" she cries. She still sounds horrified. "Oh my, that's *so* scary."

My muscles are taut hearing them talk about me, but Persephone seems to be doing a good job of lying to her mom.

"Well, that is a relief," her mother says, though her voice is so dry it doesn't sound like she cares either way. "I just came up to check on you. But since you're fine, I need to call Dr. Lederman back."

"He called you?"

"Yes. I had several missed calls while I was sorting out the issue at the decontamination center. Such a nuisance. He's incompetent without me. If you need me, I'll be in the security room. I need to find where this Monsalve girl ended up after she illegally entered the city."

"Good idea, Mom."

There's a pause, then her mother asks, "Is everything okay? You seem ... different, somehow."

"I'm fine, Mom," Persephone groans. I imagine her rolling her eyes when she says it. "Just go back to work."

I hear the bedroom door close, and I poke my head out from behind the clothes. Persephone opens the wardrobe and rushes inside.

"We've got to go. Now!" She grabs my hands and pulls me from my hiding spot. With her hands still on my wrists, she continues, "Within a few minutes my mother is going to find you on the security feeds. She'll see that you came here, and she'll see that I helped you. But ..." She pauses.

My heart is pummeling my chest. I'm ready to run again. But Persephone is looking at me strangely. Her brow is creased, like she can't make up her mind about something. Then her frown eases like she's decided. Her eyes bore into mine. I can't look away.

She tugs on my wrist, pulling me toward her. And suddenly, her lips are against mine.

For a moment, I'm frozen. My brain has stopped. I don't think to kiss her back or put my arms around her. All I do is stand still, dumbfounded by the feeling of her soft lips against mine. I don't want it to stop, but I don't know what to do, either.

Persephone pulls back, leaving me breathless.

"I'm sorry," she says, looking at the floor. "I had to do that just one time."

I don't know what to say. So I just continue to stare. Like a complete fool.

"I shouldn't have ..." Persephone mumbles, still not looking at me while I continue to gawk. "I ... I ... I guess you've never kissed a girl?"

I blink. "I've ..." I finally find my tongue. "I've never kissed anyone before."

She finally meets my gaze. Her eyes are wide with surprise. "Oh. I'm sorry. I was too forward."

Her frown returns. I don't know what is going through her mind. Does she not realize how incredible it is to be kissed by her? I cannot stand the thought of her feeling any sadness or shame, especially if it's caused by my stupidity.

I step close to her again. With a trembling hand, I cup her face, my eyes finding hers. "I'm glad my first kiss was with you," I whisper, my lips a breath from hers. And before my courage fails me, I breach the final space between us and press my lips to hers.

Her mouth opens to accept my clumsy tongue. Her fingers are in my hair, messing my braids. It is the most delicious and incredible feeling. Her body presses against mine and I shiver with delight. I don't want this moment to end.

But Persephone pulls away. Her broad smile quickly fades. "We need to go. Now! They'll kill you, Martina. I can't bear it."

Her hand entwines in mine as she leads me to the door. But it opens before we reach it.

Seventeen

DR. KATHERINE MARSHALL STANDS in the doorway. For a moment, I'm stunned. I can see where Persephone gets her beauty. They could be sisters. But that's where the similarities end. Where Persephone stands tall and proud, her mom is straight-backed, and furious. Dr. Marshall looks like she's about to implode.

There is no surprise in her eyes as they narrow in on me. I feel like an insect with the heel of a boot looming down on me.

"Martina Monsalve." Dr. Marshall's voice rumbles low and menacing.

I slowly back away.

Persephone stays where she is, glancing from me, to her mom, back to me. "Mom ..."

Her mother has eyes only for me. "I've called the guards. They will be here soon."

A million emotions dance across Persephone's face—horror, disgust, fear, anger, shame. The girl who is usually so good at acting is now revealing all. "Mom ..." Persephone's jaw tightens. "You ..." She points a finger at her mom, at a loss for words. Her face settles on one emotion: fury. She screeches, "You monster!"

Persephone charges at her mother and knocks her to the ground.

For a moment, I stand stunned, staring at the fallen figure. Then Persephone snatches up my hand again and we leap over her mother's crumpled figure before she has a chance to get up. We race down the grand staircase, through the foyer, and out into the street. My ankle barely registers any pain as I run; reduced to a dull ache in the background. Adrenaline has taken over.

We don't stop running. We ignore the astonished glances of people as we speed along Sparkle Sector paths, not stopping for anything, not even to slow down around corners.

I try to talk as we run. "Where." Inhale. "Can." Exhale. "We." Inhale. "Hide?" I exhale and pull Persephone to a stop behind a bush.

"Where can we hide?" I say again, when I've caught my breath.

"Outside," Persephone says. She eyes the path behind me, on alert. "It's the only place you'll be safe."

"We can't leave," I protest.

Persephone shakes her head, pulling my hand, forcing me into a run again. We round a corner onto the main thoroughfare.

Two guards spot us. They take off instantly, and we pick up our pace. They're several yards away from us; we still have a chance to get away.

My gaze swivels left and right, trying to find a place to hide; a way to stay in the bubble city. I need to stay to help Sebastian. I can't leave him again. But there is nowhere to hide. Every building, every door, needs an access code to enter. Walls tower over our heads, gates are unclimbable, sturdy doors are unbreakable.

We keep running.

Two more guards appear, joining the two already on our tail.

Ahead is the decontamination center. The guards will be on us before we can dress in hazsuits. We'll never get out in time. But we keep running, straight at the center. What choice do we have?

As we enter the decontamination center, we pull up short. In front stands a line of five guards bearing guns and stun batons, blocking the way to the decon stations where hazsuits are collected.

I glance behind us. The other four guards are encroaching, herding us forward.

The few people in the foyer back away. Some of the decontamination stations are occupied with people coming and going. One man exits the changing room, fully dressed and ready to enter the sterilized city. But he remains where he is when he sees the commotion. A few other onlookers watch us from the side. The guards pay them no notice. All eyes are on me and Persephone.

I glance at Persephone. She grips my hand. "Third from the right," she whispers, so only I can hear.

I look at the decon station she indicates. A woman is pulling the helmet of her hazsuit over her head. In a moment, she will seal it and leave her station out into the antechamber beyond. The antechamber that, once sealed to this side of the center, will open to the outside.

But how is that going to help me? She's already dressed in the suit. Unless … I frown. Unless Persephone means we leave the bubble without hazsuits. We could push our way past her and into the antechamber. We're both small; we could fit in the antechamber together if we're not wearing hazsuits.

Persephone nods. "You need to do it."

"Me?" My stomach drops when I realize what she's saying. I grip her hand a little harder. "You're not coming?"

"My mother will never let anything happen to me," she whispers quickly. "I've got to stay and get that evidence out. But they'll kill you if you stay. You've got to go!"

She gives me a little push toward the station. There's no time to think about it. No time to argue or consider the consequences. The woman in the station is ready to enter the antechamber.

I take off running. The guards lift their guns, pointing them at me.

Persephone runs behind me for a moment, but as she reaches the closest guard, she dives into his arms, distracting him so I can make a last dash for the decon station. Out of the corner of my eye, I see him pull Persephone backward. She struggles with him, but most of the fight has gone out of her, and she's quickly overpowered.

I leap into the station, squeezing in next to the woman in the hazsuit. She cries out in fright. She hadn't been watching the commotion in the foyer, too busy with her hazsuit, but now her eyes are wide with fear. It's easy to push her behind me. I don't even need to use force; she goes willingly.

And then I'm in the antechamber, sealing it behind me. The woman stares through her visor and the glass door of the antechamber; she doesn't move. Behind her, all nine guards have gathered, but they can't shoot, or they'll hit the woman. One of them grips Persephone's arms. The bastard. He doesn't need to be so rough.

There's nothing I can do for her now. All I can do is hope that she's right, and her mother can save her from execution. She has risked herself so that Sebastian—and I—can have a chance to live.

There's a soft beep. The antechamber is now fully sealed to the interior of the bubble city. I can exit.

A last look at Persephone shows her poised—head held high triumphantly—even as she stands in the grip of the guard. Her eyes fierce. The corner of her lips twitch into a defiant smile.

I return the smile, then turn and push through the exterior door of the antechamber. I walk down the corridor to the pedestrian exit. And leave the bubble.

Eighteen

I step out into the desert. The sun is blinding. It takes a moment for my eyes to adjust from the dark of the corridor to the sunshine outside.

I feel naked. I look down at the yellow dress Persephone gave me. It seems so flimsy now, offering no protection. With no hazsuit and no visor, I am completely defenseless.

But there's no time to worry. With a deep breath, I hurry away from the decontamination center. The guards will dress in their hazsuits and be after me in no time. I run north, to the Old City.

Within seconds, I'm sweating. I've never been this hot before. I've always had my air-conditioned suit to keep me cool outside. Inside the bubbles, the air is climate-controlled, keeping the temperature at 72 degrees. This heat is like being inside an oven. And it's everywhere. All around me. Roasting me alive. I even breathe in the heat as I run.

But I don't stop.

The door clangs open behind me, and I whip around, expecting to see the guards on top of me. But sound travels further without a hazsuit on, and the door to the decontamination center is already further away than I realized. I can move much faster without a hazsuit.

They're following me on foot. I guess they don't want to wait for the air in the vehicle chamber to circle out so a truck can exit.

There are three of them. All in white hazsuits, scanning the desert. One sees me and elbows his companion, pointing me out.

I stumble and fall to the dirt. They're running toward me. I pick myself up and take off again.

Even with my injured ankle, I can run faster than them in their bulky hazsuits. I can lose them in the Old City ruins. If I reach it.

Pop! Pop! Something ricochets off the desert floor. I yelp in terror. I look back. They're shooting their guns at me.

"¡*Mierda*!" I cry.

I'm almost there. I can make it.

Pop! Pop! Pop!

I duck my head. As if that will do any good against bullets.

Finally, the shadow of the closest building falls over me and I charge into the Old City. I leap behind the nearest building, putting it between me and the bullets. But I don't take a second to catch my breath or wipe the sweat from my brow. I keep running.

Past broken buildings, churning the dirt up from the ground, choking on the dust in the air, running in and out of shadows. I change direction, hoping the guards don't, hoping they continue north. I head east instead. That's the way the Terrene Folk went.

I can't hear the guards anymore; they're too far behind. But still, I keep running.

I run until my lungs won't let me any longer. They're burning. They're burning not only from my exertions but from the blistering air traveling up and down my windpipe. I double over to catch my breath.

My throat is ragged. Every breath hurts. The heat is suffocating, but after a moment, I realize I am getting the oxygen my body needs. I straighten up again and push on, this time at a more manageable walk that's better for both my ankle and my breath.

Where are the guards? Did they continue into the Old City? Or did they turn back to the bubble city when I lost them within the buildings? Maybe they figured out I went east. There's no knowing and I can't run anymore, so I keep a steady walking pace.

Sweat drips into my eyes, making them sting. I wipe the excess from my brow with the back of my hand, but I feel more appear in its wake.

I lick my lips, realizing I'm thirsty. But I have no water.

I duck under a fallen beam.

How long I can survive out here? I used to think the biggest threat was disease. Now, it's finding water. Finding food. Escaping the blazing sun. I know I can last a long time without food, but I'm going to be desperate for water within the day, especially with this torrid heat.

I walk in the shadows of buildings as much as I can. It seems to help a little. But sometimes I have no choice but to walk in the sun. The Old City makes it difficult to find an easy path in the shadows. Everywhere I turn, there are hills of bricks and fallen buildings blocking my path. So I'm forced to weave in and out and around, stepping in and out of shadows.

A soft breeze flutters across my skin; a slight reprieve from the heat. I've never felt the wind before. Well, not like this anyway. I felt the gale force wind that blew me off the glass bubble, but I've never felt the gentle caress of it. It's cooling kisses. It's not like the fan of an air conditioner. This feels wild, less predictable. It's here one moment, a light touch, and then it flitters away the next.

And it brings a smell with it. Or rather, several smells. Musky smells; sickly sweet smells; dusty smells. It's the scent of the desert. I breathe it in deeply; I never knew how much I was missing in the safety of the bubble cities.

Something scuttles past in front of my feet. I shriek, jumping away. It's about a foot long and has skin that looks like rusted metal. Its four legs barely lift its body from the ground as it bolts across the desert, its tail drawing lines in the sand. It suddenly stops running, just before it reaches the shadows, and flicks its skinny tongue out of its flat mouth. Then it disappears into the shade and under some rocks.

I look around in shock. Did anyone hear me shriek? Surely, the guards are still far enough away that they can't have heard.

This is a completely foreign world. Maybe I would have been safer staying in the bubble city, taking my chances with the guards. Maybe Persephone could have found a way to get me out of quarantine. Maybe if she got the evidence out before they infected me, I would have survived. But how am I supposed to survive in this fierce wilderness? I don't know the first thing I should do to help myself.

I reach the edge of the Old City. From the shade of the nearest dilapidated building, I crouch and observe the vast landscape beyond. There are miles and miles of nothing. Just dirt and sand, a few desert shrubs, and the hazy horizon.

I have no idea what to do.

I originally thought I should walk out into the desert and search for the Terrene Folk. But seeing the vast, empty expanse, I'm not too sure. There is nothing out there but sun and sand. I doubt I'll last long. If I don't find someone that can help me, I'll die of dehydration within a few days. If the steel-skinned creature doesn't eat me in my sleep first.

Maybe I should stay within the Old City. I can circle back toward the bubble city and spy on it. At least that way I'll be closer to Sebastian. I'll just have to keep an eye out for guards searching for me.

Although I still might be eaten alive by that steel-skinned creature.

The thought of Sebastian makes up my mind. I'll stay within the ruins of the Old City. Just like the steel-skinned critter, I'll find a hole to hide in, somewhere the guards can't find me. I'll keep close and hope that somehow, I'll get back to him.

I've still got the comms unit Persephone gave me. I check the battery; it's almost full. It should last a few days, and hopefully Persephone will get in contact. If not, both me and the comms unit will be dead.

I turn around, heading back the way I came, following my footsteps. Footsteps that are clearly marked in the sand.

I stop. I've been leaving a clear path for the guards to follow. Idiot! It's just a matter of time until the guards find me.

My legs feel weak and my head aches from too much sun. I sit down in the middle of the path. What's the point of going on any further? I'm exhausted. I can't walk any more. I may as well just wait for the guards to find me.

It's late afternoon. The sun still presses down on me, though now from an angle.

My eyes droop. I don't fight it. I let them close. It'll only be for a while. The guards will find me soon. At least they'll have water.

A gentle breeze plays on my skin, lifting my hair slightly to kiss my neck. It's easy to imagine it's Persephone kissing me. Her lips so soft. How can someone's lips be so soft? Her fingers had wound up the back of my neck and played in my curls, just as her kiss became more impassioned. And she had smiled at me after. A smile of pure happiness. It filled my heart with the warm golden liquid of joy. I wish I could see her smile that way again. It was like I was the only girl in the world.

It was a perfect moment—before the panic set in.

My eyes open. I can't give up. Not when Persephone has risked so much for me. Not when Sebastian is in danger. I will not lie down and wait for death.

"We won't lie down and die." The Terrene Folk's words echo in my head.

I realize my heart rate has returned to normal after the brief rest. I stand up and appraise my surroundings.

To mask my footsteps, I'll need to get off the sand. I spot a brick wall about seven feet high, a few yards back. My footsteps run alongside it. I carefully walk backward to it, putting my feet over the footsteps I've already made. It will appear as though my footsteps ended where I rested in the middle of the path. Without making more marks in the sand, I leap to the top of a rock that stands between my footsteps and the wall. I feel a small twinge in my ankle when I leap, but I keep going.

It's not hard for me to do another leap and grab the top of the wall with my hands. I hang there a moment, with bits of rock and brick digging into my fingers, until I get my footing and scramble up the side.

From the top of the wall, I can see it runs several yards away from me. *Maravilloso.* This is the perfect way to hide my tracks. I balance along the top, taking extra care with my injured ankle.

It's narrow to walk on, but my balance is good. It's only a seven-foot drop to the ground, much less than the height of my sleeping pod. I try to ignore the height and look straight ahead, but my eyes keep drifting to the ground. The sight is dizzying. The ground seems so far away.

I concentrate on each step, making sure the bricks don't crumble and can take my full weight when I step on them. And I slowly inch along.

Eventually, the wall comes to an end. I take a moment to work out my next move. The vantage point I now have helps me to plot a course that will keep me off the sand. There are a few ways I could go, with rocks, rusted vehicles, and bits of broken buildings all around. I still can't see the bubble city from where I am; another building, partly intact and taller than the wall I'm on, blocks it from view. At least that means they can't see me, either.

It's a scramble to get down from the wall. I scrape my elbow, but I ignore the sting. I leap from rock, to brick, to a plank of wood, anything that will mask my direction from the guards. It's like a game of "The floor is lava," which I remember playing with Sebastian in Colombia. We would pretend the floor of our home was made of lava and avoid touching it by jumping across furniture. My parents hated it. They would yell, "Don't jump on the furniture! *¡Pórtate bien!*" And we would giggle as we took another leap onto the sofa.

When there is nothing to use as a stepping stone, I take a few tentative steps on the sand, trying to make the smallest impression possible by walking on the tips of my toes, and then bend down to brush the marks, trying not to make it obvious that I'm hiding my footsteps. And even though the desert is scorching hot, at least the ground isn't really made of lava.

Thinking of it as a game helps me take my mind off other worries; the guards following me, Sebastian scavenging for food, my growing thirst, the ache in my ankle, or Persephone in the hands of the guards. Instead, I remember those games with Sebastian when he was so innocent, and so was I.

My mind is elsewhere, in the past with Sebastian, when I hear the murmur of voices. *Mierda.*

I dive into the shadows of the closest fractured building, my back plastered against the bricks.

The voices come from behind a wall. They're hard to hear, so they must be a bit of a distance away. I don't dare move. I pray they don't come any closer. If they circle this building, the shadows won't hide me for long.

The voices get louder. They're coming toward me. I hold my breath.

"... you think?" says a voice. A man's, I think.

"Yeah, she'll be dead in a few days regardless," says another voice. A woman's. "We'd be more useful enforcing the lockdown in Linto."

The man and woman sound like they're heading straight for me. But they don't know I'm here. I press myself deeper into the shadows of the building, though it makes no difference.

"She could be anywhere," the man says, seeming to agree with the woman.

I hear the crunch of their footsteps. They're on the other side of the wall that I'm pressed against. I jolt when I see movement, but it's just a shadow across the sand. There's a crack in my wall, near my feet. Quietly, I bend down to look through it. I see two sets of white boots pass. Hazsuit boots.

They're so close. Only a few crumbling bricks stand between me and discovery.

A metallic voice comes through a comms unit. "Report in," it barks.

"No sign of her," the woman responds.

"Check-in in fifteen," the metallic voice demands as it moves away from me. The man and woman keep chatting about their lives in the bubble city, random facts about their children's schooling, and what recipes they enjoy cooking. I don't move an inch until they have gone so far that I can barely hear them anymore.

Only then do I leave my hiding spot. I climb another wall and continue leap frogging from stone to stone, away from the voices, and back toward the city.

Nineteen

THE SHADOWS ARE GROWING larger and the ruins are darkening. The day has been long and lonely. I've never had so much space to myself before, but now that I have it, I wish I was back in my claustrophobic little pod with Sebastian. Soon, it will be too dark to see where I'm going. I need to find a place to hide while it's still light enough to see.

I spot a concrete slab, fallen from one of the buildings, tilted across the ruins in a way that creates a little cave. The gap underneath is about the size of my sleeping pod. Although with all the rubble on the floor, I doubt my sleep will be comfortable.

There's a smaller concrete slab lying flat at the entrance to the cave. I sit on it, relieved to have finally finished walking for the day.

I look down at my yellow dress. It's covered in dirt and dust and sweat stains. I finger the hem. It's still a shock to be outside in only a dress. I feel vulnerable and exposed. But not sick. Will I get sick? PMC were lying to us all along, but I still remember my Mamá wasting away with her illness. I watched every news report as they detailed her death. Her skin turning gray and her eyes hollow in their sockets. Did she and Papá die from one of those colds that Nathan told me about? Will I die the same way?

I wonder if her death was even an accident. Maybe the Colombian branch of PMC also wanted to spread fear and increase their control. Were they out to make a profit too? Did they kill Mamá with disease just so they could keep their secrets? I can't be sure of anything anymore.

Despite the heat, a shiver runs up my spine.

There's nothing I can do but wait to see if I fall ill, too.

I take stock of myself. My ankle aches from all the walking and running. The swelling has returned, but it seems to be holding up okay. More concerning is the redness of my skin. It's all over my body. It's particularly red on the tops of my knees and along the tops of my arms. But beneath my clothes, my skin is normal. Is this the start of a sickness? I do have a headache. But I thought that was due to lack of water.

There is a heat coming off my skin, and it stings when I touch it, almost like it's been burned by the sun. Can the sun burn you? I know the sun produces heat. But I know little else. I've come to realize there's so much I don't know about the world. PMC hide things from us. I can't afford educational media on my comms unit. I am so ignorant about everything.

Strange noises begin as soon as the sky darkens. There's a repetitive clicking, like millions of insects. Can there actually be that many insects alive to make such a song? But what else can it be? The more I listen, the more soothing it sounds.

I shuffle into the cave, shifting some of the rubble to make it more comfortable to lie down. I close my eyes, praying for the breeze to return, and Persephone's gentle kiss on my neck.

I spend the next day in the cave, trying to escape the sun. But there is no escaping the heat. Sweat runs down my forehead and into my eyes. I try wiping it away with my arm, but my arm is just as sweaty.

My throat is dry, my tongue parched. There is a metallic dusty taste whenever I try to swallow. My head is pounding. What is this disease? I'm going to be one of those unlucky ones that can't survive the outside.

I groan.

I've failed Sebastian. I've failed Persephone. And now my own body is failing me.

I drift in and out of sleep. Each time I wake, I hope to open my eyes to darkness, but light burns through my eyelids, so I know without opening them that the sun is still blistering on. I curse it. I hate it and its fury.

There's no comfort in the cave. There's no escaping the oppressive heat, or the harsh surrounds. A rock digs into my back. No matter which way I move, it still seems to lodge itself into my flesh.

When sleep eludes me, I watch the face of the comms unit. But no one calls. I don't dare to use it to check the news. I can't risk the battery. I need it to last as long as possible. It needs to last until Persephone calls me.

But I'm tempted. To escape the boredom. To distract myself from my thirst and the heat. But more than anything, I want to see if there's any news about Persephone and Sebastian. Have they been added to the list of infected? Or maybe the tally of the dead? Has Persephone had any luck getting the evidence out to the public? Surely she will call me if she has. But maybe … No! I can't use the comms unit. No matter how tempting it is. I have to trust that Persephone will call me when she can.

I close my eyes again, praying that sleep will take me away from my pain and worries.

By the time night arrives, I've still had no calls. I doubt my decision to stay in the Old City. Maybe I could have found someone to help me if I had kept walking east into the desert. Maybe I would have found the Terrene Folk. Maybe I would have found water.

It has become an effort to move. My muscles feel weak. My head spins if I try to stand up. I need water soon or I'm going to die. Even if I change my mind and go looking for water in the desert, I won't make it very far.

A fog clouds my brain. I struggle to think of what I should do. Through the haze, I consider walking back to the bubble city, where there's water. I'll have to drag my body back. I'll crawl if I have to.

No.

I don't want to go back there.

I can't.

My eyes flutter open.

I'm still safe in the makeshift cave. The darkness is my blanket. The day's sweat has dried on my forehead. I'm even a little cold. I wish I had a jacket, something to keep me warm. It's hard to believe that a few hours ago, I was praying for a reprieve from the heat.

I curl into myself, using my own body heat to stay warm.

I flicker in and out of consciousness. Vivid dreams plague me. Some are sweet, like showering in Persephone's bathroom, with an unlimited stream of water. Or snuggling up to Sebastian in our sleeping pod. But others scare me. The guards finding me, sometimes in the cave, sometimes they shoot me down as I'm running through the desert. Each time I awake with a gasp, cursing my decision to stay.

I should have done something different. I should have risked going further out in the desert. I should have tried to find the Terrene Folk. Nathan would have been happy to see me.

Nathan's face looks down at me, smiling. Or frowning. He's not quite in focus. And there is Jerry, the white horse, looking over his shoulder. I giggle. Jerry looks worried. His eyes are so large, bulging with concern.

The sunlight is blinding. I shut my eyes against it and drift back to sleep, into a dreamland of green and shade and water.

"Martina? Martina?"

I open my eyes, and the image of my dreamland fades. In its place are Nathan and Jerry, both with wide eyes.

I close my eyes again, smiling. Just another dream.

Then cool liquid fills my mouth. I'm coughing and spluttering, but I swallow most of it. Not a dream. A nightmare.

I look up again and see Nathan and Jerry, both still there. I rub my eyes, and the fog starts to clear. Is this real? I reach up, brushing my fingers on his chin. It feels real.

Nathan grins. "Hey there, bubble girl."

Jerry whinnies, shaking his mane. The sound makes me jolt.

"Nathan?" My voice is faint and cracked.

"The one and only," he says, shrugging. That annoying typical shrug of his.

Nathan helps me to sit up. My head spins at the sudden movement. I wait for it to stop spinning, then appraise my surroundings. I'm outside my cave, in the shadow of a brick wall. I don't remember crawling out here.

"You know, you really shouldn't travel through the desert without a supply of water," Nathan says. Wow, he's really here. This isn't a dream.

"Hmph." My head is pounding, and smart remarks aren't helping it. I reach for his canteen so I can get a proper mouthful of water. As the water trickles down my throat, my bad temper turns to gratitude. "Ah!" I breathe.

Nathan allows me time to recover. He sits next to me in the dirt with his legs crossed, just like he did the first day I met him. His hair is tied back off his face today, running down the length of his back. He wears his normal jeans with a beige shirt that sits loosely on his muscled chest. He looks good. And he's real.

"You shouldn't be so close to me," I say, wincing against my headache. "I'm sick."

"I'm pretty sure you're just dehydrated," he says, dark eyes on mine. "Drink more water. It will help."

I do as he says, taking small sips from his canteen. Slowly, I start to feel like myself again. The headache eases, and the brain fog clears. I feel my mind whirring with thoughts again as it starts to function at a normal speed.

"How did you find me?" I ask. "I thought the Terrene had moved on?"

Nathan opens his mouth to say something, but seems to think better of it. After a pause, he says, "There was a problem with a truck. We didn't get very far."

It feels like this isn't the whole truth, but maybe my mind still isn't back to normal yet. I might be imagining the uncertainty in his voice.

"But why are you here?" I ask. "Near the city?"

"We like to keep an eye on what is going on in the city," he says. "You know, to keep the community safe. We want advanced notice if they send out guards after us." He shrugs again. I didn't think I would ever miss that shrug. "We saw you run out of there like a bat out of hell, complete with the hounds on your tail."

"What?" I exclaim. "Then why did it take you so long to get here? I almost died!"

"A thank you for saving your life would be nice, you know?"

I blush. He's right. I haven't shown much appreciation. "Thank you," I murmur.

He brushes off my thanks like it wasn't really needed, then says, "I wanted to come get you straight away. But there were guards after you. We had to be careful. And then you disappeared. We knew roughly where you were, but it took me a while to find you under this rock."

"You were watching me?" I don't like the idea that someone was watching me while I writhed in the heat. But thankfully they were. I shudder to think what would have happened if he didn't find me.

"Yeah." Nathan points to the building that blocks our view of the bubble city. "We climbed up there. It's not very safe, but it's got a killer view." He gives me a wry smile. It makes me wonder if he's talking about the view of the ruins, or the view of me.

Jerry whinnies again. From my perspective on the ground, he is giant. He looks majestic with the sun behind his head, filtering through his white mane as he shakes it out. I'm in awe. It's still unbelievable that horses are real, and he seems even more dreamlike after my delirium.

"I brought Jerry to help you get back to camp," Nathan says. "You've been through a lot. How's your ankle?"

"Uh, my ankle's fine." I frown at him. "What do you mean by 'back to camp?' I can't go. I've got to get Sebastian."

"You can't stay here, Martina." Nathan frowns back at me. "The guards will find you. They're searching over on the west side, but they could head this way at any moment. I've got a short window of time to get you out of here."

"But what about Sebastian?"

"How can you help him?" he says, his voice rising. "You're not thinking of going back into the city, are you? They'll kill you, Martina. That's a stupid idea."

"Alright!" I snap, and my head pounds again. A little more calmly, I say, "Okay. I'm not going back to the city. You're right. They will kill me. How could I get in without a hazsuit anyway?" I shake my head. "But I'm waiting on ..." I hesitate. For some reason, it feels weird to say Persephone's name to Nathan. "... someone to call me. They're trying to help. I might still have a chance to save Sebastian."

Nathan does his signature shrug. And just like that, it's annoying again. "So? Let them call you from camp. Better than dying while you wait."

He's got a point. I don't know when or even if Persephone will call. And the comms unit probably won't last much longer.

"And we'll monitor things here for you." Nathan gestures to the building. "We've got a woman up there now. We won't miss anything."

"Fine," I say, sighing. I'd rather not go through the last few days again, hiding from guards and suffering from dehydration, feeling like I'm dying a slow death. So I climb to my feet. But the change in altitude quickly has my head reeling. Jerry seems to go sideways as my legs buckle.

"Woah," Nathan cries, catching me before I hit the ground. He holds me steady with one arm hooked under my shoulder and the other around my waist. I'm very aware of his proximity. His face so near to mine, not obstructed by a hazsuit visor.

My eyes flicker to his lips. And I think of Persephone's lips.

I blush. I hope Nathan doesn't notice. Surely, he won't. I'm already flushed from the heat.

"I'm alright," I grumble, pulling out of his grasp. My head has stopped spinning and I can stand without his assistance. I take a step away and compose myself. "Shall we go?"

Nathan nods and readies Jerry for me to climb up. Once I'm settled, he seats himself behind me, just like that first night I rode Jerry. Except this time, I'm not in a bulky hazsuit. I feel the blood rush to my cheeks again. The hot weather is affecting me in strange ways.

Although it's scary sitting atop of Jerry again, it's also nice. I run my fingers through his fur. The last time I touched him, I was wearing the gloves of my hazsuit. I had thought his fur would be soft, but it's actually kind of rough; a stringy, coarse feel to it. The hair flicks back into place after my fingers have disturbed it.

Nathan steers Jerry toward the north-east, beyond the edge of the ruins, and into the empty desert. Once we're clear of the rubble from the Old City, he puts the horse into a canter. I hold on tight to the saddle as the ground rushes past in a blur of stones, sand, and desert shrubs. I hope I don't topple off. We ride for thirty minutes or more before the camp comes into view. It's set up on a large plain, with nothing for miles around them. It's their own little desert oasis.

As we get closer, I realize I'm excited to see them again. I was skeptical and scared during my first stay with the Terrene Folk. They were alien; people that I could barely believe existed. Now I know the truth. They were right about PMC and their evil deeds. This time, there will be trust between us.

People move in and out of the beige tents, going about their business. Others stand to attention on the outskirts, keeping the community safe. I spot Will in the distance. He's walking with a hay bale toward the hobbled horses on the periphery of the camp. Upon spotting us, he drops his bundle. He races to meet us, his face splitting in a wide grin.

"Will!" I call, returning his grin. I'm surprised that I'm genuinely happy to see him.

"Martina!" he says, running to take hold of Jerry's reins. "Welcome back."

Nathan slides off and then helps me down, where I'm immediately accosted by Will, wrapping me in a hug. At first, I don't react, too shocked at the unfamiliar contact. People don't go around hugging each other in Neustin; it might spread germs. But I'm no longer in the bubble city. So I awkwardly wrap my arms around his lithe body. And it reminds me of being back in Colombia, where people hugged and kissed all the time. *Mi familia y amigos.*

"It's so good to see you," I say when the embrace ends.

"You too, Martina." Will squeezes my arm. "I'm glad you're not dead."

I laugh. "Me too!"

"We're all glad you're alive," Mother Jessica says as she joins our circle.

I bow my head to her in respect and shame. "I'm so sorry I didn't believe you. I know now what you said was true."

"Don't think on it another moment," Mother Jessica says, smiling. "Come now and have some food. You must be famished after spending days in the desert alone with no provisions. Now, the reason for that must be an interesting story, and one I hope you'll tell."

She leads the way into the camp. Nathan disappears to take care of Jerry, while Mother Jessica and Will join me around the fire pit in the center of their camp. It's just a pile of ash right now, so it's not adding to the hot temperature. There's a variety of stools and chairs, some blue, some red, some just a log propped up on the ground. I sit on a blue chair and Mother Jessica and Will pull up stools nearby.

Mother Jessica hands me some doughy bread and water. The bread tastes amazing. I'm not sure if it's because of the ingredients, or just because it's been so long since I've eaten anything. I wolf it down with relish.

Mother and Will allow me to eat in silence—Mother waits patiently while Will stares at me, tapping his fingers on his leg, clearly eager for me to finish eating and tell them my news. When Nathan returns, Mother asks, "Will you tell us your story, Martina?"

I look into her eyes. They're gray and bright, glowing with intelligence. The wrinkles around her eyes tell of a life of joys as well as hardships. I didn't trust her before, but now maybe I can.

Nathan and Will's eyes are also on me. Nathan has released his hair from its ties, and it flows down his back, just like Will's. Anyone could tell they're brothers. They have the same dark brown eyes with flecks of red, the same defined jaws, and high cheekbones. The main difference, other than a few years in age, is Will's face is always lit with a smile, while Nathan's is often dark and brooding.

"I might have lost everything," I finally say. My voice cracks, even though I'm trying as hard as I can to keep it together. This is what I've been trying so hard not to admit. I take a deep breath. "I don't know what to do now. Sebastian ... I might never see him again. He might be in danger, and it's my fault."

Will opens his mouth to say something, his face full of concern, but Mother stays him with a hand on his knee.

I continue, "I was able to enter the bubble city with Dr. Marshall's PIN with little trouble. A couple of guards might have been suspicious, but I was able to sneak into her house with the same code. And I met a girl there. Persephone." Heat rises in my cheeks as I mention Persephone. I try to act natural. "She agreed to help me."

Have they noticed me blushing? I swear I saw Mother's eyes widen ever so slightly. Why did she glance at Nathan? Nathan's face doesn't change, but his eyes bore into mine. What is he thinking?

I hurry on. "We went searching for evidence against PMC Life Tech."

I tell them about the pharmacists in the lab, the financial report we found, and the meeting we recorded with Dr. Lederman ordering the death of innocents. I tell them how we were captured and our narrow escape. I mention Persephone's plan to enlist the help from Daniel, the man in the media who can possibly broadcast it.

"But that was before Dr. Marshall came home and found me." I feel my cheeks burn again, thinking about the kiss with Persephone just before I was discovered by her mom. "And I had to escape. Persephone was captured. She might be killed. I can only hope that she'll be kept safe because she's the daughter of Dr. Marshall."

"She's the daughter of Dr. Marshall?" Mother repeats, her voice sharp.

"Didn't I say that?" I look from Nathan to Mother, who exchange unreadable looks.

At the thought of Persephone, I can't help feeling embarrassed. I don't know exactly how I feel about her, but I know I want to keep her safe, and I know I trust her. After everything she's done for me, I have to trust her. But I don't know what that kiss meant. I don't know if she's more than a friend. I don't even know if we'll even see each other again.

"Yes, she's her daughter," I say. I try to change the subject. "Now that I'm out here, I don't know what to do. I don't know how to keep Sebastian safe. I can't go to him. That will only put him in danger. But I can't walk away either."

I can't leave Sebastian alone. It's evident that he's more capable than I've ever given him credit for. He's been able to survive without me for the past week, but he's still got so much to learn.

Before long, he'll run out of money. Even now, he's relying on Rosa and Liam to get food. But how long can that last? How long until they get sick of helping him? What if Rosa gets caught giving away food? She won't be much help to him without her job.

He's only eight years old. Someone might take advantage of him. An image of him working in the alleys pops into my head. I almost gag. I suppress the thought; I can't think about that now. I need to figure out a way to keep him safe.

"You don't think this ... Persephone, will pull through with broadcasting to the media?" Nathan asks.

"I hope she can. But I can't rely on that." I lower my eyes. "She might be quarantined. She might be in trouble or the plan might not work. No, I can't wait for her. I need to do something now."

"Easy, Martina," Mother says, as if I'm about to run back to the bubble city right this second. "How will you know if your friend has succeeded?"

"She gave me a comms unit." I pull it out of my pocket. "She said she'd call me. But the battery is almost flat, so if she doesn't call today, then I won't know."

"We can charge that," Will says, grinning. He's been listening quietly the whole time. But it's obvious he wants to help in whatever way he can.

"How?" I ask.

"We have solar technology." Will does that nonchalant shrug he has in common with Nathan.

"That's a start," I say. "But there must be something more I can do."

"We'll think on it," Mother says, standing up. For the moment, the conversation is over.

Twenty

"HERE! TAKE THIS." NATHAN hands me a bale of hay and picks another up himself. The desert is darkening and the sounds of insects punctuate the air, although they are much quieter than the night before.

I lift the bale of hay, surprised my strength has returned. I had a good rest in the tent Mother loaned me, and I'm feeling much better after all the bread and water. Although the delicious scents wafting from the cooking fire has my tummy rumbling again, and I'm looking forward to dinner.

A woman was kind enough to lend me some clothes, so I discarded Persephone's impractical—and now filthy—yellow dress. I'm now dressed in a pair of beige shorts and a loose cream shirt that sits lightly on my skin, allowing any breeze there is to flow through it. But I still can't help feeling exposed and naked without my hazsuit.

I follow Nathan to where the horses are held under a makeshift stable made of the same thick cloth as the tents. He dumps his hay bale in front of two horses, who immediately start ripping the straw out and chewing it, their mouths flapping with delight. Nathan takes the other bale from me and gives it to the remaining horses.

I take my time to pat each of the horses. I avoid their heads, still scared they might chew off my fingers, especially now that I don't have the protection of my gloves. But I reach out, trailing long lines along their backs. If the horses notice me at all, they don't show it. They continue to chew on their food, completely ignoring me.

Despite all my worries and fears, I feel an immense joy growing in me. It's like a hot sun has taken the place of my heart and is spreading warmth to each limb. Not like the stifling heat of the desert, but one of hope and peace and freedom. The possibilities.

What if Sebastian could come outside with me? What if we could live like this, among the Terrene Folk? I've been outside for three days now, and I'm still alive. I haven't been struck down with a deadly illness. Well, not one that water couldn't fix. Maybe Sebastian can survive, too.

For the first time, instead of thinking of ways to preserve Sebastian's way of life, or to get back to my old one, I think of ways I might get Sebastian out. I can't just call him on the comms unit, because he doesn't have one anymore. By now, the guards will have confiscated my comms unit. There's a chance that Persephone can get in contact with him if I call her instead. Yes, that could work. But I don't even know how to contact her. The comms unit doesn't have her stored in the contacts.

And even if I can get a message to Sebastian, then what? How can I assure his survival out here? There's still a risk that he'll get sick. Mother said not everyone survives out here. There is still a risk of death. I don't know a lot about diseases, but I wonder if some of the medications we take daily could be of some help to transition to this life.

My mind flicks between how to make it happen and dreaming of the life we could have. Sebastian could thrive in a life outside. The Terrene kids are all happy, running around, having fun, helping with chores around the camp. They're free. They're not worked to exhaustion. They have enough food to eat. And they're healthy.

"It's nice to have you back," Nathan says, breaking my reverie. He joins me as I stroke the horse, standing a little too close. I move forward to the next horse, hoping he doesn't close in on me again. He takes one step closer but leaves me room to breathe.

I don't know how to act, not with how Nathan's looking at me; his eyes intense, the same way Persephone looked right before she kissed me.

I turn my back to him, focusing on the horse. "It's nice to touch the horses without my gloves on," I say, more to myself than to him.

I've never felt so conflicted. Here I am, contemplating a life with the Terrene Folk, seeking a way for Sebastian to join me out here. But part of me longs to be back in the bubble city. Back to my old life, when Sebastian was safe. But also back to Persephone. A life out here would be a life without Persephone. She can't leave the city. She has her whole life in front of her there. She might even have the chance to make a difference. She has her mother, her home, her money. She wouldn't want to live out here.

But all my dreams are flawed. Even if I went back to my old life in the bubble city, Persephone would never be a part of it. She's from the Sparkle Sector. I'm from The Nix. Our paths would never cross. I'm lucky to have met her once. To have kissed her. Who am I to think she would want anything more than that?

I could belong with the Terrene, though. This dream is almost tangible. It's just missing Sebastian. If he joins me, I could be happy.

I glance at Nathan. His perfectly straight hair hangs over his shoulders, reaching down his muscled chest. He deftly strokes the head of a horse, and the horse responds, extending its neck and pushing into Nathan's hand, obviously enjoying the sensation. Nathan is so comfortable with the animals; he shows a genuine tenderness to them. It's not the serious and mocking side of himself that he's shown to me. It would be nice to get to know that side of him more.

I sigh. All I need to do is figure out how to save Sebastian. Sebastian is what's important. Nothing else, *no one else*, matters.

My stomach rumbles. Well, maybe getting some dinner matters, too.

Nathan chuckles. "Was that your stomach growling?"

I flush. I didn't realize he could hear it.

"Let's head back for dinner," he suggests, nodding in the direction of the campfire.

The center of the camp is a hive of activity now. It seems like the whole community has gathered around the fire. It's a little overwhelming as people come up and introduce themselves.

"Hi, I'm Mandy and this is Jannine."

"I'm John."

"This is Vijayani and Chris."

I forget most of the names as soon as they're said. I hope I have time to learn them properly later.

Last time I was in their camp, almost no one spoke to me. Most of them avoided me. Except, of course, Roscoe the dog.

Roscoe comes bounding up to me now, his tongue lolling out the side of his mouth. Quick as a flash, his tongue flicks out and licks my knee.

I jump back from him in shock. "Gross!"

I catch Will laughing from the other side of the fire.

"Off you go, Roscoe." Nathan waves his hand, and the dog runs away again.

Now, everyone in the camp wants to meet me. They look at me with friendly eyes. Not the mistrust they had when I was in my hazsuit. They shake my hand and touch my shoulder in greeting. I feel more exposed than ever.

But again, I'm reminded of Colombia, where I was part of a family that was always hugging, kissing, and holding hands. Everyone was always smiling and laughing. But since arriving in Texas, I have been conditioned to keep my distance from people to avoid potential community transmissions in case of breakouts. Nobody touches each other. We don't shake hands. There might have been the accidental bump in the street or in line for medications, but it always brought a shock.

Until this week, the only people I had physical contact with were street fighters like Liam. But we knew we were going to make physical contact, it was never accidental, and we sanitized ourselves before and after every fight. I haven't seen a single bottle of hand sanitizer since I arrived at the Terrene Folk's camp.

I shake some more people's hands, trying to suppress the urge to pull away. I have to remind myself of how good it felt in Colombia, where I could hug my parents and cousins, not feeling like I was doing something wrong, something dirty.

I wonder if Sebastian even remembers what it was like in Colombia? Does he remember what it was like to be cuddled by our *padre y madre?* How warm it was within their arms? The happy life we had there with our whole *familia.* He must be so lonely. He's lost everyone, even me.

A continuous stream of people, their faces lit by the fire, appear in front of me, their hands outstretched. There's no hesitation. They reach straight for my hand. They've never learned to pull away from other people's bodies in fear. But they see my hesitation, so they smile encouragingly as I take their hands. Although I wish I could stop, and I long to wash my hands, I continue to subject myself to their touch, because I see their acceptance, their welcome. And I like it.

"Welcome back, Martina," says George, the one man who had spoken to me on my last visit. He holds out his hand and I take it. His grip is strong.

"It must seem pretty strange out here after living your whole life in the bubble cities," George says, his eyes soft and kind. "If you ever need anything, like the juiciest bit of meat, I can be bribed." He winks at me, chuckling.

George stays to chat about the nomad life for a while. Nathan joins in on the conversation. George tells me how they've been traveling for two months and have scavenged a variety of items in the Old City ruins, from materials and metals, to buttons and electronics, all things that can be used back at the Terrene reservation when they return.

Suddenly, George's face screws up, bunching together tightly, his eyes clasped shut. He turns his head away at the last moment and lets out a sneeze.

I shriek. It's involuntary, and so are the two steps backward that I take. My eyes remain on George as he takes out a handkerchief and wipes his nose. He regains his composure and turns back to Nathan as if nothing happened.

"Oh my god." My voice is high-pitched. "Are you sick?"

Nathan and George exchange confused looks, as if I spoke an unfamiliar language.

"Are you sick?" I repeat more firmly.

"It was just a sneeze." Nathan says. "Surely you've sneezed before?"

"Of course I have," I snap. "But people wear masks in the city, and we have quarantine procedures to make sure no one is sick." If we were in the bubble city, all of us would already be heading to the med-bay to get checked out. I glance around, as if a med-bay is magically going to appear.

Nathan tries to pat my shoulder in comfort, but I flinch away. I don't want to be touched. They could *all* be contagious. Oh god. They've all been touching me. I could be infected. What am I going to do? The disease might be spreading through my system as we speak. Already wreaking havoc on my organs, terrorizing my flesh, infecting every cell.

I back away further. I want to run away from them, but the only place to go is back into the desert. Alone.

I'm going to die.

"It's okay, Martina," George says, his eyes big with concern. "It was just a sneeze, it doesn't mean I'm sick. Perhaps it's just hay-fever or a simple cold."

Although his tone is comforting, his words are not. Hay-*fever! Cold!*

I've heard about diseases that give you both fevers and chills. What sort of disease has he given to me? I look around at the crowd, searching for other signs of sickness I might have missed before. But everyone seems fine, smiling and chatting with one another. No one is the least bit concerned that George just sneezed.

Nathan erupts in laughter; it's a loud guffaw, the kind that people turn around to see what is so funny. "Do you think you're going to get sick, Martina? Just from a little sneeze?"

People are looking at me. My cheeks flare. I cross my arms, partly in anger, but also for protection. I don't want anyone else touching me. I glare at Nathan and the stupid smirk on his face.

"I can't believe she thinks she'll get sick." Nathan is still laughing.

"Enough of that," Mother says, joining us. She keeps a few feet away from me, and for that, I am grateful. "Of course she thinks she'll get sick. With the life she's had, that is normal. Show a bit of compassion, Nathan."

Nathan blushes, hanging his head at being scolded like a child. Mother waves him away with a frown. "Go get the girl some food."

He rushes away without another glance at me.

Mother says something quietly to George. I don't hear what she says, but when she's done, George nods and also disappears. Mother turns her attention back to me.

"I apologize for their behavior, Martina," she says. "It's hard for them to understand what you've been through; living in the bubble cities, and then being exiled to a world you've been taught is poisonous."

I brush the hair from my eyes with a shaky hand. "Am I going to get sick?"

"Hopefully not," she says. "If it's hay-fever, then you can't catch that. It's not contagious. It's caused by an allergic reaction to something in the air, like pollen or dust, as well as other things. George is renowned for allergies, so it's likely only that. If it's a cold, that is a kind of virus."

My breath catches.

"I know it sounds scary," Mother continues, "but usually it's just a bit of an inconvenience. George might feel unwell with a runny nose, a cough, and a few more sneezes, but he'll recover in a week or two."

I frown, still not sure if I'll be safe.

"Let's hope it's not a cold," Mother says. "Because your body hasn't developed a resistance to such a virus, it might be a little worse for you." She glances at the ground and takes a breath before looking me in the eye. "I must be honest with you, Martina. There is a risk to you. I have seen people from the bubble cities die from a simple cold. A virus that is nothing more than an inconvenience to those within the community could be fatal to you because you've had no exposure. Keeping you safe and sheltered throughout your life may actually cause you harm out here."

"What?" My heart is pounding in my ears and I can barely make out her words. It's hard to make sense of what she's saying. I don't understand how it can be deadly for me, but not for

George. How can he be so nonchalant about such a virus if it has the capability of killing someone?

"Unfortunately, a cold is so common that you were bound to come across it at some stage out here." She shakes her head sadly. "But whether you catch it from George or from someone else later, I promise we'll do everything in our power to help you through it." Just like her words, her eyes swear to me that she will help. She watches me intently as her words sink in. *This* is what I was afraid of. This is why Sebastian can't come live outside.

My heart shatters. The brief moment of hope I had, is spent. Gone. Whisked away with a sneeze.

I can't entertain the hope of bringing him out here. As much as the lifestyle is appealing, I cannot risk his life.

I sit down on a log, too deflated for my legs to hold me up.

Mother steps away quietly, leaving me with my thoughts. I can't return to the bubble city, and Sebastian can't live in the desert. Is this our life now? Sebastian struggling to survive in the city, and me hoping not to die out here. Both of us worrying about the other with nothing we can do about it.

Will interrupts my worrying, standing in front of me with a steaming bowl. His eyes are wide with concern. He reminds me so much of Sebastian it makes my heart ache even more. "Here," he says, holding the bowl out to me.

I hesitate to take it. It could be contaminated. But the delicious aroma of the food wafts under my nose, and instantly, my mouth waters and my stomach does another loud rumble. Will grins when he hears it and pushes the bowl further toward me.

I resign to my hungry stomach and take the bowl, along with a spoon. It's filled to the brim with meat, a thick sauce, and a variety of colorful vegetables that I've never seen or eaten before. I take a mouthful.

My mouth explodes with flavor. The meat is juicy and sweet, the vegetables are firm but cooked through, and the sauce is seasoned with an array of spices I struggle to identify. Even the vegetables have more flavor than I could ever imagine.

"Is this what your food always tastes like?" I ask Will around the mouthful.

He nods. "It's good then?"

I nod enthusiastically and shovel another spoonful into my mouth. For a moment, all my problems fade away while the flavor takes over, like a symphony on my tongue.

My stomach is full before I'm even halfway through the bowl, but I'm reluctant to stop eating. I manage another few spoonfuls, but then I'm done. I'll explode if I eat any more. My stomach feels heavy and bloated. But satisfied in a way it hasn't been for a very long time.

Will sits beside me eating his own meal. "Are you finished?" he asks.

I nod, unable to speak a word. He takes my bowl and pours the content into his own bowl, then happily continues eating. I stare at the simpleness of his action. He's not bothered by germs, and he's quite content eating until his stomach bursts. I can't help but see Sebastian in him. And I imagine Sebastian beside me, even if it is impossible.

Twenty-One

I SPEND THE NEXT few days helping the Terrene Folk, busying myself as much as possible to keep my mind off other things. And although I learn a lot, it doesn't work. My mind keeps returning to Sebastian. I constantly find myself staring at the comms unit, wishing it would ring, that I will hear Persephone's voice, and find out Sebastian is okay. But the screen remains blank, mocking me.

Nathan and Will teach me about the life of a nomad. They show me how to care for the horses, feeding them, brushing them, making sure they're healthy. They show me the food stores, how to prepare the food for dinner, and even how to cook it. In the back of a truck, kept in the dark, are rations of non-perishable foods, like rice, oats, dried fruits and vegetables, and smoked meat. I learn that after traveling for two months, these stores are running low. However, the Terrene subsidize their diet with food they find on their travels. They are expert hunters and often track and kill buffalo. I'm amazed the beasts still exist.

Leaving the camp for a day and traveling further into the desert, they teach me how to find water and food. The desert is so beautiful. It stretches out to the horizon in hues of red, yellow, and orange, with patches of green shrubs and long shadows caused by hills and mounds.

Mother Jessica comes along for the day trip; she is known as the most talented water scout. And we return to the camp with plenty of spoils, from large flasks of water to edible cacti. The cacti leaves are like wide flat pads with lots of little spikes on them, and occasionally flowers and fruit.

"Here, try the fruit." Nathan peels it, handing it over with the juices dripping down his fingers.

I take the fruit tentatively, doubtful that I'll like the strange plant, but I bite into it anyway. My eyes widen in delight. The fruit is quite delicious, even though the flavor is mild.

Nathan grins at my reaction. He takes a bite of one himself and licks the juices from his lips, his eyes not leaving mine.

I look away, my heart pounding hard in my chest.

I awake to the sound of boots running outside my tent. My head feels heavy, groggy, and it takes too long to make any sense of what's happening.

I hear someone shouting commands from across the camp. Is it Mother Jessica? I can't be sure; my ears feel like they're stuffed with cotton.

Another pair of boots rush past.

I drag myself from the bedroll. Fumbling in the darkness, it takes a moment to find the entrance of the tent and unzip it. It's hard to focus on anything, but eventually I make out some silhouettes rushing around the camp.

Someone crashes into me but keeps on running. "Come on!" They yell over their shoulder. "What?" I say, steadying myself. But it's hard; my head is swimming.

Why is it taking me so long to wake up?

I stumble away from my tent in the direction the person ran. I don't know where I'm going, but there must be someone who can tell me what's going on. I weave around the tents, dodging hazards that are barely perceptible in the dark.

Roscoe bounds in front of me. I swerve to avoid stepping on him, but my foot catches on something, and then I'm falling face first.

Hands grab me around the waist before I hit the ground.

Nathan's face is close to mine. His eyes look over me, his brow furrowed. "Martina? Are you okay?"

I shake my head. "What's going on?" I find my feet and he relaxes his grip, but one hand remains on my shoulder, keeping me steady.

"Your friends are here." Nathan's expression changes from concern to anger.

"My friends?" My heart does a leap. Does he mean Persephone?

"The guards," Will says, appearing next to me. "They're heading this way."

My eyes flick to all corners of the camp, looking for guards. I almost trip again as I frantically spin round, searching for them.

Nathan steadies me. He peers closely at me. "Are you alright?"

I open my mouth, but I'm interrupted by a shout from across the camp. "They're here!"

There's people everywhere, scurrying around, pushing up against me as they hurry past. The three of us hurry along too. The movement helps my head to clear, and I start to make sense of the situation.

The guards are here. They have stopped searching for me in the Old City and have followed me here to the Terrene camp. I've put everyone in danger.

Shaking my head, the haze of sleep dissipates. I don't have time to linger. I follow Nathan and Will into the flurry of people.

There is a method to the surrounding madness. People are running in two directions. One group is going east, bringing the children with them. The other group is heading south, toward the bubble city. The latter carry weapons; guns, knives, and even shovels.

I know which group I need to be in.

I search the area for a weapon. The tent poles are too lightweight; they won't do any damage. The logs from around the fire are too heavy for me to wield. I settle on a sturdy looking cooking pot. It'll do until I find something better.

I push Will and Nathan. "Go!" I cry. "Go east! Keep safe."

I ignore their shocked and affronted looks, collecting up the pot and heading toward the city. I'm no longer wobbling as I navigate between the tents. Every cell in my body is focused on what lies ahead.

Half of the Terrene Folk stand in front of me. Their silhouettes stand tall in defensive stances, ready for the fight. The moon reflects off the blades, barrels, and handles they hold. Beyond them stands dozens of figures in white hazsuits. The guards. My blood turns cold despite the humidity.

The guards move slowly toward the camp. They're also carrying weapons. But it isn't the riffraff of weapons we have; these are city-issued pistols and stun batons.

I look at my pathetic steel pot ... and grip the handle tighter.

There's a commotion beside me. I spin to see Nathan charging out from between the tents.

"What are you doing?" We both ask at the same time.

For once, he doesn't shrug. Instead, he looks at the pot in my grip and raises his eyebrows. He's holding a shovel in one hand and a rifle in the other. "Here!" He passes me the shovel.

I stare at it. "Why don't I get the rifle?"

"Do you know how to shoot?"

I drop the pot and take the shovel.

Together, we face our enemy.

A shot fires. I don't know who shot it, or if it hits anyone, but it spurs everyone into action. The Terrene rush forward—me with them.

I raise the shovel, ready to bring it down on someone's head. To my right, Nathan raises his rifle. To my left, someone—I can't tell who in the dark—raises a thick steel pipe. And the guards raise their pistols and stun batons.

More shots are fired. I see a flash of light as a bullet leaves the barrel of a gun. There's a shriek from a camper when they're hit.

My heart beats harder. I want to run away, but I stand my ground.

A guard in front of me prepares to shoot, but Nathan already has his rifle pointed. His body jolts with the recoil when he pulls the trigger. The guard's visor smashes and he goes flying backward.

Bile rises in my throat. Is he dead? But there's no time to think about it.

I reach the line of guards.

A baton swings toward my head. It's almost invisible except for the glowing electric blue light at its tip.

I block it with my shovel. The baton hits the spade, lighting the steel face with blue sparks. It travels down the shaft, but the rubber handle prevents the electricity from reaching my fingers.

The guard comes at me again, but I block him once more. His face is barely visible through his visor, the blue light reflects off the glass, but through the blue hue, his teeth are clenched in determination. I grit my own teeth.

All those hours of training with Liam are put to use. And after all the years of manual labor, I'm stronger than I look. So when I bring my shovel backward and then swing it at the guard's head, it doesn't matter that he's wearing a helmet. His head is flung sideways, and he stumbles back.

I move forward quickly and swing again. The visor cracks. His eyes are no longer in focus. I swing one more time and he stumbles to the ground.

I snatch up his baton, spin around, and use it immediately on the guard grappling with Nathan. The guard's body convulses and then crumbles in a heap.

Nathan's eyes snap to mine. "Wow," he mouths, then rejoins the fray.

Immediately, another guard jumps on Nathan's back and starts choking him. I hesitate; I don't know if the baton's electricity will affect Nathan if I try to stun the guard. But Nathan is choking.

I drop the baton and collect my shovel again. Holding it like a spear, I stab the guard's visor with the spade end. The guard's fingers go slack, and Nathan spins around, aiming his rifle as he does.

He pulls the trigger. The guard falls. Blood darkens the white hazsuit. I'm unable to look away as the guard dies.

The moment I take to process the guard's death comes at a price. Nathan is torn away from me, engaged in a different battle, and another guard takes his place. I see her face, lit up by the stun baton she holds, her eyes furious.

But it's nothing to my fury. I charge at her, the shovel held high in both hands, and I swing. I bring the blade of the shovel down, slicing it through the night air, and lodge it in her throat. It pierces straight through her suit and into her flesh.

She gurgles, her knees buckling. She tilts backward until her back slams into the ground, sending a dust cloud up into the air. I cough. As the dust settles again, I see her body, laying in the moonlight, with the shovel still lodged in her neck.

I convulse, my chest heaving. I turn away, my dinner threatening to rise up my throat.

I don't have time for this. I need to get a grip and keep going. Save this for another time.

I'm on all fours, choking on dirt, disturbed by the skirmish around me. My eyes land on the blank stare of a Terrene woman lying on the ground nearby. Blood drips from a gash across her cheek, but she makes no move to staunch the flow. Of course she can't. She's dead. She's dead because of me. The guards followed me to the Terrene camp. If I hadn't come ...

I pull myself to my feet. I need to set this right.

I'm facing the camp. Several tents are on fire. People are running around, attempting to extinguish the flames. Mother Jessica is among them. She hastens between the fires, throwing sand from the desert floor up onto the blaze, suffocating them.

I spot a white figure in the camp. Close to Mother. I collect the stun baton from the dust and sprint toward her. The guard attacks before I'm halfway there.

But Mother is no wilting flower. She doesn't go down easily.

She sidesteps the guard and grabs hold of their baton as it swings her way. She pushes the electrical end away from her. It's a battle of strength. Mother is strong, but the guard is stronger; the baton inches closer and closer.

The guard is so intent on Mother that I go unnoticed. I forget to use the stunner, and instead, punch the guard in the ribs.

The guard lets go of Mother and turns to me. His face is lit up by the fires; bushy eyebrows and a bulbous nose. I hesitate. If I have to kill him, I'd rather not look him in the eyes while doing it. But maybe it won't come to death this time. All I have is a baton.

He lunges, his baton outstretched. It comes close enough to my head that I hear the electricity crackling. But I sidestep just in time.

I swing my baton and he blocks it easily with his own. I pull my hand away before he can zap my fingers.

From the corner of my eye, I see Mother fighting another guard.

I'm on my own.

My opponent paces, watching my movements, and I step in time with him, watching him just as carefully. We circle each other. Just as if we were fighting in The Nix.

He lunges. I step back, narrowly avoiding his hit, and aim my baton at his outstretched hand. The baton buzzes with power, but it has no effect on his gloved hand.

The guard laughs.

The gloves are made of rubber and the electricity won't conduct through them. But the rest of the hazsuit is made from a mix of synthetic materials. I need just one good hit, like the first guard I zapped, and this jerk will go down.

I'm much smaller than him. But much nimbler without a bulky hazsuit. And his hazsuit isn't going to save him. I take a few paces back as I plan my approach. And wait for him to lunge again.

He doesn't make me wait long.

I duck his outstretched hand, spring off my toes, and strike my baton on his chest. He immediately breaks into tremors. The force of my leap creates an unstoppable momentum and my body slams into his. I get a residual shock off his body, but it's not strong enough to knock me out, just enough to set my teeth chattering and make my legs wobble.

I'm flat on top of the unconscious man. I look up. Another guard races toward me. My limbs are jelly. I can't get up quick enough. The white hazsuit is almost upon me.

Twenty-Two

A VEHICLE COMES CRASHING out of the camp. It powers into the attacking guard and flattens them under its tires.

My breath catches.

"You're welcome!" Will calls from the driver's window.

My mouth hangs open. Little Will is driving one of the community's trucks, and he just crushed a bubble city guard. Like it was nothing.

He hangs out the window. His mouth raises at the corners, but it's hard to tell if it's a smile or a grimace.

He waves at me. "Get in the truck!"

I push off from the guard I stunned, my legs still wobbly, and stumble toward the truck. I haul myself into the passenger seat. Will revs the engine as soon as I'm seated. The back wheels go up and then clunk back to the dirt as they roll over the body. I wince, imagining the crunching of bones.

Will takes a deep breath, then sets his sights on the next guard to crush. He floors the accelerator and charges toward the fighting. He honks the horn.

People scatter in the beams of the headlights.

Will directs the truck toward the fleeing guards. Their white-booted feet kicking dirt up into the light as they run. Then the truck is on them. Their feet leave the ground entirely as the truck shudders, and their bodies fly over the windshield. Will hits one, two, three, guards. His face is hard with concentration and determination. He has no mercy.

I shudder. He's only thirteen or fourteen, but he's made of stronger stuff than me.

As much as I want to retch, I can't deny Will's actions are effective. The guards are on the run. They're racing away from our camp, stumbling over each other, tripping on the rocky ground, in order to escape Will's wrath.

Across the desert, another truck is doing the same.

Will continues chasing the guards, but soon, they scatter in different directions, disappearing into the darkness, white suits fading to gray then to black the further they run. Will turns the truck back toward the camp. We can't chase what we can't see.

I spot a ghost running to my right.

"There's one," I say, pointing the guard out.

Will swerves, cutting off their escape. The guard sees us bearing down on him. He raises his pistol and shoots. I duck my head, hiding under my arms. The bullets hit the windscreen, shattering the glass.

Will yelps.

I scream and whip my head up to look at him. Blood springs up across his cheek. His eyes flick to me. He's still alive.

While our eyes are locked, I feel the unmistakable thump of the guard falling victim to Will's truck. The tires ride over the obstruction.

Will's eyes fill with tears.

I lay my hand on his arm, but he shakes me off. His fingers grip the steering wheel even tighter as he drives us back to camp.

The guards have all dissolved into the night. There's no more to run down.

Mother rushes to the truck as soon as Will parks it. She wrenches the door open and pulls him from his seat. He sobs into her shoulder the moment he's in her arms.

Nathan comes forward. He's limping, but otherwise looks whole. His arms encircle Will and Mother, and he plants a kiss on Will's head.

I exit the truck and stand alone, watching the three clutch each other. My body feels so heavy that my legs can barely hold me up. I wish Sebastian was here. He'd pull me into an embrace and never let go. He'd make sure I didn't fall, didn't stumble. But I'm glad he's not here. I never want him to go through something like this.

I move away, giving the trio some privacy. But as I step, my legs crumble. My head hits the ground.

There's a muffled shout, like someone speaking through a pillow, and then everything fades.

Twenty-Three

I FEEL LIKE I'VE been sitting in a boiling pot. Sweat runs off me like little rivers and pools on the sheets, soaking them. My head aches with a constant thrum, similar to when I was dehydrated, but different, because I'm full of water this time. My head swims in it. My nose feels full of it; thick clogging water. It's hard to breathe.

My throat burns even hotter than my skin. I try to swallow, but a lump at the back causes searing pain.

"She's awake."

I wince. Nathan's whisper sounds like a shout. He presses a wet towel to my forehead. It's cool and soothing. The pressure pushes away the pain. But it doesn't last. The towel turns hot too quickly, and the pressure on my brain moves, causing even more pain.

I'm lying on my back. My body is heavy, sinking into the ground as if a weight pushes me down. I've never felt anything like this. I feel betrayed by every element—the searing heat, the sweltering water, the acrid air, the unyielding earth.

"What's happening?" My voice is a hoarse whisper, like I've aged a hundred years. "What ...?" I choke on the words. In an effort to dislodge whatever is in my throat, I cough. And cough. I can't stop, desperately wheezing in air between each cough. I'm barely getting enough air. I feel like I'm going to choke to death.

The coughing eventually subsides, and I'm spent. My body even more racked than before. I let my body relax as much as it can.

"Here, drink this." Mother is here, and she hands something to Nathan. My eyes are blurry and I can't quite see what it is. Whatever it is, I don't take it. I can't. My arms can barely move.

I just want the world to end. Let me float away from this hell.

I open my eyes; I don't remember closing them. Nathan is close, hovering over me. He's close enough to kiss. But he doesn't kiss me. He gently pours something between my lips. A warm liquid filled with herbs and spices. I expect the warm liquid to cause more pain to my throat, to burn it further, but somehow, it's soothing. I swallow carefully, trying not to anger the lump there. The liquid swirls around and down, giving me a slight relief.

I focus on breathing. Resentful and thankful of every breath. I can't get air through my waterlogged nose, so I open my mouth and let the air rage and blaze down to my lungs. It comes back out even hotter than when it went in and scorches my lips.

This is what it must have been like for Mamá when she died. Heat, pain, and discomfort.

I let my muscles turn to jelly, not trying to make them into the whole limbs and forms of a human being. And I lay back, not trying to make sense of anything, just waiting for death.

Now the sky is dark. How long has it been? Hours? Days? It feels like I've been this way for weeks. Kept alive by the soothing tonic dribbled down my throat by Mother and Nathan. Prolonging death. I wish they would let me die. Even the thought of Sebastian doesn't make me want to live. I'd be no use to him like this.

Nathan's face comes into view. His eyes wide with concern.

I narrow my own. I've had enough of this illness. I want no more of his medicine.

He doesn't force it, and then he's gone.

A cool breeze sends shivers over my skin, waking me up. It's dark outside still. Still? Is it the same night? It bothers me that I don't know what day it is, or how long I've been like this. I feel like I've aged a year.

My head is still stuffy, but the headache has subsided. I blink the crust from my eyes and take stock of my body.

I still feel weak, but no longer as if my muscles are made of rubber. My throat is still raw, but the lump has shrunk, only causing a minor discomfort. My nose has cleared so I can finally breathe through it again. I breathe in deeply. I never realized how good it is to breathe through my nostrils.

I stretch out my limbs as far as they can go. It feels good to move, but the effort quickly exhausts me. When I pull my arms and legs back in, I shift my back and curl onto my side. My body almost sings with the pleasure of a change in position. A murmur of delight escapes my lips.

"Welcome back to the living," Nathan says.

I turn my head to look at him. There's a dull glow from a torch in the tent; I'm pleased it doesn't hurt my head. Nathan looks at me with those red speckled eyes. Maybe I should feel embarrassed. He's seen me at my worst, sick and wishing to die. But all I feel is grateful.

"Was I dead?" I ask, my voice croaky.

"Almost," he says. He moves from his seat across the tent, standing quickly and heading for the opening. "I'll get Mother. She'll want to know you're awake." He leaves without another glance at me.

I gaze up at the roof of the tent. I can see the seams where the material is sewn together. A bit like me. I was falling apart, but somehow, they sewed me back together.

My mind is beginning to clear, from sleep and illness, and my thoughts turn directly to Sebastian. How long has it been since I saw him? I have no idea how long I've been ill. Did the comms unit ring while I was out of it? My heart aches at the thought. I might have missed my chance to speak to Sebastian. And Persephone.

Mother enters the tent, looking pleased with herself. She hooks her thumbs into her jeans and looks down on me with a satisfied smile.

"Now that's what I like to see." Mother winks. "A bit of color in your cheeks."

My lips twitch in the slightest smile.

She puts a hand on my forehead. "I think you're over the worst of it, kiddo." Her smile widens. "Congratulations. You've just survived your first cold."

Twenty-Four

THE COUGH LINGERS FOR several days, but the rest of my health quickly returns. I didn't think I was going to survive, but Mother said I didn't come close to death, even if it felt like it. She said my body is strong and fought off the fever with the help of her herbal medicine.

George had also been sick, but he recovered from his cold faster than me. He visited a few times and helped to nurse me. When it was clear I would survive, he said, "I'm so sorry, Martina. I never meant to infect you. I didn't even realize I was sick when I passed it on to you."

He put his hand on my arm and I had to struggle not to flinch away, reminding myself that he was no longer sick.

"It's okay." I patted his hand, trying not to seem repulsed.

After the attack, the community moved the camp, carrying my unconscious body along with them in the back of a truck. Now they are further east, but still in the vicinity of the bubble city. I'm not sure why they have stayed so close. When I asked Mother, she said, "You just worry about recovering. We'll keep you safe."

When I think of the attack on the camp, I feel sick again; my stomach churns and I shake uncontrollably. The guards' faces flash through my mind and I blink them away, trying to shut out the images. But I can't forget that I've killed someone—a guard, a person who someone will miss.

I take deep breaths, reminding myself that I'm safe for now. I replay Mother's words, "We'll keep you safe," and hope they're true.

I can't keep out the image of the Terrene woman lying dead in the dirt. She's dead because of me. I don't know why the Terrene Folk don't hate me. But they still treat me with kindness, making me feel part of their community.

Now that I'm feeling better, I can help around the camp again. I'm glad to give back to the community, and I take pleasure in doing something, anything. It feels like a lot of time has been wasted because I've never spent so long in bed. I was sick for nine whole days. Who knows what's happened to Sebastian or Persephone in that time? Nathan and Will kept watch over my comms unit, but they say it never rang. I worry about what that means.

The campers bring me things to do that aren't too taxing, like washing dishes and stitching up tents or clothes, repairing them like I did for George the first time I was in the camp.

"Good morning, Martina," Will calls, catching me on the way back from the latrine. His signature smile is back, lighting up his face despite the gash across his left cheek where the bullet grazed him. Mother had stitched it up, but he's going to have a scar for the rest of his life.

"It makes me look tough," he told me when I first saw it.

My stomach grows heavy with guilt, even now, days later. I shouldn't have let him drive that truck. I should have stopped him as soon as I realized he was driving. Or I should have turned the wheel, or covered Will, or pulled his head down, instead of just ducking my own. He could easily have been killed if the guard had better aim.

Every time I look at Will, I see Sebastian's face punctured with a bullet. I shake my head, trying to clear it of such morbid thoughts.

I wave back at Will, forcing a smile. He's got Roscoe in tow, who immediately runs and jumps up on me. I give him a scratch behind the ears in greeting.

"Do you want to fetch cacti with me?" Will asks.

"Sure," I say. "Let me just grab my comms unit. It's on charge. I'll meet you at the horses."

I jog to the center of camp where it's connected to a solar charging station. It's rare I leave it unattended, but it needed to charge, and I needed the toilet. I check the face, but no calls were made. Still.

Every time I look at the comms screen, a small hope blooms in me, just to be squashed seconds later when I see the blank screen. My worries for Sebastian continue to grow.

Now that I have the luxury of charging the comms unit, I use it to check the news for any sightings of Sebastian or Persephone. But there has been no mention of them. Further deaths from the Azutine virus have been reported, as well as increased restrictions in The Nix, confirming that Dr. Lederman's plans are being carried out. More will continue to die unless I do something about it. I don't know what has happened to Persephone or the evidence we had. I need to figure out another way to get the truth out there.

I ponder my options on my way to the horses, but I stop short when I see Nathan leaning against the pole they're tied to.

Ever since my fever broke, I have been avoiding Nathan. I let his little brother get shot. Every time I see him, I can't meet his eyes. I'm afraid of what I'll see. But I can't go on avoiding him. So I approach him, looking at the ground.

"What are you doing here?" I ask.

"What are *you* doing here?" he says.

I look up and see him smirking. I duck my head again, watching my feet as they twist in the dirt. "Will asked me to come along."

"Yeah, he asked me too." Nathan shrugs and starts saddling his horse; his muscular arms lift the saddle effortlessly.

I consider backing out of the trip, going back to my tent, and hiding from everyone. But I can't stand the thought of being bored any longer. And I need to face Nathan at some stage.

"Ready to go?" Will asks. He's on his horse, waiting for the two of us to mount.

Nathan glances at me but quickly looks away. I drop my eyes as well, pretending to be busy with Jerry's saddle, while out of the corner of my eye, I watch Nathan mount his horse in one graceful movement.

I'm not quite as graceful getting up on Jerry, but I'm getting better at it and manage the mount on the first try. I sit on top, grinning despite myself.

"Heeya." Nathan gives his horse a squeeze with his legs and it takes off at a canter. Will and I spur our horses into movement too, following behind.

We spend the day collecting cacti and searching for other edible plants and wildlife. The tribe sometimes eats reptiles, like the steel-skinned creature I saw in the old ruins, so we also look out for them. We search for water, too. It's a precious commodity out in the desert, so no matter what the purpose of a trip is, it's always worth looking for water.

I keep my distance from Nathan, often placing Will between the two of us. Occasionally, I catch him looking at me, but his gaze drops quickly, probably thinking about how much he hates me for letting Will get hurt.

The three of us work quietly, harvesting prickly pear from a large cacti bush. We wear thick gloves to protect us from the plant's spikes and use knives to cut the fruit away from the pads.

We take a lot of the pads, too, storing them in hessian sacks to take back to camp to cook into soups and stews.

Will and I find ourselves working a little further away from Nathan, so I take the opportunity to talk to him without Nathan hearing.

When I look at Will's face and see the scar on his cheek, guilt turns my limbs heavy.

"Will ..." I hesitate. "I'm sorry I couldn't protect you." My voice is barely a whisper.

"I can protect myself," he says, smiling. "I saved you, didn't I?"

The image of the guard under the wheels of Will's truck makes me shudder.

"You sure did." I smile weakly. "Thank you, by the way."

He shrugs and quickly looks away, back at the cacti he's cutting. He puts on a brave façade, but I can see the killing affects him too.

"Will? Do you know why the Terrene Folk are staying close to Neustin? After the attack, I thought they would leave this area." It doesn't make sense. They know PMC is aware of them now, watching them, so why not run? No one in the camp will tell me why, not George, and certainly not Mother.

"I thought you'd want to be close," Will says. "You know, to be near your brother?"

"Of course, I do. I'm glad we're still nearby, but I'm sure Sebastian and I aren't the reasons you've stayed around."

"They don't tell me anything." Will shrugs, his eyes still averted.

"You suspect something, at least?"

Will's mouth is a firm line as he cuts the pads from the cacti. I frown. I hoped that Will would tell me something, but he's brushing me off too.

"And how did they get Dr. Marshall's PIN?" I persist. "And what's the purpose? Have they been going inside the city?"

Will lowers his head. His long hair falls in front of his face, so I can't read his expression. But I glimpse something in Will's eyes before they disappear behind his hair. Guilt? Pride? I can't be sure.

I try to change direction with my questions. "Do you think they can help me get the evidence out?" I allow a little of my desperation to seep into my tone. Once the Terrene have done whatever they're here to do, they'll leave, and I'll go with them. I can't survive out here on my own, I know that now, as much as I hate to admit that I need them. This is my last chance to do something that might help Sebastian.

Will nods. "They might." He's still tight-lipped, but it's something. After a moment, he says, "You should speak to Mother Jessica about it." He nods decisively. Then he moves away to a different bush to collect more fruit.

What is the community hiding? I'm convinced there is something more going on and they're keeping it from me. Are they using PINs to go inside Neustin? But to what end? Maybe they're stealing from the city. I wonder what the bubble cities have that they don't. Medicine? But the Terrene don't take meds every day like we do in the bubbles. Maybe there are different medicines they still need. That makes some kind of sense. But why wouldn't they just tell me that?

"Will is loading up the horses," Nathan says, "so let's finish this bag and then head back."

I was too busy pondering to notice Nathan until it was too late. Now I can't avoid him without being rude. He sets to work beside me. I continue to work without speaking.

Nathan breaks the silence. "I feel like you're avoiding me, bubble girl?" His voice is quiet enough that Will won't hear it where he's working.

"What? No." I shrug, then curse myself for shrugging exactly the way he does.

"Oh, okay then." He nods, smirking. It's obvious he doesn't believe me.

I keep my hands busy, cutting at the stems of the pads to release them from the rest of the bush and placing them into the hessian bag.

"Is it because I laughed at you when George sneezed and then you got sick?" Nathan asks in a rush. "Because I'm really sorry about that. It was stupid of me, and you had a right to be scared."

I look up in shock. I hadn't expected an apology from him. "No, no it's not that," I stammer. How do I explain that he hasn't done anything wrong? That it's me that needs to apologize to *him* for getting his brother shot?

I stare at him, my mouth gaping. He waits patiently for me to continue, but his gaze makes it even harder for me to put my feelings into words. I try to grasp at any of the thoughts speeding through my mind—his rich brown eyes, Persephone's lips, Will's scar, the community's secrets, Sebastian. Like a life raft, I grab onto the thought of Sebastian.

"I'm just missing my brother," I say, and it's not a lie. I miss him with every beat of my heart and it makes everything else harder to bear. If I knew Sebastian was safe, it wouldn't matter that I was out here in the desert and about to leave Neustin, possibly forever. Suddenly, all the emotions I've been suppressing, all the fears and sadness I've ignored, come rushing to the surface.

I'm shocked when a tear rolls down my cheek. I quickly brush it away with my forearm, mortified that I'm now crying in front of Nathan, after everything else.

"I understand." His eyes are soft with pity.

¡*Puta vida*! I can't believe how pathetic I am, crying like a fool. But the tears won't stop.

"You don't understand at all," I snap. "I'm losing my brother, and I don't know if he's going to be okay without me. You've still got your brother; you have no idea how I feel." I sink to the ground. I tear off my gloves and my hands fly to my face, wishing I could stop the tears, but my body racks with sobs instead.

"I do understand, Martina." Nathan places a hand on my back, but I shrug it off. My body crumbles further, bunching myself up as if that will protect me from the pain I'm feeling.

Sebastian is alone. Abandoned. Helpless. And I'm out here collecting cacti, doing nothing about it.

"Hey, are you guys ready?" Will calls from where our horses are waiting.

My breath catches. I hope Will doesn't come over and see me falling apart; it's bad enough Nathan is a witness.

"Almost," Nathan calls back. "Why don't you go on without us? We'll be along soon."

"Sure," Will says. I don't look up, but after a moment, I hear the hooves of his horse trotting away from us.

Nathan says nothing for a while. He sits patiently beside me, just letting me sob. I wipe at my eyes, willing myself to stop crying. Slowly, I do.

After a few minutes, Nathan says, "It may not seem it, but I *do* know how you feel."

"How could you?" I ask. "You see Will every day."

"Because I once had a little sister too."

I blink at him through my tears.

"Her name was Tahnee." His voice is grave and thick with sadness. "She was only six years old when she died."

"How?"

He takes a shaky breath. "My family were living on the outskirts of the reservation. There's good farming there, but it's very open. Not a lot of protection. The village was miles from our house, but we liked it out there. We were still part of the community, and we had our land that we tended. We were happy.

"But PMC saw the Terrene as a threat. We had survived deadly plagues and droughts and throughout all, the Terrene Folk still thrived. Until PMC came to wipe us out. We think they came from Nalbuquer. That's the closest city to the reservation, but we're not sure.

"Our house was the first to be attacked, since it was on the outskirts. We weren't even there. Well, my parents and Will and I weren't. We were all in the fields. But Tahnee had gone back to the house to fetch us some lemonade. She was so proud she was allowed to go alone; she'd never been old enough before. I remember her puffing out her chest as she waddled away." He smiles, but his eyes glisten.

"Then I saw the smoke. I didn't hesitate. I just ran. The smoke was coming from our house, and the closer I got, I realized it was on fire. There were two PMC guards in their hazsuits, watching and laughing. They didn't see me coming.

"I didn't think. I unsheathed my machete as I ran. The first one went down easily. I got him in the back. The other one was able to stun my father with his baton, and my father dropped, but my mother got the guard. She sliced him right through the throat.

"Then I heard the screams from inside the house. Tahnee was stuck in there. I tried to get her out. But the flames were out of control."

I can't keep the horror from my face.

Tears fall freely from Nathan's eyes. I reach out and hold his hand. There isn't anything else I can do.

"The roof caved in and the screaming stopped." His breath shakes. "I couldn't save her."

He falls quiet. I stare at him, not knowing what to say. There are no words that will make it better. I hear those little girl's screams, even though I wasn't there. I imagine them as Sebastian's. I try to push the thought away; it's too horrifying.

Nathan quietly sobs for a moment, and I wait for him to stop, just like he waited for me.

Eventually he says, "My family doesn't live on the farm anymore. As soon as my dad recovered, they moved closer to the village. There's more protection there. It was my mother's family's land, so it broke her to leave it, but they didn't feel safe there anymore. There wasn't enough work for me and Will without the farm, so we came out with Mother Jessica to scavenge and hunt instead."

"I'm sorry," I say. "I didn't know."

He puts his hand on top of mine and squeezes my fingers. We sit in our own thoughts for a time until eventually Nathan stands, picking up the sack of cacti. Silently, I follow him back to where our horses wait.

I stroll through the camp, looking for Mother Jessica. Now that I've decided, I won't back down. I can't wait any longer, I can't wait for Persephone's call, and I can't wait until the Terrene leave for their home. While we're still stationed nearby Neustin, I need to act. But I need help.

I stalk with purpose, past tents and campers, until I find her.

She's ringing out clothes and hanging them on a line strung between two tents.

"Can I help you, Mother?" I ask her, picking up a wet shirt.

"Thank you," she says.

As I hang the shirt on the line, I say, "I need your help, Mother Jessica."

"I wondered how long it would be until you came to me."

"So, you know what I'm going to ask?"

"I suspect."

I can't see her face; a beige towel blocks my view.

"I can't leave here without doing something to help my brother … and the other citizens of the bubble city." I keep the clothes in place with wooden pegs. "I know you care. Just like the other Terrene care. And I hope that you all will help."

"Go on." I hear from the other side of the towel.

"If we can get the evidence that I collected out to the citizens, that will have the biggest impact. I know you have access to get inside the city." I take a guess. "Dr. Marshall's was not the only PIN you've stolen."

I come out from behind the towel to face Mother Jessica. She nods in confirmation but keeps her lips pressed tight. She focuses on her work, not looking at me. I reach for another shirt.

"I know I can't go into the city again," I admit. "I'm too easily recognized. But maybe someone else can. I think they've been going in anyway." She doesn't nod this time, but a twitch in her cheek gives the truth away. "They can find out what has happened to my friend, Persephone. She has the evidence. They can help her get it out to the people."

Mother finally stops what she's doing and looks at me. Her eyes are hard. I feel like a child under her stare. I understand why everyone calls her Mother; she has a look that makes me respect her like my own Mamá.

"So, let me get this straight," she says, her hands on her hips. "You want someone to risk their lives in the hope they can find some evidence your *friend* has, then somehow—and you don't know how—get that evidence broadcast?"

"Basically, yes," I say, taking a deep breath. My heart weighs heavy asking for more help, especially after putting the Terrene in danger already, but I'm desperate. And I believe my plan will help both them and me. If PMC is exposed, they'll have bigger things to worry about than hunting the Terrene Folk.

"I hope you have a backup plan, girl?" She shakes her head and turns back to her work.

"I do, actually."
That stops her. She turns back, giving me her full attention.
"Go on," she says.
"I'll need everyone's support."

Twenty-Five

THE WHOLE TRIBE IS gathered around the fire. Most have finished eating, but a few still pick at their food. Either way, when Mother stands up, she has everyone's attention.

"Thank you for gathering tonight," she says. "I know things have been tough since the attack and we haven't had one of these since we said goodbye to those who fell."

Remembering those who died in the attack makes it even harder for me to say what I need to say. To ask of them what I have to. Although I told Mother Jessica my entire back up plan, she can't decide for the entire community. It's up to me to convince everyone to join me, despite the danger it poses them.

Although I have begun to acclimatize to the heat, my palms sweat. And my throat gets scratchy again, like my cold is returning. I cough a few times to clear it.

"I will not speak much tonight," Mother continues, "I'm going to let our young friend, Martina, speak instead. She has something to propose to you. And I hope you'll give it some serious thought. She has told me what she plans, and I believe they align with our values. Therefore, she has my support."

I release my breath. I didn't know Mother supported my idea until now.

Mother says, "We will take a vote after she has spoken."

Her support gives me strength again. I step forward, but instead of words coming out of my mouth, I cough instead. I swallow and try again.

"Thank you …" I cough. "Thank you for hearing what I have to say … You don't know me well, and … and I'm still getting to know you too … but anyway, you've been so kind accepting me into your community." Cough. "I wish I didn't need to ask this …" I look down at my hands. "I know I've already caused so much trouble for you." There's some murmuring from the crowd, but it's soft and gentle, like they're comforting me, not condemning me. I raise my head again, looking at the crowd. "But I need to ask this of you. It may put you at risk. So, I understand if you say no … but I hope you'll say yes."

I take a breath and clear my throat again.

"Dr. Lederman and PMC Life Tech have been killing people inside the bubble city. And as you know, they've killed people in this community, too." Everyone is looking at me. For a moment, I forget what I am saying under their gaze. But then I think of Sebastian. "I want to do something to stop them. I was able to gather evidence that proves beyond any doubt that PMC and Dr. Lederman have been plotting these deaths. However, I have no way of getting that evidence out to the community.

"Mother Jessica has organized someone to try to retrieve it." I nod to George, standing a short distance from the fire. He nods back. He has agreed to take on the mission, despite its perils. "That mission may fail. The evidence may be lost."

I try to gauge the reactions of the crowd, but it's impossible to tell what they're thinking.

"So, I have another plan." My voice is shaking. "We'll help distract the guards in the bubble city, and hopefully the evidence can be found … recovered. It will also help to educate people within the bubble city. Maybe they'll question what they've been told."

"What are you proposing, Martina?" someone calls from the back. I can't see their face in the shadows.

I steady myself, planting my feet wider, and focus on projecting my voice. "I want us to surround the city. My intention is for everyone inside to see that people can survive outside."

The community erupts. Calls of "No!" and "Yes!" pierce through the noise. It's hard to tell what the dominant feeling is; no one is happy, but there are a range of other emotions flittering across their faces, highlighted by the flames of the campfire. There are frowns of fear and anger and confusion, eyes wide with hope and surprise, quivering lips and mouths twisted in hatred, and heads held high in determination and defiance.

One woman pulls her child closer, wrapping her arms all the way around him. My arms feel empty without Sebastian.

Two men argue, hands gesturing wildly.

A young couple grip each other's arms, staring intently into each other's eyes as they speak quickly, nodding their heads.

My eyes land on Nathan. His eyes are dark black holes, letting no light out of them. He's not speaking to anyone; he's staring straight at me.

Then he nods.

I give him a grateful smile.

Will stands a little behind him. On his face I see hope; his smile wide and his chest puffed out.

After a time, Mother raises her hands and says, "Settle down!" As they quieten, she says, "Let's hear the plan in detail and then we can discuss and vote."

The crowd turns to me again and I share my ideas. There's some back and forth, with many raising questions and concerns. Some are worried about what to do if the guards attack or try to chase us off. I try to convince them they won't do that, not in front of the citizens of the bubble city. Besides, the plan is to be speedy in our approach, before the guards get wind of it and keep us from reaching the city.

"What about the children?" a man asks.

"We can't leave them behind," a woman called Jannine says.

"Well, we can't bring them with us!"

"If we leave them behind," George says, "there is a bigger risk the guards will attack them without the whole camp to protect them. They could use them to lure us away from the city."

"I agree," Jannine says. "PMC won't kill children that are camped right in front of the bubbles. The citizens won't stand for mass genocide."

George nods. "And the entire camp will be there to protect them if they come with us."

Eventually, it's decided the bigger risk is to leave the children at the camp where they would have less protection.

It's easy to see which way the community will vote after the long discussion. So, when Mother asks for the people to raise their hands if they agree to the idea, it's not a surprise that most people hold up their hands, including Mother, Nathan, and even little Will. God bless him.

Twenty-Six

It's almost dawn.

I'm working as efficiently as I can in the dark. The plan is to be among the ruins of the Old City before day breaks, hoping the guards won't spot us until it's too late.

I glance at the comms unit and wish for the thousandth time that I could use it to call Sebastian. I huff at the uselessness of the wish and continue with my work.

It's been two days since I addressed the tribe. Since then, we've been busy finalizing the plans and packing up camp. The tribe needed time to prepare because they knew we wouldn't be coming back to this camp. But now, the day has finally come.

When everything is packed, it feels like the Terrene Folk take a collective breath. They look at each other, smile, pat each other on the back, hug the children. I stand among them feeling the love that is their strength.

Will comes through the crowd and wraps his arms around my shoulders. He holds me so tightly that I can't move my arms, even though I try. I laugh as I struggle out of his grip, and he laughs too—a little nervously—but when I look at him, all I see is strength in his face.

"Take care," he says.

"*Y tú también, hombrecito.*"

Nathan passes us and gives me a nod. I nod back.

And then we're moving. People mount horses and climb into trucks. I climb into the cargo bed of a truck with several other campers. Will joins me, but Nathan rides alongside us on Jerry. With a bark, Roscoe leaps into our truck, curling up at Will's feet.

At this time of night, the air is at its coolest. Tonight, it's weighted with electricity. There is a nervous energy, but also a swell of excitement.

Everyone is silent as we ride, broken only by the occasional hushed voice or child's cry.

I spend the trip fiddling with my hair. Despite tying it back, my curls keep getting loosened by the wind. I brush it from my face until it gets too unruly, and then I tie it back again.

On the horizon, the sky is turning from black to a deep blue. It won't be long until the desert is streaked with light. I hope we're not far from the ruins. My back faces the direction we're traveling; I try to twist around to look without disturbing the person sitting next to me, who has somehow fallen asleep. I gawk. My veins are wired with anxiety, my eyes alert to every movement. I can't imagine being able to sleep through this journey. Even Roscoe has his eyes open, although his head rests on Will's feet.

A child sits nearby. Am I putting him in jeopardy? I hope not. I hope this helps all of us. I don't want any of the Terrene to get hurt, not for me, not again—but I can't save Sebastian without their help.

I keep glancing at the child, praying he'll be safe. Maybe I should never have suggested this plan. It could all go wrong. But I had to do it. For Sebastian. I'll do anything to keep him safe, even if it means putting the Terrene in danger, even if it means ... No. They won't die. I won't let that happen.

I send up another prayer, for the child and for Sebastian.

Across from me, Jannine also whispers a prayer as she clutches her hands together. Beside her sits a man, another child in his lap held tightly.

I glance at Will. His brow is creased with worry as he peers into the dark.

I clutch my own hands together and continue to pray.

Please keep them safe.

A slip of pink highlights the horizon just as I feel the terrain under the tires change, and the truck starts a decline. We're close.

The horses move to the front of the pack and the trucks slow to form a single line so they can travel through the ruins. The people on horses scout the way, making sure it's safe for the rest of us to follow. That's what we'd planned.

As we enter the ruins, I look up at the tallest building still standing. I can't see them, but I know our sentries sit up there, watching us. They don't signal that anything is wrong, and the convoy continues forward.

I keep my eyes peeled for any danger as the sun continues to rise and the sky begins to glow orange, now spreading over our heads. I peer into shadows, look down corridors of bricks, glance around corners, straining my ears for any sounds of danger.

A child cries and is hushed immediately.

I barely breathe.

I gauge we're over halfway through the ruins by the location of the largest building. We're going to make it.

A fire erupts with a large whoosh of wind, the same color as the burning horizon.

I drop to the floor of the cargo bed and take Will with me. It's a squeeze with all the other passengers, but we stay that way. I peer over shoulders to see the danger. A truck has exploded up ahead.

The horses at the front whiny in fear. Hoof beats slam the dirt. Engines roar as the trucks increase speed. Roscoe barks into the air.

My heart jolts. We've been discovered.

The truck accelerates so quickly past the fire that I almost miss the person burning within it, trapped in the overturned front seat. My stomach lurches. Another person has died because of me. Others escaped the blast and run alongside our vehicle. One jumps on our tailgate, hitching a ride.

I turn in my seat, no longer worried about disturbing anyone; we're all wide awake now.

Another explosion goes off, just in front of our vehicle. The truck's tires raise in the air. It lurches to the left. Then comes crashing back down on all four tires with a bone shattering *thump*. It continues striving forward. The only way out of this is to continue.

The trucks race on.

I see white hazsuits ahead. They stand on the ruins, holding guns, looking down on us. Their suits glow where the rising sun hits them.

"Keep your head down," I scream to Will, pushing him behind me.

The shooting starts. With each ping on metal, I duck my head. People scream—terror ripping from their lungs. The windshield shatters, but our vehicle keeps moving. There's a truck in front and behind us too. We're still together, but we're sitting ducks.

We can't go fast enough.

I rise to my feet, balancing on my toes like I learned when dancing salsa.

"What?" Will shouts above the fray.

"Keep down," I scream again.

And then I leap.

I time it perfectly—a little thrill runs through me with that knowledge—and I crash into one of the guards. Both of us fall backward off the wall he stood on. His body breaks my fall, cushioning the ground. He groans below me as I scramble off him, but he doesn't move. I go to leave, but then stop. I turn back to him and quickly unscrew his helmet, tearing it off his head. Let's see how he copes with that.

I jump back onto the wall, running along it toward the next guard. He doesn't see me coming.

I push him.

He falls toward the vehicles. I hear the now familiar crunch as the tires crush him. I don't have time to think about his death. His comrade sees what I did and lunges at me. I recoil. Slip. And fall from the wall, too.

My whole body shudders as my backside hits the ground. The wind is knocked from me. I'm dimly aware that the trucks are coming, tires bearing down.

Twisting into the fetal position, I squeeze my eyes closed. I wait for the tires to crush me.

They miss by inches.

Just as I think I'm out of harm's way, the guard jumps down from the wall and runs at me. I scramble away, backing up as quickly as I can, away from the guard and the other vehicles coming toward us.

I'm not fast enough.

He kicks me hard in the side. While I arch in pain, he leaps on me, pinning me to the ground. His hands wrap around my neck.

I wheeze, choking on dirt with any air that gets down my windpipe. I'm going to suffocate.

Through his visor, I see his lips curl back, his eyes glowering.

His weight holds me in place. I can't move.

Looking around for some kind of escape, I spot another guard up on the wall—pointing her gun down at the trucks. Right at

Will. The sun penetrates her visor, lighting up her face. Her gaze is steady, her jaw set. She's going to kill him.

"No!" I scream in my head, unable to get it out of my lips.

The rush of adrenaline gives me more clarity. I remember Liam teaching me how to get out of this hold. I trap the guard's right arm in both of my hands, arch my back, and roll. He loses his balance and before he knows what's happening, he's below me.

A shot rings out.

Who is shot? Wildly, I look around and see the guard on the wall re-aiming.

I can't swallow, I can't breathe, my heart is in my throat. Who did she shoot? Will?

Adrenaline takes over my body. I jump to my feet and take three quick steps backward—out of the guard's grasp—collecting his discarded pistol as I go. He doesn't move from the ground when I point it at him. So, I turn and run, chasing after Will.

I see the truck, but I can't see Will. It's hard to see anything. There's too much dirt in the air and the world is still shrouded in shadow, the sun not yet high enough.

Then I spot it. A leg jutting over the edge of the tailgate. Limp. Familiar boots.

Will.

She shot him.

Is he ...? He's dead? Will's dead.

I almost choke on my heart.

I look up. The guard on the wall is taking aim again.

My feet stop running and plant themselves wide instead.

I don't know how to use a gun, but I copy her stance, pointing the gun at her. I squeeze the trigger.

It misses.

The guard looks toward me, alerted. She re-aims—at me this time.

I shoot again.

A moment later, her body jolts. A red stain grows on the stomach of her white hazsuit, and she falls backward.

I look at the pistol in my hand—shaking. I try to connect the shooting with the trigger I pulled, but it feels removed. The death doesn't affect me the way it did with the shovel. When I killed the guard with the shovel, I felt it reverberate up my arms as the spade edge lodged in her throat. I was repelled by it. I choked on it.

This is different. It's too distant. Not as personal. I just squeezed a trigger and the next moment the guard fell ... like I didn't even do it.

But I did.

It takes me a couple of breaths to recover. Again, I look at the pistol in my hand. So strange that such a small thing can cause so much damage, so much pain and death. My knees tremble, but I don't let them collapse. There is too much at stake.

I keep moving.

Others from the trucks have followed my lead, jumping down and attacking the guards. If they had considered us easy targets before, they are swiftly being proven wrong. The Terrene Folk are a strong and determined people. They won't lay down and die. *We* won't lay down and die.

I feel a knot in the pit of my stomach. *But what about Will?*

Another explosion has the horses skittering. They run off but I can't see Nathan with them. I might have gotten both brothers killed.

The explosion doesn't meet its mark, doing no damage, and our procession goes through the fire unscathed. I keep running alongside our vehicles, skirting around the fire. Roscoe runs past me, still barking. I don't know how he ended up behind, but he leaves me for dust and catches up to the trucks ahead, sprinting alongside them.

There are no more guards ahead that I can see. I glance over my shoulder. I can't see any behind either—but with so many places to hide, that doesn't mean we're safe.

We're well past the largest building, which means the end of the ruins is just up ahead.

Then I see it; the edge of the glass bubble, rising above the ruins.

The horses up ahead fan out. They've reached the land between the ruins and the bubble city.

Two shots from behind signal that at least one guard has survived. A bullet hits the dirt by my feet. I jump away from it.

A look over my shoulder confirms the guard is preparing for another shot. I have nowhere to go, so I just keep running, hoping I'm out of range.

I hear the shot, and instinct makes me jump and hunch at the same time, making myself as small as possible. There's a whoosh of wind past my face and a rock ahead explodes.

Then I'm out in the open. Before me is the bubble city. Four domes reflecting the sunrise.

I turn back to my assailant. They stand in the middle of the ruins; the white hazsuit contrasting against the rubble. But they don't follow. They can't be seen chasing us. Not in front of the entire bubble city.

The truck closest to me slows enough for me to jump aboard the back, and then we speed off again, heading closer to the bubbles. A few people pat me on the back, asking if I'm alright as I sit down in the cargo bed. I shake my head while my chest heaves. Will's smiling face floats across my mind. What have I done?

Twenty-Seven

I BITE BACK TEARS as we approach Neustin.

Will had the most infectious smile, and now I'll never see it again. I picture him sitting cross-legged in the dirt with me the first day we met, somehow drawing out a smile from me even though I was grumpy. How will I face Nathan? His brother is dead, and it's all my fault. It was my plan, and now that sweet boy is gone.

The community regroups right in front of the Sparkle Sector. I select a spot where we can glimpse the business district through the glass. That'll annoy Dr. Lederman.

The horses arrive first, and I see Nathan dismount.

"Nathan!" I scream and launch myself out of the truck before it's come to a stop.

He's OK.

He glances at me as I run toward him, but he's distracted—searching the crowd for his brother.

Dread pools in my stomach as I watch him walk toward the vehicles, about to discover Will's limp body. He has already lost a sister. What will it do to him to lose his brother too? It's not fair that Will is dead. Not someone so young, so kind. Is this the price for Sebastian's safety?

As I approach, I grab his arm. "I'm sorry, Nathan. I couldn't save him."

His eyes flick to mine in terror before he frantically pushes his way through the people. He screams, "Will!" as he weaves past people hugging and kissing, sobbing and mourning. I follow until he reaches the truck Will was in.

Blood is smeared across the side.

My hand flies to my mouth. My stomach lurches.

"Nathan?" His name is called.

Nathan spins around and suddenly his arms are wrapped tightly around someone, and he's laughing and crying at the same time. Will. He's alive.

"Nathan, I'm ok," Will muffles into his shoulder.

How? ... How?

A sob escapes my lips. My knees are so weak they barely hold me up.

I stare at Will, dumbstruck, as Roscoe yaps at our ankles. "I thought ... I thought she killed you."

They both turn to look at me. Will's smile isn't as radiant as normal; tears pool in his eyes. But he's smiling. The smile is faint, but it's there. And it's infectious. I find myself smiling too.

"Jannine pulled me out of the way," he says, and his smile falters. "But ... then she ... she got hit, Martina."

My smile fades. I press a hand to my chest. "Oh. I'm so, so sorry. Did she ...?"

Will shakes his head. "She's gone," he whispers.

I open and close my mouth, no sound coming out. The relief I feel seeing Will alive is outweighed by the guilt and grief on my shoulders. My fingers tremble with the horror that I've caused another death. But something else weighs me down, more than the horror and grief. The shame that I'm pleased it's not Will. Jannine gave her life for Will. And I'm glad she did.

I wrap my arms around my body to shield myself and hide from my shame.

There are more people dead. Jannine and whoever was in the flames. Plus the guards. Guards that I killed with my own hands. It's my fault they're dead. I didn't know them, but they're dead because of me.

Who else will die before this is over?

I look at the Terrene Folk. Parents clutch their children. Tears stream down faces, making tracks on their dusty cheeks. A man holds his head in his hands, blood running from a gash on his forehead. A woman has collapsed on the ground, sobs wracking her body, and her friend sits beside her with an arm around her shoulders.

But Will is alive, and so is Nathan ... And I'm here to save Sebastian. Whatever it takes. No matter the price. No matter how much I wish it didn't cost so much.

"Alright, people," Mother calls. She stands proud and tall in the midst of trucks, horses, and people. "Let's get on with this plan."

George has already disappeared. In fact, he didn't come with the main convoy; he left earlier in the night and should have already entered the city in his stolen hazsuit. I peer through the glass, but of course, I don't see him.

The city is still quiet. Most people are probably still in bed. I look forward to them awakening, not only to the day, but to the truth of the world.

People crawl and climb back into trucks while others remount their horses. I return to my allocated truck next to Will. Jannine no longer sits across from me. Only a smear of blood remains. I stare at it.

"They took the bodies away," Will whispers. "We'll give them a ceremonial cremation later."

I nod, swallowing down my anguish.

We leave a contingent sitting in front of the Sparkle Sector, setting up a small camp there. And despite their grief, they sit proud; backs straight, heads high, while I sit in the truck with my shoulders hunched.

We have prepared signs on canvas, planks of wood, and any spare material from the camp. The Terrene Folk hold them high.

We're not sick!

We can survive!

PMC lied!

We won't lie down and die!

A few more of us are left in front of the Linto quarter as we head to the south around the city. Linto is still in lockdown, so we don't leave many people there. With each person who leaves our convoy, I wonder if they'll be safe. Will our gamble pay off? Will the children actually be safer with us? Or should we have left them behind? For the millionth time, I wish I had just gotten down from the bubble before the storm hit—none of this would have happened.

We keep circling and my heart yearns, calling to my old home, calling to Sebastian. I lean forward in my seat.

We pass the decontamination center from where I've entered and exited the city a thousand times. The doors are firmly shut. No one is preparing to exit at this hour of the day, but soon it will be abuzz with activity. I wonder if people will still go to work on the windows with us sitting outside. Maybe that will be my chance to see Sebastian.

And then we're passing the dirty windows of The Nix.

My breath stops. My eyes frantically search through those windows, darting back and forth.

There is more activity inside this quarter; people need to get up early to earn a living. But I can't make out any faces through the grime and dust on the outside. And to them, we probably just look like a dark blob.

I direct our convoy to stop where I know the main square sits a little beyond the glass. I try to see inside, but it's useless. It's too dark inside with the sun still too low to lighten it, and the windows are too filthy.

"We need to clean the windows," I say to no one in particular. "They can't see us."

Half of the remaining convoy continues north, toward the Bama quarter, while the rest of us start to unload and set up an impromptu camp. I can't tell if anyone inside has noticed us yet, and I want to make a big impact, so hopefully, those lives won't be in vain. I beg for a portion of our precious water and take it to the window with an old cloth.

"Will, Nathan, come help me," I call as I approach the bubble. Squirting a small amount of water onto my cloth, I start scrubbing the glass. I do the section in front of my face and a little higher, just enough of the window for the people inside to see us out here. I'm glad I don't need to climb under the bubble to wash the underside.

Will comes up with another cloth and I squirt some water on it. He sets to work beside me, and Nathan works diligently on the other side of him. Before long, others from the camp take notice of what we're doing and join us.

It's not the best window cleaning I've ever done—the glass isn't streak free and sparkling—but it's clean enough to allow us to see inside; and more importantly, the people inside can see out—*they* can see us.

A child holding her father's hand stops in the street to stare at us. Her eyes widen. Her father tries to tug her along, but she doesn't move, forcing him to look at what has distracted her. His body jolts when he registers the sight of us, outside, with no hazsuits. And his eyes grow wide.

Others stop walking, too. They stare, point, not comprehending, unsure of what it means. Some back away. Others come forward, curious to see if it's a trick, or to see how we're alive.

Their eyes roam over the camp, the dozen of us outside without protection. They read our signs. Eyes widen even further.

We clean a large section of the bubble and can now be seen easily. But we stay close to the window, staring inside, back at those that look out at us. My back straightens, and I lift my head high, stretching on the tips of my toes. I search the crowd for Sebastian and his favorite robot mask, but I can't find him. I try not to let the disappointment deflate me. So I stare furiously through that window, willing people to understand, to realize they've been lied to. And to stand up against it. I want them to revolt against PMC Life Tech.

Some people shake their heads, disbelieving. They turn away from us. Others stay at the window for a period, watching us with curiosity, wasting away minutes and hours, like we're strange and unusual animals that they can't figure out.

People point at the horses. As much in awe and disbelief as I was once.

Some citizens jump away from the window when Roscoe runs toward them and bounces up with his paws against the glass.

And they point at me, talking to each other, gesticulating. They know who I am, that much is clear. They know I'm the girl from the news, the girl who escaped quarantine. They probably think I'm sick and diseased. So I grab a sign saying, "I am not sick," and hold it high. I scream it, "I am not sick!" I know they can't hear me through the glass, but I yell it again, anyway. "I'm not sick. I'm not sick. I'm not sick!"

When my voice is hoarse from shouting, and my arms tired from holding up my sign, I retire to a chair with the sign propped at my feet. Others sit too. Some grip each other's hands, some are curled in grief, more stare in through the glass bubble with scowls on their faces.

Mother pulls up a seat and sits beside me, watching the news on a comms unit.

"Have they reported it?" I ask.

"They can't keep this quiet, girl," Mother says with a smirk.

A satisfied grin spreads across my face, too. Maybe the plan is working.

I pull out my own comms unit and switch it to the news. Videos of the protesters are broadcasted across the city, including videos of me, screaming into the bubble.

I look up at the city, searching for the cameras trained on me. I hadn't noticed them earlier. My attention was solely on the people and the protest, but now I see them. Two large black industrial cameras pointed right at me.

I wave.

"... with signs stating, 'We're not sick,'" the reporter is saying through my comms unit. "It is unknown where these people have come from, other than one young woman, who is from our very own city. Martina Monsalve went missing two weeks ago during the storm. She was believed dead. The city conducted a search for her in the hopes she could be saved before she succumbed to disease. However, it looks as though she's thriving."

They air the shot of me waving at the camera from moments ago. Then the video changes, showing the inside of the Sparkle Sector and their curious onlookers, watching the Terrene Folk that sit in front of their bubble.

I look up and see people around the camp exchanging shy smiles.

It's happening. And it's going to change everything. Hope surges through me. Surely, Sebastian will see the news soon and will come to the window. I can't wait to see him.

Throughout the day, I alternate between sitting and walking in front of the bubble holding my sign, shouting at the cameras and the onlookers inside with defiance. But no matter what I'm doing or saying, I constantly search for Sebastian in the crowd. Tía Rosa stops by briefly and waves, probably on her way to the diner. Liam and his girlfriend—Kelly?—arrive and make funny faces at me. Even Old Henry shows up to have a gawk. I mouth, "Where's Sebastian?" to my friends, but no one seems to know. They shake their heads and mouth back, "I don't know." The crowd continues to grow until it looks like the entire population of The Nix has gathered to watch us. Except Sebastian.

Maybe he's at work. But there's no sign of the buses. There's no sign of any movement in or out of Neustin. No one seems to be leaving the bubble city at all. They must have the entire city in a kind of lockdown.

We stay there all day. When the daylight starts to fade, a dread like a darkening storm cloud weighs down on my heart. Where is Sebastian? There's been no sign of him. Hours have passed. If he's seen the news, surely, he should have come to wave at me by now. *If* he's seen the news. I doubt there's a person alive in the city who hasn't seen the news by now. Maybe he can't watch it. Maybe he's out at work, even if there's been no sign of buses. Or maybe something, *someone*, is stopping him.

My stomach churns, hoping he is safe and healthy.

An image of a man, with his flesh moldering and rotting away, flashes through my mind. That poor man from Dr. Lederman's presentation. My blood turns to ice. What if they've got Sebastian? Are they doing that to him?

These thoughts plague me. They drag me down into a darkness that the desert sun cannot penetrate.

I try to wait patiently. I try to convince myself that everything we're doing is going to help Sebastian. But I'm full of worry. The longer I wait, the more impatient I get. Standing and protesting isn't enough. I can't stop pacing, searching the crowd of onlookers for that familiar robot mask.

"Martina! Martina!" Nathan jogs toward me. "You'll want to hear this."

I reluctantly pull my eyes away from the crowd and jog back with Nathan. He takes me to Mother, who is hunched over a comms unit. I peer over her shoulder to see it. Looking out from the screen is George. Gone are his worn clothes. He now wears a clean-cut business suit. And his dusty hair has been washed and styled. He looks like an entirely different person. Almost like he belongs in the Sparkle Sector.

"That's great, George," Mother is saying into the unit. She glances at me over her shoulder. "Here's Martina. I'm sure she'll be interested in your other news."

George nods at me. "I have news of your friend, Persephone. She's alive and safe."

My legs wobble with relief.

"She has been under house arrest since you escaped. From what I've been told, she hasn't had access to anyone outside her household. That's why you haven't heard from her. But you were right. Her mother kept her safe from any real harm.

"I don't know if she still has the evidence. But I have someone in her household helping me. A disgruntled employee that is happy to sell out Dr. Marshall and help Persephone in the process."

"Oh my god." My hand goes to my heart. "That's great news, George. Thank you so much." I hesitate before asking, "Have you been able to find out anything about my brother?"

Pity dulls his eyes. "I'm sorry, Martina, I haven't. They don't talk about anyone from The Nix quarter here, and it's too difficult to sneak in there with this PIN. People would question why a man in a flash suit is in the quarter. It could jeopardize our other plans."

Mother shifts in her chair.

"I understand," I say, though I can't hide the disappointment and worry from my voice.

George says to Mother, "I'll check in again soon." Then he's gone from the screen. And I'm left with a hollow feeling in my chest. Even though I'm standing right beside the bubble city, I don't feel any closer to Sebastian than I did when I was in the middle of the desert.

We take turns to sleep. There are always a few people awake to keep watch and ensure no guards sneak up on us. It's my turn to rest, and although it's difficult to fall asleep, I feel myself dozing off just as my comms unit starts vibrating.

I startle awake. I've waited days and weeks for this comms unit to ring. Uncertain if it's real or a dream, I let it buzz in my hands for a few seconds. My drowsy eyes scan the screen and my thumb fumbles to hit the answer key.

"Martina." Persephone's face fills the screen.

"Persephone," I breathe. "You're okay?"

"You were worried about me?" Her lips slide into a teasing smile. "I told you I'd be alright."

"But Dr. Lederman ... Persephone, he could have killed you anyway, despite your mother."

She snorts. Somehow, she makes even that seem delicate. "He wouldn't dare. He wouldn't want to cross my mother and lose her backing."

I stare at her. Absorbing her words, but more than that, absorbing the sight of her. Memorizing the shape of her lips and eyes, the lines of her nose and jaw.

"It's all happening, Martina," Persephone says. "George is here." The camera spins to show George standing in the corner of her room with a young maid. He looks up when the camera falls to him, but then goes on talking with the maid. "Liza sneaked him in here." The maid looks up when her name is mentioned, and then Persephone turns the camera back to herself. "I'm giving him all the evidence. He's going to get it to the media."

"That's unbelievable," I say.

"Be prepared for anything. We don't know what PMC will do."

"I'd love to see Dr. Lederman's face when he realizes he's doomed, and all his secrets have been spilled." I picture his smarmy face and imagine shock and desperation crossing it. No amount of antiwrinkle injections can mask that. And he'll have nowhere to hide once we're done with him.

Hope warms my gut like a heated pillow. I imagine Sebastian living healthily and happily, free from undue medical costs, able to afford food and an education; rising higher than a window washer, to become something that won't break his back. And maybe I can return to him. Even if he can't risk coming outside, I could go back to him.

Like a splat of bird poo messing up a newly cleaned window, a niggle of fear tarnishes my hope. So much can still go wrong. What if George can't get the evidence to the media? What if Dr. Lederman finds out somehow and intercepts it? What if something happens to Sebastian? If something hasn't already happened to him ...

My hope dissipates, and I have to swallow my fear before it engulfs me.

"Tomorrow, Martina." Persephone's voice is full of conviction. "It'll go live tomorrow." I focus on her determination, her tenacity, and allow it to feed my own. Now's not the time to fall apart or hide in fear. If hope eludes me, then I must rely on sheer grit instead.

260

Twenty-Eight

THE WAITING IS KILLING me. But all I can do now *is* wait. After my call with Persephone, I can't find sleep again. So I stay on watch, ensuring PMC doesn't unleash their guards. They don't.

Too many people know about us now. PMC can't attack us without people asking why. We've done our job well, just standing in front of the bubble, showing up and being counted. The Terrene Folk paid for this with their lives. There's nothing more I can do from this side of the glass … except wait.

I'm constantly watching my comms unit between scanning the windows for Sebastian. Checking the time; waiting for another call; wishing the news would change from images of us to images of Dr. Lederman and PMC ordering the death of innocents.

It's 11.30 when I check the time. And it's still 11.30 when I check it again. I groan.

"Stop pacing, Martina!" Mother calls. "It's not going to make anything happen faster and you're just stirring up the desert." She gestures to the chair next to her. "Please take a seat. I'm sick of breathing in your dust."

I huff and stalk over, plonking down on the chair.

Mother hands me a flask of water, which I gulp down greedily.

"You would risk everything for Sebastian, wouldn't you?" Mother asks.

"Yes, I would," I say, without hesitation.

"Just like Nathan would do anything to keep Will safe," she says. "And so would I." Her eyes penetrate mine, but I don't understand the message she's trying to portray.

"What's your point?"

"It's just something to remember." Her eyes turn back to the glass bubble, where people are still gawking at us from inside.

She must be angry at me for putting her people in danger. Or maybe she's referring to something else. I peer at her out of the corner of my eye; her long, gray-streaked hair is tied back, allowing me to see her face fully. But it gives nothing away.

I look around our impromptu camp. Will is playing with Roscoe. He has a stick that he throws for the dog, who chases after it and brings it back with a goofy smile. I scan the rest of the campers. Their anger has dissipated; grief and mourning taking its place while they wait.

"Where's Nathan?" I blurt when I realize he's missing.

Mother raises one eyebrow and her lips press even tighter. "He's gone on an errand."

My stomach churns at her cryptic words. Mother knows something that I don't. What kind of errand can Nathan be on that has Mother tight-lipped and speaking in riddles?

Her hawk eyes watch every movement inside the bubble. My eyes flick back to the bubble too, searching the crowd for some clue to her words. But all I see are masked faces and curious eyes.

I open my mouth to demand more information when her comms unit buzzes. Her eyes flick briefly to me before she answers the call.

George appears on the screen. He doesn't waste time on greetings. He says, "It'll be on the news at midday."

I check the time on my own comms unit—11.52. Only eight minutes until we change the lives and beliefs of thousands.

Mother nods. "Noted."

"It's as damning as Martina said." George's tone is serious, but satisfaction drips from him. And I feel it too, the gratification that Dr. Lederman and PMC are at an end. "And phase two is ready if needed."

"Also noted."

My eyes widen. Phase two? I look at Mother, but she's looking determinately away. She signs off the call, standing up before I have a chance to ask about phase two. She turns her back on me and calls to her people. They stop what they're doing instantly, all turning to face her.

"Thank you all for your bravery." Mother's voice projects across the camp. "We've uncovered the evidence that Martina found—" she gestures to me, but still her eyes avoid mine, "—and it will be aired at midday. Be prepared for anything. Arm yourselves in case the guards come for us. People will do anything if they're desperate. We can't rely on this ending peacefully. But we can rely on the fact that things will never be the same.

"Today will change history. Today we free thousands of people, while also freeing ourselves from persecution. We will no longer be hunted. We will no longer bow to *their* rules. Today we change the future.

"In seven minutes. It airs."

As Mother turns away, the camp erupts into conversation and activity. Any weapons stashed are brought out and readied to use. I hope it doesn't come to that. I don't want anyone else to die because of what I set in motion.

I turn back to Mother. *What's phase two?* But she is back on the comms unit, calling the other camps around the bubble city, warning and rallying them too.

With one of the stolen stun batons in hand, I approach Will. Roscoe sits patiently beside him.

"I hope you don't need to use this," I say, and hand him the stun baton. Bile threatens to rise up my throat. The picture of a gun aimed at him flashes through my mind. "But just in case."

He takes it, looking at it with a seriousness I've never seen from him before. "Thanks, Martina."

I pull my comms unit from my pocket, tilting the screen so Will can watch with me. It's almost time. I switch it on with trembling fingers and click into the news portal. We don't need to wait long.

A soft chime rings and the news begins.

"Today we bring you some disturbing, horrifying, news," the male reporter begins. "I am Daniel Stevenage, and this is the midday news."

This must be Persephone's friend, Daniel. He mentions the discovery of documents and footage that are damning to Dr. Lederman and PMC Life Tech. He looks directly at the camera with an appearance of professionalism and confidence, but his voice quivers with apprehension. He knows the gravity of the news he's disclosing.

The screen flicks to images taken from the executive report, the profit made from compulsory medications, the death toll and active cases, a graph that shows the decline of sales over time. Then they air the footage taken from inside the cupboards of the boardroom.

It's blurry and shaking, partially obscured from the edge of the cupboard, but Dr. Lederman's face is clearly recognizable.

"There has been unrest in both the Linto and The Nix quarters," he says in the clip.

The clip is edited, and it jumps to him ordering the deaths of civilians. "We need to increase fear in the population."

A woman out of view of the camera asks, "So, more deaths?"

Dr. Lederman responds, "Yes, and a public scare." The image freezes on Dr. Lederman's face as he says "Yes" and Daniel clarifies, "As you've just seen, Dr. Lederman has sanctioned the death of individuals within our community for the purpose of making a bigger profit on medications for the Azutine virus. He even provides further details on who should be selected to infect."

It flicks back to the image of Dr. Lederman. He shows no remorse or shame as he says, "Select two or three people from a public place. More people will be concerned they have contracted the virus from being in the vicinity, and they'll be rushing to the med-bays as usual."

People around me from the camp are gasping. Even though I had told them of Dr. Lederman's actions and the corruption within PMC, they're still shocked to see his blatant disregard for human life.

I glance up from the comms unit and into the city beyond the glass. There's still a crowd at the window watching us. But some are turning away. Some have their eyes glued on their own comms units. Their faces are twisted in horror, mortification, disbelief; mouths gaping, brows furrowing.

Then others start to notice something is amiss. They turn to their neighbors. They want to know what's wrong. They see them with their comms units, so they watch over shoulders, standing on tiptoes to see, craning their necks around strangers.

The news shows the pictures of the man labeled "Subject 2" that was purposely infected with the deadly Azutine virus. Daniel explains that with each day, the man further declines in health, but we can all see that for ourselves. "And by day six, the man passed away," Daniel says. They don't show the photos from day five or six, but I remember them. And it curdles my stomach; the flesh rotting off their victim.

I pull my eyes away from the screen and look at the city. There is some kind of commotion. The crowd surges in different directions, like clouds in a storm, pulled and pushed by a raging wind. But instead of wind, it's a guard.

The guard tries to get the crowd to disperse, but they're not as pliable as usual. They've seen the evidence against PMC and the guards get their orders from PMC. A few people leave, but most keep their ground, arms crossed over chests, and heads shaking adamantly.

And then it happens. A woman slaps the guard across the face and, before he can recover, a man pummels his fist into the guard's gut.

Some of the crowd scatters, but many stay, anger rising. They feed on it. And it quickly spreads, just like an infectious disease.

The crowd yell and scream at the guard. More lash out violently—all fists and feet; punching and kicking. Beaten and bruised, the guard tries to escape the crowd, who chase him down with fists and shouts.

I look away.

The report has ended, but the chime sings again, and the report is repeated. It's already done its damage though. Repeating it will make sure it spreads to every corner of the city, poisoning every citizen against PMC Life Tech and Dr. Lederman.

I pocket my comms unit and turn back to my fellow campers. Will smiles. I see others smiling too. They're congratulating each other, hugging, laughing, crying. I feel numb. No, that's not right. I feel too much, so much that I can't tell *what* I feel. It's turmoil inside me. My heart feels heavy with guilt from the loss of life, yet it still burns with hope. My blood boils with anger, and yet my limbs are limp from sadness and exhaustion.

Overshadowing everything are my thoughts of Sebastian. Where is he? The news has broken; he should be safe. But what if they've already done something to him? If PMC or Lederman haven't got to him, someone else might. Anyone could have taken advantage of a young boy with no one to look out for him.

I need to get inside the city. And if I can't do that, I need Persephone or George to go looking for Sebastian.

I phone the last number that called me, the number that Persephone called me on. It rings ... and rings. No one answers. It rings out. I try again. And again. But my calls go ignored.

I slam the comms unit off with a stab of my finger.

Staring through the window once again, my fists clenched, my jaw tight, I search the crowd. Then I spin away and storm across the desert to where Mother Jessica stands, talking and laughing with a group of people.

"I need to contact George." I interrupt their conversation, my voice desperate.

The group stop talking and look at me. Mother turns to me with forced patience.

"Excuse me." Mother waves her apology to the others and steps away to talk with me more privately. I feel someone at my side and see Will standing nearby. His back is straight, and he stares at Mother too, as if he's on my side and he's here to back me up. I give him a grateful smile.

"Have you been in touch with him?" I ask.

"Not since before the broadcast," Mother says, her face a mask, revealing nothing.

"I need to find Sebastian." Her secrets don't matter to me now; only Sebastian does. "He hasn't shown up at the bubble window. He hasn't called me. Something's wrong."

Mother's eyes soften slightly, but she says nothing.

"I need George to find him. Or Persephone. With everything going on inside, it shouldn't matter if they're wearing fancy clothes in The Nix. They don't need to hide anymore; they can go in there and find him."

Mother inhales deeply. "George might not be able to help."

"What does that mean?" I snap. "You know something I don't. I don't care what it is. I just want your help. Mother! I need your help, please. *Por favor*!"

Her eyes flicker with pity again and dread fills me. Does she already know my mission is useless? Does she already know that Sebastian is dead?

I grab Mother's arm. The contact helps keep me standing. "Is he dead?"

"I don't know. I truly don't know, Martina. But if you haven't seen him ... well, it's not a good sign."

"Then help her, Mother!" Will cries. "She would do it for you."

My heart swells with appreciation for Will. But Mother doesn't sway. "It's not that easy. There are other things at play." She shuts her mouth tightly. She doesn't seem very motherly anymore, just calculating and guarded.

Mother looks at the clock on her comms unit. It's been over an hour since the broadcast. What else has George got to do?

I open my mouth to ask when my own comms unit buzzes. It vibrates in my hand for a moment before my brain catches up and I make sense that it's a call coming in.

I answer.

Twenty-Nine

AT FIRST, THE IMAGE is blurry, just a fuzzy blue, like the camera is held too close to the subject. Then it pulls back, and the blue becomes a t-shirt. The camera pans up and Sebastian's face appears.

He's not wearing his robot mask. His mouth is contorted in pain, and he's twisting and turning, not paying attention to the screen.

A hand grips his shirt at his shoulder, holding Sebastian tightly in place in front of the screen.

"Sebastian," I exhale. He's alive. My heart sings. But my eyes flare with anger at the hand that holds him captive.

Sebastian's eyes flutter open at the sound of my voice. His face fills with shock.

"Martina!" His eyes are wide with fear. "*Lo siento*, Martina." The hand yanks at his shoulder and his eyes water.

"What do you want?" I say through gritted teeth.

Mother and Will hear my hostile voice and they move closer to watch my comms unit.

"I want *you*, Martina."

I suck in a breath. I recognize the voice. It's been all over the news today. For years I've heard that smug voice giving false health announcements. I don't need to see Dr. Lederman's face to know it's him.

"Fine, let's talk. Let him go." My voice comes out stronger than I feel. But my hands are shaking, partly in terror, partly in rage.

"Not so quickly," Dr. Lederman purrs. "Let's make a bargain."

I want to say "Anything!" but I hold back. Instead, I say, "Go on."

Muffled sounds come down the line. The image tilts as the screen is adjusted and Dr. Lederman comes into view. Despite his stretched skin, his face is a mask of fury. His brows don't furrow, but his blue eyes are steely, showing his rage, even if his muscles won't. And those malicious eyes make me shudder. He's the cause of hundreds, if not thousands, of deaths. And he has hold of my little brother.

He keeps his grip on Sebastian's shirt, although now most of Sebastian is out of view. He continues to squirm, causing the camera view to tilt and sway as Dr. Lederman keeps it focused on himself.

Nice one, *hermanito*. Don't give in.

"Come into the city." His artificially plumped up lips twist into a snarl. "I have a camera crew ready to take your testimony. You'll tell the city that the video is fabricated. That I never said those things. They can see it's edited. They can see the poor quality. Some already doubt its validity."

"What good would that do? Have you seen the crowds? They believe it. You're done for!" The words are already out of my mouth before I catch them. I kick myself. The last thing I want to do is anger him further when he has Sebastian by the scruff of his neck.

But the minister has the gall to chuckle; I've never heard anything so sick, so egotistical. "You're the one who started this. They'll believe you. You're the face of this revolution. You'll see how gullible they are. You will admit that you tried to extort money from me by doctoring that video. You'll say you're confessing because you see the damage it's causing now, and you want to prevent any further bloodshed."

Mother grunts beside me. I ignore her.

"Even if they believe me, won't they think I'm infected?" My tone is calmer now, as if I'm considering his proposal. I need him to believe it will work so I can save Sebastian, but if I give in too easily, he'll see right through me.

"You'll tell the city that you were infected," he continues, "but I cured you. That, due to the resources of PMC Life Tech, we were able to save you."

"But why would I try to extort you if you saved me?"

"Because you're a little bitch," he spits.

His words are like a slap in the face. My cheeks smart with the sting of them.

He regains his composure before saying, "You'll explain your desperation to help your little brother." He tugs at Sebastian's shirt and snarls, "And that won't be a lie, will it?"

I can't walk away and leave Sebastian, and he knows it. I have no doubt that he will kill Sebastian if I don't agree to his bargain. He's already proven he's a ruthless killer.

"And then you'll let us go free?" I ask.

"I'll let *Sebastian* go free." He corrects me as if he's talking to a child. "You'll be in custody for the crimes you've committed. The citizens will want justice for forging that video."

I swallow my outrage, my pride. I clench my jaw and say, "I need better assurances for Sebastian. You'll provide for him. You'll give him an education. He'll be set up with a place in the Bush quarter." I know I'm reaching, but if I don't ask, then Sebastian will still be broke and hungry. I need to create a future for him.

Lederman chuckles again. "You have audacity, girl!" He nods. "Fine, but it'll be the Bama quarter, not Bush. We can't have an orphan flea in the Bush quarter. PMC Life Tech will provide him a home, food, and pay for his education."

"Done!" I say before he changes his mind.

"You can't," Mother gasps.

"Shush," Will murmurs.

Dr. Lederman lets go of Sebastian. He even pats his shoulder. I still can't see Sebastian's face, but I hear him sobbing in the background.

"It'll be okay, *hermanito*," I call to him.

"You'll be met at the decontamination center," Lederman says. "Use your personal ID code. Don't shake, Martina." And then he's gone.

I blink at the blank screen, no longer displaying any part of Sebastian. I take a second to wish him back, and then I turn my attention to my mission.

"Martina," Mother says. Her voice is already raised, telling me I can't go. I ignore her and storm off.

Mother and Will follow me.

"... jeopardize everything we've done," Mother says, but I'm barely listening. "It'll all be for nothing."

I head toward the decontamination center.

Mother grabs my arm. "I can't let you go." I try to shake off her grip, but she's stronger than she looks, and she holds on tightly.

"I can't stay." My eyes fix on hers. I'm not asking to leave. I'm not seeking permission. I'm telling her I'm going.

"No!" Mother grips harder. "This isn't up for debate. I can't let you tell them it was all a lie. It hurts our cause too much." She calls over her shoulder, "Chris, Graeme, please retain Martina in her tent."

My eyes go wide.

"Mother, no!" Will calls.

I tear my arm from her grip, shoving Mother as hard as I can. She falls backward, dust flying up as she hits the ground. I hesitate, worried I've hurt her, but I have to get away. She can't keep me from saving Sebastian. She can't really think I would ever leave Sebastian to that monster.

"Run, Martina!" Will shouts as he drops to the ground beside Mother.

I look up and see the two men charging toward me. I take off, running all the way to the entry of the decontamination center that leads into The Nix. When I reach it, sweat is pouring off me and my breath is ragged. The two Terrene men stop following me once I'm within the shadows of the glass bubble. They return to the camp, too afraid of the city guards to follow me any further.

I look back at the camp. It's tempting to turn back. After everything they've done for me, I don't want to betray them. They're good people and they deserve better. Will this jeopardize their freedom if I say the video was doctored? The truth that we can live outside will still be out there. There's nothing I can say that will take that truth away now because the citizens can see it for themselves.

Still, my chest feels tight as I turn back to face the pedestrian entry to the center, crossing myself in prayer as I do.

It looks the same as it always has. But I've never been so scared to look upon this door before. The thick steel is a prison, ready and waiting to entrap me.

I take a breath to steady my nerves, squashing the voice telling me to run. I take several steps forward, stopping right in front of the security pad. My fingers shake as I reach out to enter my PIN. The door swings open and I step inside.

My eyes adjust to the darker interior of the center. An empty corridor stretches out, ending in an individual decon station. The corridor seems a lot wider than when I've walked down it before, because this time, I'm not wearing a bulky hazsuit: just a shirt and shorts.

I reach the chamber and strip off my clothes, stuffing them into the decontaminator machine for washing. I'm left standing naked.

I go through the normal process of showering and scrubbing away any contagions. I wonder if this process does anything at all. Can it wash away any trace of the cold I had, or other diseases that may have stuck to me while living outside unprotected? I do it anyway, hoping I won't infect anyone inside.

As I exit the shower and move through to the scanning chamber, I am fully aware that someone will be watching this time. I want to cover up my breasts, but instead, I hold my arms out wide with my head held high, letting the scanner run over me. It gives me the all clear, but I wonder how accurate it is given the cold I had.

There are strange clothes waiting for me on the sterile side of the chamber—a pair of orange cotton trousers, and a matching shirt. It's the same clothes they give to criminals. That's what I am now—a criminal, and a prisoner.

If I had any lingering doubts about my status, they shatter as I exit the decontamination center. A row of guards wait for me outside. They stand in a line, blocking my way. There's eight of them. They're dressed in hazsuits; I guess they aren't taking any chances that I might be infected. Beyond them, a small crowd has gathered, clearly wondering what is going on to warrant eight guards in hazsuits.

Among them is a news crew; their large camera pointed right at me.

The guards might be in hazsuits, but PMC has taken no precautions to protect the rest of the community from me. The crowd are wearing only their normal face masks and no other protection. If I really am infected, they're at risk. But neither Lederman nor PMC care about anyone from The Nix.

A guard steps toward me. "Let's go," she growls. She takes my arm in a firm grip and marches me out of the center.

The guards surround me; two in front, four behind, and another grips my other arm. Even if I break free from their hold, there's no way I'm getting far before one of them runs me down.

The crowd parts as we approach. Some stare, eyes wide. Others point. I hear them saying, "That's the girl from outside," and, "She was the one they said was contaminated." Some of the people hurl insults at the guards.

They march me straight through The Nix, the news crew following, all the way to the Linto quarter. And we don't stop there. They keep walking at a steady pace, past the middle-income homes, past the people now ignoring the lockdown; they stand at the edges of the roads, allowing us to pass but watching carefully as we do.

More guards meet us as we enter the Sparkle Sector. Can't put the rich people at risk. We travel through the metal corridor, under the sign stating, "Bush quarter," and the streets change to the walled mansions of the rich and influential. I look at the faces of the people who watch me here and I wonder which of them work for PMC; which of them knew PMC were killing people for profits. I wonder if they're scowling at me or at the guards.

I'm led straight to the PMC Life Tech headquarters. The black marble runs the entire length of the foyer, bearing down on us. I feel as small as a mouse, but the walls are closing in anyway. The cold rock sucks away all the light and any hope.

I shudder.

I am ushered into a lift with four of the guards. It's not one of the central lifts, but one that climbs the outside of the building. We only just fit as the glass doors slide closed.

As we rise, I look over my shoulder to see the Sparkle Sector laid out before me. I've seen the view before, of course. It's just like the view I had atop of the bubble. On the day everything changed. The day I was torn away from everything I had known.

That day I had looked down on this tower, only seeing a building, not knowing the corruption and evil held inside. I have since learned the truth, but now I have to convince the city that it was all a lie. I will allow the city to return to its blindness, to continue to be manipulated by PMC ... if it will save Sebastian.

I hold my head higher, pushing down my guilt.

Thirty

THE LIFT REACHES ITS zenith, and with a soft clunk, the doors open directly into a large meeting room. It has a white marble table, with white chairs surrounding it. Large windows ring the room, looking out over the Sparkle Sector, making the room bright and airy.

There's no sign of Sebastian.

A different news crew is already here and filming as I enter. Two of them stand in the corner, one with the camera on his shoulder, the other holding a microphone and staring right at me.

I sneer at them.

Sitting at the head of the table is Dr. Lederman. He wears one of his expensive suits, his shirt too tight as usual. Today, his tie is a vibrant green—the color of sickness. More importantly, he doesn't wear a hazsuit or face mask. He knows I'm not a threat to his health.

Seeing me, he promptly stands up and adjusts his jacket. He inclines his head and gives me his version of a smile. It doesn't reach his eyes. With the amount of antiwrinkle injections he's had, I'm not sure it could.

"Martina, welcome to PMC Life Tech," he croons, as if we're old friends.

I try to mimic his smile, but my lips curl in a grimace. "Dr. Lederman." I stop a few paces before him, causing my guards to stop too. "Where is my brother?"

"Right down to business then?" His lips twitch, trying unsuccessfully to smile a little wider.

My only response is to hold his gaze.

"He's safe." Lederman waves his hand in a gesture that says I have nothing to worry about. "I hope you're well? Would you like a drink?"

My lips purse.

His eyes trail up and down my body. I can't help but feel violated. Soiled.

"It's a shame to see you in orange, Martina." His plump lips turn downward. "The yellow dress I saw you in last time was much more flattering." He huffs when I still don't answer. "You're going to have to talk if you want to help your brother."

"I know that," I spit.

"And you'll need to be convincing."

"I will be."

He turns to the news crew, beckoning them to come closer.

"No," I say. I don't know where my commanding tone comes from—inside I'm shaking like a leaf—but everyone stops. "I won't do anything until I see my brother and I know he's safe." I cross my arms over my chest. "And I need reassurances that you'll follow through with your promise."

Dr. Lederman's eyes drill into mine, but I don't budge. Eventually he nods at my guards and two peel away, disappearing into the lift.

Lederman returns to his seat and waves for me to sit too. I remain standing, and he doesn't push it further. He leans back in his chair with an air of nonchalance. His beady eyes remain on me, casually trailing over my body, making my skin crawl.

The room is silent except for the slight buzz of electricity feeding through the lights. I avert my eyes from the smug face of Dr. Lederman, staring at the empty table instead. I count the seconds.

After some time, Dr. Lederman says, "I'm so glad you've decided to come forward." He looks between me and the camera crew. "Your confession will save a lot of lives. To think that we've been killing people just for profit." His tone is incredulous, and he shakes his head sadly, playing up to the camera. "We're here to save people! Not hurt them. PMC Life Tech, myself especially, hope that people don't stop taking their life-saving medications *just* because they believe this footage is real."

I twist my fingers around each other, wishing I could strangle Dr. Lederman's over tanned throat.

"You've hurt many people, Martina. Innocent people."

I keep silent, biting my tongue, reminding myself that I'm doing this for Sebastian. But it churns my stomach thinking of all those innocent people Dr. Lederman has hurt, and now I'm going to take the blame for causing people harm.

"... just to get to me," he continues to drone on. "To extort money and steal from those that would help you and others in your community."

He watches as my fingers curl into fists. His lips spread into the biggest smile he can manage. Which isn't much.

He's baiting me. He's purposely making me angry. To torture me, I suspect. It takes all my strength not to tell him exactly what I think of him. I want to scream the truth. To say that footage is real, that everything reported today is true.

I calculate how far away he is from me. The guards stand at my side, not in front of me. If I leap fast enough, use all that strength I've gained over the years of manual labor, all the fighting skills I learned from Liam, maybe I can get to him. Maybe I can kill him.

"... provided shelter for you after fleeing from Colombia ..."

My fantasy fades to hear him still talking. I want to rip his tongue out.

"And gave you a job," he continues. "But you had to take advantage of those who live honestly."

Now he's lying about our arrival in the city; Sebastian and I had no help from PMC, we forged lives for ourselves out of nothing. I don't know how many more lies I can take. I look out the window to the glass dome above and send out a prayer instead.

The sound of the lift interrupts my prayer. My body jolts; it's ascending again. Sebastian! I spin around to face the lift. The guards stiffen at my movement, making sure I'm not going to attack. But I just want to see my brother.

The glass doors rise and there he is on the other side, two guards on either side of him. As if an eight-year-old could over-power even one guard.

My heart leaps at the sight of him. I don't care about the guards—when the doors open, I run to Sebastian. One guard makes a grab for me, but I slip through their fingers and wrap my arms around Sebastian before they can do anything about it.

He's in my arms. I touch his back, his shoulders, his face, his arms. I bury my face in his hair, smelling the sweet scent of curry spices that still linger from the restaurant below our pod. His skinny little arms circle my back and hold on tight. We're both sobbing. My tears dampen his hair.

"*Hermanito*," I breathe.

Sebastian grips me tighter.

For a moment, everything else fades away. There's no such thing as PMC Life Tech, there's no camera crew waiting to take my false confession, no guards, and certainly no Dr. Lederman. There's just Sebastian and me, gripping each other and crying.

"You've seen him now," Dr. Lederman says, behind me.

I reluctantly look over my shoulder, once again aware of the danger. My tongue stings with distaste at the thought of it, but I need to confess this lie. I look down at Sebastian. His dark round eyes, so innocent, peer back up at me.

I kiss his forehead and brush his hair away from his face. Then I kiss his head again as I squeeze him tight one more time.

I'm stalling, but I don't want to let him go. Is this the last time I'll ever get to see him? To touch him? Smell him? My fingers convulse in his hair. They revolt against letting him go.

Dr. Lederman clears his throat, and I sob in response.

I hear Lederman open his mouth to speak, but I interrupt, "You swear he'll be looked after?" My voice is thick from crying, but it's still full of venom. "You swear he'll have a home, education, money for food and clothing?" My tear-stained eyes bore into Dr. Lederman's.

"Yes, he'll have all that," Lederman says with an impatient sigh. "He'll have more than you could ever have provided him."

"Prove it."

Lederman rolls his eyes impatiently, then clicks something on his comms unit, bringing a screen down from the ceiling. The screen shows Sabastian's credit balance. It's climbing every second.

"As you can see, we've already organized a sizable investment in Sebastian," Lederman says. The screen changes to show a beautiful townhouse near the edge of the bubble city. "These are the Longworths. They live in the Bama quarter and they've agreed to have Sebastian stay with them." A friendly looking man, woman and child stand out the front of the house, smiling into the camera. "... for a price." The screen flicks again, now to show a school. "I've taken the liberty of enrolling Sebastian in the Bama Sector School. Do you approve?"

I swallow. It's everything I want for Sebastian—money, opportunity, a safe home. Tears well in my eyes again, but it's not from happiness. They're tears for myself. I will miss him.

I nod to Lederman.

"Right then." He gestures to the camera crew.

My muscles sag. My fingers lessen their deathly grip on Sebastian, but it's still an effort for me to disentangle myself from him. Sebastian doesn't want to let go either. It feels like a knife piercing my heart as I push his hands away.

I step back from him. He stands there, limply, looking sad and alone. So alone. His tiny body gone slack with defeat. His eyes, rimmed with red, are wide and pleading. I don't want to leave him, but this is the only way I can keep him safe.

I squeeze my eyes shut, steeling myself for what needs to be done. Tears roll freely down my cheeks. I open my eyes again and take another step back.

A guard lays their hands on Sebastian's shoulders, gently pulling him away from me.

A sob bursts out my lips. But then I turn my back to Sebastian, and nod to Lederman again. Malice flashes in his eyes as he waves me toward the camera crew.

"We'll have you stand by this window," the reporter says, gesturing to the side of the room where she's standing, "so we can see the city behind you." The reporter is a woman, dressed immaculately, just like my Mamá would be if she were still alive. Of course, they wouldn't get Persephone's friend, Daniel, to do this report.

I wipe my eyes and nod, moving around the large table to do as they say. Three of the guards move with me.

I realize that everyone in this room is aware of the lies I'm about to spin. They're all complicit in Lederman's games. They can clearly see that I'm being blackmailed and they're not doing anything to stop it.

Despair turns to anger and disgust. How can they let this happen? Just stand by and watch?

My stomach feels leaden. Because I'm no better. If I go ahead with this, I am condemning everyone in this city. I am betraying the Terrene Folk. PMC will keep on killing people, and it will be all my fault. Just so I can save one person. How many people will die so Sebastian can be safe? How many am I willing to sacrifice? How many is too many?

All of them.

I'd sacrifice all of them to save Sebastian.

The truth crawls over my flesh like a swarm of beetles, but I can't deny it. No matter how much it repulses me, how much I hate myself for doing it. I will do anything to save Sebastian.

My spine goes taut. I lift my head high and resolve settles my stomach. I will say these lies. I will save Sebastian and I will condemn myself. Even if guilt eats me from the inside out. Even if it means other people will die because of me.

I deserve to go to prison for this. I'll be charged with fraud and that's exactly what this is. I'll be condemned for hurting people, which is exactly what I'm doing. But it's worth it. I feel my body turn to steel. My little brother is worth all of it.

I glance back at him. As usual, his dark hair flops over his eyes; eyes that watch me with trust and love. I wonder how he'll look at me when he realizes what I've done. I turn away from him. It doesn't matter. At least he'll be safe.

I reach the reporter and look out the window at the bubble and the city below. Three of the guards stop a short distance behind me. The reporter directs me into place with her hands on my shoulders. My skin crawls under her touch. Then she turns to the cameraman to ensure he's in position. He gives her the thumbs up and she turns back to me, holding out a microphone.

"Martina," she says, "in your own words, please tell us what you'd like to say to your fellow citizens."

I glance at the cameraman, and at the large camera with its dark lens staring me down. My heart beats faster and the back of my neck tingles. I glance at Dr. Lederman again. He stares back expectantly.

"I … I …" I falter. "The video …"

"Help her out, would you!" Dr. Lederman says.

The reporter nods and speaks into her microphone. "Martina, you leaked the video of Dr. Lederman, is that correct?"

"Yes." I swallow the lump in my throat.

"How did you come across this video?"

"I made it. It's …" This is it. I'm really going to do this. I glance at Sebastian, his innocent eyes watching me. He'll have an amazing life, and this is all I have to do to make it happen. Just one little lie. One little lie with lethal consequences. But Sebastian will be safe. I take a deep breath. "It's not real. *Perdón.* It's all made up and Dr. Lederman is innocent." I say the last few words quickly, spitting them out of my treacherous mouth.

Dr. Lederman's eyes sparkle with glee.

"And why would you do such a thing?" The reporter asks with clipped precision. A professional reporter. Just like Mamá. But Mamá would never be part of such a thing. Not like me. I wonder what she's thinking of me right now in heaven. Would she be happy I'm saving her only son? Even if it means so many others will die?

I look down at my hands before answering. People who watch this will probably think I feel guilty, and I do, but not for the reasons they think. "To blackmail him."

"I see," the reporter says. "So you fabricated the whole video?"

I nod.

"And the report, too?"

"That's correct, yes," I whisper.

The reporter asks something else, but I can't hear what she says over the drumming of my heart. My eyes catch Sebastian's.

His lips are trembling. Does he understand what I've done? I've condemned myself and everyone else in this city to save him, to give him a chance in life. And although I'd do it again to make sure he's safe, I can't help wishing I hadn't done it.

I think of Rosa struggling to make ends meet in the diner; of poor Old Henry working his aged muscles to the bone; of Liam and the other kids training in the street so they're not robbed of all they have; of the Terrene Folk dying for my cause. Today I haven't helped any of them. I've doomed them. After all the times they've helped me, I couldn't repay the favor—not at the expense of Sebastian's life. I've let everybody down.

The reporter is waiting for my response, but I have no idea what she asked. I just gape at her, opening and closing my mouth; the only sound coming out is a strange croak.

"Some water might help," Lederman says in a sickeningly polite voice.

I nod at the suggestion.

A guard steps away from the others and pours a glass of water. When he returns, he stands unusually close—between me and the reporter. In confusion, I look into his face through the hazsuit visor.

George winks back at me.

I almost drop the glass, but my fingers grip a little tighter before it slips through them, although some water sloshes over the edge. I hear Lederman guffaw. He finds my nervousness amusing.

George still stands between me and the camera crew, as if waiting to take the glass back. He holds my eyes, trying to tell me something I don't understand. But I do know he's here to help.

What have I done? I betrayed the Terrene Folk, when all along George has been here, trying to help me. And he's still trying. If only I stalled a few more minutes so he could carry out his plan.

I take a sip of the water and hand the glass back to George. His nod is almost imperceptible, but I catch it, bracing myself for whatever his plan is.

He moves, and I duck.

The glass leaves his fingers, flying through the air and crashing into the visor of a guard behind me. Water drips down his hazsuit. The perfect conduit to increase the shock when George strikes him with his stun baton. The guard's suit sparks with electricity and he convulses spasmodically. He shudders to the ground.

The other guard reacts slowly, caught unprepared. He tries too late to hit George with his baton; George is already on top of him, beating him in the stomach. George lets go with another zap from his stun baton and the guard flops to the floor.

George grabs my hand and we bound right over the top of the boardroom table. Dr. Lederman backs away, fear flashing in his eyes, and the camera crew cower in the corner.

And there is Sebastian. The last guard stands with him by the lift, a hand on his shoulder holding him in place. As I leap off the table, I change my trajectory toward the last guard, intending to use the momentum to flatten them. They back up nervously when they realize my intention. At the last moment, I see through the guard's visor and into the dark pools of Persephone's eyes.

I skid to a stop, just short of hitting her.

"How?" I mouth the word, but there's no time for talking.

Persephone has the lift door propped open and the four of us squeeze inside. George slams the button to close the doors.

As the glass doors inch together, Dr. Lederman stands on the other side. His initial shock is gone and a deathly rage stands in its place. He brands me with his stare.

Thirty-One

THE LIFT DESCENDS TOO quickly for my liking. When we exit, the guards will be on us. I grip Sebastian's shoulders way too hard. He doesn't complain, but I force my fingers to loosen.

I look out of the glass walls of the lift, down at the streets below. Guards are rushing toward the PMC building. Dr. Lederman must have sounded the alarms. We're fugitives now.

Persephone's eyes flick to mine. They're hard to read. They're aflame with something—fear or bravery or concern. It's hard to tell. But I missed seeing them.

"We need to get out of this lift," I say, tearing my eyes away from Persephone's. "We can't wait 'til it reaches the ground."

"You're right," George says, and presses the button for level three.

The lift slows as it approaches the level. Outside the glass doors is a dim foyer. No guards. I exhale in relief. Maybe we'll find a way out of this mess. Find somewhere to hide until PMC has been torn down by the people—but will that happen now after they've aired my false confession?

I tap my foot impatiently as the lift settles and the doors finally slide open. I burst out of them before they're fully open, Sebastian in tow, my hand gripping his.

In front of me is a glass wall with a large room beyond. I squint through the glass, but it's hard to make out what's on the other side; it's a blur of darkness pinpricked by the occasional spot of light.

Persephone goes straight to the security pad and enters a PIN. The glass wall slides in the middle, admitting us into the dark beyond.

There are no overhead lights, but we navigate easily due to the small lights that sit inside glass cases. There are rows upon rows of cases, the lights showing the contents of their shelves; beakers, test tubes, jars. It seems like there are endless shelves, endless beakers.

They must be samples of some kind. Diseases? Cures? Medications? I'm tempted to ask Persephone if she knows anything, but now isn't the time for chatting.

My body tenses as we walk down one aisle, away from the entrance. I squint into a case; it holds a row of test tubes filled with a yellow liquid.

A shiver runs down my spine, leaving my toes and fingertips tingling. Persephone and George are safe in their hazsuits, but what about me and Sebastian? As long as everything stays in their cases, we'll be safe.

"Be careful, but hurry. *Rapido*," I whisper to Sebastian.

We pick up speed, heading for the other side of the room, hoping there's an exit. George and Persephone's large hazmat boots thump loudly as they jog, echoing throughout the entire storeroom. That's why I almost miss the sound of the door to the storage room opening. But I do hear it beep as a PIN is accepted.

I freeze.

A whoosh signals the doors sliding open.

"Shh." I hold my finger to my mouth and duck to the ground, pulling Sebastian down with me. George and Persephone go to the floor too, with a slight clunk as they do; it's impossible for them to move silently in their lumbering suits.

Footsteps echo through the large room. There's more than one of them. By the heavy boom, boom, boom of their steps, I guess they're also wearing hazsuits. I can't tell quite how many there are; the echoes make it sound like there's a hundred of them. It's probably just five or six.

We need to leave. I barely breathe as I consider our options. I can't see any way out ahead, but behind, I spot a soft green glow. It could be an exit sign, but it's hard to tell. I shuffle forward to get a better view.

"We know you're in here!" A voice calls through the gloom.

I stiffen again. They must have heard my movement.

"Come out, come out," they say, as if they're playing hide-and-seek with children. "Come out. We won't hurt you."

I recognize the voice but can't place it. It's obvious its owner enjoys having power over others; the taunt and glee clear in their voice.

The footsteps grow closer as the guards move among the rows of cases. I glance toward the green glow again; I still can't tell if it's an exit sign or something else. Maybe it's just a beaker of green that the light is reflecting off; not a sanctuary at all, but a death trap. However, if I don't do something now, and fast, these guards are going to find us in no time.

Still gripping Sebastian's hand, I leap to my feet.

We run.

I don't care about the cases and their deadly contents. I don't care about the noise we make; they're going to hear us anyway.

Now that we're making more noise, the echoing makes it harder to pinpoint where the noise is coming from. We could be anywhere in the storeroom. But it also makes it harder to know where the guards are, too. All I know is there's so much noise bouldering around the room—and my head—that they must be moving too.

I glimpse a white hazsuit in the glass's reflection. I spin around, expecting to see a guard right behind us, but it's only George and Persephone. My heart is in my throat. I swallow it down and pull Sebastian around another case of samples.

Persephone makes a noise, like a desert mouse shrieking. I look up to see a guard at the other end of the aisle. He's coming toward us. I skirt around another case, putting it between us and the guard, and the others follow. But the guard knows where we are; he calls to his comrades, his voice reverberating down the room.

I look up at the green glow. It *is* an exit sign. George follows my sightline and sees the sign too.

"You go that way." George nods in the direction of the exit sign. "I'll try to distract them. Give you more time to get out."

"Be careful," I say. I want to tell him not to go, to stay close, to not put himself at risk. And if I was alone, I *would* tell him that. But his plan is the best chance we have. And I'll take that chance, for Sebastian's sake.

I don't look back as I jog toward the light. I keep my head low, pushing Sebastian's down too, hoping they don't see us as we duck behind and around cases, making our way to the back of the room.

"I saw them! Here!" It's George that shouts. I don't know where he is now, but I trust he's leading them in the opposite direction from where we're heading. The thumps of boots pick up speed, heading to George's position.

We slide into another aisle and stop dead.

A guard is already halfway down it. He halts too, clearly surprised.

I use his surprise to our advantage. Letting go of Sebastian's hand, I charge at the guard. I aim low. The guard sees what I'm about to do, and instead of attacking, he steps backward, unsure of himself. I leap.

My shoulders crash into his legs, and he topples backward with me on top.

That's the thing about me. People underestimate me. I might be small, but I'm powerful.

Persephone doesn't waste a second. She grabs Sebastian and leaps over both of us. I knee the guard in the groin before clambering off him. He sucks in a sharp breath. I glimpse his face through his visor. It's screwed up in pain. A small satisfaction at causing that pain gives me a spurt of energy as I chase after Persephone and Sebastian.

Sebastian looks back at me as he runs.

"I'm here, *hermanito*," I choke out between hurried breaths.

I catch them quickly because Persephone is so cumbersome in her hazsuit. It's a problem. We'll never outrun them while she's wearing it. But we don't have time to stop so she can take it off either. I reach for Sebastian, quickly running my hand over his face and hair to ensure he's okay. He's puffing from the exertion, probably from fear as well, but he's fine. He can keep going.

"Mar-ti-na," the voice of that first guard singsongs across the room and the echoes take it up like a chorus.

Persephone's eyes widen in recognition. "That's Guard Debbie," she whispers.

Then something smashes, and the tinkling of glass makes music that goes along with her terrifying song.

My nerves turn to ice.

She has smashed a case.

A case filled with unknown, potentially deadly, substances.

Persephone looks at me with eyes as wide as saucers. She grabs Sebastian's shirt and thrusts it over his mouth. I pull my own shirt over my mouth and hope the thin fabric will provide some protection.

"Stop running, Martina," Guard Debbie says, "and you'll be given medical treatment." There's another smash. Another case broken. More deadly toxins in the air.

Of course, she and her guards are all protected in their hazsuits. Only Sebastian and I are at risk. But the door is just there. The exit sign glows brightly, only a few yards away.

I hesitate, but Persephone pushes me on. "Let's go," she yells.

She's right. We have to take the chance and hope the toxins are too far away to have any effect. The break happened on the other side of the room, nowhere near us. I think. I hope.

Persephone doesn't allow me to think more about it. She slams her hand down on the exit button before barreling through the door.

The light beyond almost blinds me after the dimness of the storeroom. We all falter a moment, but don't stop running. It's a stairwell, and we trip and stumble down the steps as quickly as we can.

We're almost down one flight when I hear the door swing open again. I see a guard looking up and then down. He spots us. But it's not a guard after all. It's George.

A sob of relief escapes my lips, but I swallow it. No time to relax yet. They're coming.

We go down another flight and the door to level two looms ahead. Persephone is in front and she doesn't stop to check what's on the other side.

It opens to some kind of lounge.

A handful of people sit inside, reclining in armchairs and loitering by a small kitchen. All of their heads snap up at our entry. Some gasp in shock. We give them no heed and storm through the room.

"Hey aren't you ...?"

I push past the woman addressing me.

There's another exit, an archway leading out to a foyer, and we don't hesitate on our way there. George lumbers behind us, causing another round of gasps.

The foyer has several more doors leading off it and the other set of lifts. This must be the center of the building.

Persephone chooses a door, and we follow her through. This one leads to an auditorium and we stand at the top, looking down on hundreds of chairs with a stage at the bottom. I exhale when I realize it's empty.

There are two exits, one on either side of the stage, indicated by the lights above the doors. Persephone starts off for them, but I grab her arm.

"No, let's hide here a moment," I say. "Hopefully they'll assume we kept running and go through those doors looking for us. Then we can double back and find a different way out."

She nods. George catches up to us as we duck below the line of chairs and start to crawl. Making our way along a row, getting some distance between us and the entrance.

"Take off your suits," I whisper, realizing the large helmets can probably be seen over the top of the chairs, bobbing up and down as they crawl. There are two soft whooshes as their helmets unseal and are discarded.

Both Persephone and George are wriggling out of their suits, like worms writhing on the ground, when a click signals the opening of the door to the auditorium. I grab Persephone's ankle to hush her. George stills too.

I hold my breath.

The lights in the auditorium aren't bright, but I can still see Sebastian clearly. His eyes are wide as they hold mine. His lip quivers. Slowly, so slowly, I remove my hand from Persephone's leg and place it on Sebastian's hand instead. He seems to take some comfort from it.

"Where'd they go?" A guard calls.

There are sounds of them rummaging around the auditorium. I don't dare lift my head to see where they are.

"You two take the left," a guard orders. "We'll take the right." There's a series of thunks as they charge down the steps of the auditorium toward the stage and the exits on either side. After the doors clunk shut, we all take a moment to breathe, not moving from where we are.

I strain my ears to make sure they're gone. I hear nothing.

I pull Sebastian closer and squeeze him tightly. Unsure if it's to comfort him or for my own sake.

Persephone and George shuffle the rest of the way out of their suits. An impossible task to do silently. The suits rustle and squeak as they twist and squirm their way out. As Persephone pulls the suit down, I quickly look away. She's almost naked now, wearing only a black singlet and tight shorts that could possibly be underwear. Heat rises up my neck.

"Should you keep the boots on?" I whisper. But both Persephone and George shake their heads.

"I can run faster barefoot," Persephone says.

George is also in a black singlet with shorts. He looks relieved to be out of the suit as he runs a hand through his red hair. He gives me a lopsided smile.

I grin back at him, although we have little to smile about right now.

I stand up. "Let's go."

I pivot. And my stomach turns to lead.

Thirty-Two

A GUARD STANDS A few chairs down. He stops creeping toward us when he sees me stand, and instead, he jumps onto the seats. He lunges forward.

I shriek, backing away. I trip on Persephone, who's still on the ground, and stumble backward. My reflex is to grab for Sebastian and he falls backward too, both of us landing with a hard smack.

George is on his feet and faces the guard, who takes another leap at George's middle. But George is ready. He uses the guard's momentum to lift him into the air and throw him over his shoulder, slamming him down on the row of chairs behind us.

It's the attack I should have done if I didn't back away like a coward.

The guard is dazed, but conscious. He immediately fumbles to stand up.

"Go!" George screams, and we take off. We scramble over chairs and each other. Persephone, now free of her suit, shoots like a rocket along the row of chairs ahead of us, not hindered by her lack of shoes, and up the steps of the auditorium.

George stays behind, grappling with the guard. Both are grunting as punches are thrown. Sebastian trips on the step and falls. I tear my eyes away from George and focus on Sebastian. I pull him up and push him on, up the auditorium steps. We're almost at the top when the guard lets out a whelp.

There is quiet behind us. A quick glance shows George, stun baton in hand, climbing off the fallen guard.

When George sees us hesitating, he again yells, "Go!" and bounds up the stairs in large leaps, covering the distance in seconds.

We dash through the door, back into the foyer area. Instead of returning to the lounge, we opt for another door that displays a sign indicating it's another stairwell. We pass the first floor and head down to the basement.

The scent of the basement fills my nostrils well before we've reached it. A thick chemical smell, possibly a disinfectant. I expect the door to open to another laboratory or a hospital ward. Images of dying people, doctors, pharmacists, and guards flicker through my mind. Or another storeroom that will put us all at risk. I dread what we'll find.

I open the door and stand for a moment, stunned. The room is full of soft, relaxing lighting. Its walls are decorated floor to ceiling with blue tiles, and a large body of water occupies the middle of it. So large that you could house a hundred sleeping pods. The water sits still and empty, a whisper of steam rising from it.

"What is it?" My voice echoes around the room. I shiver. More echoes, just like the deadly storeroom. I can't begin to imagine what this water is used for. It's much larger than a bath, but it has the same scent as the decontamination showers. Maybe it decontaminates masses of people at once.

Persephone raises her eyebrows in surprise. "It's a swimming pool."

"What's a swimming pool?" Sebastian asks.

I shrug, looking down at him. "Sebastian," I gasp when I notice the blood running down his leg. Kneeling in front of him, my hands glide over his body, desperately trying to locate his injury.

"I'm fine, Martina." Sebastian tries to push me off, but I don't let go. "I just scraped my knee when I fell."

Through a tear in his trousers, I see the cut just below his knee, a sharp but shallow gash and a graze across his skin. It doesn't look bad, but guilt floods me anyway. "*Lo siento mucho, hermanito.*"

"I know where we are," George interrupts. "Follow me."

There's a large entranceway to the left of us, but George ignores it. His bare feet patter on the tiles as he walks around the swimming pool. He stops at a door, almost hidden in a nook at the back of the room. We follow slowly, making sure not to slip on the damp surface.

The door opens to a corridor, but this one isn't like the pristine halls on the upper levels. This one has plain concrete walls with pipes and wires running along them. Fluorescent lights flicker overhead. It's almost like somewhere you'd find in The Nix, except there are no people.

We're not running any more but walk quickly, following George, trusting him to navigate this subterranean world. I quickly lose track of where we are and where we've come from; we take so many left and right turns. George could leave me here, and I doubt I could find my way out. But we haven't seen or heard anyone else down here, so my heart rate starts to lower and I feel I'm finally getting oxygen back into my lungs.

Then we turn a corner to find a man in a business suit.

Thirty-Three

THE MAN HAS HIS back to us. He looks completely out of place here in his tailored suit amongst the dusty floor and pipe-covered walls. But he doesn't seem to be waiting for us. Something else is keeping his attention. I realize he's fiddling with something on the wall.

George continues his approach, and I assume he's going to attack the man from behind. But the man hears us approaching and spins around.

"Nathan?" I cry.

Nathan stands before me in an expensive suit, typical of the fashion in the Sparkle Sector, with his hair neatly tied back. He looks like a different person to the rugged nomad I've gotten to know outside.

"What?" Nathan stares at me. "Ah, Martina ..." He swallows and looks at George for explanation.

"What are you doing here?" I demand.

Nathan looks at Sebastian, who's clutching my arm and peeking around my body. Then they roam to Persephone. His eyes harden. "You're the rich girl, huh?"

"I'm Persephone." Persephone tilts her head, looking down her nose at him. It probably won't help him like her any better, but it makes me proud of her anyway. She holds out her hand to shake his. "Good health to you."

Nathan looks at her hand, his eyes narrowed. He doesn't take it.

Persephone lowers her hand, but maintains eye contact with him.

Nathan blinks at her a few times and then turns to George. His voice is hard as he says, "What are they doing here?"

I roll my eyes and repeat, "What are *you* doing here?"

Both men ignore me. Instead, George tells Nathan, "We busted Martina and her brother out. Persephone knew where we could find some guards' hazsuits and once we were suited up, it was easy to pretend we were guards. A few white lies and we found ourselves as Sebastian's escorts to see his sister. Of course, it all went to hell once we found her." He winks at me. "And we've been chased through the PMC building for the better part of an hour. Found ourselves down by the pool. Didn't do any swimming though." He grins at his own joke. "Wondered if you might still be down here."

"What is going on?" I ask through gritted teeth. My patience is wearing thin from all their secrets and avoidance of my questions.

"I'm almost finished," Nathan says, turning back to the wall. I try to peer over his shoulder. He flicks some buttons on a device that is fixed to the wall, but I have no idea what it does. "Done." He closes a lid over it and turns back to us.

"Good," George says. "The guards might follow us down here, so we'd better get going."

Nathan says, "They'll have bigger things than us to worry about soon. Still, we'd better get out of here quick."

George and Nathan exchange knowing smiles as Nathan hurries to pack up his tools.

My heart quickens. "What does that mean?"

"We've set explosives to blow the whole place down," George says casually, his face beaming with pride.

"You've set explosives to blow up the bubble city? Is this phase two that Mother Jessica mentioned?" My voice is icy calm, but a war is brewing inside of me.

Nathan avoids my eyes, looking at his tools, to the ground, the wall, anywhere but me.

"Yep!" George says gleefully, rocking back on his heels. "Well, it'll blow up this quarter anyway. We don't have enough explosives to do the whole city. But this will be enough."

George is completely oblivious that *I'm* about to explode. He carries on as if it's a brilliant idea that's not going to hurt anyone.

I glance at Persephone. Her eyes blink with the realization of what this means for her, her family, her friends. Everyone she knows is at risk. She shivers, and I'm sure it's got nothing to do with the small amount of clothing she's wearing.

Sebastian grips my hand in both of his. I squeeze back.

"I trusted you," I growl, low and threatening.

George stops his chattering to stare at me, but my attention is on Nathan. The boy who I opened up to, who I told the story of my parents and my narrow escape from Colombia. I trusted him. How could I be so foolish?

"We've got to go," Nathan says, slinging his bag of tools onto his shoulder.

He steps to leave, but I stand in front of him, stopping him in his tracks.

I stare daggers. His expression is unreadable.

"We had to do something," Nathan finally says.

"People will die."

"But the Terrene will be safe." His jaw sets. "I've got to look out for Will. I can't let what happened to Tahnee happen to him."

"What about Sebastian?"

"They had taken you, Martina." He runs his hands through his hair, messing it up. "We couldn't let you say it was all a lie. We've come too far." He sounds exasperated, as if I should understand why he has betrayed me.

"But you planned this *before* Dr. Lederman called me."

He shrugs. "We needed a backup plan. He's evil, Martina. Of course *he* was going to have a backup, so we did too."

My fingers curl into fists, even the one holding Sebastian's hand. I let go when I realize I'm squeezing his fingers too hard.

Nathan goes to leave again, but seeing my anger, he continues, "Martina, you were going to deny that video is real."

"She already has," George says gravely.

I feel everyone turn to stare at me. I bow my head, tears pricking at my eyes.

"Really?" Nathan says, his voice rough. "No ..."

I nod, looking back up at him. He meets my stare. And his expression turns dark.

"See!" He slams his fist into his palm. "I had to do something to protect the Terrene. We can't let PMC keep pursuing us and killing us." His eyes seek mine, as if for understanding. "This will destroy PMC headquarters. We'll have them on the run."

Persephone inhales sharply.

"I'm not going to let you do it," I say. Even though I hate what I've done, I can't let him do it. Not when I've already condemned so many people. I can't stomach any more death. "I'm not going to let you kill hundreds, *thousands*, of innocent people. They're not all like Lederman." I shout my last words.

Nathan shakes his head furiously. Persephone shakes her head, too, in disbelief, her face crumbling in horror.

"You can't stop it," Nathan says.

"I won't let you," I shout.

"The bombs are already set to blow," Nathan says quietly.

I gasp. That can't be true. But I glance at George and he nods in confirmation.

"I can't believe you did this." I point my finger in turn at Nathan and George. "How much time do we have?" Maybe I can stop them. Maybe I can still find them and disarm them.

"Enough time for us to get out of here," Nathan says.

"Which is precisely how long?" Persephone demands, finally finding her voice.

Nathan checks the time on his comms unit. "Thirty-nine minutes, precisely. So can we go now?"

Thirty-nine minutes. Thirty-nine minutes until thousands of innocent people will have their death warrants signed. Many may survive being exposed. Some might not get sick at all. But not everyone. Not everyone can survive a cold, or the other diseases Nathan, George, and the Terrene Folk take for granted outside. I almost died. Will Sebastian survive?

My Mamá's wasting face floats before me. I hear Papá's sobs as I crawl away from him, escaping out of the Colombian bubble city. Both are gone. Dead. Who else will die today? Who else will now share our fate? Who will lose their parents, just like Sebastian and me? A life struggling to make ends meet, with no guidance, no love. Just the two of us.

I pull Sebastian to me, holding him tightly.

"I think we should go, Martina," Sebastian whispers.

"Yeah, me too, *hermanito.*" But where to? George and Nathan obviously intend to escape outside the city. But what about Sebastian and Persephone? They might not survive outside.

If the bombs are only set to blow up the Sparkle Sector, it means the other sectors can be sealed and we'll be safe. If we get there in time. And if we're quick enough, maybe we can save some other people, too.

I turn to leave. Nathan grabs my arm to stop me. I try to shake him off.

"Don't touch me," I growl, and he grips tighter.

He looks hurt, but says softly, "Where are you going?"

"To save my brother," I pull out of his grasp, "and other innocent people." I stride away with Sebastian and Persephone, leaving Nathan and George to make their own escape out of the city.

I hear George mumble, "Let her go. We've got to get out of here."

I don't look back, but my heart aches.

As we travel down the concrete tunnels, I worry we're never going to find our way out before the bombs detonate. But an exit isn't that hard to find after all. Attached to a wall is a ladder, and in the roof is a manhole. It's got to lead somewhere, and we can't stay here, so I climb.

I push off the manhole cover, revealing the streets of the Sparkle Sector above.

"This is it," I call down before climbing out onto the street. I reach down to pull Sebastian up, and Persephone after him.

There aren't many people in the street, but the ones that are stop and watch us. Some point, recognizing me. I guess I'm infamous now. Everyone seems to recognize my face.

I stop to catch my breath, then shout, "There's a bomb!"

People look at me strangely. Maybe they don't hear me or don't understand.

I take a deep breath and say more calmly, "Someone has set this place to blow. You need to get into one of the other sectors."

They murmur to each other, exchanging glances, but no one rushes off.

"Hurry!" I shout, but I don't wait for them. I run along the street, dragging Sebastian and Persephone with me.

We enter the main square, where there are more people milling about. Some are in cafes, others are strolling by. But a large portion of them are facing a platform.

Belatedly, I hear what they hear. Dr. Lederman's voice. Then I see him, standing proudly on top of the platform, guards at his sides, speaking into a microphone. He's come down from his tower to address his fellow Sparkle Sector citizens.

"We have proof that this video was doctored. It's a fake." His smarmy voice projects across the crowd from loud speakers. "Martina Monsalve is the culprit. She did it to blackmail me."

Behind him on a big screen is an enlarged image of me in my orange prison attire.

"It's not real," my image says, the words echoing around the square. "*Perdón.* It's all made up and Dr. Lederman is innocent."

I turn to Persephone, desperate to fix this, to take it back. She's staring at the screen in horror, as if this is the first time she's hearing this, even though she was in the room when it happened.

"Take Sebastian and run." My voice is urgent. "Get out of this sector. Go to The Nix."

Persephone looks away from the screen and turns to me. She shakes her head.

"It's your only chance," I say firmly. "And Sebastian's. Do this for me."

"No Martina," Sebastian says.

"What are you going to do?" Persephone asks.

"I don't know, but I can't let all these people die, or ... maybe die. I have to help them. And maybe I can help the Terrene people as well—take back my confession." I turn to Sebastian. "Go with Persephone." He shakes his head, crying. "Don't worry, *hermanito.* I won't be long. But I have to do this and you won't be safe if you come with me. Trust me, okay?" He looks to the ground, tears falling from his cheeks.

Persephone tugs on my hand, indecision crossing her features.

"You have to go," I beg her. "I'm the only one who can do this. Please, get Sebastian to safety."

She presses her lips against mine in the briefest of kisses. And then she's gone, tugging Sebastian away with her before I have a chance to react. Sebastian looks back but lets Persephone lead him away.

I stare after her, stunned for a moment, my lips tingling. It gives me strength, although my legs wobble and I'm not sure if it's from the kiss or from what I'm about to do. But it makes me take a step toward the platform. And another. I don't stop until I'm within the crowd.

I couldn't do this if I didn't trust her to keep Sebastian safe.

"We are searching for Martina Monsalve and we will bring her to justice." Dr. Lederman slams his fist into his palm.

"I'm right here," I shout over the heads of people in tailored suits and sparkling dresses.

The Health Minister's head snaps to me. "You!"

Everyone turns. The people closest take a step away. I wonder if they think I'm infected. Maybe it's my orange jumpsuit that pegs me as a criminal. Whatever the reason, I hope they still believe me.

"Dr. Lederman is the liar," I cry. The camera crew that had been live-streaming Lederman's speech, now turn their cameras to me. I must look a mess. Sweat runs down my face, my hands are stained with Sebastian's blood, and I'm red-faced and panting. I probably look like I do have an infectious disease. No wonder people are looking at me warily.

But I don't stop. I point my finger at Lederman. "*You* are killing the people you've sworn to protect. *You* have done it all for greed. *You* are the plague on these lands."

With each sentence I shout, I take a step closer to him. It feels good to say the truth.

Lederman waves his hands at the guards, directing them to capture me.

"For years, you've tricked these people. And I won't let you do it any longer." I turn to the crowd, trying to get the words out before the guards stop me. "Our lives have not been our own. We've been manipulated, lied to, and killed. The truth is, Dr. Lederman and PMC *have* been infecting people on purpose so they can line their pockets with your money."

Two guards are close, edging toward me, but I dart deeper into the crowd to avoid them.

"I was coerced into that confession." I point to the screen. "Lederman threatened to kill my little brother. But I want you to know the truth."

Another two guards are closing in, but surprisingly, they're blocked by others in the crowd who give me the chance to keep speaking. "You're a liar," someone shouts. "Let her speak," someone else calls.

"They've denied that people can live outside the bubble cities and have been hunting and killing off the people that live out there so you wouldn't know about it. Those people now surround our city and they're seeking vengeance."

"Give them Lederman," a woman shouts.

Others in the crowd stir, shifting toward Dr. Lederman.

Lederman takes a step back, his eyes flicking back and forth, clearly aware of the danger he's in.

I hold up my hands to halt the crowd from jumping him, or rushing out of the city. "But," I shout a little louder, trying to hold their attention. "But, there are still diseases that can kill us outside. We need to be careful."

People glance at each other, confused. I know it's a lot of information, but I don't have long to tell it before the bombs explode.

"We can't just rush outside and survive, we might die. And ... we might die if the bubble collapses." I look around, making eye contact where I can. Then I look directly at a camera. "Listen carefully," I say gravely. "There is a bomb set to explode."

Gasps. Wide eyes. Dropped jaws.

"It's going to bring down this sector, the Bush quarter. You need to evacuate. You need to get into the other sectors and seal them."

People start to move. But some continue to stare.

"Where?" someone asks.

"Who did this?" asks another.

"Why?" a woman next to me shouts.

"Go!" I scream. "You need to get out of here."

Hands grip my shoulders, holding me in place. The guards have caught up to me.

People are finally starting to disperse, but not quickly enough. "Hurry!" I shout, struggling to get free myself. "Hurry. Go!"

The hands tug at me sharply and I look up to see the face of Guard Debbie behind her visor, a glint of satisfaction in her eyes. She drags me out of the square.

"Hey, no!" I cry as she drags me backward. "You're going to die, too. There's a bomb. You need to get to the other sectors."

Others now take heed and are rushing back and forth around us, but Guard Debbie ignores me. She doesn't even look at me. She's determined to carry out her orders.

I squirm and kick and twist, but it does me no good. Her hold is firm. Besides, I'm exhausted, and part of the fight has gone out of me now I know Sebastian is safe.

Instead of the PMC building, she drags me behind the platform, where Dr. Lederman is waiting.

He has lost his smug expression. Now he scowls with open hatred. His brows furrowed as much as they can.

"You are really testing my patience, girl," he says, as if I'm a child. Yet he's the one with lips pouting like a sulky kid. "If you had just let it be, everyone would be safe."

"You know that's not true," I say.

He paces. "Everything I've done was for the good of the city. It was in everyone's best interest to stay safe, to take their medications, to stop the spread of diseases. I did what I had to, to keep as many people as safe as possible. So many people are going to die because of you. They'll go outside and they'll die. And this bomb!"

He spins to look at me. "How long do we have, Martina?"

I shake my head. "I don't know."

"Must be a bit of time, else you wouldn't have stuck around." He shrugs as if it's not a problem. "I take it the bomb was Mother Jessica's idea?" He tilts his head in question, then he scoffs when my eyes widen. "You didn't think I knew about her?" He reads my confused expression again. "Oh, I see. You just didn't know she was behind the bombs. It's not the first time, you know."

I freeze. Colombia. Were the Terrene responsible for the collapse of the Colombian bubble? Could they have traveled that far?

"Don't you see that it's your friends that are the liars, Martina? They're the ones hurting and killing people."

I shake my head, but I can't deny it. He's right. They have been lying to me. I remember the sly looks Mother exchanged with Nathan and George. How they avoided my questions. The tight line of her lips as she kept her secrets from me. It dawns on me, clear as day now. That's why the Terrene didn't move on. That's why they stayed close to the bubble city, why they had access codes to get inside, why they knew all about the workings of the city. And why I had seen Nathan walking through the desert that day. He was preparing for an attack on the city.

It all makes sense now. This has been their plan all along.

As I stare at Dr. Lederman, my heart breaks in two. It feels like it's tearing one side of itself from the other. I had trusted them, but just like Lederman, they never told the whole truth. And just like Lederman, they hurt people too.

They're no better than PMC.

My legs give way. I would crumble to the floor if it weren't for Guard Debbie still gripping my arms.

Were they responsible for killing my parents? Did they cause the Colombian bubble to collapse?

"Silly girl." Lederman tut-tuts. "And now you're going to pay for their treachery." He nods at something behind me.

I look over my shoulder. Another group of guards are coming toward us. I don't know how many there are. But it's not them that has caught my eye.

Between them is the dark mop of hair and innocent eyes I know so well. Sebastian. He isn't struggling, but they grip his shoulders as if he is.

I let out a strangled cry.

Behind him is Persephone. She's not as placid as Sebastian. Her body twists in their grasp, she bucks and hisses, and struggles with all her might. She kicks, landing a decent blow on her captor's leg. Her captor lets out a grunt and then slaps her across the face. She gasps, but doesn't stop.

Dr. Lederman walks around me to meet them as they're dragged forward. He stands too close to Persephone for comfort. She stares daggers back at him.

He takes her face firmly in his hand.

"Oh, my dear," he croons. "I never did like you much. You've always been a troublemaker. I told your mother as such, but she wouldn't listen. She insisted you'd be brought around. I love being right, but it breaks my heart a little. You would have been a great asset to our team, and it would have kept your mother happy. Too bad you're such a nosey little bitch." He squeezes her face and then pushes her away.

"Where's my mother?" Persephone says, her eyes blazing with fury. "Wait until she hears about this. She'll kill you if you hurt me."

"We won't hurt you," Lederman says, "but I can't say the same about your friends."

She tries to attack him as he dismisses her, but her guards hold her back.

"You bastards!" she screams.

Lederman approaches Sebastian.

"Don't you touch him!" My screams join Persephone's. "Don't you dare touch him." I pull and tug, but Guard Debbie's fingers are like steel clasps.

Lederman pulls Sebastian to him as if he's a proud father. Sebastian faces me, the health minister's hands resting on his shoulders. Dr. Lederman almost looks affectionate and protective; a total facade.

"Isn't he such a nice little boy?" Lederman strokes Sebastian's hair, one finger trailing down his face. Sebastian's lower lip trembles, but I can tell he's trying to stay calm. "So young, so innocent. It would be a shame for anything to happen to him."

My shrieks turn to pleads. "Please, don't. Don't hurt him, please."

"Wouldn't it be awful if Sebastian died?" Lederman's eyes open a little wider, as if he's merely curious of the answer. Then he pulls something out of his pocket. It shimmers and glints in his hands. Something metal and glass.

He holds it to Sebastian's neck.

A syringe.

"No." I'm sobbing, reaching out to Sebastian even though he's too far away.

The piercing needle almost brushes the delicate skin of Sebastian's neck—it's so close. I don't know what's inside it. It could be any number of deadly viruses. The liquid is so clear it could be water. My heart skips—perhaps it is water, and this is all a bluff. But I know Lederman isn't bluffing. He doesn't need to.

Lederman leers at me. "It didn't have to come to this, Martina. We could have finished with all of this already. Sebastian would be off to his new life in the Bama quarter, safe and sound. But no. You had to make things difficult. I have a mind to stick him with this needle right now, just for the trouble you've caused me."

He sneers at Sebastian and my heart stops. He looks back at the needle, his eyes darkening. "This isn't like anything you've ever seen before. It's a new biological weapon we've been experimenting with. Supposedly it can kill its victims within seconds. A neuro-toxin that can cross the blood–brain barrier and shut down the brain almost instantaneously."

The needle edges closer and closer. "Do you understand what that means, Miss Monsalve? He doesn't stand a chance if he gets pricked with this. So just do what I tell you and he'll live. Simple?"

I swallow. "Yes. Yes, I'll do anything."

"Tell me where the bomb is."

My blood goes cold. I can't tell him where the bombs are because I don't know. I feel my voice thicken as I say, "I ... I ... I don't know."

"Don't play games with me, girl."

"I'm not, I'm not." I raise my palms to him. "Please ... please ... I don't know. I really don't. All I know is there is more than one. I don't know where they are. I swear. *Lo juro por Dios.*"

The needle rests on Sebastian's neck. "Tell me!"

"*¡Por favor!*"

Then a bomb goes off.

Thirty-Four

THE EXPLOSION ROCKS THE entire city. My ears are still ringing when another goes off. And another. The noise is deafening. My eyes dart up to the glass bubble, expecting it to crack.

"You stupid girl," Lederman shouts over the noise. I tear my eyes away from the glass ceiling and fix them on Lederman. And in the blink of an eye, he presses down on the syringe. The clear liquid disappears; squeezed into Sebastian's veins.

For a moment, I'm paralyzed.

He didn't do it. Surely, he didn't do it.

But the syringe is empty, and Lederman lets it fall to the ground.

I watch as it bounces on the marble.

Sebastian squeezes his eyes shut briefly. When he opens them again, they're bloodshot. Already.

Please don't let this be real.

"Martina." My name floats from Sebastian's lips.

"No!" I scream. My body jumps to life again. I thrash at Guard Debbie's hold, using all my energy and power into getting free—my eyes never leaving Sebastian's—but there's nothing I can do. I watch as his body goes slack. His knees bend, crumbling beneath him. They hit the ground. Then his torso leans to the right—falling, falling—until his tiny body is slumped on the ground.

My own knees collapse under me, and my body slumps—falling, falling—in Guard Debbie's grasp. As if I'm dying with him.

And I guess I am.

Sebastian.

I'm dimly aware of another explosion, closer this time, rocking the foundations we stand on. My arms are released from Guard Debbie's grasp, and I fall the last few feet to the ground.

I crawl to Sebastian. My face slick with tears.

I pull him into my arms, cradling him. "*Perdóname, hermanito.*"

He looks up at me, but the effort seems to tire him and he closes his eyes.

"Give him the vaccine," I yell, not taking my eyes from Sebastian. His body is limp. His breath shallow. I put my hand on his cheek, caressing it, and his eyelids flutter open at the touch. But his eyes don't focus.

"The vaccine!" My voice is thick with tears. "Please! I'll do anything."

I tear my eyes from Sebastian's in search of Dr. Lederman. But he's gone. And so are the guards. There's only Persephone. Standing alone.

"I need the vaccine," I say.

Persephone shakes her head, blinking back tears.

I look back at Sebastian.

"*Todo va a estar bien,*" I whisper to him, holding him tightly. "We'll make you better. *Todo va a estar bien. Te amo, hermanito.*"

I rock him in my arms as his beautiful eyes slowly close, and the rise and fall of his chest ceases.

"*Todo va a estar bien.*" I curl my body over his, my sobs shaking us both.

"I did the video," I say between sobs. "This wasn't meant to happen ... I lied, so ... so ... he wouldn't ... It was all for nothing."

I feel Persephone's hand rest on my back.

"Martina," she says.

I flinch away, holding Sebastian's limp body tighter.

"Martina, we have to go."

I shake my head. "I can't ... I won't leave him."

A loud crash makes me jolt. I look around through tear-filled eyes.

Buildings tremble, slowly caving inward, and bricks fall. I finally realize the danger I'm in. The glass bubble has held so far. But for how long?

"We need to go." Persephone pulls at my arm.

I try to lift Sebastian's body, clutching him to my chest, but my legs are too weak to stand, and I crash back down to the floor. I can't breathe.

He can't be dead. He's just sleeping.

A shadow falls over me.

"Let me help." The soft voice is Nathan's. My heart skips a beat. It's both horrified and relieved he's here.

He leans down and deftly collects Sebastian into his arms.

I'm too stunned to stop him or even keep my grip on Sebastian. I thought Nathan had escaped the city, but he's here. And he holds Sebastian's lifeless body.

There's a loud groan, a creak, and a piercing crack. I turn toward the noise. Above us, the glass is breaking. A piece falls away; glittering and giant.

"Move!" I cry.

I push Nathan forward as I leap to my feet, adrenaline taking over. I need to get Sebastian out of here.

We run.

The glass hits the ground behind us, shattering into a billion shards sparkling like glitter sprinkled across the square of the Sparkle Sector.

Sebastian's body is jostled as Nathan takes the lead with Persephone a step behind him, skirting around debris and wreckage. My feet follow his; my eyes follow the little fingers that flop down from where Sebastian's cradled.

I'm aware of people running around me. They're shouting and calling as they help each other out of the quarter. How many heeded my warning and got out before the bombs exploded?

There's more creaking overhead. People scream in terror, running for the connecting quarters with their arms over their heads. As if that will offer much protection if glass falls on them.

Persephone is falling behind. With a glance back, I realize why. She still doesn't wear any shoes. Her feet are being torn apart with each step on the broken glass. She leaves bloody footsteps in her wake. But she doesn't stop. Her face is fractured by pain, but she keeps going.

I look forward again. Nathan still runs with Sebastian in his arms. I don't want to lose sight of Sebastian. But I can't leave Persephone.

"Go on ahead," Persephone says when she sees my hesitation.

Sebastian's little fingers, the flop of his hair, get further and further away from me, as I slow.

Instinct makes me run back to her. I sling her arm over my shoulder, giving her some of my strength to lean on. It's tough as my legs still feel wobbly, but somehow, I keep standing. Even though all I have to live for has gone.

We struggle forward toward the connection to the Bama quarter, one labored step at a time. The world falling around me.

Something catches my eye and I spin toward it.

Dr. Lederman.

He runs across the square with Guard Debbie and his personal guards, the ones that watched while he held a needle to Sebastian's neck.

Rage burns inside me.

He killed Sebastian.

He has to pay.

My feet take a reflexive step toward him, but then I realize he's running in the wrong direction. He's not heading toward either the Linto or Bama quarters. He's going to get himself killed.

He's going to the decontamination center, I realize. But he has to go through the heart of the Sparkle Sector to get there. Surely, he must realize the danger of falling glass and buildings and the fire burning across his path. He won't reach the decontamination center before this whole place falls apart.

There's no need for me to seek vengeance. The city is going to do it for me.

I turn away. I need to get to Sebastian who's waiting for me in the Bama quarter.

Only stragglers are left within the Sparkle Sector now. A few dashing toward the connecting tunnels. The Bama quarter is only a few yards away. Nathan waits just beyond the threshold, Sebastian's body still in his arms.

A clunk makes me look up. Someone has activated the security door to seal off the sector. It's coming down from the ceiling.

I drag Persephone along as quickly as I can.

There's more creaking, cracking, smashing and rattling around the bubble. But my focus is on the exit. I don't look over my shoulder to see if I'm about to be crushed.

Glass crunches under my feet while Persephone leaves her bloody footprints.

The security door is almost halfway down. It won't be long until we're sealed out.

Persephone bumps and jiggles against my shoulder.

It's almost closed, only a few feet from the ground. We won't make it in time.

I almost give up, resigned that Persephone and I will lose our lives too.

But it's not dropping any further. Hands keep it from going down. Several sets of hands of Sparkle Sector citizens. The door groans with the strain.

We reach it and I slide Persephone from my shoulder, practically throwing her underneath the door. My body swings itself under too.

The door closes behind me with a clang.

Everyone jumps back from it as it seals into place.

The crowd around me burst into applause, people laughing and patting each other on the back. A joyful sound while I sit on the floor, looking up at Sebastian, still lying limp in Nathan's arms.

Nathan bends down, gently laying Sebastian on my lap.

I brush a strand of dark hair from Sebastian's forehead to see his peaceful face.

A tear slides from my cheek onto his.

"*Lo siento*," I whisper.

Thirty-Five

THE SKY IS A brilliant blue, completely clear without even a wisp of a cloud. How dare it be so cheerful when storm clouds rage in my heart.

I wait alone in the desert, just outside the Bama quarter, refusing to look at The Nix bubble. I can't stand to look; it will only bring back painful memories.

The sun glints off the glass atop the Bama bubble. It's been newly cleaned. I wonder who worked on it. It shines almost as much as the Sparkle Sector once did. It seems so long ago that I was cleaning bubbles. Once so excited to be promoted to abseiler. It feels like a dream. Like somebody else's life.

My eyes flick to where the Sparkle Sector bubble once stood. It's now just empty space. I can't see the rubble it's become. From here, it's just empty air. More blue skies—mocking the tempest inside me.

I hear the clang of the decontamination center doors and my attention flicks back to the Bama quarter. Three people in white hazsuits exit and head toward me. Even though I expect them, I can't stop my heart beating faster at the sight of the pharmacists. I'm still scared of them. I think I always will be, after what they've done. Except for the one in the lead.

Persephone.

As she approaches, I fall into step beside her.

"Good health to you." Persephone nods and smiles briefly.

"Good health," I mumble. I'm not sure how to act around her after everything we've been through. We've barely had time to talk, and when we have, it's been awkward and too polite. Like we're strangers. Like we never kissed.

We approach the tents that are set up at the edge of the Old City, entering the largest one, while the other two pharmacists disappear into different tents. Inside is a row of camp beds. An array of people lounge on them—Old Henry, Liam, his girlfriend Kaylie, and a handful of others from the bubble city. They stop chatting when we enter.

"How's my favorite patient?" Persephone smiles as she approaches Old Henry.

He chuckles. "I'm fine."

"We'll see about that." She pulls out her thermometer and holds the barrel to his forehead. The thermometer beeps and Persephone checks the reading. "Looks good."

"So I can go?" he asks eagerly, ready to jump out of his bed.

"You can go."

Old Henry slides off his mat and out the door, whispering conspiratorially to me. "I hate hospitals." But his eyes are twinkling as he says it.

I try to smile, but the best I manage is a slight twitch of my lips. It's hard to smile these days.

Persephone moves onto her next patient. She's clinical as she works. But also kind. She's completely in her element. This is what she wanted—to help people hands on, while still utilizing her pharmaceutical skills. I'm happy for her. Even with my pain, I'm glad for her.

When she reaches Liam, she pulls out a syringe from a medical case. I see the glint of the needle and my knees go weak.

I see it piercing Sebastian's skin. The liquid disappearing into his veins. Sebastian's eyes going wide, questioning, "Why didn't you keep me safe?" Then he topples to the floor.

The ground tilts, and I feel myself tumbling. The floor rushes up, even as I stand upright. The edge of my vision blurs, going black.

I squeeze my eyes shut, but still, tears well in them.

I can't stay in this tent any longer. Rushing outside, I breathe in the hot desert air, letting the blue skies wash away the images.

I sit down on a rock to catch my breath, hanging my head in my hands. After a few minutes, the tears finally dry. The heat turning them to salt on my cheeks. But I still want to cry. I always do. I doubt this will ever change.

I hear the tent flap open. Through my fingers, I see Persephone approaching.

"Are you okay?" she asks.

I sit in silence, my head still in my hands. Wanting her to go away. Wanting her to stay. Finally, with a sigh, I say, "I'm not sick."

"That's not what I meant."

My hands lower from my face, but I don't reply.

She sits down beside me, turning so she can see me through her visor.

"They've had all of their vaccinations now," Persephone says. "You all might need a couple of booster shots to remain healthy, but you shouldn't be susceptible to any of the common diseases found out here."

"*Gracias,*" I murmur. My thanks feels hollow. I don't know how to fully express my gratitude. What she has done is beyond thanks. Since the Sparkle Sector collapsed, she has worked tirelessly to help citizens from *all* the quarters to live outside. Researching the diseases, finding vaccinations in the archives, testing, and nursing the people that have fallen ill.

After a moment of searching for something else to say, I blurt, "You look tired."

"You really know how to compliment a girl." She chortles.

My face burns red.

"I am tired," she says, looking into the distance.

I follow her gaze and watch a group of children playing tag, screaming, laughing, kicking up dirt. I smile despite myself, but it quickly fades when I think of Sebastian, wishing he was one of them.

Persephone continues, "The first wave of people to leave the city are just finishing their course of vaccinations, and the second wave are starting to get symptoms from their vax, so I've been running around like crazy checking and treating people. It feels never ending."

She sighs and sinks into her body. "There are some people who refuse to take the vaccinations. They believe it's another ploy from PMC and it's going to kill them. Or it's just another scam for more money."

"But isn't the city paying for it?" I ask.

"Yep. But they don't believe us when we tell them that."

I shake my head. For years they've trusted the wrong people. Now that people are truly trying to help, their trust has evaporated. It all feels so sad, so unfair.

"We advise them not to leave the city without the vaccinations, and some of them listen to us."

"What about the ones who don't listen?" I ask. "The ones that leave without getting vaccinated?"

"Some of them will survive. You did. Well, you survived that one disease anyway. But some of them will die. I just ... I can't force them. I won't be like PMC ... but watching them leave, especially the ones with children ..." Through the visor, her face is torn with sorrow, her eyes glistening.

"Of course," she says with a shrug, "there's also people that are migrating to other bubble cities, and for them life won't change much at all."

"But not everyone is leaving the city, right?"

"No, not everyone. Some are scared, like your friend Rosa and her husband. They don't want to risk getting sick out here."

Poor Tía Rosa. I'll miss her. She was so kind to me and my ... I shake my head, trying to clear my thoughts.

Persephone turns her stare to the glass bubbles. "And some don't believe PMC have done anything wrong. They want everything to stay the way it was."

"Because of me?" My voice cracks. "Because of the lies I told to save Se ... him."

She doesn't say yes. But she doesn't have to.

It was all for nothing. I went against everything I believe. I betrayed the Terrene Folk, and I betrayed myself. For nothing.

My hands feel empty. So empty ... without my little brother's hand to hold.

"I'm so sorry, Martina." Persephone's voice catches. "You told me to keep him safe, but I couldn't stop them ..."

My face turns to stone. I can't talk about it anymore. I can't talk about him.

The silence is heavy as I think about where everything went wrong.

What could I have done differently?

The thickness in the air is broken by a dog barking. Roscoe runs past the tents toward the Old City ruins where Nathan waits. He glances at me. When he sees me looking, his face turns as blank and barren as the desert, hiding whatever he's feeling. He quickly looks away.

"Have you spoken to him?" Persephone's voice is barely audible.

"No," I say. "We avoid each other."

She says nothing. I don't know if my words have comforted her or hurt her.

"I don't blame him for …" I squeeze my eyes shut. "But he still betrayed me."

Persephone knows this. I don't need to spell it out to her. She saw the destruction of her home. People she knew died. People are *still* dying. She'll never forgive Nathan for that. I don't blame her.

Persephone says, "So you don't know if it was the Terrene who caused the collapse of the Colombian bubble city?"

"No," I say. It makes my skin crawl to think about it; that these people I had become friends with could have caused my parents' death. But I'm still not convinced it wasn't PMC Life Tech either. "I asked Will, but he doesn't know."

"Or he won't admit it," Persephone says.

"I believe him," I say firmly. "He doesn't know."

Persephone hesitates before saying, "What about Mother Jessica?"

Just the mention of her makes me angry. I welcome the anger. Feed it willingly. It's a distraction from the pain I'm feeling. I don't think Nathan would have bombed the city if it wasn't for Mother. I don't know who's worse—Dr. Lederman or Mother Jessica. I can't look at her without fury blurring my thoughts.

"She says it wasn't the Terrene Folk," I spit. My words are like venom. "But after what she's done, I can't trust a word she says."

We sit in silence for a while. Persephone eventually asks, "Have you heard anything from the clean-up team?"

I know she's not really asking about the team who is sorting through the rubble that was once the Sparkle Sector. She wants to know if they've found Dr. Lederman buried among it.

I shudder. "They've found some of his guards, but they haven't found him yet."

"Maybe he did escape."

"He couldn't have." I shake my head. It's incomprehensible that he's still alive. Impossible. "He was running into the fires, through buildings that were falling down. There's no way he could have made it out alive."

"But what if he did?" Persephone looks at me briefly—one emotionally charged look—and then she glances away.

What would it mean if he survived? Nothing. Nothing to me. He has disappeared from my life. He can't do me any more harm. He's already taken everything from me.

But who else could he be killing? The doubt niggles at the corner of my mind. I squash it. Lederman is dead! He didn't survive. I won't even consider the idea. How can he be allowed to live when my little brother is dead? He has paid the price for his evil crimes.

"He's dead," I repeat out loud.

Persephone doesn't contradict me. But she doesn't agree either.

"I'll check your vitals," she says, collecting her thermometer and stethoscope again. She leans over me. Her fingers gently brush my skin as she adjusts my shirt so she can put the cool stethoscope against my chest. And even though her fingers are gloved, my skin still burns at her touch.

Her face is close to mine as she listens; only the thin sheet of glass between us. I try not to, but my eyes flicker to her lips. I remember the soft feel of them upon mine.

My fingers itch to reach out and touch her again. But I hold back. I'm scared that if I take her hand, she'll reject me. But I'm even more scared that she'll choose me. I'm scared she'll shed her hazsuit, risk infection, and live among the Terrene Folk with me. They'd never let her in the bubble city again. I can't ask her to give up everything; her home, her work. She said that her work gives her purpose. I won't let her give that up for me. I'm not worthy.

No. I can't take her hand. I can't kiss those lips or run my fingers through her hair.

So I pull away.

At my movement, she sighs and leans back too.

"You seem healthy," she says, and starts packing up her instruments, keeping her eyes averted. "I don't know how much longer I'll be able to keep coming out here."

I swallow. This had to happen eventually.

"My mom wants to relocate us to Norleans so I can continue my studies there. And of course ... well, she doesn't approve of my work. So, she's dragging me away."

"When?"

She finishes clasping her bag. "I don't know. But soon."

I can't stop my fingers this time. They take her gloved hand, give it a gentle squeeze, and then let go.

Persephone's smile doesn't reach her eyes. After a moment, she stands and collects up her medical bag.

"May you stay healthy and safe, Martina."

My eyes don't stray from her as she walks back to the bubble city, her hazsuit boots stirring the desert as she goes.

Author's Note

Although this book can at times draw comparisons to our experiences during the Covid-19 pandemic, it is a work of fiction and I did not intend it as a political statement. The truth is that I came up with the concept of people living in sterile bubble cities long before anyone had ever heard of Covid. However, thanks to living through a pandemic, I was able to take some inspiration from the experience and add in details to make the story more realistic, like lockdowns, face masks, and constantly using hand sanitizer.

I am not a health expert, and you should not use this fiction as a guide for your own health. Please seek health advice from health professionals and make informed choices when deciding to use medications or get vaccines.

And I wish good health to you.

Nikki

Martina Needs You

Did you enjoy Plagued Lands? Please consider leaving a review.

Reviews will help get Martina's story to more readers. So please, help keep Martina's story alive by leaving a review on Goodreads, Amazon, or the digital storefront of your choosing. Martina thanks you and wishes you Good Health.

Note: Reviews are incredibly important for indie authors, helping them reach new readers and sustain their livelihoods. What's cool is that writing a review is a simple and free way to support the authors you enjoy. Every review counts and it doesn't need to be long; one sentence is enough unless you feel the urge to write more. It can be as simple as, "I loved this book." So if you have the time to leave a review, I will forever be grateful.

Acknowledgements

My biggest support has been my sister, Krystie. She has been my alpha reader, amateur editor, cheerleader, sounding board, counselor (on more than one occasion), the first person I call with good news (or bad news), and my bestfriend. Thank you for everything you do for me. I'm so lucky I got you as a big sister!

Special thanks go to Alice Hanov. I couldn't have done this without your help! You generously give me your time and assistance and are a constant inspiration to me.

Thank you to my amazing Life Coach and NLP practitioner, Dr. Kim Brown. Without you, I'd still be sitting on my couch, too scared and depressed to write a word. You helped me overcome my limiting beliefs and to strive for my dreams with confidence and determination.

Thank you, Liz Harrington, my incredible editor. I learned so much from you that no other editor will ever have to work on my stories as hard as you did. You made me a better writer.

Thanks to Linda Monsalve, who checked the Spanish (all mistakes are my own) and lent me the use of her surname. You helped inspire Martina's character, but you're much nicer!

I'm eternally grateful for Alan and Ian at the Book Designers for my incredible cover. It's more gorgeous than I could have ever imagined.

Thanks to my supportive friends, Jill, Shaz, Monique, Petula, Emily, Fan, Katherine, Carina, the "It's 5 O'clock somewhere" crew, Elise, Alexandra & Patrick (who also lent me the name of his dog, Roscoe), and the #NoJudgement girls, Nicole, Susan & Michelle. My work colleagues at my day job. All have supported me in many ways, whether it was reading my book, boosting my confidence, or being an ear when I needed to vent.

My Family, especially my Mum and Dad, my brother, Trent, and my sister-in-law, Kosoma. And of course my sister, Krystie, who was already mentioned (she's been such a big help, she deserves two mentions). You all believed in me, even when I struggled to believe in myself.

My beta readers who were among the first to read the book (and unfortunately, the worst version of it): Bree, Rob D, Lucy, Joan, MK Whiting, Amber, Niamh, Boektuin, James, Duncan, Lucia, Eliana, and Charity. Thank you for putting up with typos and poor character arcs to help shape this into something great.

Thank you to the amazingly supportive community on bookstagram and other platforms. For every person who has shared, liked, and commented on my posts to show their support. I am so very grateful.

And the biggest thanks to you, my reader. You're the reason I do any of this. Thank you for taking a chance on me and Plagued Lands.

About the author

Nikki Brooke, an Australian science fiction and fantasy author and scriptwriter, is a vocal advocate for bisexual representation in literature and cinema, drawing from her own journey of self-discovery as a proud bisexual. Nikki's talent has garnered recognition, with accolades such as finalist in the 7th Annual Launch Pad Prose Competition and semi-finalist in the Screen-Craft Cinematic Book Competition, along with the publication of her short stories in various anthologies.

Nikki has lived in London, England, and Austin, Texas USA but grew up in Melbourne, Australia, where she currently lives with her two dogs, Osiris and Apollo. With names from ancient mythology, it's no wonder they believe they are in fact gods and are allowed to do anything, including wreaking havoc. Nikki lets them get away with it. As well as writing, Nikki enjoys reading, watching films, swimming, dancing, learning to speak Spanish, and she especially loves having adventures; which is where a lot of her inspiration comes from.

Follow @nikkibrookeauthor on facebook, instagram or tiktok for regular updates. Subscribe to Nikki's newsletter so you don't miss any news. Join at nikkibrooke.com/newsletter

CHOOSE FREEDOM

Plague Warriors, sign up to the newsletter below for news from the rebellion against PMC Life Tech!

nikkibrooke.com/newsletter

@nikkibrookeauthor

Get updates about the sequels to Plagued Lands, behind-the-scenes content, competitions, and games.